Etc

can

etc

Laugh .

AMEN

H. Male

HOWARD MALE

ISBN 978-1-908318-88-6

PALACE PARK PRESS

www.acornindependentpress.com

PRAISE FOR
ETC ETC AMEN

'Etc Etc Amen is smart, thoughtful, funny, original and never less than well observed. It is also, most importantly, a tremendously enjoyable read.'
Graeme Thomson (arts critic and author of Under the Ivy: The Life and Music of Kate Bush).

'A thundering good read. Howard Male has linked power chords with esoteric philosophy and skullduggery in an intriguing and compelling manner.'
Johnny Green (author of A Riot Of Our Own: Night and Day with the Clash).

'Very enjoyable, ambitious, and thought-provoking. Velvet Goldmine meets Michel Houellebecq.'
Chris Roberts (writer for Uncut and the Telegraph.)

'Really astute and funny. The KUU 'bible' passages are clever and ridiculous in a pleasing way. You write with such clarity and originality about the music press that I laughed out loud several times. Is it ready for publication? I can believe that. Is it something really special? I can even believe that too.'
Patrick Neate (Whitbread Prize winning author of Twelve Bar Blues).

'It is highly original and darkly funny. The world of the KUU and The Tripod remain in my mind like some strange dream. I'm sure it will continue to gather fans.'
Justin Adams (musician and record producer.)

ABOUT THE AUTHOR

Howard Male was born in Cambridge in 1958. He's been a painter, a musician, and in more recent years a music and arts critic for *The Independent on Sunday*, *The Arts Desk*, *Songlines* and *The Word*. He lives in deepest South London with his wife Marcia and his cat Karnak. He's found that the quickest way to get rid of Jehovah's Witnesses is to tell them he's a KUUist.

To Marcia

Etc

etc

AMEN

PROLOGUE

When Zachary C noticed his audience were no longer beguiled by his best Zachary B smile, he arranged for his chargrilled-sweetcorn teeth to be replaced by a mouthful of ultraviolet-sensitive acrylic. Much to his delight, shop windows, car windscreens – even a puddle he awkwardly traversed on the way to the gig – all threw back at him a grin of searchlight intensity.

On arriving at the Kings Theatre, Portsmouth, he found Fountain – his backing vocalist wife – immersed in her own reflection in the dressing room mirror. He sat down beside her and grinned his new grin.

"Perfect," he said to both their reflections.

He waited for Fountain's agreement – or at least some acknowledgement that he'd spoken – but she was far too busy assembling her own stage persona to indulge him.

Zachary C flashed his fluorescents for a second time. "So?"

Fountain continued to ignore him. The application of turquoise eye shadow required her full attention. She lifted her chin a fraction to better inspect her shimmering lids.

Fountain Penn's tragedy (apart from Ma and Pa Penn's African-American predilection for inventing new Christian names) was that she had once sung backing vocals for Zachary B, but was now singing backing vocals for Zachary C. In other words, she had once performed with the Now, but now she was performing with their tribute band, the

1

New Now. Yet for fifteen months this Detroit girl from the projects *had sung with Zachary B.* She had even endured the infamous Trafalgar Square concert.

"Well?", Zachary C persisted.

Finally Fountain relented and granted him an audience, but with her smile on the edge of laughter it was unfortunately a comedy club audience.

"It's the teeth isn't it?" said Zachary C.

"No, the teeth are great."

"So what is it then?"

"Okay, it's the teeth."

"But you just said the teeth were great!"

"You're not going to let this go are you, Zac. The teeth *are* great. It's just that they're…" Fountain strained for the gentlest way to put it. "It's just that they're not you."

"Thanks."

"Don't sulk, baby."

"So whose bloody teeth are they then – Brad Pitt's?"

The empathy Fountain had found hard to muster in the first place turned into a bluntness more in keeping with her personality. "Well, you did ask. I'm sorry sweetheart, but they're just not working." The eye shadow was returned to her bag, the lipstick unsheathed. "Every time you flash those things at me, it just gives me the creeps. They do have different hues, you know. Now can I get on?"

"Different what?"

"Hues. *Shades.* Like with paint. Ivory white, seashell white, dove white, you name it. Anything's got to be better than goddamn Nuclear Flash White."

"Okay, okay. I get the picture. Jesus." Zachary C closed his mouth.

"Phew, that's better," risked Fountain. "Now I can take off my sunglasses."

Poor Zachary, she thought. How much longer could he go on doing this for? She'd answered the ad in *Melody Maker* back in… 1995 was it? He'd recognised her as soon as she'd stepped into the rehearsal studio – and no one had recognised her in years. "You're in!" he'd laughed, before she'd even sung a note. And of course the fans loved seeing a living breathing member of the Now, in the New Now.

When Fountain went to the loo, Zachary C treated himself to another quick examination of his teeth. *What was her problem with them?* Next on the list was his hair: he wasn't balding exactly, it was the thickness. Although he dyed it *(coal black, cat black, black-bloody-hole black)* it had become as insubstantial as candyfloss. One day the wind machine was going to send it flying off into the audience like tumbleweed on a mission. However, in other respects he was in good health. He did all the right things: he ate the right food; he'd cut back on the booze; he exercised regularly. Yet several nights a week on stage trying to *be* Zachary B, was causing gravity to press down on him more mercilessly with each day that passed, manifesting itself in a dull ache here, and a sharp twinge there. The great man himself had been saved from the undignified task of performing his own sexually charged music as a sixty-year-old, by dint of the fact that he was dead. Why did all trains of thought eventually lead Zachary C back to this cold hard fact, which in turn led him back to the crime scene photos he'd made the dreadful mistake of googling a few years ago? Memory is wilfully perverse, so while countless childhood daytrips to the seaside remained tantalisingly just out of reach, those chilling photos were always springing up unbidden in his mind's eye, making him dizzy with nausea.

Despite all the KUU bullshit, he'd been a huge Zachary B fan. Suddenly he remembered the LSD-induced epiphany he'd had at Zachary's 1972 concert at the Rainbow: that just as slack-jawed cavemen had once believed the wind was created by agitated trees waving their branches about, he had believed – at least for one vertiginously exciting moment – that it was Zachary B who radiated the light that the greedy spotlights then vacuumed up.

PART ONE

A number, a dream, a coincidence can affect me obsessively - though not in the sense of absurd fears but as fabulous (and on the whole rather bracing) scientific enigmas incapable of being stated, let alone solved.

Vladimir Nabokov

Extraordinary how potent cheap music is

Noel Coward

1

Marrakech, February 2007

The street was so narrow that when a scrapheap of scooter wove past her in one direction, and a distressingly overburdened donkey nudged past her in the other, August almost stumbled into the path of a small oncoming truck. It responded with an abrasive blast of its horn. *Shit! Why didn't I change flights and travel out with Damian? Why am I always trying to prove something?* She searched her bag for the map she knew she'd put in there only minutes earlier, but her blind hands recognised only her water bottle, guidebook, camera and purse. Did she want a henna hand tattoo like the one the teenage girl was showing her? *No-no, not now.* She gave the desperate apologetic smile she'd have cause to fall back on many times over the next few days.

That morning, August had been surprised to find it warm enough for shorts and T-shirt despite the fact it was still only February. However, the rising hubbub outside her riad brought on a creeping sense of vulnerability, so she went for a blouse, linen jacket and jeans instead. After a ten-minute mull over earrings she had found herself on the disconcertingly uneven street. But having escaped the unapologetic stares of the Riad Bahja's thickly moustached owner and his small coterie of female staff, there now seemed to be a whole city's worth of people intent on giving her one kind of attention or another, with none of it welcome.

Still no map but... sunglasses! She put them on as if she were a welder donning goggles: now she felt more protected. Although of course they made little difference. The stall holders, snake-charmers and fortune-tellers still approached her as if they could make direct eye-contact, even though they couldn't – looming into her field of vision with colourful merchandise or just their colourful selves. It was still early in the tourist season and so every Westerner represented a possible feast after the famine. August noticed that women in particular were targeted as potential buyers of rugs, vases, spices and all manner of gaudy trinkets and tired tat (including models of the KUU Tripod of varying size and quality). She saw a woman single out a particular brass lamp. The stallholder rushed to get it down from its particularly high hook (even though countless identical ones were piled high on the ground).

Just as she found her map, August realised she no longer needed it: the apex of the KUU Tripod was visible from just about any part of the old city, and all she had to do was keep it in her sights until she reached it. As the structure's revolving globe winked an indifferent star of sunlight at her, she cursed herself for becoming flustered and determinedly set off towards it. Within minutes, meat, fish and vegetables replaced tourist temptations, as narrow streets narrowed further into unnamed alleyways, which, in turn, became mere passageways not wide enough for even the smallest of vehicles. She wasn't sure if this more hassle-free world made her less or more nervous.

The windows of Marrakech buildings rarely faced the street. Instead, they looked inwards onto central courtyards, leaving outer stone walls to soak up the heat and keep the interiors cool. This emphasised the impression that the city was a gigantic maze, its blind walls only occasionally punctuated by small inscrutable doorways behind which might be a palace or a brothel.

August momentarily panicked when she thought she'd lost sight of the Tripod. Then there it was, just a hundred yards away, looming above her. She was relieved to be free of the labyrinth of biblically ancient streets, standing before this vulgar yet oddly austere symbol of the civilised world. It seemed an age since she'd last seen anything this dazzlingly twenty-first century (even though it was only 24 hours since she'd last been lost in Canary Wharf). The whole structure of the KUU Tripod was wrapped in glass, exposing the eleven floors within. A steel exoskeleton of three turquoise legs crossed to form a cradle for the revolving globe at the building's apex. It wasn't an intimidating piece of architecture by modern standards, but it still towered above the mostly squat, raggedly utilitarian structures surrounding it. And to the consternation of many of the locals, it was a metre taller than its nearby rival, the stolid tower of the Koutoubia Mosque - the tallest mosque in Africa. Was this a deliberate provocation? This was one question August was planning to ask the KUU Foundation's Leader Who Is Not A Leader, tomorrow. Which was precisely the reason for her surprise visit today: it never did any harm to catch your subject off guard. After all, the KUU Foundation claimed it had nothing to hide.

She was wondering just how much of old Marrakech had to be razed to the ground to make room for this glass pseudo pyramid, when a rush of anxiety threatened to make her turn straight back the way she'd just come. *Get a grip – this is what you're here for!* She got out her camera: maybe taking some photographs would calm her down. A few minutes and a few deep breaths later, she'd regained her composure sufficiently to approach the building. The doors gave an electronic sigh, delivering August into a spacious concourse, electric with human activity yet disconcertingly quiet. Something about the building's acoustics sucked the sound away, creating an underwater ambience. But there was air, vaguely scented air in fact – sandalwood with a hint of lime? It seemed even brighter than outside. August was tempted to put her sunglasses back on. Adding to her visual disorientation were searchlight beams of African sunlight

9

ricocheting in every direction, creating fleeting rainbow affects wherever they came to rest. She joined the queue at the security desk. The T-shirts worn by the two girls who guided her through the check-in procedure were a welcome reminder of the domestic and down-to-earth (she'd half expected KUU officialdom to be clothed in the iridescent one-piece costumes favoured by the denizens of old science fiction movies). One girl's T-shirt was emblazoned with the words **Entertain the Possibility**, the other's asked the question, **Tri-Curious?** As the Tri-Curious girl checked her passport, August tried not to stare at the perfect curves of her eyebrows, which looked like they were drawn on with a compass.

Once she'd been through the BodySearch X-ray machine she moved on to the enquiries desk that was adjacent to the central lift shafts and service ducts. T-shirts were clearly the anti-uniform here: the old Moroccan gentleman who looked up wearily from his computer had the words **Don't Pray, Dance!** incongruously written in glitter across a T-shirt that was too big for his slight frame.

"Yes?" he asked.

"Is Mr Merrick around? I'm from London. I'm here to interview your... er... Leader Who Is Not A Leader, tomorrow but thought I'd just come by to say hello?" She hated herself for adopting an Australian interrogative speech mode. But she'd already decided how to play this: she wouldn't be sarcastic; she wouldn't be impatient; she wouldn't be patronising and she would be respectful. It wasn't going to be easy.

"Aah yes, London." The man's face brightened. "I have a cousin in London." A white-punctuated-with-gold smile flashed briefly. He consulted the screen, spoke to someone on the phone, and then directed August to the lifts. "Level 10. Entertain the possibility, and the possibility will..."

"Yes-yes. Thank you." She was slipping already – *be polite, be polite!*   The glass-walled lift granted August a tantalising glimpse of each floor as it passed silently. She was still mentally chastising herself for snapping at the man at Security when the doors slid back and she found her hand being rigorously shaken before she'd even stepped out.

"August! Delighted! Barney Merrick. Although we like to just use first names here. How was your flight?"

"Oh, you know…"

"We weren't expecting you until tomorrow. I hope they didn't give you the run-around at the airport. I could have sent someone to pick you up if you'd given us a bell."

August took stock of this middle-aged man who didn't seem to want to let go of her hand. Obviously eyebrows were going to be the theme of the day: why would someone who took so much care over their hair (a lacquered-back silver helmet) and smart but casual clothes (navy-blue linen suit, open-necked white shirt) let their eyebrows get so out of control? He'd look at least ten years younger with a bit of judicious pruning.

August felt the presence of Merrick's hand in the small of her back as he ushered her into a boardroom dominated by a large triangular glass table.

"How's your accommodation? We hear so many stories…" continued Merrick. The window-walls offered a 360-degree view of the Medina. The snow-tipped Atlas Mountains to the south looked suspiciously like a painted backdrop. "If there are any problems, you can always stay with us here. All our guest rooms have Wi-Fi-enabled TV/PCs. It's not La Mamounia, but it's clean and functional."

"I'm fine where I am, thank you," August replied with as much warmth as she could muster.

After twenty minutes of small talk, she decided it was time to address Merrick and the other two younger male KUUists who had joined them, on the reason for her visit. The atmosphere turned from genial to awkward as soon as she placed the portable digital recorder on the table between them: this was the impartial witness she carried with her everywhere. She always felt more confident as soon as its tiny red light started blinking. Conversely the three men became less confident, exchanged nervous nano-glances as their smiles stiffened. But Merrick only took a moment to regain his composure. "I'm afraid you're not going to get much of interest on your little machine today, my dear. And in all honesty, as we weren't expecting you until tomorrow…" His tone hardened. "Was your surprise visit designed to catch us off guard?"

"Not at all. I was at a loose-end and so thought I'd drop by. Maybe chat with a few visitors and staff – get a bit of background material. I wasn't expecting you to just drop everything…"

Merrick turned away, ostensibly to admire the view. "Well, it might all be academic anyway. I'm afraid the Leader Who Is Not A Leader has a touch of gastric flu – one of the downsides of living here. Obviously everyone else will do their best to accommodate you. So if you'll excuse me…"

August bit her bottom lip – *where to go with this next?* "Do you have a mobile, Barney? So you can keep me informed of developments? You do realise that the KUU Foundation is up shit creek, whether I get this interview or not. And trust me, it's only going to get worse. But if the world hears your side of things first, there's a chance for damage limitation."

August suspected that the young man who leant over to whisper in Merrick's ear was a lawyer, despite his chinos, Jesus sandals and red **You Can Laugh** T-shirt. Merrick turned back to face August. "The World. I see. I hadn't realised you were here representing *the World*. Well, good for you, my dear. Nevertheless, there's still nothing I can do. Perhaps if you come back tomorrow… In the meantime do make use of our extensive leisure facilities – there's table football, cafes, shops…"

"Thank you Mr Merrick, but…"

"Barney. Please, call me Barney. If it's more sophisticated entertainment you want, we have art classes on Level 5 where there's also a small library of KUU-related books and an Internet cafe. Level 7 offers virtual reality booths;

pretty state-of-the-art, I'm told. And on the Lower Ground Floor there's the dance floor and swimming pool. There are also shops and cafes on Levels 6 & 8. We…"

"Thanks, *Barney*. I'm sure when my photographer Damian gets here we'll…"

"And no chains, I hasten to add – that would be very un-KUU. So you'll have to wait until you get back to England for a Starbucks fix or a Big Mac." This time Merrick's guiding hand landed on August's shoulder as he escorted her back to the lift.

"No, really. I think I'll just get back to my riad."

August had begun to find the sterile ambience of the KUU Tripod oppressive: did every floor have a different smell, or was it her imagination? The smell as the lift passed through Level 5 reminded her disconcertingly of the dentist, and made her feel momentarily woozy. She wanted to get back to reality, even if that reality was as unpredictable and overwhelming as the streets of Marrakech. But it was still only ten-thirty; Damian didn't arrive until early evening. So she steeled herself for taking a look around, after all.

Being compulsively methodical, August began by exploring the lower-ground level, with the idea of gradually working her way up.

Every shade, shape and age of humankind seemed represented in the divers, paddlers, splashers and screamers crowding the triangular swimming pool. But the density of noise, the smell of chlorine, and the feeling that she might be thought voyeuristic, made her quickly step back into the corridor in order to follow the bass thuds to the adjacent dance floor. She was surprised to find this area just as densely populated, despite the fact it was still only mid-morning. A *Saturday Night Fever*-style chequered dance floor flashed red, blue, yellow and white, and Rihanna's *Umbrella* acted as a reminder that you were never far from a ubiquitous pop song. A digital jukebox boasted more than 200,000 songs on its database (with more being added everyday at the request of visitors). It was accessed via touch-screen and visitors were allowed one selection each which, the screen promised, would be played sometime within the next two hours. If no selections were made, the computer went into random play: August was delighted to hear Lieutenant Pigeon followed by Issa Bagayogo. The strobe lights made her feel less self-conscious about people-watching.

Eventually, after a necessary dance to *Lady Marmalade*, she began to tire of avoiding attempts at sustaining eye-contact from lone middle-aged men, and she headed back to the lift.

On returning to the ground floor she was disconcerted by the KUU subtext of an English lesson that was taking place in the main auditorium. The tutor and his students were engaged in a call-and-response repeating of various KUU non-commandments and maxims.

"You can laugh."

"*You can laugh.*"

"You can doubt."

"*You can doubt.*"

"Etc etc, Amen!"

"*Etc etc, Amen!*"

So she stayed in the lift and let it take her up past the accommodation levels, where two women with mops and buckets were labouring away, and onto Level 4, which appeared to consist entirely of a forest of old fairground games. One-armed bandits and Space Invaders machines stood in ordered ranks, and a dozen table-football tables were all in use. A bar running the length of one wall was already doing a steady trade, but the fug of cigarette smoke and other sour male odours made her step back into the lift. *Now what was this?* The Surreal Therapy Department. She went back to dentist-scented Level 5. Another diverse mix of people were making photo collages out of pictures from old magazines. Their tutor was a pleasant-looking pony-tailed young man in a baggy purple shirt and faded denims. He saw August and gave her a wave and a smile. "Care to join us?"

"Another day perhaps. Wrong floor." She cursed her English reserve. Where had this shyness come from? Certainly not her parents.

This was more like it: Level 6. The smell of fresh coffee was instantly subsumed by a hundred other smells: cumin, garlic, chargrilled meat, and cinnamon. Just as Merrick had promised, it was free of any familiar shops or eateries. There was a Turkish coffee house, a Mexican fast-food joint, a Japanese sushi bar, and, slightly incongruously, a tiny independent bookshop. The bookshop's window display consisted solely of copies of *The KUU Hypothesis* and Ayaan Hirsi Ali's *Infidel*. August had only recently just finished Hirsi Ali's book and it had simultaneously broken her heart and filled her with hope. She wondered whether any other bookshop in the world had dared to display it so boldly.

Limited floor space meant each food outlet only had a couple of tables in front of it. August opted for Japanese, selected some sushi and a beer, and found herself a table from where she could comfortably watch the people around her, as well as the city below. She felt like a time traveller looking down from this pristine structure at the chaotic bustle of just another day in Marrakech. Because of the triple-glazed glass, a cacophony of battling car horns came through as just distant muted toots.

The strong Japanese lager worked its magic, giving August a temporary sense of expansive well-being. Perhaps there really was hope for mankind if all these different cultures could coexist under one roof like this. *Hope for mankind? Get a grip, girl!* But nevertheless, it was amazing what the KUU Foundation had achieved in little more than a decade. So what had gone wrong? Twelve suicides scattered across the planet in just two short months: London, Tokyo, San Francisco, Mexico City, Amsterdam, and now Marrakech. All linked by method, and the fact that a copy of *The KUU Hypothesis* was found in close proximity to the victims. She wondered if victim was the right word for someone who committed suicide. To any reasonable person, the KUU non-belief system seemed perfect in its open-ended inclusiveness and its refusal to lay down rules. August felt it offered more hope and practical wisdom than any other political ideology or organised religion that she'd ever come across. So what was going wrong?

On a more personal level, August decided that if things didn't pan out with her newspaper feature she'd just enjoy herself. Maybe even give Surreal Therapy a try. When her mother had told her to try to have a good time, it was clear she suspected her daughter wasn't capable of having a good time, but she'd show her! After all, only two hours earlier she'd been in heaven, sitting on the roof of her riad, drinking coffee, and taking a disproportionate pleasure in opening and deleting her emails. As she had closed her laptop, she'd heard an inadequate PA-system turning the muezzin's call to prayer into a distorted howl that seemed to fill the whole cloudless sky. She remembered thinking that it sounded more like the plaintive cry of some wounded or lovelorn mythical beast, rather than a joyful invitation to praise Allah as the one true God, but at least the sound's eerie omniscience had reminded her of the fact she was in a thrillingly alien city on the threshold of a brand new day.

Extract from *The KUU Hypothesis* by Zachary Bekele

A Disorganised Non-Religion

There is no entrance exam or ceremony involved in becoming a KUUist, unless you'd like to invent one. Needless to say, if you did, it would be for your own personal use only. Every faith refugee, agonised agnostic and entertainer of the possibility is welcome to join this disorganised non-religion.

The KUU HYPOTHESIS
An Introduction

Coincidences are often entertaining and intriguing. Sometimes they even generate feelings of indefinable and unquenchable expectation: what did that confluence of events mean? Was I meant to meet that old friend today of all days? But these feelings soon pass and we move on. But perhaps coincidences are more than just coincidences. Perhaps they are the subtlest form of supernatural phenomena visited upon us by a benign force wanting to challenge our narrow perceptions of the world around us.

The Naming of the KUU

The naming of The KUU was almost accidental. But then a synchronistic chain of events cemented its aptness. But let's start at the beginning.

In the beginning was the acronym,
and the acronym was -

The KUU

The **K**nowing **U**nknowable **U**niverse

This precise yet imprecise definition of my proposed deity needs to be meditated upon a word at a time.

The Knowing

The first word suggests we are speaking of something that demonstrates intelligence. Knowing also suggests knowledge beyond intelligence; beyond our comprehension. The implicit implication is all-knowing

Unknowable

Unknowable because this is all guesswork; that's all religion ever is. So we need to be happy with just unresolved guesses. We need to stop needing answers, or turning our wild guesses into answers and then getting defensive if anyone dares suggest they are just guesses.

Universe

This third element symbolises that which we find impossible to grasp or understand. The universe is an undeniable reminder of the incomprehensibility of life and our fragility and contingence. We have more knowledge than we've ever had before, but with each step forward, the universe recedes two steps. By ending this definition-within-a-name of my bespoke non-faith with the word "Universe", I acknowledge and embrace the limits of my understanding and accept how farcically insignificant we are in the face of the vast holy unknown and wholly unknownable.

Extract from
The Life and Death of Zachary B
by Paul Coleridge

Warm Beer and Wan Music
23rd August, 1971

After a couple of hours spent flicking through dog-eared LPs in Soho record shops, I found myself on Wardour Street. I did a cartoon double take as *Rock On's* bulbous red logo blinked arrhythmically at me from above a blistered brown doorway. I stopped, backtracked a few feet, and, without giving myself any time to talk myself out of it, rang the bell. I was buzzed in (twice – I was new to all this) and found myself climbing some unfeasibly steep stairs, like those in an Amsterdam pension. At the top of the stairs was a small landing and three inscrutable plywood doors, one of which – the unpainted one – was slightly ajar. I wiped the sweat from my forehead, switched on *cool and confident me* and boldly crossed the cracked linoleum threshold into my new life. But doesn't everyone act it before they can become it? Doesn't everyone, in a situation like this, summon an actor to play a better version of themselves for as long as it's needed? Perhaps because of my uncharacteristic spontaneity in ringing the bell in the first place, my confidence was bolstered for just long enough to make a good impression. However, Jake Golding (who I would later learn was the features editor) didn't make it easy. He wasn't even aware of what a life-changing moment in time he was sharing with me, as he looked up briefly from last week's *Melody Maker*.

"Be with you in a mo. I can't believe they've done a spread on that Colin Blunstone poof." He was addressing no one in particular, scanning the competition as if it were a schoolboy's scrappy homework. As my presence had been noted, but not fully acknowledged, *cool and confident me* ebbed away to leave *wobbly-legged and embarrassed me* facing the music editor. What was I thinking of? What was I doing here? I then made the mistake of looking down: because I'd not planned on doing this, I'd made no effort with my appearance. The pink scoop-necked T-shirt with its ghost of an iron-on Stones logo was okay. But I was wearing shorts – for anyone over eight or under twenty-five, an absolute no-no regardless of the temperature. It was as if I was seeing their slippery nylon unpleasantness for the first time – although at least the elasticated waistband was hidden beneath the hem of my T-shirt. Then there was the horror of my feet: tan Clarks sandals. I'd had them since school! Their latticework straps made them look like week-old Danish pastries.

I tried to control my escalating anxiety by pretending to read a flier I'd picked up from Jake's desk. The rest of the high-ceilinged open-plan space was deserted apart from two men chatting conspiratorially, their feet up on their desks. A static ionosphere of smoke lingered above them, illuminated by weak shards of sunshine, which had somehow made it through the grime-laminated windows. It was the first time I'd even smelt grass never mind smoked it. The atmosphere pleased me. I wanted to be a part of this.

So I pulled myself together, my T-shirt down a little, and my shorts up a little, just as Jake - perhaps out of a dawning sense of my throbbing discomfort - creaked out of his chair to introduce himself. He claimed, unconvincingly, to remember the pieces I'd sent him weeks ago.

"Yeah, that *Hunky Dory* review – you really got the essential vibe of... er... what's-his-name?"

"David Bowie."

"Yeah, of course, David Bowie, the one-hit-wonder *Space Oddity* dude."

Because Jake expended so much nervous energy keeping his shoulder-length red hair out of his eyes, it clearly left him no time to deal with the improbably large sideburns doing a pincer manoeuvre on his narrow freckled face.

He introduced me to Barney Merrick (offhand), Andy Morgan (friendly), and the only person doing any work, Debora, typist and tea girl (sweet but shy) who had just appeared with a tray of mugs. He then led me down a short passageway to what he proudly – or rather, mock-proudly – called The Music Room. No, it wasn't a delightful sun-filled space dominated by a grand piano. It was a cork-lined cubbyhole containing three orange plastic chairs and a rudimentary shelf supporting a dusty turntable and a pair of speakers. A beaming Jake told me that The Music Room also served as The Drugs Room and The Private Meeting Room. We were clearly there for all three of its functions as he handed me a flier, rolled a joint and unsheathed *LA Woman*.

I was disappointed when he asked me what qualities I thought I could bring to *Rock On*? I took a tentative drag of the joint, stifled a cough and resisting the temptation to go with, "Well, I'm a fucking genius, Jake," and instead opted for, "Well, Jake, I think I can offer new blood... new blood and a spirit of adventure. You see, I have an explorer's attitude to music – the heart of darkness, and all that. There's just nothing around today that says, this is now – or even better – this is tomorrow. So, er, yeah..."

My gift-from-the-gods speech tailed off when I noticed Jake wasn't even listening. He was staring myopically at something on the cover of *LA Woman* he'd apparently never noticed before. But the fact I'd stopped talking refocused him.

"Look, as I said, we liked your stuff... er... Paul. And to be honest, we're too fucked to move a muscle here, what with the heat and everything. So why don't you just give us three hundred words on that lot…" With an effete wave of his hand he indicated the flier I'd forgotten I was still holding. "We'll see how you handle it, and take it from there."

So that was that. I got my lucky break reviewing the grim-sounding Axe Grinder whose morose, unsmiling faces glared up at me from the crumpled piece of paper I now looked at with renewed curiosity.

But let's backtrack a bit. What made me want all this in the first place? That's easy enough to answer: my older brother, Phil the DJ. He'd get back from gigs in the early hours of the morning, burst into my room with the electricity of the night's music still animating every muscle of his skinny body, and with a DJ's dexterity whip Captain Beefheart from my Dixons deck and throw on the white-label James Brown I just *had to hear*. Then he'd breathlessly berate me in a good-naturedly manner.

"Paul, Paul, *Paul* – how can you listen to that stuff, man? It's just white boys getting black music wrong. They're just trying too hard, man. Trying to be spaced-out and different. Look, dude, get your lug-holes round this…"

He'd dance lankily around the space between my bed and wardrobe as if he needed to emphasise how much better this music was than the stuff *I* listened to (which he said was music to read sci-fi novels to). And he was right. There was a natural fluidity to the music Phil force-fed me while still high from DJing. But I could never admit it to his face. I'd just go back to my paperback, pretending to continue reading about killer plants taking over the Home Counties, while James Brown's kick-drum forced its rhythmic will on my consciously stilled feet. This weekly Friday or Saturday night ritual played itself out in much the same way for a couple of years.

"Oh come on, Paul – listen to that *sax solo*. And the bass and drums are so *out there*."

"Yeah, it's okay," I'd say. "But what's it about? It's about nothing. He's just singing about sex and dancing isn't he? The lyrics are crap."

"So what are the lyrics of bloody *Take Up Thy Stethoscope And Walk* about then, Paul? If you want meaning, I'll give you meaning—"

With dizzying speed, *I Got a Feeling* was put back in the box and *Say It Loud I'm Black and I'm Proud* filled the room with its urgent, necessary message and its jumping, syncopated beats. He knew he'd got me: a record which so joyfully and succinctly demanded racial equality had to ace a record which self-indulgently documented some art school hippy's mescaline meltdown – however much the gatefold-sleeve artwork resonated with my imagination.

I envied Phil's certainty when it came to music. I was still finding my way, following trends, making sure I liked the *right* thing and belonged to the *right* tribe. But Phil just didn't care. From Miles Davis to Ray Davies, if the barometer of his tapping foot liked it, that was all that mattered. Before the stylus had completed its final graceful journey back to its cradle, Phil would be ruffling my hair (because that's what older brothers did) and taking himself and his box of 45s off to bed. More because I wanted to have the last word than because I needed to hear anything else, I'd put the Small Faces or Floyd back on. But they'd always seem stuffy and stilted after whatever Phil had played. Rock was theatrical, intellectual or macho posturing, whereas Soul and R&B were life, love, pain and lust made manifest in music. That's why Zachary B was different. His father was Ethiopian. Although he left Zac and his English mother and returned to Ethiopia when Zac was only ten, he would send Zac LPs of Ethiopian music. I still have a cassette Zac made for me of one singer in particular: Mahmoud Ahmed. The influence was never explicit in Zac's music, but it was there nonetheless – the musculature, the otherworldliness, the spookiness.

But back to Axe Grinder. After an evening spent in the simian company of a few hundred bikers and hippies, I dictated my honed hatchet job (appropriate don't you think?) to the lovely Debora from the communal pay-phone in my Peckham bedsit.

And so it began. For the first few months, I loved the idea I might discover some astonishing new band that would change the direction of popular music etc. But I quickly realised such finds were rare. All I'd ever see was denim-clad rockers trying to emulate Rod Stewart or Deep Purple. Warm beer and wan music. Twenty-minute guitar solos pouring like treacle into my begging-for-mercy ears. My body-temperature pint tasting like it was better suited for sprinkling on my chips on the way home. Where was the charisma and glamour associated with singers my parents listen to? Frank Sinatra, Tony Bennett, Billie Holiday? Or the power of the jazz and soul pioneers Phil worshipped: Little Richard, Ray Charles, Sam Cooke? This was what Britain needed in 1971 – a bit of soul and a bit of showbiz pizzazz! I'd scribble down song titles slurred by the singer and distorted by the beleaguered PA, and ache to leave through countless uncalled-for encores. Occasionally, rather than phone in my report, I'd catch the bus to Piccadilly Circus and deliver it by hand. I got used to climbing those tricky stairs three at a time, and pushing open the never-locked door (there was no breach of security expected from the accountant or the dressmaker who shared the communal landing) before slapping down my increasingly predictable copy on Jake's straining donkey of a desk.

"So how's it going, man?" he asked, one morning, clearly at a loose end. I'd turned up with a review of some art student folk singer who had been heralded as the next Bob Dylan (the third *next Bob Dylan* that month)

"Oh, you know, so-so. I'm still waiting to hear something which really blows me away."

"So what was James Blake like then?"

"Well, you know. He's like Bob Dylan."

"Great!"

"No, not great. Dull, very dull."

"Get out of the wrong side of the bed did we?" interjected Barney.

"Not at all. It's just that I like the Bob Dylan we've already got. He more than satisfies my Bob Dylan requirements. So I don't feel the world needs a second third-rate one, or even a third second-rate one."

I handed Jake my review and turned to leave. I really didn't feel like listening to any of Barney Merrick's sarcastic asides, but he reeled me in anyway.

"I do believe you're already sounding a little jaded, Paul."

Jaded, no. Bored, yes. That bullshit speech I'd given Jake a few months back (it already seemed like a lifetime ago) had more than a grain of truth to it. I really was greedy for something new. And perhaps even the deferred glory of discovering something new.

Hendrix was the only rock artist Phil had time for. The night we heard, on Radio Luxembourg, that he'd died, we stayed up all night playing his stuff.

"You know me, Paul," Phil began. "I don't like to talk about this shit, really. It's music – what's to say? You're the words guy. But Hendrix was the future, and now the future's been cancelled." Phil looked down at his beer can, absentmindedly swilled its contents around before tipping the last metallic drops into his mouth. "Do you know what? His death is kind of up there with the death of Martin Luther King or even Jesus. I mean it, man."

"Oh come off it, Phil."

"No, really, I mean it. Think about it: we both dug him – he was black music and white music. Okay so some cats didn't get it, or couldn't deal with it. But that's always the case with the greats. It's a fucking tragedy man. A fucking tragedy."

I have fond memories of that night at Phil's squat, listening to the screams and howls of *Electric Ladyland* until the dawn chorus made itself heard over the crackle between the tracks. Then we both crashed out on the damp double mattress which, besides his stereo and his DJ gear, seemed to be all Phil owned. So yes, I was the words guy; I was the one who escaped. But after five months of missing the last tube, and spending half what I'd earned for a review on the cab home, I was already dissatisfied with my lot. Seeing my name in print above my cigarette-packet-sized reviews was no longer enough. So I asked Jake for a more prestigious assignment, knowing exactly what I wanted that assignment to be.

Extract from *The KUU Hypothesis* by Zachary Bekele

Be Graciously Ignorant

All is conjecture and wishful thinking. The KUU is just an inspired guess. I was led to this guess – and convinced to expand on this guess – by a number of what I have decided to call Knowing Unknowable Universe incidents (KUU-incidences). The word "Unknowable" graciously admits ignorance. It is the safety catch in my name-with-a-built-in-definition. If all religions started with this premise – which is intrinsically part of the KUU name – then there would be nothing to fight over. Etc etc, Amen!

The Dazzling Surface of Science

Scientists invent bizarre hypotheses such as parallel universes, just as their ancestors invented bizarre gods. They know as little as their ancestors, but dress up their ignorance in "facts" which create a dazzling shiny surface of apparent knowledge. Scientists have contributed immeasurably to society, but they've not made a dent on some of the central mysteries of mind, soul or creation.

The Knowing Unknowable Universe
is a Phrase not a Personifying Name

It offers hope with the Knowing, takes it away with the Unknowable, and then plunges you into the infinite Universe at the end. It is one part conjecture to two parts an embracing and admission of limited knowledge. By contrast, science and other religions would have you believe that we and our world are two parts understood to one part mystery. But why should we suddenly have all the answers now, any more than we did two hundred or even two thousand years ago?

2

Marrakech, February 2007

"That grilled squid's fucking delicious!"

It had only been half-an-hour, but Damian was already tiring August. It wasn't so much the fact that every sentence he uttered included the words: fuck, fucking, or fucked, it was the fact that this extravagance of expletives was obviously an affectation. This young man was clearly ex-public school trying to be Streatham High Road. And what was it with goatees? What did these boys think they were saying about themselves with their carefully delineated patches of facial hair? Damian's effort was particularly risible in its desert-scrub sparseness and the fact it was two shades more ginger than his mousy shoulder-length hair.

They were eating in the Jemaa El Fna. At sunset dozens of long trestle tables transformed the square into a huge open-air restaurant where food sellers competed with charm and guile for the opportunity to feed the crowds. Tables were assembled around a central cooking area hung with swaying acetylene lamps and manned by all-male crews in pristine white hats and coats.

Damian's hashish-heightened senses were already busy perceiving the clouds of lamp-lit smoke issuing from the butane gas cookers as a visual manifestation of the primal blues the gnawa musicians were playing a few yards away. Every shout, clang, and sizzle of food preparation added perfect offbeat percussion to the cyclical music that already occupied a sonic terrain somewhere between harmony and dissonance. Although Damian was disappointed that the neat twist of newspaper he'd bought had only contained enough hash for a couple of joints, he knew that even if he'd been completely straight, all this sensory input would have still made him feel stoned.

"This is fucking superb!" He shovelled another dripping spoonful of lamb-something into his mouth. "Four hours ago I was in London and it was pissing it down and cold as fuck. And now..." He plucked at his plain white T-shirt and waggled his scarily-white shorts-clad legs in August's general direction. "Fucking amazing!"

August did her best to keep any note of condescension out of her voice. "I take it this is your first trip abroad then?"

"No, no, of course not. You know, I did Europe and shit – in my gap year. But this is, you know, different. We're in Africa for fucks sake. Yet it took no time at all to get here. That's what's freaky."

August stared at Damian with the detached fascination of an anthropologist as he took a lump of sausage from one plate, and some deep-fried eel from another, while cracking and peeling a hard-boiled egg by rolling it under the heel of his hand – all in the time it took her to take one tentative sip of sweet mint tea.

"So, are you into the KUU then, Damian?"

"Yeah, of course. Who in their right mind isn't?"

"Have you been nudged lately?"

"Not lately, I have to say. Though if you're watching out for it, it's not gonna happen. You know – don't push the KUU, and all that. But I've had some great cosmic nudges in the past ..."

He was clearly waiting for August to persuade him to relate his favourite KUU-incidence. As she was more comfortable as a listener than a talker, she put him out of his misery. "Well, go on then, let's hear it."

"Yeah, well, the best one was back at college. It's a bit of a long story so just tell me if I'm boring you. Me and a couple of mates, Dave and Jess, were getting stoned, watching TV..."

"As you do."

"Yeah, as you do. You know Derren Brown, the mind control dude? Well, he was doing this trick of making bookmakers at a greyhound race pay-up on a dog that came last in a race. Anyway, we start riffing and Dave says, 'So, which greyhound would come last?' And I reply, quick as a flash, 'the three legged one.'"

Damian started giggling, but quickly composed himself. "As we were all stoned this was the funniest joke we'd ever heard. But anyway, as soon as the programme ended I stuck on a *League of Gentleman* DVD – it was probably just the first thing that came to hand. We're about ten minutes in, and Jess sat up straight on the sofa and pointed at the screen. 'Wasn't that a three legged greyhound?' she said, kind of freaked out a bit. There'd been this scene of a group of carnival freaks barging into this woman's house. It had all happened very quickly, but me and Dave hadn't seen any greyhound. But because we're KUUists we needed to check to make sure. So I rewound about thirty seconds, pressed pause, and, sure enough, there's this fucking three-legged greyhound bounding up the stairs – the picture was a bit blurred but there was no question he was one leg short of a full set. We couldn't believe our eyes..."

"Interesting..."

"No, wait, that wasn't the end of it. Jess said that to complete our KUU set, all we needed was to see a real three-legged greyhound. So, a few weeks later, I got a call early one Saturday morning. It's Jess. She had this Saturday job in a shop in Covent Garden. She was meant to be off that weekend, but the owner has asked her to come in because his other girl couldn't make it."

At this point Damian paused for effect, except the effect was lost on August who wasn't experiencing the same sense of profound expectation that Damian had hoped she was. But once again, August politely gave him his cue anyway.

"And, so?"

"Well, apparently this girl was always coming up with one excuse or another for being late, or not coming in at all. But on this occasion she'd opened her front door... and... Yeah you've guessed it – there was a fucking three-legged greyhound standing on her doorstep! So the girl decided it was her duty to take it to the local police station and so wouldn't be able to get into work before lunchtime. When Jess called me on her mobile to tell me all this, I told her to get her arse over to this girl's place to take some pictures! Fucking brilliant, eh? You know that bit in the book about KUU-incidences having to involve the most unlikely elements in order for them to be, you know, valid? So, how many times do three-legged greyhounds crop up in life?"

"Or conversation, or TV shows," interjected August, smiling. She was warming to Damian just a little, now that he was showing a bit of KUU spirit. And his KUU-incidence had been fairly impressive and amusing.

"And the tripodic KUU is a 3 legged GOD and this greyhound was a 3 legged DOG – brilliant, eh?"

"You can't teach an old god new tricks."

"Exactly... Hey, nice one!"

With a theatrical flourish, one of the waiters held a teapot high in the air with one hand, and their glasses low with the other. He then poured a long arc of tea into each glass without spilling a drop.

August continued to sip slowly at the comfortingly hot liquid. She still wasn't feeling hungry. "So what were you before you were a KUUist?"

"Catholic."

"And?"

"Well..." Damian thought for a moment. "It was when I read they were officially thinking of scrapping limbo..."

"Sorry?"

"You know – the doctrine of limbo? Purgatory or whatever you want to call it. I mean, they can't do that can they? That's like destroying some amazing listed building or sacred monument – no, worse – it's basically admitting that all that stuff we were brought up to think was the Holy Word can just be gotten rid of on the whim of the powers that be. And because this is coming right from the top – from those who supposedly have a hotline to the Almighty – well, I just thought, that's it, enough already. It's all bollocks anyway, isn't it?"

August didn't answer at first: an answer of either yes or no somehow didn't seem appropriate. Eventually, she picked up a piece of calamari from Damian's plate and popped it in her mouth. Smiling, she looked him straight in the eye and said, "Maybe."

Damian laughed. "Yeah. Maybe. KUUism always has the answer."

Momentarily, August felt sorry for Damian. He seemed genuinely hurt and confused in his disillusionment with the Catholic Church. But then his face relaxed again. He looked around at all the rising smoke backlit by a miniature universe of gas lamps. "I fucking love this place. Is there a more atmospheric place to eat on the entire planet?"

"But there's trouble in paradise."

"Yeah, of course. So what do you make of all that shit?"

"The suicides? Well, it's scary isn't it? And the Leader Who Is Not a bloody Leader has gone back on his word regarding my interview. And then there's Barney Merrick. I didn't get a good vibe from him *at all*."

"So you've been to the Tripod already?" Damian looked disappointed. August decided not to acknowledge it. "I thought it might be useful if I did some groundwork. I don't want to just do some one-hour hack job. I came here with the idea of letting them tell their side of the story. I wanted to be on their side, but if they're closing ranks, what can I do?"

"I can't believe I'm going to be the first person to photograph the Leader Who Is Not A Leader in, what, twenty years? Thanks August."

"Don't thank me, it was the paper who decided to send you. Maybe they thought that as you're such a Born-Again Questioner it might make you a useful go-between."

August's eyes were beginning to sting from the smoke. When Damian, on impulse, asked a passing trader how much an ostrich egg cost, she decided it was time to call it a day. "Look, I'm really tired, Damian. Would you mind if we?…"

"No, no. No problemo. I'm a bit fucked myself."

August continued to scrutinise the young man who was now taking an age to count out the right amount of dog-eared dirhams for the patiently smiling egg man.

"Can I just say something, Damian?"

"Yeah, of course."

"Were you aware that you use either the word fuck, fucking, or fucked, just about every time you open your mouth?"

As soon as August had spoken, she regretted it. Damian looked crestfallen.

"Do I? Sorry." He crammed the crumpled excess notes back into his pocket while simultaneously trying to deny a monkey on a chain purchase on his left shoulder.

"Don't apologise. I just thought you should know. You could be quite an agreeable young man if you could cut down on the fucks."

He gave the monkey's owner a handful of coins. "Yes. I see what you're saying."

August tried to temper her outburst with a touch of joviality by continuing, "It's not big, and it's not clever," in her best schoolmarm voice. "And I don't think it will be a particularly useful talent if you are going to help me oil the cogs of communication at the Tripod."

"Okay, okay! Enough! You've really starting to fuck me off, now!"

For a moment August was taken aback, but then she registered Damian's broad, schoolboy grin.

"Stop fucking with me!" She replied, laughing and relieved.

"Well, fuck you!"

"No, fuck you, motherfucker!"

They both doubled up with laughter. Damian wiped the tears from his eyes. "That's some laugh you've got there."

"It runs in the family."

As they wove their way back through the crowds, trying not to avoid eye-contact with the transvestite belly dancers, August mentally chastised herself for being so prudish: *I'm only twenty-five but I'm acting like I'm sixty-five. What's he – five years younger than me? But it's a very important five years; he's still a boy.*

"So, do you normally write about stuff like this?" asked Damian, interrupting August's self-chastising internal dialogue while neatly sidestepping an oncoming scooter whose rider looked about ten-years-old.

"Not really. I write about books…"

"Book reviews?"

"No, no, that's far too labour intensive. It's kind of upmarket gossip about the publishing world. Up-and-coming trends, that kind of thing."

Damian looked sceptical. "And there's a demand for that?"

"Amazingly, yes. I do a weekly column and other bits and pieces."

"So why did they send you here?"

"I asked to be sent. Well, I begged actually. I want to branch out. And this is personal too, so… Look, can we just walk now? It's been a long day."

"Yeah–yeah, of course, sorry."

Stopping to get their bearings, August and Damian noticed two women in a small cave-like workshop, one standing, the other seated, their hands intricately busy with some kind of needlework. They looked up briefly, but without curiosity. From their dispassionate demeanour, August imagined this work was what they'd always done and always would do. A skin-and-bone cat insinuated itself between the seated woman's feet before disappearing under her robe. It reappeared a moment later with a scrap of something red hanging from its mouth. August turned away, not wanting to know what that something red was.

★

August's first thought on waking the next morning was that she was never going to get used to her log-like pillow. Her second thought was that she couldn't wait to show Damian the view from the roof – her discovery, her roof. The interview with the Leader Who Is Not A Leader still looked doubtful, but Merrick had phoned her at 8 a.m. to say he was willing to see her at midday, which was better than nothing.

The Riad Bahja, like most riads in the Medina, was an improbable cross between a B&B and a palace. Two storeys housed eight apartments, which were built around an ornately tiled central courtyard. The courtyard contained a stone fountain (apparently inoperative), two small orange trees (which looked artificial but weren't) and a couple of tatty wicker chairs. The impression of period opulence was completed by stained glass in the gothic arched windows and plush Moorish furniture and fittings. As August crossed the courtyard to knock on Damian's door, she wanted to believe all this stuff was *real* but she knew nothing was further from the truth. Just as the modern British pub is encrusted with reproduction sepia photographs and fake horse brasses, so this gorgeous place with its Arabian Knights exoticism, was – like most things on early twenty-first century Earth – just an illusion. August knew (thanks to her *Rough Guide*) that what seemed like it had been there for centuries, was probably no older than a decade. Since the early 1990s, money had poured into Marrakech from foreign investors and property developers. Crumbling, neglected town houses were converted into the Westerner's dream of tasteful Arabic ostentation, and even by the mid-90s you could still buy a palace in Marrakech for the price of a studio flat in Battersea. This was why it had been relatively easy for the KUU Foundation to get permission to flatten a sizeable chunk of abandoned real estate and build the KUU Tripod.

While some locals, and a liberal contingent of expats, mourned the destruction of a whole neighbourhood, the Moroccan government just saw Big Money upfront and Big Money from future tourism. However, they did allegedly take the largest back-hander in Morocco's history to get the city to bypass a ruling made in 1985 that no building, unless it was a mosque, could exceed the height of the tallest palm tree. Despite its pride in its past, just like everywhere else, Marrakech wanted to become a part of the future. And there was no better way to do that than to have an instantly recognisable piece of cutting-edge architecture redefining your skyline.

"I want to show you something," said August with girlish glee, as she stood on the threshold of Damian's room. She was determined to dispel any lingering notions of fustiness he might have been harbouring about her from the previous night. Damian was about to rub some sleep from his eyes when he found his hand in her hand, and his bare feet following hers up the short run of stone steps to the roof.

"I've already asked them if we can have our breakfast up here," August said. "You won't believe the view."

"Nice."

"Nice? Just nice?"

"I'm not really a morning person, August. Maybe it'll be 'fucking amazing' once I've had a coffee or two."

They sat down and, within moments, had coffee and pastries placed in front of them. August was simultaneously impressed and embarrassed that Damian had wasted no time in obliquely referring to her comments the previous night on his swearing. She changed the subject. "You haven't told me your thoughts on the suicides." She was relieved that Damian sat forward in his chair, all previous concerns forgotten, and began to get stuck in to what was obviously his favourite subject of the moment.

"Do you know what freaks me out the most? That each victim used the exact same handgun – a Smith and Wesson, Model 340 revolver. It's a tiny gun, J-frame, less than four inches in length…"

"But it does the job," interrupted August, curtailing Damian's depressingly enthusiastic cataloguing of the gun's spec.

"It's also weird that each gun had two spent-cartridges and not just one…"

"Why so?"

"Oh come on, August, keep up! Usually only one shot is fired when someone shoots themselves in the head?"

"Sorry. Yes, of course. But where did you hear about the two-spent-cartridges? I knew it was the same gun, but…"

"Oh, you know – websites. Maybe it's all bullshit – there are always conspiracy theories around shit like this, but it's a very odd thing for someone to make up. Most conspiracy theories go somewhere: they have their own internal logic; they make some kind of sense. But this just…" Damian threw up his hands in a vague gesture of defeat. "And no suicide notes. Not one of them left a suicide note. I checked up on the statistical likelihood of that, and found out that in Canada and Mexico, for example, between 15% and 37% of people leave notes. For the elderly it goes up to almost 50%. Another site recorded that in Hungary, New Zealand, and Sweden figures were between 10% and 43%. So, although it's not as high as I might have guessed, it's a lot higher than zero."

"You have been doing your homework." August patted Damian's hand.

He tried to disguise the pleasure he felt at getting her approval by wolfing down the last of the cinnamon pastries while simultaneously telling her what else he'd found out. "Yeah, well… thank Google not me. But it tells us, statistically speaking, that at least a couple of these victims *should* have left notes. And also there have been few statements from family and friends. I think the father of the nineteen-year-old in Tokyo just said his son was a good kid and loved football and computer games. Plus, of course, all the usual stuff about it being a complete shock."

"What we can do is look into the background of the Marrakech victim, Malika… something or other."

Damian brushed crumbs from his shirt. "Let's see if we can find an address for the poor kid on the KUU Foundation website."

Although August was touched by his enthusiasm, she still needed to know more about him before letting her guard down.

"So anyway, Damian. Are you a practising KUUist?"

Damian leant back in his chair slightly, a look of mild surprise on his face. "What the fuck's a practising KUUist? There are no rules to obey, no substances to not eat or not drink, no rituals to fit into your weekly diary…"

"Just testing," August interjected, pleased to have hit a nerve. "But what about the Eleven Non-Commandments?"

"Well, it's all good stuff isn't it? Who could argue with any of it: you can laugh; you can doubt – just those two non-commandments alone strike at the very heart of every other religion. Laughter and doubt are the two things that make us human, yet they are conspicuously absent from, or frowned upon in…"

"I'll take that as a yes then," said August, smiling.

"Okay, I see where you're coming from. You were just wondering how seriously I take The KUU. In that case, I suppose I'd have to say… pretty seriously."

Damian looked uncomfortable. August felt sorry she had pushed him into having to defend his non-faith. Casual KUUists teeter on a tightrope of spider's silk. But the passionate KUUist is close to being a walking contradiction. Over the past decade, KUU sects had sprung up which wilfully reinterpreted and distorted the philosophy of *The KUU Hypothesis*, the most prominent being the Coup KUUists, the Doubting Doubters, and the So & Sos (The Solipsistic Socialists – or the SS to their detractors). They shared the view that there was a great deal of wisdom in *The KUU Hypothesis* but that its apparent open-mindedness actually veiled a deeply conservative faith-based subtext. They interpreted non-commandments such as, "you can doubt" as meaning, you *can* doubt – but under the weight of all the KUU evidence it would be ludicrous to do so. They also used the enigma of the Third Near Proof to go that extra step towards being the complete antithesis of KUUism as most people understood it.

August recounted some stories she'd heard about the Coup KUUists and Damian laughed. The convivial atmosphere was restored.

"Yeah, they're absolute nut-jobs. For one thing they place most of their hopes on the missing Third Near Proof."

"Putting all your eggs in a basket that probably doesn't even exist, is never a good idea."

"Exactly. Do you mind if I smoke?"

"Yes I do, sorry."

"No problem." Damian quickly returned his tobacco and papers to his canvas shoulder bag. "Look, when I reread *The KUU Hypothesis* – obviously I'd read it in my teens, everybody does – I realised, as an artist, that I'd let myself down. I'd suffered from a failure of the imagination. It takes guts to take on board some of that stuff, but if you don't go along for the ride then you're just a victim of a culture that has annihilated your ability to think outside the box, as they say. So where do you stand on all this?"

Like most journalists, August didn't like having the tables turned on her, but she knew it would happen sooner or later, so she was ready with an answer.

"It amuses me."

"Okay…"

"Okay, what?"

"Just… okay."

★

42

Damian's camera made him a far greedier consumer of form, colour, incident and detail than he ever was when he wasn't taking photographs: as he focused the lens, the lens focused him. As he stretched up, crouched down or swung around, his eye revelled in every confusing refraction of sunlight in the dazzling concourse, delighting in the incidental ambiguities he was able to make new pictorial sense of – and then with a perfectly timed, whirring click – freeze in time. He found his senses further disorientated by the fact they weren't used to computing a triangular space – both horizontally and vertically. Even the floors were made of reinforced glass so that, as you looked up, you could see the progress of people's feet making their kinetic patterns everywhere. Damian felt it was like being in a computer simulation of a building rather than the real building itself. He trained his camera on anything and everything as he followed August towards Security. Barney Merrick's hand curled slowly into a fist as he watched their progress on one of fifty CCTV monitors, but he managed to stop himself from bringing it down hard on the desk in front of him.

Extract from *The KUU Hypothesis* by Zachary Bekele

The Liberating Certainty of Uncertainty

I will not be pushing *The KUU Hypothesis* with the usual passionate conviction that accompanies a new manifesto, for the simple reason that passionate conviction is one of the human inclinations *The KUU Hypothesis* questions. KUUism proposes a third choice (KUUism generally involves the third option, as you will learn) between the diametrically opposed opposites of scientific truth and religious faith – our two life-support systems. I am an idealist who doesn't believe in ideologies. My only passionate conviction is that passionate conviction is dangerous.

Vagueness as a Virtue

I will therefore resist the blinkered bloody mindedness and rampant egotism that seems necessary to get new ideas accepted, adopted or discussed because the very nature of this non-religion (non-religion because the dictionary defines a religion as a belief) is that it shouldn't be blindly believed in. Its vagueness and uncertainty are its main virtues. However, I will sometimes adopt the forceful tone of the preacher – or if you prefer, the scientist – purely for rhetorical purposes. So I'll start – as expectations dictate I should – by rhetorical proclaiming:

The ideas in this book could save the world! Etc etc, Amen!

That felt good. Now all I have to do is deliver.

Extract from
The Life and Death of Zachary B
by Paul Coleridge

Men Will Be Boys
May 1972

This book is really *for* Zac as much as being about him, God rest his soul. But it's more of a tribute than a biography. If you want all the anorak minutiae then look elsewhere. There's countless biographies by callow young hacks who weren't even born during the reign of Zachary B. They'll tell you about every tour and record and every group member and groupie, but they won't give you the real Zachary B. Phil Kirby's *Zachary B – Man and Myth-maker* isn't bad (at least Kirby interviewed Zac once or twice), but avoid *The Star Guru* by Ray Gunner, *Rock God, Stone Idol* by James Renton and *The King B's of Glam: Bolan, Bowie and Bekele* by Steve Oliver. They're inexcusably exploitative and full of schoolboy errors (everyone knows Bowie didn't play Stylophone on *Do the Rocket!*)

So...

In the beginning was the Warhol-meets-flower-power 'happening' on the South Bank in the summer of 1967. I was up in London for the day with a couple of schoolmates and we were handed this screen-printed flier. As far as I recall, Zac was one of about six acts, only two of which were singers. The Small Wonders were a troupe of dwarves dressed as astronauts whose act consisted entirely of throwing a large inflatable silver moon to each other. Then there was some skinny mime artist doing the usual invisible wall stuff. And, last but not least, nothing could have prepared me for the prepared-piano played by a naked woman painted bright blue from head to toe (her act was prematurely cut short by some passing bobbies).

Eventually, Zachary Bekele strolled onto the stage with an acoustic guitar. Vocally, he was part Scott Walker and part Marvin Gaye, although he wasn't yet confident enough to live up to such lofty comparisons. His long, thick hair was tied back in a Native American plait and he was wearing a purple velvet tunic brass-buttoned-up to the neck, and vibrantly clashing scarlet loons. His songs already mixed strong melodies with funky riffs, despite only having a half-asleep percussionist and a double-bassist as back up.

He went down well, although it helped that the other acts were either pretentious nonsense or just plain run-of-the-mill nonsense. I even kept the flier, feeling sure I'd come across his name again. A year later, he'd become Zachary B. He shrewdly realised that, in Britain, an unpronounceable foreign name was, commercially speaking, the kiss of death. But Zac was proud of his Ethiopian roots and so didn't want to pick a sparkly new name at random. So he just let it be B. It's a name that still sounds cool today in its graffiti-friendly hip-hop brevity. Here's a snippet of pop trivia for you that isn't in any of the other biographies: Zachary's English mother chose his first name. He once told me (with a mixture of pride and ironic detachment) that it was Hebrew and meant, *Remembered by God*.

From the earliest interviews, it was clear Zac had a keen intellect, which makes pop music an odd career choice, but of course our lives often choose us, rather than the other way around. He said of his childhood, "I was a bookworm as well as a rock 'n'roller, so C.S. Lewis and Jerry Lee Lewis were both guiding lights." It was a well-practised line, but the sentiment rang true.

When I first suggested an interview with Zachary B to Jake, I claimed that – like the rest of the *Rock On* staff – I was indifferent to his disconcertingly funky and insidiously commercial style. I just thought he had *something*. Jake saw through my ruse, but indulged me nevertheless. These were desperate times.

Rock On folded in 1984, so I won't hold back in telling the truth about the paper. I never even spoke to the editor, Nick Hyde (or was it Hider?) in all the years I wrote for them. I just remember a ruddy lump of a man with a toothbrush's worth of pigmentless hair in each rosy ear, occasionally glimpsed when his office door was ajar. As for the rest of them, Jake was okay, but the others suffered from the kind of self-importance which breeds paranoia. They didn't form their opinions by open-mindedly listening to the band in question, they formed them by covertly finding out what their colleagues or even their readers thought. Perhaps they'd have followed their gut instincts if they'd had any guts, but they didn't. I sometimes wondered who *did* stick their neck out in the first place, to create the thumbs up or thumbs down the rest of them would then go along with. A typical office conversation would go something like this:

"You don't *really* like Wizzard do you, Paul?" Barney would say incredulously, nonchalantly twiddling his biro.

"Yeah, they're okay. Roy Wood's a good songwriter and their singles are epic," I'd reply, trying not to sound defensive.

Andy then had to weigh up Roy Wood's credibility score (plus-points for being in the Move, minus-points for dressing like a Zulu scarecrow and being on *Top of the Pops*) to decide whether to back-up Barney or side with me. When it comes to music, men will be boys until the day they die, but the real irony was how few readers *Rock On* had anyway. Let me put it like this. It was the most independent of all the rock rags – and this was before independent was the buzzword for trendy and cutting edge. Back then independent just meant you had no money. BZ (Before Zac) the only way you could have got a more obscure music paper was by writing it yourself and just handing it out to your friends. So you could say (and damn it, I am saying it) I rolled up just in time to save their sorry arses. Although, in retrospect, I realise I was taken on so Barney and Andy didn't have to go and suck up to the Pop Ponce of the Month. But having taken the plunge with Zachary B, Jake decided he wanted two-thousand words: if *Rock On* was going to have this prancing pansy in its hallowed pages then he wanted something in return. And so Zac became the cover story and *Rock On* suffered an unprecedented and deeply unsettling doubling of its circulation. This was only the beginning of its tragic downward spiral towards commercial viability.

★

And then there I was, outside Zachary B's Powis Square basement flat. This time when the buzzer buzzed I took the Pavlovian nudge and pushed open the door. Thick velvet curtains shut out what little daylight might have otherwise crept in. Further visual disorientation was created by numerous candles on every available surface, creating the illusion of a low-slung miniature galaxy of flickering stars. As my eyes acclimatised, I realised I was in a picturesquely cluttered, unusually long room. Moroccan rugs covered the floor and walls. The whole of one wall seemed built out of LPs. African masks made threatening eye contact from the darkest corners. Several crowded bookshelves name-dropped Golding, Huxley, Jung, and Camus. More prosaically, a Flying V guitar leant against a Marshall amplifier, and a partially dismembered drum kit seemed to be trying to escape from a walk-in cupboard.

I was so busy making sure I didn't knock over any candles or crush any esoteric artefacts underfoot, that I didn't realise there were people at the far end of the room. A flashgun flared and the words "five minutes" were apologetically fired at me by a suddenly silhouetted hunchback. Then a main light went on and this gothic vision turned into a photographer struggling with a malevolently misbehaving tripod. To his right, Zachary B reclined on a mass of cushions, playing the role of the exotic foreign prince for all it was worth. The photographer gave up on the tripod and resumed his photographer's dance in a semicircle around him.

Years later, I realised Zac was most in his element at times like this. He was being worshipped just for *being* – for just exuding Zachary B-ness as a platonic absolute – rather than having to speak, talk, sing or do anything else the rest of us have to do in this world to make our presence felt. For most of us, there is a dismaying disjuncture between our wonderful complex souls and our lumpy, deeply compromised physical selves, but not for Zachary. Zachary knew that if his soul could be as transcendent as his physical beauty, he would be perfect. I watched in fascination as he pushed an errant curl from his forehead while letting others take their rococo course down the side of his face. He was his own sculptor, making last minute adjustments before the camera caught the finished masterpiece.

Well, not finished exactly, because Zachary B was always a work in progress. One minute the predatory sex god, the next, the androgynous siren (luring innocent seafaring teenagers to their deaths on his jagged rock). Then his Gibson Les Paul played a supporting role for a few shots, becoming a machine gun aimed at the camera (don't mess with Zac!), a hugged stand-in for the female form (Zac has a sensitive side too!), and then finally a between-the-legs phallus (so the older girls could giggle at the crude symbolism while teasing the younger girls for not getting it.) The cleansing white light of the flashbulb blessed each transformation, turning it into a future iconic image for thousands of pastel-pink bedroom walls across the land.

"Could you do something more interesting with your hands?" the photographer implored, knowing he was pushing his luck.

"I could wrap them around your neck," came back Zachary's deadpan response. "Seriously though, you must have captured my soul by now."

I was actually grateful rather than irritated that my interview had been delayed. It gave me more time to acclimatise to the thinner, headier atmosphere of Planet Zachary B. During this photo session, I studied Zachary as a zoologist might study an exquisite endangered species. Beauty is often found in the unusual or the different; it's the model with the asymmetrical smile you remember. So I looked for Zachary's flaws. I would eventually discover that his strong features were commonplace in his father's Ethiopia: the deep-well depths of those almost-black eyes and that clearly defined bone structure would have gone unremarked upon in a land where everyone glides along the dusty streets as if they are catwalks. But here – in this moment and in this place – Zachary was otherworldly. Beauty is not just in the eye of the beholder, it also depends on where the beheld and the beholder are from. However, it was a close thing for Zachary: this was the guiltlessly racist 1970s. But because his mixed blood tempered his Ethiopian physiognomy (narrowing his nose and thinning his lips, giving him a safer, more Mediterranean look), the dude could *pass*, as they used to say. Zac told me that as a child he'd once removed a plaster from a grazed knee and noticed how pleasingly pale the revealed skin was. From that moment on, he dreamt of covering himself from head to toe in sticking plasters so that he could then tear them off, one by one, to be reborn with the paper-white skin of his school friends. Yes, beauty is also in the eye of the dominant culture. Eventually, the photographer stopped begging for more time and packed away his stuff. As he did so, Zachary questioned him about his family. Although he didn't seem to listen to the school sports day anecdotes that followed. Then the photographer gave a funny little curtsy and backed awkwardly out of the room.

Zac carefully put down his guitar, as if it was a baby rather than a musical instrument, and then collapsed back into his cushion ocean. He raised a heavily bangled arm in order to signal that I should sit down beside him.

"*Rock On* – am I right? You were a little early..."

"Er... Yes. Sorry, was I?" I wrestled my portable cassette recorder from my bag.

I shakily pressed down the two square buttons: "Play and Record." I didn't think I'd said it aloud, but Zac's laughter told me otherwise.

"Are you sure you know how to operate that thing?"

"Er... yes. Yeah. Of course."

"Sorry about all that photo session nonsense. Part of a day's work at the moment. All very tedious."

Before I could answer, a strikingly beautiful black woman appeared in a billowing white trouser suit, carrying a tray on which three glasses and a bottle had been placed. A Siamese cat was following her, but then it changed its mind and trotted back out again. The tidy ropes of hair elaborately piled high on her head miraculously remained in place as she placed the tray on the floor in front of us. She was almost as extraordinary looking as Zac. It was as if an inspired sculptor had boldly sliced off both her clay cheeks with a pallet knife in order to create the most aerodynamically honed face I'd ever seen. She gave me a brilliant white smile, introduced herself as Jody, and then knelt down by Zac's other side. To my horror, I found myself blushing at the thought that I didn't deserve to be breathing the same air as these two higher beings, but fortunately they were too preoccupied with each other to notice.

"What have you done to your hair? And your eyeliner's all smudged!" She talked to Zac as if he were a child, not giving him time to respond, fussing with his clothes and gently chastising him for messing up all the fine-tuning she'd done on his appearance before the shoot. When she had finished attending to Zac as if he were a flower arrangement, she offered me a limp hand to shake, and those honed cheeks to pretend to kiss. I think I got through the ritual without seeming too gauche.

"Nice to meet you, Paul. I'm afraid it's been a pretty crazy day – but then that's not unusual at the moment," said Jody.

Was she African or West Indian? There was a trace of American in her accent too. She went over to the huge stereogram (its coffin-like appearance enhanced by those ubiquitous candles) and slipped the as-yet-to-be-released *An Eye For An Eye* from its paper inner sleeve before handing me the gatefold cover. It was indescribably thrilling to be hearing it before anyone else. Possibly because of this it has remained my favourite Zachary B album to this day. And the sound that that stereogram had! Many times I failed to adjust the crude treble and bass knobs on my own cheap deck to replicate it.

As the conversation became more relaxed, in direct relation to the amount of rum we drank, I found out that Jody was in fact from Jamaica via America. I also found out that Jody had her own fashion business, and that Jody had done most of the interior decoration in the flat herself, and that Jody... well, you get the picture. I was keen to talk to Zac about the new album, but Jody seemed to think I was there to interview her. Not in a bad way, I hasten to add. She was simply more comfortable talking to strangers than he was. However, I did eventually come to realise that Jody was Zac's filter system; she worked out who could be trusted and who couldn't. And Zac clearly adored her, and had no problem with her holding court while he doodled away on the guitar and occasionally interjected.

"Last month Zac took me to the Bahamas to celebrate our third year together. We were thinking Paris – where we met – but Paris is a bit predictable, don't you think?" She paused to light a Pall Mall. "What was the name of that club again, Zac? The one Mick Jagger goes to?" Zac shrugged, but she wasn't expecting him to answer anyway. "Do you know something, Paul? I didn't even know who he was – Zac, I mean. But you liked that didn't you, baby?" She looked over to Zac. This time an answer was expected.

"I wasn't that well-known then anyway, so…"

"Zac played me one or two of his tunes, but I can't say I was that impressed," continued Jody, laughed a warm, open laugh, her head thrown back. "But I like what you're doing now, sweetheart," she added quickly, patting his knee and smiling conspiratorially at me.

Eventually, Jody left us alone and I got to ask Zac about the new album, his influences, and all the other stuff that we music anoraks find so desperately important.

"We did the album at a great little studio just outside Paris. We wanted Visconti, but ended up with this new guy, Justin Hammond. Fortunately, he got where I was coming from, and we laid down the basic tracks in just two weeks. Six weeks to add strings and overdubs. Like the elephant noises on *Ghost Lover*."

"Elephant noises?"

"We ran them backwards. Very spooky in a pachydermic kind of way."

"How do you see yourself in relation to say, Bowie or the Sweet?"

"The Sweet!" Zac recoiled in horror. "Builders dressed as princesses. And they don't even write their own stuff. Bowie's cool. He'll be around for a while. But Zachary B and the Now are edgier and funkier than any of them."

"But you wear the platform boots and makeup. You're playing the game too…"

"We have to sell records," Zac replied flatly. He seemed momentarily thrown by my rum-fuelled front, but hid it well. "But we're not really glam, now, are we?"

He always turned questions back on me, flatteringly implying that I was intelligent enough to work the answer out for myself, but then he'd answer anyway. "Look, my roots are in Stax, the Stooges, African music. You can't get more rock 'n' roll than African music can you? But this is a business. You do what you've gotta do…"

"Including dressing in women's clothes?"

"Come now, Paul. I expected more from you than that." Zac ran his hand down the wide lapel of his red satin jacket as if he were stroking a cat, before adding "are you threatened by all this then? Of course you're not. I enjoy dressing up. You should try it sometime."

I changed the subject. "You're from Chelmsford, aren't you? Don't you take inspiration from any British bands?"

"I was *born* in Chelmsford, but what does that mean? I'm a half-caste. My mother, bless her, still lives there. And of course I love bands like the Stones and the Kinks. But we're about soul music from Saturn. Vibes from Venus!"

We were back to the rehearsed script, but I was thrilled that, as far as I knew, this was the first time Zac had made public the fact he was mixed race. Intentionally or unintentionally he'd given me an exclusive.

We talked for about another hour before Zachary's concentration began to flag.

"I know it's one of those awful, unanswerable questions, Zac, but what inspires you?"

"What inspires me?"

"I only ask because I know you won't give me a predictable answer."

"Well now you've set me up for a fall…"

"I'm sorry, I'm new to all this…"

"Don't panic, I'm only teasing. It's not so much a case of being inspired as being receptive. When artists say they are inspired by a woman or a landscape – do you know what? I don't believe them. Or rather, I don't believe they're a real artist."

"How do you mean?"

"Well, it's not as direct as that. When I'm composing, the music feels like it's coming from another universe…"

"Now you're really losing me…"

"Look, if you're any good at what you do, especially with anything creative, it shouldn't be hard to do it. The idea of the struggling artist – apart from in a financial sense – is bullshit. It just flows out of you or through you. Sometimes I don't work out what a song is about until years after I wrote it. The point is, it doesn't seem to come directly from me."

"So you're saying it's some kind of divine inspiration?"

"Your words not mine. All I know is I rarely feel a part of the process when it's going well, but painfully part of the process when it isn't."

"So what do you believe, spiritually speaking?"

"I believe it's time this interview came to an end." Zac hand-signalled to me to turn off the cassette machine. "It's getting late my young friend. And that's a big subject, but it's been a pleasure." He scrutinised me, narrowing his eyes. "I like you. We'll do this again."

He looked about himself, like an old man in need of his nurse. "Jody. Jody! Can you show our young friend out?"

Jody instantly reappeared, as I struggled up from the quicksand of cushions. I bent to receive a gentle handshake from Zac, who remained semi-reclined, and Jody showed me to the door.

"I hope you got what you came for, Mr Coleridge." I detected a veiled note of aggression in her voice. I was disappointed that after such a pleasant evening I was still being treated as the enemy.

"All I came here for, Jody, was a good interview," I replied, still emboldened by alcohol. I needed her to know her tone hadn't gone unnoticed. She seemed taken aback by my impassioned response.

"No, of course not. I'm sorry, Mr…"

"Paul. Call me Paul – you have been all evening."

"Yes, Paul. Sorry, Paul." She nervously tucked escaped ropes of hair back under ornate hairclips. "You have to understand Zac doesn't have a great relationship with the media. You know how they like to pigeonhole everything. Most of our attempts to get them to just come to a gig have been ignored."

"Yes, it pisses me off too," I said, thinking of *Rock On*.

All of a sudden Jody looked incredibly tired.

"Just one live review in *Sounds* and two single reviews in *Melody Maker* is not much to show for three years of hard work. If it wasn't for the radio airplay we'd have given up by now,

"Look, Jody," I began, straightening my back, instantly finding myself comfortable in my new role as Zachary B's champion. "Hopefully that's all going to change now. Get Zac to announce at Sunday's Roundhouse gig that they'll be a big feature in next week's *Rock On*. That'll send their sales through the roof. And then they'll be eating out of your hand."

She looked at me with a mixture of mild astonishment and lingering suspicion. I knew what she was thinking, so I quickly added, "Yes, I know *Rock On* hasn't shown any interest in Zachary before, but the-times-they-are-a-changing. They're beginning to realise which side their bread's buttered on."

Her tensed features softened and she laughed. "Yes, I like that – which side their bread is buttered on! Well thank you, Paul." She seemed to look at me with new eyes: was this the same nervous young man she'd met for the first time earlier in the evening? The funny thing was, this me was a new me to me too. Yes, it was partly the drink and the excitement, but I also felt a seismic shift had occurred in my personality. I turned back to see Jody's elegant silhouette giving me a graceful, cheery wave from the door she still held slightly ajar.

I floated back to Westbourne Park Station. Even some verbal abuse from a group of dead-eyed skinheads (Get yer 'air cut yer fuckin' poof!) couldn't wipe the stupid grin from my face. I couldn't believe my own chutzpah. I had gone from nervous first-time interviewer to single-minded media champion of Zachary B, in the space of just a few hours, and I felt entirely comfortable in my new glowing skin.

The iced air magnified my tipsiness, and by the time I got back to Peckham I felt stupidly drunk. Even when sober, mounting the creaky stairs up to my third-floor room without disturbing the landlord, was dauntingly difficult. Mr Koumi, a sallow Greek Cypriot who owned the hairdresser's on the ground floor, hated any noise after ten, and it was well past midnight. I usually took off my platform shoes before ascending, but in my less than lucid state I forgot. I was rewarded for this heinous crime by the frightening vision of Koumi, all chest hair and pickled-egg eyes, scowling at me from his doorway.

"How many times! How many bloody times! Show a bit of consideration, boy. You know I'm in bed by nine, what with my back and everything!"

"Sorry Mr Koumi. Shoes – I forgot to take my shoes off."

"I can see that! I don't know how you can walk in those bloody things!"

He retreated into his flat, cursing multilingually, slamming the door behind him.

How different the brutally lit interior of my room looked to me now, compared to when I'd left it this morning. Then it had simply been my reality. But since languishing in Zac and Jody's cushioned and candlelit wonderland, my rented wallpaper (vertical wavy lines of chewing-gum pink, French-mustard yellow and dog-shit brown) seemed to press in on me malevolently from all sides. Surely I deserved better than this?

Mr Koumi's cat, Demis (named after Demis Roussos) was curled up at the end of my coffin-narrow bed. He lifted his ginger head in greeting. I rubbed him under the chin, and just managed to spoon some globs of Kitikat on to a saucer before passing out on the bed.

The next morning, I was eased out of sleep by the intermittent buzzing of my faulty two-bar electric fire. A white rum hangover is a rum thing indeed – even my eye sockets ached. But nothing could take the edge off the excitement I felt as the memories of the previous day came skipping back. I lay there for an hour staring at the white stippled ceiling (the only relief from the haranguing wallpaper) smiling to myself. I couldn't believe how much time Zac had given me – two C90's worth. Eventually, I got up, heaved my prehistoric typewriter onto the bedside table that doubled as a desk, and pressed Rewind followed by Play.

★

Jake was so pleased with the interview ("Blimey, who'd have thought he was a darkie!") that he wanted me to expand it. Some American singer-songwriter had cancelled a UK trip and so there was a page that needed filling. Why didn't I go and have a word with Zac's manager, Nick Valentine?

★

"Crisp?" As a concession to good manners Nick Valentine lowered his feet from his desk as he proffered the almost empty bag of Golden Wonders. People say, don't trust someone whose eyes are too close together, but what if they're too far apart? Valentine's eyes also bulged slightly, making him look simultaneously bovine and reptilian in his purple three-piece suit. "The single's doing great – no thanks to you guys," he said.

My albatross of a hangover made me uncharacteristically blunt in reply. "Hey, don't tar us all with the same brush."

"Whatever you say, kid. Anyway, if the airplay keeps up it'll be top ten by the end of the month. Then there's a UK tour in January to coincide with the second album..." He drew the last life from a cigar before vigorously stubbing it out in an onyx ashtray. Then he resumed his default position: feet on desk, hands clamped behind his head like a sunbather. A blonde in a Day-Glo pink miniskirt flounced in, put a pile of post on his desk, and then flounced out again. "Have we sent you the album yet?"

"No, but Jody played it to me when..."

"The forty-piece orchestra on the title track will blow your mind. We just need some good press from the right people to seal the deal, if you get my drift." I ignored his spiel.

"So who is the real Zachary B?" As soon as the words were out, I realised my question was as clichéd as all the guff he'd been spouting. Valentine didn't even try to conceal his boredom. "Well, don't let all that peace-and-love bullshit fool you. He needs fame even more than he needs money."

The unflattering picture Valentine painted of the man he was supposed to be promoting surprised me. My next question sounded even more naive. "But surely the music's the most important thing?"

"Sure, kid, the music's important…" Valentine repeatedly stabbed the stud of his ballpoint pen into his desktop, clickedy click, clickedy click. He was clearly born bored and needed the heightened reality of the music business just so to feel something. "Don't get me wrong though, kid. The guy *lives* to play music. But if you're that talented you're gonna want people to hear you. It comes with the territory."

And so it continued in fits and starts for half an hour. Valentine was clearly relieved when I said I'd got all I needed, but just as I was leaving he brightened up. "Hey, kid." This kid thing was intensely irritating; he was from Canvey Island not Coney Island. "Anytime you want to interview Zac, just call. He was on the phone earlier saying how well yesterday went. And Zac's not an easy man to please. Rock 'n' Roll!"

"Er, yes. Rock and roll."

He was about to say something else when both phones rang simultaneously. He reached for another cigar before answering either of them.

Extract from *The KUU Hypothesis* by Zachary Bekele

Entertainment as Enlightenment

The central idea of *The KUU Hypothesis* is that a connection can be cultivated between The Knowing Unknowable Universe and the receptive "entertainer of the possibility" on Earth. By entertaining the possibility that unexplainable events such as coincidences are in fact Cosmic Nudges from the KUU, you may in turn be entertained, and enlightened while also increasing the likelihood that more of these events will come your way.

The Evangelical Agnostic

If you are reading this, you are probably a sceptic, atheist or agnostic, rather than a believer. Believers already have their holy instruction manuals and would have little use for this ragbag of deliberately uncommitted musings. But if you *are* a believer, please forgive me for underestimating you. I'm part evangelical agnostic and part woolly-minded fantasist myself, so we are not that dissimilar.

A Born-Again Questioner

I'd like to pre-empt your suspicions that KUUism is like all the other spaced-out homemade religions that you may have encountered. All the events and ideas relayed here are grounded in reality in all its deceptively banal details. I am just a born-again questioner with a novel interpretation of the facts.

Everything is Remarkable

If something seems to defy the laws of physics it is no more or less fantastic to a child than the sight of ripples spreading on a pond from where a thrown stone has landed. The child has no sense of what *should* be possible: the dropped toy could just as easily float away as fall to the ground. Unfortunately traditional education methods prevent our wide-eyed children from becoming wide-eyed mystics.

3

"I will continue to try to persuade The Leader Who Is Not A Leader to grant you an interview but, in the meantime, I'm more than happy to answer any of your questions," said Barney Merrick, as he slowly poured mint tea into August and Damian's glasses and then into his own. "To be honest, I'm slightly hurt at how little interest you have in me." He affected a sulky expression. "Without my efforts there wouldn't have even been a KUU Foundation or even The KUU Hypothesis itself."

Merrick told August and Damian more about the KUU Tripod as he took them down to the Lower Ground Floor. They found a table with an unrestricted view of the swimming pool. Soundproof glass prevented the poolside hubbub from disturbing them. After a few minutes, a square-set man in a shiny grey suit joined them. Merrick stood and shook the man's hand, before introducing him to August and Damian. "This is my friend and business associate, Ramadi."

Ramadi shook Damian's hand, but when he turned towards August his hands remained resolutely at his sides and he merely gave her a shallow bow. It crossed August's mind that this Muslim tradition of never touching a woman who wasn't your wife, said a lot about the innate power that men felt women had over them. Perhaps it was what led so many cultures to subjugate women in the first place – male

63

paranoia had a lot to answer for. But there was no point in taking offence. So she just let the moment pass, feigning gracious acceptance of her Untouchable, Unclean status. However, she had to elbow Damian in the ribs to prevent him from taking offence on her behalf. But Damian had taken an instant disliking to Ramadi anyway. It was the man's face. It was so deeply etched with lines that at first Damian didn't notice the diagonal scar that bisected his right cheek, no doubt the result of some backstreet knife fight. How could you not be wary of someone like that? But what really upset Damian was that he resented the fact that Ramadi looked like the quintessential suspicious foreigner of the adventure stories he'd read as a child. He was trying his hardest to be politically correct in this overwhelming place, and then reality would go and throw him a curve ball like this.

Merrick began talking about his Arab friend. "Without Ramadi none of this would have been possible. He oversaw the whole project and made sure everything was okay with the... er... locals. And of course it would have been twenty times more expensive to build the Tripod in London."

Ramadi slowly removed the cellophane from a fresh packet of cigarettes while Merrick continued to sing his praises. Once his cigarette was lit and his gold Pierre Cardin lighter was returned to his breast pocket, he interjected in clear, precise English. "Sometimes it is difficult for foreign investors in Marrakech. There can be ill feeling towards what are sometimes seen as colonisers, but at least Mr Merrick is not French!" Even Damian laughed at this.

Merrick smiled. "Ramadi was brilliant with the local workmen. It's still the Middle Ages here when it comes to building methods – which, of course, are no use with a structure like this – so we could only use them to clear the site. There had to be some hefty baksheesh otherwise we would have had a revolt on our hands."

"Mr Merrick wisely agreed to the sacrifice of a ram," said Ramadi, smiling. "It is something we do to celebrate a new wife, a new car, a new building, or whatever. The ram has to face east and… but I shall spare you all the details, as there is a lady present. But it was a wonderful party for everyone – the local people, some government officials. It was the wise thing to do." Ramadi raised his coffee cup to Merrick in a salute. "Showing a willingness to fit in, is everything in our culture."

Damian could see that August was poised to ask a significant question by the way she was sitting forward in her chair, both elbows on the table. "I have to ask you this, Barney. Were you being deliberately provocative making the KUU Tripod a metre taller than the mosque?"

"Now, where did that suddenly come from?" Merrick laughed. He exchanged a knowing glance with Ramadi. "You know, you're the first journalist that's ever thought to ask me that. Good for you, my girl! As a matter of fact, yes, no, and kind of." He settled into lecture mode. "We took as our example the Dome of the Rock – do you know it? It's an exquisite building in Jerusalem. It was the first Islamic structure to be built there – around AD 700, I believe – following the capture of Jerusalem by the Muslims. The designers made absolutely sure it was the best advertisement possible for Islam by building it a metre taller than the highest local Christian edifice, the Church of the Holy Sepulchre, the place where Jesus is said to have been buried. They also gave it a much grander gold dome, significantly twenty-eight centimetres wider than the church's dowdy old stone one."

"Nice one," interrupted Damian.

"Well, that's only half the story," continued Merrick, searching his pockets for something. "On the wall of this provocative structure were the first words from the Koran ever to be made public. In essence, these words stated that Mohammed's people thought Jesus a decent enough chap, and they wished him well and all that, but they nevertheless doubted very much that he was the Son of God."

Merrick seemed to forget what he was looking for in his pocket as a young mother wrapped in a red towel distracted him. She was walking her toddler along the near side of the pool and seemed to sense Merrick's distracted stare. Her retaliatory glare instantly woke him from his trance. He continued from where he'd left off without skipping a beat. "But you've got to laugh, haven't you – my dome's bigger than your dome! That's why we couldn't resist getting in on the joke. Of course if you take the globe – our symbol of Earthly unity – off the top, our structure comes in at just under the height of the Mosque, but if people want to make trouble they'll make trouble. We just couldn't resist teasing all those thin-skinned believers just a little bit."

"Like Salman Rushdie did, you mean," said Damian

August quickly interjected. "So how does Marrakech feel about the KUU Tripod now, ten years down the line?" She directed the question at both men.

Merrick turned to Ramadi, who half-smiled and took a deep breath. "I won't lie to you. It has not been easy for many people here." He turned to Merrick. "What you have done here is... how you say... provocative. But at the same time, the people here want progress. They want to be a part of the twenty-first century." He shrugged. "It is just a pity that..."

"I think what my good friend, Ramadi, is trying to say is that the Tripod is an insult to Islam," interrupted Merrick. "But then what isn't? And it's no consolation to them that it's also an insult to Christianity, Judaism, Scientology, science, or any other belief system you care to mention." Ramadi laughed and Merrick continued. "It doesn't matter how many times I tell my friend, Ramadi, here, that KUUists are obliged to entertain the possibility that the Koran is the truth, the Bible is the truth, or Richard bloody Dawkins is the truth. The "great" religions: Christianity, Islam, Judaism – want unshakeable belief from their people, and nothing less." Merrick lightly slapped Ramadi's back and the two men once again shared a companionable moment. "See how easy it is for two men to love and respect each other. But once religion comes in to the equation, all these good feelings are forgotten."

"I think *you* think that we Muslims take ourselves more seriously than we do," said Ramadi. "But many of us drink on the quiet, or don't pray as much as we should. And we too get tired of being ranted at by gentlemen with long beards on the television. We are only human..."

"Human?" Damian stroked his negligible goatee with exaggerated thoughtfulness. "If only all of you were so reasonable."

Ramadi gave Damian a look of almost fatherly concern, and then took a deep breath. "What you people call an Islamic terrorist is usually just a naive young man who has been won over by strangers on an Internet chat room. It's as simple as that." He gave a resigned shrug of the shoulders. "These boys know very little about Islam and care even less. You must understand there is no doctrine behind it – all this madness – no set ideology. Just dulled minds and hardened hearts trying to impose some kind of meaning on the world and their own lives. It's very tragic."

"You said it." Damian looked like he wanted to say something else, but he thought better of it.

"Just one more question," said August, trying to repress the image of Peter Falk as Columbo that had popped into her head. "Could you tell us a bit about yourself and your role in the KUU Foundation, Barney?"

Merrick stiffened. "To be honest, I like to keep a low profile. I have a good life here, just acting as genial host. I don't want that to change. So I'd be grateful if we could just stick to discussing the KUU Foundation and its interests in world unity and peace."

August was about to protest, but Merrick's face told her he wasn't going to be persuaded into saying anything else, not at this juncture at least. So instead she followed her right hook with a left jab. "Okay, fair enough. Let's talk about the suicides then."

But Merrick was more prepared for this line of questioning. "Tragic, tragic. What else can I say? But if there is one religion – or non-religion in our case – which has no responsibility for its practitioners, or members, or whatever you'd like to call them, it's KUUism. We have the skeleton of a philosophy but, as you know, it's primarily a philosophy committed to its lack of commitment to the very ideas it puts forward." As Merrick warmed to his subject, his tone became more mellifluous. "It's about freeing yourself from what binds you and becoming a Born-Again Questioner. So we can't be held responsible for people who get lost along the way."

Circling the table, taking photographs, Damian became fascinated by how August slowly came to life doing her job. It was as if she were playing the tennis match she'd only previously been warming up for. Her whole posture had changed. Her eyes burnt with the need to know. She was born to interrogate; he was glad he wasn't Barney.

"Look, I don't mean to be rude, Barney," she continued. "But I didn't come here for a KUU sermon. In the last two months, a dozen KUUists have gotten lost along the way, as you euphemistically put it. And the KUU is somehow involved. You or your staff must have at least known Malika Zrihan, the Marrakech boy who died? He must have visited the Tripod?"

"Hundreds of KUUists along with the merely curious, bored or hungry, pass through these doors every week…" Merrick thought for a moment before adding, "But, yes, I'm not going to deny that Malika was a regular visitor… ."

"Why would you deny it?" asked Damian, surprising himself with this spontaneous interjection, as he ran through the pictures he'd just taken on his camera's tiny screen. The edge in Damian's voice clearly riled Merrick.

"Indeed. Why would I deny it? Look, Malika was a sweet boy, but troubled. All we can do is lend an ear. We have over thirty KUU counsellors providing support for what we call belief refugees…"

"Belief refugees?" Damian put his camera back in his bag.

"Those who are in the process of throwing off the shackles of Islam, Judaism, Christianity, or whatever," continued

Merrick. "It's a difficult time for them. It can be painfully hard to let go of a faith when you've grown up with it; when you've been immersed in it since birth. Some of these poor souls are saying goodbye to their family, their job, even their whole community – never to return. Not through their choice, but because family or friends refuse to have anything further to do with them. Regrettably, because of the demands placed on our limited resources, it becomes impossible to spend as much time as we'd like with each individual. And some are needier than others."

"But you can't get needier than someone who commits suicide," said August, trying to keep the anger out of her voice.

"I can understand why you're upset, August, but directing it at me won't help matters. Shit happens." The American expression sounded absurd delivered in Merrick's precise upper middle class accent.

Ramadi was looking increasingly uncomfortable, repeatedly clicking his cigarette lighter open and shut.

Merrick continued. "Every charity is under-funded and we receive no financial help at all. We get some income from paying guests visiting the Tripod, who, I hasten to add, only make up 50% of people staying here. The remaining rooms are for those seeking sanctuary. Our other main source of income is *The KUU Hypothesis* itself of course. Sales have been growing exponentially in recent years."

"Praise be to the Internet," said August.

"Indeed, indeed. The Internet has made a huge difference. Although both *The KUU Hypothesis* and Paul Coleridge's controversial little memoir have always sold steadily.

"But to get back to Malika."

"Yes of course. Well, I spoke to the young man on a couple of occasions, if memory serves. After one of our counsellors, Alice Cooper, thought a word with me might help him."

Damian interjected. "Does Alice know she has the same name as a...."

"Shhhh!" August glared at Damian.

Merrick ignored the interruption. "Sometimes would-be KUUists seem to want, or need, a more direct connection to... . to the beginning I suppose. I was there, you see. It helps them to..." Merrick smiled. "Not believe, obviously. But it helps them to connect."

"So what was your impression of Malika? Did he seem unstable? Depressed?"

"Not at all. He was bright, lively. Full of KUU spirit."

"So why do you think Alice thought Malika should speak to you? Obviously this wasn't standard procedure."

"Indeed not. Getting an audience with me could be compared to getting an audience with the Pope. I jest of course. But, yes, I am a busy man."

Merrick at last found what he was looking for in his pocket; a small battered tin from which he took a wodge of tobacco, which he lovingly fed to his pipe. Delay tactics, thought August. The man had talked himself into a corner, and was trying to think of a way out.

So would it be possible for me to speak to Alice?"

"I've no idea. She's no longer with us."

"Is she still in Marrakech?"

"Sorry, I can't help you there either, but I doubt it."

"Was there a problem?"

"I'm afraid there was. She had become less and less patient with would-be KUUists who were having difficulties breaking away from their faiths. It's impossible to emphasise enough how hard it can be for some people to let go.

August finished her coffee and then addressed her final question to both men, a note of disbelief in her voice. "How can you two work together? You're obviously not a KUUist, Ramadi, yet you've been working with Barney for, what, ten years now?"

Ramadi smiled the smile of the spiritually self-assured; the smile of someone blessed with the patience and grace mere non-believing mortals can only dream of possessing. "My friend here has a good heart." It was now Ramadi's turn to pat Merrick on the back. "And I believe that somewhere deep in that sceptical heart of his, he does believe in God. But, at the end of the day – as you people say – it doesn't matter what he decides to call that God..." Ramadi paused for a second before delivering his holy punch line. "Because that God is Allah."

Both men laughed.

"That explains everything," said Damian, under his breath.

Extract from *The KUU Hypothesis* by Zachary Bekele

Do Car Crashes Exist?

The scientific mindset is an insidious influence in every area of our lives. It is part of our hardwiring that the unexplained is not worthy of our attention unless it's in the form of escapist entertainment: if you haven't seen it, then it doesn't exist. Yet the fact that you may never have witnessed a serious car crash doesn't mean car crashes don't exist. Most people keep it to themselves if they think they've seen a UFO or had a supernatural experience, for fear of ridicule. However, the one form of unusual occurrence that we don't feel self-conscious about discussing is coincidence. After all, coincidences are just coincidences... aren't they?

The Subtly Supernatural

But what if coincidences are the subtlest form of supernatural phenomena? Because of their subtlety, they may surprise or even astonish us, but we don't necessarily question their meaning or significance. The astute reader may be wondering what is in these pages if not some quantifying and defining of the Knowing Unknowable Universe. The answer is imaginative conjecture and nothing more. If I do appear to make any definitive statements, please understand that I am just hypothesising and improvising around a theme. I could have begun every sentence with the words "I entertain the possibility that..." but that would waste both your time and mine.

Extract from
The Life and Death of Zachary B
by Paul Coleridge

The Stiff Little Men Span and Clattered
September 1972

An Eye for an Eye entered the lower reaches of the charts the first week of its release (perhaps partly thanks to my article) and then, like a stoically determined mountaineer, finally got a foothold in the Top Ten in October. The final frontier was reached by the next single, *Sensimilija*; a kind of *Strawberry Fields* with a Jamaican lilt. When it was released in March '72 those toothy Radio One DJs thought the title was the name of some foreign chick. But then those headphoned morons thought grass was something the gardener dealt with, and smack was something you did to the satin-clad bottoms of your female fans. So *Sensimilija* got round-the-clock airplay until the phone calls started flooding in from middle-class, middle-aged, middle-England claiming the record was corrupting the nation's youth by promoting marijuana. Once banned it became irresistible to a generation baffled by the outright hypocrisy of their puritanical yet *Carry on Nurse*-loving parents. Censoring *Sensimilija* was just the stamp of disapproval the record needed. In fact, The Sensimilija Incident, as it became known (as if it were a Hollywood conspiracy thriller) was the turning point. It made Zachary B and the Now seem edgier than all the camp competition bolstering their male, as well as their female, fan base.

The only person at *Rock On* who seemed on the same wavelength as me was Debora. One day she leant over her typewriter to whisper that she had a soft spot for Marc Bolan – after all he had written a song about her! She even dropped the H at the end of her own name to align herself more perfectly with her song. Barney and Andy may have been only five years older than me, but musically and idealistically they were from a different planet. I was born in 1955. My generation were (drum roll please...) The Children of the Future!

During the Sixties, fact and fiction seemed to become delightfully blurred. While Factual-man was taking one slow-motion giant leap for mankind, Fictional-man was going where no man had gone before. And while the USS Enterprise had warp drive, our very own Concorde wasn't that far behind, hurtling through the blue faster than the speed of sound. We knew, in our bionically replacable bones, that one day all sci-fi would become sci-fact, but we needed a soundtrack for our dreamed-of future and supersonic present. Fortunately, musical instruments and effects had kept apace with rockets and jet planes, and so Roxy Music, Bowie, Bolan and Bekele were able to make us feel the full thrill of the age we lived in. Or as they say, if Zachary B hadn't existed, someone would have had to invent him. Meanwhile, Jake, Barney and Andy were trapped in a past crippled by both post-World War Two austerity and post-Vietnam cynicism. Their earnest hippy singer-songwriters and self-indulgent rock experimentalists were the musical quicksand from which they had no will to escape. Once, when I was delivering a Gilbert O'Sullivan piece I'd done on autopilot, I had a bit of a barney with Barney on this very subject. Barney always tried to start an argument about music whenever I visited the office. It was presumably his way of creating a brief distraction from the daily lack of grind. Or maybe he just envied the fact I wasn't stuck there all day like he was.

Barney gained his reputation as a journalist with a series of self-financed (or rather, parent-financed) trips to Africa in the late Sixties to explore tribal music. *Rock On* had humoured him by publishing these pieces, perhaps thinking it would add some kind of exotic kudos to the paper. And it did to a degree. *The Times* reprinted them and *Rock On* got name-checked. But that was several years ago, and Barney was still playing the part of the world-weary explorer to the hilt, despite the fact he'd probably not even been south of the river since.

"It's the artifice of the whole thing..." Barney puffed away on the long stemmed Moroccan sebsi pipe he claimed Hendrix had given him at the Speakeasy in '67, but everyone knew had come from a stall on Portobello Road. He looked up at me from under his thick thatch of blond shoulder-length hair. It was the same look he always gave me: could he be bothered to even have this discussion? Okay, he'd humour me just this once. He took a deep breath. "The way theatre has crept into music is just so *vulgar*."

"Oh come off it, Barney. Music's always been a part of theatre and vice versa. Judy Garland was about theatre, Little Richard was pure theatre."

"Yes, but that was then, this is now. Rock is a primal force. It shouldn't be about raiding the bloody dressing-up chest and prancing about like a fairy. It just cheapens the whole thing. Really it does."

"But music is just another form of entertainment. It's great that musicians are making an effort again..."

"They're making an effort to disguise their complete absence of musical finesse. They're a bunch of charlatans, the lot of them."

Andy's head swivelled backwards and forwards between us, as if he was watching us play tennis from the sidelines. But, for once, he took my side. "You've lost me, Barney. What do you mean, cheapens the whole thing? Part of the fun of rock is its cheapness. Just look at the New York Dolls."

But Barney ignored him. His beef was with me. As he paced the office's crooked avenues delineated by unopened parcels of LPs, skyscrapers of old issues, and arbitrarily angled desks, he spoke with the authoritative precision of the lawyer his parents had wished he'd become. "Yes, but that's good cheap. Bowie, Bolan and what's-his-name – it's all just so premeditated. With The Dolls you get the feeling they couldn't be any other way; they were *born* in those clothes, with that hair. They sprung fully-formed from New York's steaming vents; gloriously degenerate superheroes of the narcotically dispossessed!" Barney paused on this high note, tapping pipe ash into one of the numerous ashtrays strategically placed around the office so that no one ever had to move a muscle to use them. It gave me a chance to speak.

"That's bollocks, Barney, and you know it. It's just that bands from across the pond *seem* more romantic and heroic. Our rock musicians had to *create* exotic personas to capture the public's imagination: when you're born in Beckenham or Hackney you have to self-mythologize a bit, whether it's by wearing Japanese kabuki clothes or saying you were once a wizard's apprentice…"

"And how pathetic is that? Making up a life to cover up for how provincial your own life is."

"It's not pathetic; it's fantastic – we should all do it! If you don't like your life then why not invent an alternative? Or give yourself a new name even?"

"What, like Gilbert O' bloody Sullivan?" he sneered, tamping down another wad of Clan into his ludicrous pipe.

The mention of Gilbert O'Sullivan was cruel. I had unofficially become *Rock On's* pop correspondent, which sometimes felt no better than being the tea boy, but I hid my annoyance as best I could. "If all you can do is mention a granny act who has nothing to do with the artists we're discussing, I shall take that to mean your fatuous little argument has run out of steam, Barney. So I'll be on my way."

I often found myself speaking in the vernacular of whoever I was in conversation with. As I reached the door, Barney fired his parting shot. "And they can't play. Bolan only knows three chords."

"That's their genius!" I surprised myself with this simple but paradoxical truth. "It's not about musical excellence as Olympic sport, it's about whether you can dance to it or not."

"Dance? The very idea makes me feel quite queasy…"

"It's about innocence and joy, Barney. The era of the twenty-minute guitar solo is over, my friend."

I understood why Barney thought Zac and his ilk were trying too hard. But it was because they had to. In retrospect, glam was a product of desperation. All of its practitioners had been looking for a way into the music business for years. Glam said, *Notice me*! It was evolution; it was needed.

★

I didn't see Zac again until early Autumn when I tubed it over to the band's rehearsal studios in Camden. They were preparing for an extensive tour of the UK, followed by a few tentative dates in the States, and Jake had suggested I did a behind-the-scenes piece. That first Zac-fronted issue had sold four times more than any previous issue (Zac's Roundhouse audience had been as good as their word) and every day Jake received requests for back copies written on pink scented paper.

As I entered reception, I heard raised voices followed by a loud crash. But the girl at reception didn't even blink a false eyelash at the din going on in the background. She gave my press pass a cursory glance and nodded in the direction of a set of double doors at the end of a short passageway. The doors opened onto a long windowless room at the end of which, to my astonishment, Zac and one of the band were wrestling amongst the debris of a collapsing drum kit. I recognised the second man from photographs. It was the keyboard player, Brian, with his Ziggy Stardust hairstyle. Clutching his injured shoulder, he angrily pushed aside the hi-hat that had fallen across his chest. They hadn't even noticed I'd come in.

"The keyboard riff *is* Cosmic Blood Brothers!"

Zac was backing away, brushing dust from his yellow silk jacket, clearly not interested in continuing the fight.

"And *An Eye for an Eye* – that was my chorus!" continued Brian, trying to square up to Zac, who refused to be squared up to.

Zac composed himself. "I'm sorry, Brian, but I'm not discussing this any further. Yes, you do your bit. But it's not the essence of the song, the spirit of the song." Zac flicked some curls away from his face. "And if you don't like it – and forgive my bluntness here – you can just fuck off."

"You'd like that wouldn't you?" Brian snarled. "Then everything would be just rosy in Zac's little garden. And anyway. Essence? Essence? What the fuck's essence, man? You're so full of shit!"

I was feeling increasingly uncomfortable so I noisily cleared my throat, but the sound died in the dead acoustics of the space. So I tried speaking instead. "Er… excuse me… I'm from *Rock On*."

The band looked like they'd been caught planning a heist as all heads turned towards me in unison. Zac spoke first. "Hey, Paul. Great to see you again. Forgive the boys. A lot of fuss about nothing as usual. Let me introduce you. The dude with the Zappa moustache is bass player Spike. The one with the girlfriend is Colin the drummer…" A dead-eyed blonde was draped around Colin's neck like a feather boa. "…And that's Brian, my truly brilliant keyboard player. Say hello to Paul Coleridge, ace reporter," concluded Zac.

I shook their hands. Brian was still rubbing his shoulder. Colin had disengaged himself from his girlfriend (who had sunk into a grimy old armchair) in order to reassemble his drum kit. But Spike, with his motorcycle-helmet-shaped perm, was the only band member who managed anything like a warm greeting. He vigorously patted me on the back.

"I dug what you wrote, man. Brilliant!" His round frizz of hair vibrated as he spoke, as if it were carrying the charge of his excitement to a million fibre-optic ends. "It's ace you've been a fan since the start. All that over-night-success bullshit; we've been touring for two years solid. And you know that, man. You know that."

I was about to reply when Zac placed a hand gently but firmly on my shoulder.

"Come. We need some quiet and privacy."

"Ponce," Brian muttered, as Zac steered me away from the rehearsal room, through a broom-cupboard of a kitchen, into a kind of games room. A black and white TV flickered away silently in the corner. A mortally-wounded dartboard, its colours mashed into oblivion by a million half-hearted games, hung on the wall. But it was the table football that attracted us. I was about to have a game of table football with Zachary B. How surreal was that? I got a feel for the handles, rocking from one foot to the other, while Zac got us grey coffees from the drinks machine.

"Just let me get these things off." He slumped down onto the brown vinyl bench that ran the length of one wall, and extricated himself from his turquoise platform boots. "I wouldn't normally have all the gear on just for a rehearsal, but as you were coming I made a special effort."

"I'm touched."

"Don't be. I'm just being the consummate professional. Okay, let's go!"   He sprang a ball into play. I was having a game of table football with Zachary B! The stiff little men span and clattered, the ball changed course every half-second.

"Sorry about all that, Paul." Zac said, obviously referring to the fight. "It's just petty jealousies. There wouldn't even be a band if it wasn't for me, and they know it. They also know that I could replace any one of them tomorrow – that's the bottom line." Suddenly Zac doubled up with laughter. I stopped playing. "Jesus! I'm talking in fucking showbiz clichés! But that's my world now – it's inescapable. I'm surrounded by walking, talking clichés: the seedy greedy manager, the jealous fucking keyboard player, and the possessive girlfriend. Are you a cliché rock journalist too, Paul Coleridge?"

"I hope not. I'm not sure what or who I am, to be honest."

"Good answer."

But Zac was right. When you saw the rest of the Now on *Top of the Pops* they might as well have been doing the ironing for all the charisma or stage presence they had. Yes, they could play, yes they wore all the right gear, but they weren't essential to the show as individuals.

In the few seconds since I'd stilled my players, the ball had crept over to Zac's side. Without warning, Zac – having spotted the ball's drift – sent it rocketing past my first line of defence. However, my second line of defence whacked it back with equal force but more accuracy. Goal!

"Nice shot!"

Over and over again, my synchronised team fired balls straight through two lines of Zac's shuttling left-and-right men, leaving Zac helplessly watching as each ball rolled nonchalantly into the goal and then back into the mysterious hidden depths of the table.

Eventually Zac cracked. "Shit!" He jumped back from the table, simultaneously letting go of the handles as if a live current had just passed through them. "Fuck!"

Something of an overreaction I thought. I was about to offer my commiserations, but he'd already got another ball into play. He twisted, twisted again, and then volleyed it into the back of my goal before I'd even begun to position my men. "Nice one," I offered generously, ignoring his unsportsmanlike behaviour. After all, I was playing table football with Zachary B!

We played the best of five, which then became the best of seven when Zac realised he was going to lose, which then became a victory for Zac after I decided to let him win. Then Zac suddenly needed to get back to rehearsing.

"What about the interview?" I asked.

"I'm sorry, Paul. It doesn't feel right just now. Call Valentine. We'll do it soon, I promise. I have to say, I loathe doing interviews."

"But I've got a feature to write…"

"To be honest, Paul, your editor just said you were coming down to check out the rehearsals. No mention of an interview. The boys will have calmed down by now, so it's back to work." I was speechless. He sat down and eased his feet back into his towering boots, and then he lead me back to reception.

"You put up quite a fight there. We must have a rematch some time. And the interview, of course."

Once again, I found myself covertly studying his face. The only thing that gave it a subtle asymmetry was his left eyebrow. It rose to indicate a variety of emotional responses: surprise, curiosity, bemusement, resignation – any excuse and it sprung to life. Now his eyebrow semaphored vulnerable concern as he waited for my assurance that he'd been forgiven for not doing the interview.

"I'll cobble something together," I said. "I'll build the feature around the fact you don't like doing interviews. It'll add to your mystique."

"Excellent! You'll go far in this business."

Luckily I'd got a few standard questions in during the table football: Was there a change of direction with the next album? No – give the kids what they want; were the rumours about film offers true? Yes – he was looking at scripts, but hadn't committed to anything yet (the standard pop star response as it guaranteed a flurry of offers even if the pop star hadn't yet been offered anything); did he have a special message for all the fans out there? Yes – keep watching the stars! All the usual bullshit, in other words. I was a model of discretion and made no mention in my piece of the fight I'd witnessed. The iconic image of the perfect pop star is perhaps as powerful as stained glass windows were to our ancestors hundreds of years ago. The individual depicted becomes more than human – separate from other humans – so that when you meet them it's difficult to take on board the idea that they might be as mortal and flawed as you are. So despite the hour we'd just spent as two blokes playing table football, afterwards we reverted to Pop Star and fan again. It would be a while before our conversations stopped being stilted and stillborn things.

Did the Mystery Man angle of my article actually influence the way Zac began to play that role from then on? Definitely, I would say. As the press became greedy for any morsel of wit or wisdom that spilt from his lips, it made perverse good sense to button them. Because an interested media is also a fickle media, and Zac knew that they could turn on the spin of a less than perfect single. And not talking to them kept them hungry. But it was good news for me too because, apart from some guy from Rolling Stone (he still needed to whore himself to the States) I was the only journalist he'd speak to. And Zac was wonderfully amenable. He'd even answer the surreally silly questions teen mags like *Popswap* and *Jackie* demanded responses to. Although these flimsy publications mainly catered for a demand for A4-sized images of all the pretty boys of the day, they had to keep up some pretence of providing reading material too:

Favourite colour – turquoise.
Favourite food – Yorkshire pudding and banana fritters.
Favourite place – England (of course!).
Favourite record – today it's Rescue Me by Fontella Bass.
Favourite TV Shows – The Ascent of Man and Man About the House.

Had enough? No, I thought not. Although we turn our noses up at all this stuff, we secretly lap it up. Perhaps we think that all these useless shards of trivia will somehow build into a meaningful mosaic, and therefore give us a glimpse into the very soul of our otherworldly heroes. Or is that just me? Favourite toothpaste, Biblical figure, footballer, *Star Trek* character, pet, film, indigenous Australian marsupial, colour of sock, post-Impressionist – we did the lot.

Extract from *The KUU Hypothesis* by Zachary Bekele

My 10 Ground Rules While Creating *The KUU Hypothesis*

1. KUUism couldn't be yet another inflexible set of instructions from on high.

2. KUUism shouldn't propose moral absolutes. Most of us already know in our hearts what's good and bad, even if we don't behave as if we do.

3. *The Bible* has commandments so *The KUU Hypothesis* would have non-commandments – written in sand and not stone.

4. While the world's religions cower under the weight of their own solemnity and piety, KUUism should wear its spirituality lightly.

5. KUUism should be incisive yet vague, issuing stray sparks to light the flame of the imagination, rather than pedantic rhetoric to dull the mind into obedience.

6. The existing religions have brought about so much pain, suffering, guilt and death that their mirror image would surely be an improvement.

7. Let there be humour! Sometimes the muse likes to amuse. But if the reader guffawed at the serious bits while remaining stony faced at the jokes, then that was fine too.

8. Rejoice in inconsistencies. For just as the inconsistencies in other holy books prove that they were written by men and not God, so the flaws in KUUism would guarantee it was never taken too seriously.

9. KUUism can't be sexist because the other religions have covered sexism so comprehensively. The only hope this planet has is to let women have a go at the controls for a few centuries. Etc, etc, Amen!

10. Let the mind wander; let the mind wonder.

4

Marrakech, February 2007

Damian kept changing his mind about August. He'd met women like her before: fine-tuned, blinkered careerists who treated men as if they were either boys or thugs – and interpreted everything they said as if they had some hidden agenda to hurt or deflate. But, it complicated things that he found her physically attractive. It was partly the way she dressed: quirkily mixing and matching in an art-student-with-money kind of way. He also liked the way her eyes looked permanently half-surprised (or would curious be a better word?). And she was quite funny when she relaxed a bit. Yet they'd spent nearly three days in each other's company and he still didn't feel she'd let any of her defences down, not even for a moment. She was hiding something, but what? He thought he'd make a good woman: his instincts about such things were usually right on the nail.

Damian was beginning to wonder if they'd made the right decision turning down Ramadi's offer to be their guide. Just crossing the road in this city was an act of either blind faith or defiant bluff. He could only assume that the ghosts of zebra-crossings (sand-erased grey and lighter grey stripes) had been laid down by some early more reasonable civilisation, because all modes of transport ignore them without conscience. As August and Damian tentatively stepped off the pavement into the traffic an old man shouted out to them, "You have to get the traffic to respect you!" He was right. You had to stride out confidently, believing that it was more important that your fragile frame of flesh and bone got to the other side, than it was that any one of these ferocious vehicles got to their destinations a minute or two sooner than they otherwise would have done if they hadn't slowed to let you cross. Damian had never felt proud of himself after crossing Oxford Street, but here there was a definite sense of achievement if you didn't flinch at the angry horn blasts, and you reached the distant shore of pavement in one piece.

Yesterday when they'd got back to the cool of their riad, Damian had sent private messages to a number of Coup KUUist forum members asking if they knew Malika Zrihan's address. This morning there were three replies. It was out beyond the city wall, so they took a taxi. Malika's family lived in what was called the new city to the north-west of the Medina. August told Damian that much of the area was built by the French in the 1930's (so that was who put down the zebra crossings, thought Damian). Many of the properties retained an atmosphere of that colonial period. It was mostly tourist-free and inhabited by middle-class Moroccans and settled expats. The Zrihans lived in one of the modern concrete apartment blocks just off the main boulevard.

"Jesus, a fucking McDonalds." Damian found himself almost physically recoiling at the sight of the acidic yellow-on-red logo that cancelled out all the crumbling beauty around it.

August resisted the temptation to bend down to stroke a cat when she noticed how filthy it was. The city teemed with these forlorn, long-eared creatures that schizophrenically begged for attention, only to then panic and disappear into the nearest hole in a wall if you tried to oblige them.

"Moroccans believe cats are possessed by human spirits," said August as they watched the animal run ahead of them, and up the steps into the apartment building. "Whereas dogs 'scare away the angels,' quote-unquote. It's because

Mohammed loved cats. Apparently he once cut off his own sleeve rather than disturb the cat that was sleeping on it at the time."

"You mean *the* Mohammed?

"The very same."

"That's something my mum would do."

"Mine too. Aren't cat lovers pathetic?"

Needless to say, the lift wasn't working. Damian thought the building differed little from run-down apartment blocks he'd seen in several European cities. Only the hot motionless air on his bare legs, and the sand in his sandals, told him this wasn't Hackney or Amsterdam.

The door was opened by a woman who August thought didn't look much older than her. For some reason, it always surprised her when she met women her age with children. It was as if she had suddenly been made aware of a parallel life she might have had. Although, of course, there was still time for all that. She silently chastised herself for expecting someone in full burka. Sara Zrihan was wearing jeans and a faded yellow T-shirt.

"It is good that you come. Welcome," said Sara, ushering them in.

The apartment was larger than August imagined it would be, and free of all the Moroccan bric-a-brac-ish stuff that she'd seen everywhere else. A purple three-piece-suite was grouped around a wide-screen TV and a glass-topped coffee table. Unlike her male counterparts – who were often fluent in English, French, Spanish and Arabic – Sara, like most Moroccan women, only spoke Arabic (apart from the few English words she'd offered in greeting). Damian was both astonished and relieved when August immediately began to converse with Sara in her own tongue. There was no reason August should have told him she spoke Arabic, but he would have told her, he thought to himself. To begin with, August kept Damian up to speed with quick asides as to what Sara was saying, but once the conversation became more involved she said she'd fill him in later. Sara poured them tea to go with the generous spread of pastries and fruit she'd put before them. "Malika was a good boy and a happy boy. There is no reason for what they say he did."

"But did you even notice any change in his mood leading up to the day he… the day he died?" asked August.

Damian was glad he wasn't the person having to question this poor woman. He was also touched by the empathy that flowed from August towards Sara.

"He was the same as he always was: playing football during the day, on some chat room at night. Maybe going to a café to meet friends…" continued Sara.

"Was this a particular chat room?"

"I don't know. Maybe, sometimes. He liked to listen to music. He liked rock music. Arcade Fire. He liked Arcade Fire."

"Do you know anything about the KUU, Sara?"

"Of course, yes. Malika was obsessed with the KUU, but we just thought it was a phase. We didn't want to make a big thing out of it. My husband said the boy would find his own way back to Islam when he was ready. This KUU thing was just a fad."

A thought suddenly crossed Damian's mind. He leant over to August. "Can you ask her if we can take a look at the computer?"

August looked at Damian sharply. She then put her hand on Sara's knee by way of an apology for interrupting her flow. Eventually, she asked Damian's question and he was directed by Sara to Malika's bedroom.

Damian was moved by how similar the room looked to his younger brother's room: posters of footballers and Lara Croft on the wall, several pairs of trainers in varying degrees of decrepitude along one skirting board. After awkwardly thanking Sara in French (thinking she might understand it better than English) he tentatively sat down in front of the screen. A Post-it note stuck to the screen gave him the password. He looked through Malika's favourites until he found a link to the Coup KUUist website chat room. He signed-up as a member under the name Holy Joe and began checking some of the discussion topics. Ten minutes later, August looked around the door to say that Sara had made another pot of tea for them. "Two minutes," he responded impatiently.

For the next hour or so, Sara advised August on the best places to eat and – at Damian's request – the best places to hear Gnawa music. Sara relaxed a little and even laughed a couple of times. Damian complained of stomach ache and disappeared off to the toilet. As they were leaving, August handed Sara her card, and thought of one last question.

"The gun, Sara. Do you know where he got the gun from?"

The tears that Sara had managed to hold back for two hours now sprung forth, and August wished she'd kept her mouth shut.

"No. No, I've no idea. Please, you must go now. I'm sorry, I'm sorry."

★

The KUU Foundation's website opened with a CGI animation of Zachary Bekele mounted on a rearing white horse, red cloak flying behind him. The turquoise letters K, U, and U congregated above Zachary's head before growing into the words they stood for. One of the ambient passages of Zachary's instrumental album *Laughter in the Dark* looped continuously in the background. August clicked on chat room and a list of topics appeared:

To believe or not to believe?
Guitar String Theory
Where is Helen's butt?
Zachary wants us to push!

And so on. Countless KUUists with pretentious or silly pseudonyms came and went, virtual fights broke out, religious extremists hurled extreme abuse, and August and Damian began to buckle under the weight of all the never-to-be unresolved arguments on the meaning of all things Zachary Bekele, and all things KUU. Both of them were already familiar with the site, but there were always new conspiracy theories being expounded, new rumours circulating, and new squabbles erupting.

"This is depressing," said August getting up from her chair and throwing herself on the bed. "I'm pooped."

"One more thing to try," said Damian, fishing in his shoulder bag. "Malika's Word files." He held up a silver disc as if it were an Olympic medal.

"Where did you get that from?"

"Where do you think? While you were playing good cop with Sara, I went back to the kid's PC and downloaded all his Word files – it took bloody ages. Windows 98, for fuck's sake."

"So you didn't have a dodgy tummy then?" August was fully attentive again, sitting on the edge of her bed, looking over Damian's shoulder as he clicked on various files.

"No, just dodgy moral scruples. Now let's see... Bingo!" Damian opened a file helpfully named "KUU forum" and started scrolling through pages. "Jesus, there's tons of it. But this is exactly what I'd hoped to find. Some people just tap out their chat room stuff straight into the public domain, but English was a second language to Malika which meant he treated it with a bit of respect, unlike most of these illiterates... Anyway, he didn't want to look stupid so he spell-checked everything in Word Pro before he posted it. Even better, he's cut and pasted some of the dialogue he's responding to into this file as well..."

"So what are you looking for?"

"I'm not sure, but I'll know when I find it."

"Isn't that a U2 song?"

Before Damian continued his scanning and scrolling he turned to face August. "Bit of a confession. I do know what I'm looking for actually. There was a topic, a big one: thousands of hits, called "To push or not to push." It was a debate on the 11th non-commandment – Don't Push the KUU. The whole caboodle had been removed the last time I looked. No one on the forum seemed to know why. But only the site owners could have removed it. I thought at the time it was a bit odd – KUUists not being into censorship and all that…"

"Hey, hang on there. You said you were just KUU curious. You're beginning to sound more like a Coup KUUist."

Damian looked sheepish. "Well, I like to keep track of what's going on. Zachary said the KUU should be an organic ever-changing thing. Always open to new ideas…"

"Or regressing back to old ideas," August snapped back. "The Coup KUUists just want to turn KUUism into just another bloody religion like all the rest, don't they?" August had surprised herself by how passionately she felt this issue. She stared at Damian through narrowed eyes.

"Hey, give me a break. If it wasn't for me, you wouldn't have all this stuff in the first place. This looks *very* interesting." Damian began to scroll more slowly. "There's three guys here – or at least I think they're guys, don't you just hate all this self-nicknaming bullshit? Anyway, they're talking to Malika about some kind of 'final affirmation.'"

Damian continued searching for another ten minutes. Eventually, August leant forward. "Why don't you put 'final affirmation' into the find-and-replace thingy?"

"Good thinking, Batman… Hey, now we're getting somewhere…" With every click of the mouse the software leapfrogged to the next occurrence of the ominous phrase 'final affirmation'.

"Hey, what's this…" Damian shifting over slightly so that August could read what he'd found. "I think we're getting warmer."

Aladdin Cave
Joined: 24 Jan 2004
Posts: 16
Location: undisclosed
Posted: Wed Jun 20, 2007 11:45 a.m.
Post subject: To Push or not to Push

I'm a believer, I just can't bloody help myself. The glam god Zachary was sent to us to preach non-belief to tease us. The KUU wants us to believe, and when we believe it will give us the **final affirmation**.

Diamond Dog
Joined: 01 Aug 2006
Posts: 681
Location: Bristol
Posted: Wed Jun 20, 2007 11:55 a.m.
Post subject: To Push or not to Push

Give us a break AC! Its all that shit that Zachary was getting away from. If you want to push the KUU then that's your business mate, but check your book first – it's a mugs' game. If you want the KUU to nudge you then just forget about the KUU. It worked for me.

Navelgazer
Joined: 03 Sept 2005
Posts: 122
Location: Maastricht, The Netherlands
Posted: Wed Jun 20, 2007 12:12 p.m.
Post subject: To Push or not to Push

I wrote something on another thread about this. You're really on one today aren't you ;) Cheer up, AC!

Aladdin Cave
Joined: 24 Jan 2004
Posts: 16
Location: undisclosed
Posted: Wed Jun 20, 2007 12:17 p. m.
Post subject: To Push or not to Push

Don't you worry about me, Navelgazer. I have a purpose now. The KUU Hypothesis is clued-up if you know where to look. PM me and I'll put you in touch with this real wise dude. He'll see you right. This is the real shit and its big believe me.

Malika
Joined: 24 Feb 2006
Posts: 32
Location: Marrakech
Posted: Wed Jun 20, 2007 12:35 p. m.
Post subject: To Push or not to Push

AC is cool. PM him, you won't be sorry. My life and the way I think about it has changed. I can't wait for the big day – **the final affirmation**. I can't say any more. I shouldn't have even said this much. We must all make our own journey towards the truth of revelation.

Diamond Dog
Joined: 01 Aug 2006
Posts: 681
Location: Bristol
Posted: Wed Jun 20, 2007 13:30 p.m.
Post subject: To Push or not to Push

Feeling those {{{vibes}}} Malika. You've really got it bad, haven't you (whatever it is!) Keep buzzin! You really know how to get this old dog thinking....

HellsAngel
Joined: 09 Dec 2006
Posts: 1
Location: Bristol, UK
Posted: Wed Jun 20, 2007 14:12 p.m.
Post subject: To Push or not to Push

You atheist MOTHERFUCKER FAGS will burn in God's holy hell, fuck you!!

An hour later, August and Damian were still hunched over the laptop going through Malika's Word Files of dialogues he'd had with fellow KUUists. Nietzsche's Cloak, Nudge-addict, the Great Deflator and others each adding their own cliché-ridden, telegrammed responses to various discussions which may, or may not, have led to Malika's death. Every few posts Malika made a sincere and heartfelt comment, and then nothing. The Word document finished. Malika's last post simply stated that he couldn't wait for the Final Affirmation because he trusted that the KUU would deliver him from doubt.

Damian turned to August who was lying back on the bed with her eyes shut. "Are you okay?" he asked.

"Just disappointed. And tired. What hope is there when even something as open and positive as the KUU can get so twisted up like this?"

"We just can't resist belief. It's in our genes. We're like moths to the eternal flames of Hell."

"Quite. And we still don't know why Malika killed himself, or even *if* he killed himself."

Damian leant back in his chair and stretched out his arms. They'd reached a dead end. Several dead ends in fact: each name was a pseudonym except Malika's; they had no idea who Malika was sending private messages to, and they didn't know what advice or wisdom was being passed on to him. "What did you make of Malika going on and on about

The Three Near Proofs? All that dice and Lego stuff?" asked Damian. "I think it might be the key…"

"Me too. But how?" As Damian didn't get a response from August, he turned around. She was sitting up and looking out of one of the small windows into the shaded courtyard. As usual, she responded to his question with a tangential thought rather than an answer, "What is it with these Coup KUUists anyway? I know they're extremists, but what's their angle?" She closed the heavy wooden shutters. Damian was still reading forum dialogue. "Enough," she said, leaning over his shoulder and closing down the laptop. She wished she could switch herself off with the same completeness. "You didn't answer my question, Damian."

You didn't answer mine, thought Damian, but resisted saying as much. "The Coup KUUists? Well, essentially they think Zachary Bekele missed the point. When he stumbled across – or was led to – depending on your view – the idea that the word "kuu" sounds like the word "coup". The Coup KUUists think Zachary should have understood this to be the only important Cosmic Nudge: the vital message that revolutionary action is required in order to sweep the board clean."

"Shit," said August. "Where are these people coming from?"

It was a rhetorical question, but Damian thought he'd answer it anyway. "Like all religious fanatics they need definitive answers, so they went and found definitive answers between Zachary's lines. Or rather, by choosing only one or two lines to focus on."

"You're being very profound all of a sudden."

Damian grinned. "Look, you've only known me three days. I'm full of profound shit like that."

"Of course you are. And you're right. Perhaps most people just don't have the strength of character to revel in the chaos and mystery of the universe. We're all born craving answers. Why is the sky blue? Is there life after death? We need to grapple back some kind of control as we free-fall through life. Perhaps we're simply not ready for the KUU."

"You're right. It's about control; it's about needing to *know* the Knowing Unknowable Universe. Shit, August, I feel we're almost there."

"So near and yet so far."

"Here, catch!" Damian threw August her bag. "Let's go eat. I'm fucking starving."

THE ELEVEN KUU
NON-COMMANDMENTS

(Or Gentle Suggestions)

There had to be eleven because the decimalists have had their own way for too long. The rigid thought matrices we all unwittingly collude in, dictate that ten is order and nine or eleven is disorder. And from the decimal comes the binary, from which many of our troubles stem.

You Already Know What Not To Do!

These are non-commandments because we shouldn't need to be commanded to do what is in our best interests. Five million years of evolution have been overlaid by a few thousand years of cultural distortion. So these non-commandments don't cover killing, fornicating or coveting oxen. They're concerned with the individual's well-being, sense of self and relationship with the *possibility* of a spiritual realm.

The Non-Commandment Chart

If you think any of my eleven suggestions trivial, evil or just plain dumb, then here's a couple that didn't make God's original top ten but were nevertheless given to Moses at the same time. Firstly the peculiarly superficial:

"You are to make tassels for the four corners of the cloak in which you wrap yourself." **(Deut. 22:12).**
And then the somewhat harsher:

"A man whose testicles have been crushed or whose male member has been cut off is not to be admitted to the Assembly of God." **(Deut. 23:2).**

Each is given equal weight in the Bible, yet the former is just sartorial advice while the latter is banishment from Heaven for someone who has already suffered an extremely painful misfortune. Given their absurdity, maybe my alternatives will come as a breath of fresh air.

THE ELEVEN NON-COMMANDMENTS
(OR GENTLE SUGGESTIONS)

1. **YOU CAN LAUGH**

2. **YOU CAN DOUBT**

3. **MEDITATE ON THE MYSTERY OF MUSIC**

4. **ENTERTAIN THE POSSIBILITY, AND THE POSSIBILITY WILL ENTERTAIN YOU**

5. **REJECT ORGANISED RELIGIONS. AND IF YOU'RE AN ATHEIST, REJECT THAT TOO!**

6. **EMBRACE AND DELIGHT IN THE HELLO OF THE COSMIC NUDGE**

7. **FORGET ABOUT LOVE; EMPATHY AND RESPECT ARE THE REAL DEAL**

8. **THE PARADOX IS A PANDORA'S BOX**

9. **THE THIRD WAY LEADS TO THE KUU TRIPOD**

10. **DON'T WORRY ABOUT DEATH – IT'S NOTHING**

11. **DON'T PUSH THE KUU**

Next we will consider each of these non-commandments in more depth.

Extract from
The Life and Death of Zachary B
by Paul Coleridge

Stalker Status

December 1973

Between 1972 and 1975, I was one of only two journalists Zachary B would talk to. Consequently, my credibility as a music journalist improved and I got to do more of the jobs I wanted to do. No more Mud interviews for me! But oddly enough, whenever I did get a prestigious assignment, something went wrong. Lou simply didn't show up, Iggy was spectacularly incoherent, and worst of all, when I got sent to New York to do Bowie after a Madison Square Gardens concert, the painfully thin Thin White Duke collapsed from "total exhaustion" just after the curtain went down. There were no funds to pay for me to hang around and wait for him to recover, and so that was the end of that. But at least I still had Zac.

By the end of 1972 he was even turning down *Top of the Pops*. This could have backfired horribly, but Valentine got Zac's record label AMT to finance a short promotional film for *Strange Camille* which TOTP had no choice but to show. This 16mm exercise in pseudo-surreal self-indulgence (Zac and the band fisheye-lensed into otherworldliness on Hampstead Heath) kept the song at Number One for six weeks.

Whenever I got the call, the pink Rolls would roll up with Zac's chauffeur, Clive, at the wheel and we'd purr across the grey-green worm of the Thames to Zac and Jody's new Swiss Cottage pad. I was surprised they hadn't got somewhere larger sooner, but Zac spent so little time at home, that moving wasn't a priority. It was Jody who eventually found the five-bedroom Victorian property, sufficiently tucked away to not draw too much attention from the fans.

As soon as I arrived, the greyhounds would offer slavering licks to my face and hands it seemed rude to refuse, and Jody would laugh unselfconsciously at my stupid jokes. Jody clearly delighted in the longed-for luxury of a bay-window's worth of daylight caressing walls of yolk-yellow and powder-blue. The homely austerity of stripped floorboards was broken up by casually angled Turkish rugs (of a much better quality than the cheap Moroccan ones in the Notting Hill flat). Zac only became excited about the new place when he realised his in-storage Ernst and Magritte would finally get the wall-space and light they deserved. To begin with, the new house changed Zac for the better. For one thing, he became more relaxed and less wary of me. He even asked me for feedback on tracks he was working on.

The glass and blonde-wood loft studio looked unsightly from the road, making a mockery of the house's elegant Victorian façade. Zachary gleefully told me that the builders had begged him to make it a basement studio to save them lugging all the heavy equipment up three flights of stairs. "Their exact words were, 'Bloody Nora, you're off yer rocker mate," he said in his best Ealing Comedy working man's voice, as we climbed the spiral of wrought-iron steps up to his new playroom. "But I wanted to look at the stars while I worked. And what was I paying them for?"

With only a rectangle of sky visible through the skylight, and the mixing desk festooned with knobs, faders and flashing lights, it was like being in the cockpit of a Boeing 747. When Zac pushed up the faders and a new song jet-engined into life, my fanciful conceit was thrillingly enhanced.

"What do you think? Is the police siren overdoing it?"

"Well, the Sweet did do something similar on—"

"Of course they did! That's got to go then."

Put Your Glam Rags On blasted from two sets of paired-up speakers at a searing volume. Objective criticism is impossible when you're in pain, but it was pointless asking Zac to turn it down. Eventually, I worked out that when Zac played a track this loud it meant he wasn't convinced by it himself and wanted to cover up its flaws with bombast. Jody would sometimes join us. She and I would sit at the back on the old leather sofa Zac had saved from Notting Hill. She'd leaf through *Cosmopolitan* while moaning about the lack of black models in its pages (but nevertheless seeing something every few minutes she had to have), while I scribbled down any verbal gems Zac came out with (it was generally too noisy to use the cassette machine). During those early visits, I'd be brutally honest whenever the embryonic beginnings or over-laboured end of a song disagreed with me. But I soon learnt this wasn't a good idea.

"It's a bit of a mess, actually," I once shouted above the electric storm. "The horns are over icing the cake a bit."

"WHAT?" Zac shouted back.

"It's great," I U-turned.

At first I thought fate had saved me, but then something about the expression on Zac's face suggested he'd heard what I'd said and was giving me the chance to either retract my criticism or have the guts to repeat it.

"YEAH, ISN'T IT! THOSE HORNS ARE PURE STAX!"

Zac slowly pulled down the stereo faders and the thundering track disappeared over the sonic horizon.

"Brilliant." He sunk back into his chair. "I love songs that fade. It's like they could have gone on forever, but…"

"Yes, like at the end of *Get It On* when the sax starts soloing. You're not even aware there's a sax on the track until that moment…"

But Zac wasn't interested in pursuing a theme if it was no longer his work being discussed. He leant over and pressed Rewind and the large spools of two-inch tape whizzed round like something from an old spy movie. Zac was about to press Play for the tenth time on the same mix when Jody and I protested in unison.

"No-oooooo!"

"Not again, pleeease, Zac?" Jody added with real feeling. Our protest wasn't unreasonable. We'd been listening to this song for hours. First there'd been the bare bones of drums and bass plodding ever onwards, then two hours of Zac trying to crank maximum oomph from a battalion of Les Pauls without it turning into a soup of distortion. And then, finally, back to an isolated snare drum that needed an injection of compression and reverb before it could be thrown back into the mix to fend for itself.

Zac laughed. "But it is brilliant, isn't it."

Not a question, a statement. No false modesty – or modesty of any kind for that matter. Although Zac generally suppressed outward displays of emotion – responding only with a half-smile or that errant eyebrow – when he did laugh, it was an open-mouthed cackle that bent him double.

He tipped back the last drops of a bottle of Southern Comfort and swung round to face us, grinning broadly. We fired back matching smiles, knowing it was what he needed from us. He was finished for the day. "As ever, your feedback was appreciated, Paul," he said. "Jody's great but she'd rather be listening to Diana Ross or something, truth be told."

"I know when I'm not wanted." Jody gave Zac one of her chastising punches on the arm and kissed him on the cheek. I don't know how much time she spent in the studio with Zac, but I got the feeling that when I visited she made a special effort to come up. Perhaps she appreciated seeing a different face around the place. There was rarely anyone else in the house, apart from other band members and a cleaner whose face I never saw because she was always disappearing into rooms rather than coming out of them. "Yes, I'd better make a move too." I said.

But then Zac brightened up. He wanted me to hang out for while longer. He'd got another hit under his belt, and so it was time to bitch about the limitations of his contemporaries.

On such occasions he'd always pay for my cab home if Clive had gone off duty, so I indulged him. He hit Play, and *Put Your Glam Rags On* once more shook the room.

"Bowie would give his dodgy right eye for this one," he said, nodding his head to the music as he assembled a joint with the care of a traditional basket weaver.

Usually, when he lined up other musicians to pick off one by one, Jody and I would just look at each other, look at Zac, and then all three of us would fall about laughing. It was all part of the Zac charm; the Zac crack. For example, he predicted that *Brave the Spotlight* would be number one for a month and then it ended up staying at the top for six weeks. In the early days, we loved him for it. But over time his bravado acquired an unpleasant edge. As drink and cocaine fed his ego, wit left the building, leaving homophobic jokes, weak double entendres and feeble puns to take centre-stage. "Roxy Music? Poxy music, more like. Bryan *Fairy* and Poxy Music. Ha!"

Ferry wasn't even gay, so the joke didn't work on the most basic level. That was the funny thing about glam-rock. Ninety per cent of those musicians plastered on the mascara and lipstick because it actually helped them pick up chicks.

Eventually, even Zac became bored with his jokes, and then it would be time to play me a new demo and ask if I thought it was a hit single or not. "Honest opinion. No bullshit."

Zac would lean back, sunbathing in the hot aural blast of his own creation (on this occasion, *Ride to Saturn*). It was depressingly formulaic. Was it fate – or Zac's devilish sense of humour – that gave me this second chance to have the guts to speak my mind? Zac waited for my hyperbolic assurance that this was indeed another three-minute masterpiece.

"The production's *really* muddy and I'm not sure about the guitar solo." Zac had his back to me and didn't respond, so I dug myself in deeper: the solo was, quite frankly, disappointingly clichéd and even a little out of tune. And wasn't the chorus a direct lift from a T. Rex B-side? I said all this to my feet. When I looked up, Zac was pacing up and down like a man who refused to believe his doctor's diagnosis that he only had six months to live. "You're wrong you know. That solo was perfect. Maybe the vocals could come up in the mix a bit. But otherwise…"

I never heard the last of it. Zac brought it up at every opportunity, usually as a long-running private joke, but sometimes with barely suppressed anger, "Well you didn't even like *Ride to Saturn* and that spent four weeks at number one, so what the fuck do you know?"

What the fuck did I know, indeed. I was never as forthright with my opinions again. But Zac was Zac: the temperament came with the territory; if I didn't like the beat, I could get out of the studio. I didn't see Zac again for six months. Then, for the first time, Zac rather than Valentine summoned me to Zachary Mansions.

★

The way the fans tracked my progress up the front drive reminded me of semi-curious cows staring at passing hikers. When I first visited Zac, I found this attention thrilling. I was an important person by proxy. One girl might ask me if I was Zac's friend. The bolder ones would say things like, "Tell him Jane Morris loves him," or, "Ask Zac if he's horny". Sometimes I even got propositioned. But eventually even "no comment" was no longer necessary: they knew they'd get nothing from me.

The door opened just wide enough to let me in; Jody led me straight up to the loft studio. Something was amiss. Zac immediately embarked on an anecdote he'd clearly been dying to tell someone of the male gender, and I suppose I had to do. He'd just got back from a gig in Paris, and there'd been this girl…

"You'll love this one, Paul."

"I somehow doubt it."

"Don't be such a… whatever it is you're being. Anyway, we're back at the hotel and she goes for a shower while I crash out on the bed, but she's gone for ages. Eventually I realised I couldn't hear the shower. I was about to check things out, when she reappears. And guess what?"

"I don't know. Was she naked?"

"Was she naked? Oh, come on, Paul – what kind of bloody anecdote would that be! Try again."

"She was... oh, I don't know... dressed as a knight of the Round Table?"

"That's better. Now at least you're trying. But, no."

"Okay, okay. She was invisible apart from the towel wrapped around her? She was wielding a six inch dagger and shouting, 'Death to the Rebel Prince of Glam Rock?'"

"You're kind of close with that last one. Okay, I'll tell you..." Zac paused for dramatic effect, as he loved to do at such moments. "She was dressed from head to toe as Ziggy fucking Stardust! I kid you not. She'd even painted the lightning bolt across her face – rather crudely though, I have to say. But the overall effect – including a convincing copy of one of those Freddie Burette one-piece things he wears – was still pretty amazing. I'd noticed earlier she'd got the hairstyle and shaved eyebrows – but loads of girls do, so I didn't think anything of it. And she was as skinny as hell, so it kind of worked."

"So what did you do?"

"I'm afraid I just laughed. And I just couldn't stop laughing. I was a bit out of it anyway, so it really freaked me out. I mean, what was she thinking? Did she think she'd turn me on? Anyway, she burst into tears, gathered up her real clothes and left. But that was nothing compared to when..."

"Look, Zac. Did you just ask me over to tell me more sordid tales of your rock 'n' roll lifestyle or was there something else?"

I found these stories embarrassingly adolescent and an insult to Jody. In some ways Jody had become more of a friend to me than Zac. Back in November, the Now had been in Germany for some gigs and a TV show, and Zac had asked me if I would mind keeping Jody company on her birthday because, for the moment, she'd had enough of life on the road and had decided to stay at home. I confess I was surprised. Was there no one better suited to the job or closer to Jody? However, the fact of the matter was that Jody had no family in the UK and nearly everyone else she normally hung out with was going on the Germany trip. What a weird night that turned out to be.

The evening started out okay, each of us stretched out on our own sofa, a huge heart-shaped box of chocolates (a guilt gift from Zac) on the coffee table between us. And there was plenty of gossip to catch up on. But then the deep-pile cream rug got ruined by a 45-sized wine stain, caused by Jody halfway through her second bottle. I offered to clean it up, but she just gave a who-cares shrug, spilling more vivid red drops as she did so. There were more important things on her mind and she was building up to telling me all. Then the dam burst.

"Like every other motherfucking asshole he's led by his goddamn dick! One day I'll goddamn kill him, I swear! Do you think he really believes I don't know what's going on?"

I didn't know what to say. I'd never seen Jody – or anyone for that matter – that angry and upset before. I ineffectually stroked her shoulder, although she didn't seem to notice. She knew Zac still loved her, so why was he doing this? At first her mantra was that some of him is better than none of him, but halfway through the third bottle of wine, stoic resignation got chased from the room by fierce, inconsolable anger. Eventually, just the fact of my presence seemed to help her a little. "You're very sweet, Paul. I don't know what I would have done tonight if you hadn't been here. If only Zac was more like you."

"I don't know about that, but thanks anyway." I tried to suppress a blush, but that made my face burn even more fiercely.

"Why haven't you got a nice girlfriend? Or are you keeping her a secret from us?" Jody seemed relieved to escape her own troubles for a moment.

"I wish…" I began, taking a greedy gulp of wine. But then I forgot what I wished and went off in a different direction. "You've hit the nail on the head, Jody. I'm sweet. I'm always just *sweet*. But, you know…" The wine brought the confessor out in me too, and it was something of a relief. "I just don't seem to be whatever it is girls or women want. What do they want, Jody?"

Jody laughed so heartily that she was forced to put down her glass before it further speckled the rug.

"I'm serious. I really need to know."

"I don't think they know themselves half the time, sweetheart. But maybe you shouldn't be quite so… er… sweet then. But someone will come along soon. You're a perfectly presentable young man."

"What's that supposed to mean – perfectly presentable?"

"Okay, so you're not my type, but you're going to be somebody's type."

"Oh, I see. Got you."

"Now-now, don't sulk, Paul. Otherwise I'll have to send you home. To be honest, Zac and I wondered if you were, you know…"

"You're kidding!"

"It's the truth. It was just the way you… You're so, you know, obsessed by Zac. And you've never mentioned any girls…"

"I don't brag, if that's what you mean," I said, probably sounding snootier than I meant to. "Although I've got nothing to brag about," I added quickly, to stop myself from sounding conceited. "Look… it just gets embarrassing after a while, if you're not… It's easier to just avoid talking about it." I could see Jody was wishing she hadn't raised the subject. "Hey, don't worry about it," I said, reassuringly. "Or rather, don't worry about me. Is there any more?" I held up the empty wine bottle. "I'm beginning to enjoy myself."

The second half of the evening went more smoothly. We didn't mention Zac, we drank more wine and watched some films on Zac's new video machine. Jody told me he'd had it imported from Tokyo at a cost of nearly fifteen-hundred dollars. We laughed ourselves senseless when the machine started making an awful clunking noise and then stopped altogether.

So, yes, I could see Zac through Jody's eyes. And as he told me his Ziggy in the shower story, I noticed he wasn't looking as dapper as usual. Yes, he was twinkling subtly in a black trouser suit with gold paisley detailing on the lapels and sleeves. But the awful silver highlights in his hair brought to mind the glistening slime trails of snails. And, of course, he hadn't just asked me over to tell me about Ziggy Stardust Girl. So was there something else? He leant forward so that our foreheads nearly touched – as was his way when sharing a confidence.

"I've got this weird fan, Paul," he almost whispered. "She's *always* outside the house, day and night." I suppressed a smile. Yes, Zac had a stalker, long before the media had even coined the phrase. It was immediately obvious part of him was secretly thrilled to have the undivided attention of some blinkered obsessive. But, yes, part of him was also genuinely frightened. So I indulged him a little.

"I'm sure she's harmless," I offered.

"That's easy for you to say. But even after all the others have gone home she'll still be out there, looking up at the house. She was still there at four in the morning last night. What kind of person behaves like that?" He gave an involuntary shudder as he reached for the old tobacco tin he kept his coke in. "And then there's the letters. Not the usual stuff – the hearts and kisses, the pink paper, the psychedelic watercolours. Or even the pervy photos. This was really weird stuff, Paul. Dark stuff."

After a lengthy silence that I was clearly expected to fill, I said, "Why don't you just speak to her?"

"Are you mad? That's exactly what she wants!" Then he acted as if a thought had just struck him, even though this was surely why he'd summoned me in the first place.

"Maybe if you spoke to her, Paul? Could you? *Please.*"

"Is she out there now?" I asked, hoping with all my being that she wasn't.

"I don't know. I've not looked. I've only been up half an hour. She was there last night though."

I told Zac that there'd been the usual gaggle of girls (or should that be giggle of girls?) when I'd arrived, but I hadn't noticed anyone behaving suspiciously. I really didn't want to go back out there, demand their attention in a head-masterly manner, and then ask them which one of them was the nutcase.

"Look," I said. "Even if I did speak to her, it would just make her the centre of attention and add fuel to her fantasies." Zac sulked. "What about the police?" I offered.

"What's the point? She's not actually *done* anything. They'd just say I was being pathetic."

"Well, aren't you? Just a little?"

"Thanks a lot, Paul. You just don't get it, do you? This whole rock star thing already freaks me out, without all this extra pressure." I tried to steer Zac's thoughts elsewhere. It seemed like a good opportunity to ask him about his family history for a feature I was planning for a French magazine.

Zac had never hidden his upper middle class background. In fact, he rather played on it. But he hadn't planned on the *NME* finding out that his father, Girma Bekele, made his fortune "acquiring" icon paintings from Ethiopian churches and monasteries and then selling them to European collectors at a huge profit. Girma even sold works back to the Ethiopian Studies Museum in Addis Ababa that he'd bought them from in the first place, several years previously. By the early 1970s, he'd made enough money to set himself up as a legitimate art dealer. Several run-ins with the law in both London and Addis Abada gave the *NME* license to paint the man as some kind of notorious criminal mastermind – or "art pirate" as they put it. But, once the story was out, Zac embraced it for adding a further layer of romantic intrigue to his pop star persona.

"Water off a duck and diver's back. I might even call the next album *Art Pirate* in my dad's honour," he said when I mentioned the *NME* piece. I pushed him further on the subject of his father. "I always thought Daddy was a bit dull. I knew he bought and sold paintings. but I didn't know there was a shady side to it. Good for him! Hey, let me show you something." He jumped to his feet and descended the iron steps in what seemed like two easy leaps. At the end of a short hallway we arrived at the master bedroom.

"My dad sent me this for my 18th Birthday."

On the far wall above an Art Deco dressing table was a small square painting of an Ethiopian St George on a white stallion. There was no dragon, but on the Saint's right was a monk looking up at him adoringly. Both men wore calm, gentle smiles. But the most unusual thing about the painting was the St George himself. Not only was it rare to see a black man looking heroic in a painting that belonged in a museum. It was also unusual to see a figure in a pre-Renaissance painting that looked like a rock star. It was the hair that did it. St George sported a rudimentary afro with dreadlocks sprouting from it like Medusa snakes.

"It's fifteenth century. Beautiful isn't it?"

"Doesn't it bother you that it's probably stolen property?"

"Oh Paul, you're such a killjoy. It couldn't be more loved or appreciated than it is here. Look at the condition of it – it probably would have rotted away altogether if it had just been left in whatever Godforsaken hovel of a church my father found it in."

★

A week later, I dropped by the *Rock On* office to pick up my backstage pass for the Wembley gig. Andy and Barney had just been told they were going to have to swallow the bitterest pill of all: *Rock On* was getting a full-colour cover. The other three serious rock weeklies would never have dreamt of going colour, so essentially this meant the paper was aligning itself with the glossy teen mags.

"Are you happy now?" Barney barked, tossing me the smaller format, colour *Rock On* with Roy Wood dressed as Father Christmas on the cover.

"Ecstatic," I replied, grinning.

"We wanted Mott to do it, but Hunter refused to wear the Xmas gear," shouted Jake from the other end of the office.

"Hey, Jake," Barney interjected, smirking at me. "If you'd wanted someone to dress up as Jesus, you could have asked that Zachary B freak."

I ignored him. Barney had become even more of a self-parody with his Harris tweed suit and a moustache he was trying to wax-train into two Daliesque curls.

Jake sauntered over. "Do you fancy doing Barry Blue next week, Paul?"

"Can't I'm afraid. I'm writing a screenplay for Francis Ford Coppola."

"Great. Can you get it to us by the 3rd?"

★

I was milling around the half-acre of stage, trying not to get in the way of the beer-bellied roadies, heavily-bearded technicians and teenage girls (whose fathers were either beer-bellied roadies or heavily-bearded technicians, hence their backstage passes), when I noticed one girl who didn't look like she belonged there. For one thing, she was still in her school uniform (all the others had changed into their *Topshop* togs). For another, she stood alone yet seemed unfazed by her isolation. I was so busy scrutinising her, I failed to notice she was staring fearlessly straight back at me as if she saw my focused attention as a challenge. The only way to save face was to walk over and introduce myself. But she got in first. "You're the writer – the one who's always at the house."

There was a note of condescension in her voice. I tried to think of an answer more interesting than just yes, but then realised she was still talking.

"Why doesn't he answer my letters, Paul Coleridge? He must realise I'm not like all the other..."

I heard the word "tarts" in my head but she hadn't actually uttered it herself. I cleared my throat – a nervous habit that always preceded my attempts at gravitas – and jumped in at the deep end. "You know you could get into a lot of trouble. Zac is a very busy man. He doesn't have time to answer all the letters he gets from fans. And you're really not doing yourself any favours by..."

"Zac is a very busy man." She did a disturbingly accurate impression of my self-important tone. "Sorry, I shouldn't make fun of you should I, but you know what it's like. I can tell from your writing that you love Zac just as much as I do." She repeatedly brushed a lock of mousy hair from her face that a devilish breeze was fighting for control over. "I'm not doing any harm, you know. I don't even shout stuff out to him like the other girls do. Some of them are so *crude*."

I was fascinated by how calmly she put forward her case; her rationale for why she did what she did. I looked out over the thousands of soon-to-be-occupied seats and wondered at the power of music and the power of one man. Thinking myself cunning, I pretended I'd forgotten her name. "Yes, but?..."

"Helen. Helen Wheeler," she interjected, impatiently. "You don't have to trick it out of me. I sign and address everything I send to Zac, so he can write back if he wants. He really should write back at least once – it's only polite." She smiled warmly. "I'm a nice girl. Zac would like me, don't you think?"

"Er... yeah, I suppose so. But you're going about this all in the wrong way..."

"So what's the right way, Mr high-and-mighty music writer? He's part of a different world from us. I'm not going to just bump into him down at the local disco." She was right. This girl stood no chance on Earth of ever getting herself into Zachary B's head or heart. I stared at her open, pretty face and comprehended the absurdity and tragedy of her situation. Then she caught me off guard again. "So what is it with you and Zac? What is it about him that holds you in his thrall?"

Thrall: what an unusual word for someone so young to be using in everyday conversation. Thrall, *enthralled*... I pulled myself back from my drifting thoughts and considered how to reply. But before I could respond, she had disappeared back into the bustle of the busy and the expectant.

★

Perhaps I should have said something to Zac about meeting Helen, but I didn't want to freak him out before such an important gig. There was a lot at stake. Sales of the last single hadn't been great. And as the single was the ad for the forthcoming album, *The Slim-Hipped Hipster and the Juxta-Posers*, this didn't bode well. Yes I know, not the greatest title in the world, but there'd been a recent trend for long album titles. I thought it was beneath Zac to follow such fashions, but he claimed he was being ironic, so that shut me up.

Before the concert, Zac was unusually relaxed, so I got back to the subject of his family. As mixed-race relationships were even less common in the 1940's than the 1970's, how did his parents meet? He talked to both our reflections in the dressing room mirror as he put on his makeup.

"My dad was in the Merchant Navy during the war. He got invalided out, and found himself in Liverpool where he met some Nigerians in a pub who mentioned an African underground music scene in London. They gave him the addresses of a couple of clubs and off he went."

"So your dad was a musician before he became an art dealer?"

"Yeah, he played sax in Ethiopian military brass bands before the war. Anyway, he arrived in London on May 7th, 1945..." Zac paused for a moment to see if the date meant anything to me. I looked blank, so he continued. "May 7th was the day before VE Day – the end of the war. He had no idea. So the next day there's my dad with a second-hand sax he's just bought in Denmark Street, stumbling across the crowds gathering in Trafalgar Square. And, above all the raucous noise, he hears this strange music. He weaved his way through the crowd, following the sound, until he saw a six-piece band – five black guys and one white – playing this weird mix of calypso, hi-life and American jazz: congas, shakers, clarinet, trumpet… he was hypnotised. The guy with the shaker notices Dad's sax and persuades him to join them. It was that kind of day, you know – spontaneous, joyous and chaotic." Zac looked blissfully distracted for a moment, as if these were his own memories.

"So then what?"

"Well, I think he just ended up playing with the band for the rest of the day and half the night, trying to get a decent tune out of this battered old sax. He never bored of telling me about Nelson's Column all lit up by searchlights. And all these crazy white folk dancing in the fountains. But he soon found out London wasn't always like that…"

"So where does your mum come into all this?"

"He's blasting away, in a world of his own, and this tipsy white girl literally runs right into him. She drops her handbag and everything. He helps her pick up her stuff and then gives her his biggest, whitest smile. The next thing he knows she's giving him a huge smacker on the lips. They were married three months later. Mum had just come up for the day with some girlfriends to join in the fun. I don't think she imagined she'd end up finding herself a husband, and certainly not an African husband. She was only eighteen."

"Wow!"

"That story meant something different to me each time my dad told it."

"How do you mean?"

Zac poured himself another drink to delay answering. But then he spoke plainly. "He was black and she was white – a big deal back then. It was the end of the war; there's no way she would have kissed him like that under any other circumstances. Everyone was kissing and hugging everyone else, everyone was drunk, and everyone was fearless and jubilant…"

"So what are you saying?"

"I think I'm just saying how weird life is. It's funny how tenuous and contingent on chance even the very fact of our existence is. It was tough for my parents. The pressures eventually drove them apart. Perhaps they shouldn't have been together in the first place."

"You can't say that."

"I just did." There was a tightness around Zac's lips, a sadness in his eyes.

I shifted the focus of our conversation. "So what happened with the band? Did he continue to play with them?"

"Yes he did." Zac brightened a little. "There were a few student dives and jazz clubs where the Black Aces were popular. They even supported the African Rhythm Brothers – the biggest of those bands. But there was no real money in it, so he ended up working for British Rail, just like every other disillusioned immigrant. Until he got into art."

★

The Now reigned supreme that night. Watching the show from the wings, I felt both the sheer muscle of the music being pumped out, and the waves of love gusting right back from the ocean of fans. Girls fainted faster than the bouncers could drag them from the crush of the crowd, their faces streaked with tears and flushed with lust.

In the dressing room afterwards, Zac collapsed into an armchair like a victorious boxer after a prizefight. As Helen Wheeler wasn't amongst the fans trying to squeeze their way past the bouncers into the room, I decided to continue to keep her presence at the concert to myself. Eventually, a handful of the girls were let in. Valentine had picked the lookers like a football coach chooses his team ("you, *you* and you. You three, and... er... you,"). The chosen few tumbled into the room and Valentine locked the door behind them.

They immediately froze, finger-splayed hands shooting to gaping mouths. Where were the words to express what they felt? What were they even doing here? As part of the screaming crowd they'd been liberated and empowered by their vast numbers, but now there was just a few of them in this intensely male space. And there was their god, finishing a can of Red Stripe.

As if responding to a director's cue, Zac got to his feet and crossed the room with the precise liquid movements of a predatory cat. He extended his hand to the headlight-lit bunnies for kissing or shaking. The pretence was that now everyone was equal. The reality was very different.

Zac spoke. "Alright then, girls? Find yourself somewhere to perch. Did you all enjoy yourselves?"

They all answered at once.

"Me and Cath saw T. Rex but they were rubbish compared to you"

"Are you and Marc Bolan friends?"

"Are you and Jody splitting up?"

Zac took a deep breath. "So many questions, so little time. Brian, some champagne for the girls? After all, this is a special occasion. We've got some advance copies of *The Slim-Hipped Hipster* around somewhere, for one or two of you lucky ladies..."

And so the circling, the ensnaring and eventually the consumption of the prey began. The band's easy laughter and cheeky grins told the girls they were in safe company. But if they'd looked into the eyes of these men asking them their names and how far they had travelled, they would have seen the focussed meat-lust of hyenas. I felt sorry for them, sitting there on upturned beer crates, knees pressed together, trying to take it all in. Eventually, when their excitement became tempered by wariness (and perhaps guilty thoughts of parents waiting by phones), the band and road-crew shrewdly moved things up a notch. Joints appeared followed by lines of coke. Programs, LP sleeves and coyly exposed body parts were signed as part of an unspoken pact. And yet sometimes Zac could be a real sweetie to his fans.

Once we were up late in the studio and he realised his wardrobe-sized fridge was dry of a particular cider he was inordinately fond of. When he didn't have something, nothing else would do, so I drove him to an all-night off-licence (Zac never learnt to drive – he said he didn't have the temperament for it). So picture this: we're walking towards the off-licence, Zac's in a purple crushed-velvet robe and twinkling Moroccan slippers and all of these kids just appeared from nowhere, like Dickensian street urchins in a sentimental musical. Zac loved it. He knew he wasn't going to be mobbed because he had somehow – and this is the only way I can explain it – cultivated an untouchable aura. He was magisterial in his demeanour and so the fans treated him accordingly. When we got to the off-license, a shoal of girls bustled in behind us, giggling and chattering with barely controlled hysteria. The middle-aged Asian proprietor was horrified, but Zac took control of the situation. He turned to the pressing throng, raised both loose-sleeved arms in the air, and spoke to them as if he were the Mother Superior of a strict Convent school.

"Now, now, girls, calm down. Everyone back outside – let's be having you. Once I've got my booze and fags I'll come out for a chat."

The girls backed out of the shop like a film rewinding, and we were left alone with the baffled shopkeeper. Zac went back outside; I paid for everything and followed. Then came a moment of panic. The girls were on the other side of the road, silently gathered round something, or someone, and there was no sign of Zac. I ran over, expecting to peer over adolescent shoulders only to be confronted by a torn-to-shreds Zac. But instead, Zac was crouched down with one ear to the road, as were a few of the girls.

"Can you here anything?" Zac whispered urgently. "Can you hear the white noise of distant, bubbling molten iron? Beneath those double yellow lines, beneath the tarmac and the concrete, beneath miles of rock and earth – at the very centre of our world – between our feet and Australia – is a molten mass of iron the size of the moon. That to me is *amazing*. But, hey, there are autographs to sign." Zac jumped to his feet. Relieved to be back on solid ground again (so to speak), the girls scrambled to get notebooks, pictures and flushed skin under Zachary's busy pen.

But back to the hyenas with champagne bottles. It was time for me to leave. This scene wasn't my style. Some of the things I was told about – and in some cases witnessed – during Zac's teen idol reign, I still find distasteful to think about. Yes, there was funny-weird stuff as well as weird-weird stuff. For example one of the Now only ever sought sexual congress with members of rival bands. And Colin told me it was often easier to get a blow job than a mug of tea after a gig. And he generally looked like he would have preferred the tea.

Extract from *The KUU Hypothesis* by Zachary Bekele

1. YOU CAN LAUGH

Laugh With Us or at Us

You can laugh with us, at us, or at yourself. All laughter is welcome except for the evil cackle of the mad scientist. Most religions ignore laughter because it's the Great Deflator. Laughter is a weapon; satire can be a sabre; the arrogant and the vain can be defeated with razor-sharp wit. So try employing the deflating laugh rather than the impotent curse.

Laughter the Leveller

If you hear someone laughing, without seeing them, it's impossible to tell where they're from. A laugh sounds the same in all languages, yet it's also an idiosyncratic expression of an individual rather than his clan. The laugh says, "I am the same as you".

Laugh With Us, or Against Us

As a KUUist you should expect mocking chuckles and self-satisfied smiles from those who doubt your doubting. But they can laugh away! By doing so, they inadvertently join you in spirit with their giggles.

The Survival of the Wittiest

Since the 1960's we have known that chimps and other animals use tools and even language. But they don't make jokes. So what is humour's evolutionary advantage? Wit also means cunning, and both qualities can help you find a mate, in order to pass your sense of humour onto the next generation.

Laughter and Happy Astonishment

A Cosmic Nudge promotes laughter and happy astonishment, so perhaps that's what the KUU wants to promote in us? Vanity and Ego are human weaknesses yet they're desirable qualities in most deities, along with vengefulness, lack of mercy, jealously, racism, sexism and all those other Old Testament neuroses. In keeping with all these personality traits, your average trad-god also has no sense of humour, which means that His more ardent followers also have no sense of humour. How ironic that a quality we so welcome in our fellow human beings is so absent in the one whose image we are allegedly made in.

A joke explained loses its power to amuse
A deity explained loses its power to amaze

5

Marrakech, February 2007

A sudden spike in the din of the street made Damian's question inaudible to August, so he asked it again. "So why August?"

"Crazy parents. Well, kind of crazy. I was actually born at the end of July, but I was expected in August and they'd already got their heart set on August."

"And July is a bit…"

"Exactly. I used to hate the name August. It's a man's name, after all. And don't *ever* call me Augie. But at least it's different. Did you know it also means to be extremely dignified or majestic?"

"Kind of, I think – 'The August Queen of Sweden' – that kind of thing?"

"Yep, you've got it." August grinned and lifted her chin a little for extra magisterial effect. As they'd heard nothing from Merrick (apart from an email circular inviting them to his weekly introductory talk at the Tripod the following day), they'd decided to take a look around the city. It wasn't even ten yet, but it was already hotter than yesterday. They wandered off down one of the streets that led away from the Djemaa el-Fna. As the noise from the square began to fade, the goods for sale became less enticing. A woman shrouded in black, with just a letterbox slit for her eyes, sat cross-legged before a pile of shrivelled lemons. Further on, they encountered a frighteningly thin man with a face like a scrotum who had nothing to offer but a broken chair. Some children began following them, until Damian clapped his hands at them as if they were a flock of pigeons. The oldest of the boys gave Damian a ferocious, hate-filled look, which shocked him. It was as if the boy had torn off his mask of innocent mischievousness to reveal his true self. He gave some kind of signal to the others and they all ran away laughing. Damian felt disproportionately disturbed by the incident.

"Little fuckers," he said, fishing his water bottle from his bag. He couldn't believe how insolent and relentless these kids could be; so hell-bent on making him feel uncomfortable for having money.

"You can't let them upset you." August accepted the bottle, and drank more from it than Damian felt was polite. "They'll win every time. Just ignore them."

"But they make themselves so unignorable! It drives me nuts."

If the reds of this red city were the only colours in the spectrum, Damian would have been happy: from rich Venetian reds to sunset golds; from fresh-scar-pink to baked-bean-orange. It was a palette borne of the colours of the earth and the clay of the buildings. Yet transformed by age, light, shadow, time of day and time of year, it was a richly varied alternative rainbow. This was the first place he'd been where his preference for monochrome photography felt like mean-spirited art school posturing. The colours in his photos would end up only coarse approximations of all these delicious hues, but at least he would try to capture them. At first they weren't sure what the next lone trader was trying to sell. From a distance it looked like a crumpled old coat. But as they drew closer they noticed a black fog surrounding the object, half obscuring it from view. Perhaps exclamations of horror are affectations – responses learnt from films and TV – because neither of them screamed, "Oh my God!" or "Jesus Christ!" No deity's name was said in vain as it dawned on them what they were looking at. They just stood there, silently horrified. It was a camel's head, or what was left of a camel's head. It looked almost large enough to weigh as much as the skin and bone man who sat cross-legged behind it. The black fog was formed of a million tiny flies, through which larger flies could be seen, combing the landscape of the rotting head like a speeded-up murder squad looking for evidence on a hillside. The camel's one visible eye and lolling tongue were getting the most attention from the flies.

There was no question in Damian's mind that the trader was taking pleasure in the shock his "merchandise" was engendering. He gave a thirty per cent teeth, seventy per cent gaps grin, as he beckoned to them with a finger that had suddenly appeared from beneath the folds of his robe. Damian realised that August had already slowly moved away, leaving him still held under the spell of the old man's will. A word forced its way up from the man's chest.

"American?"

"No, English."

"Aah, English. And your wife?"

"She's not my wife. She's English too. I really don't think…"

The old man prodded the camel's head with his finger and a thousand flies momentarily dispersed, giving Damian a sickeningly clear view of the head, as if he'd just pulled his camera into focus. The goofy smile of apparent contentment on the camel's fat lips emphasised its grotesqueness.

"Good soup. It make good soup."

"I don't doubt it," said Damian, forcing a smile. He then realised his turn of phrase was unlikely to have made any sense to the man, so he quickly added, "Yes, good soup. But no thank you."

The man issued a joyless cackle. With much effort, he leant forward and plucked the remains of the camel's eye from its gloopy socket and held it out to Damian.

"For you. A gift!"

That was it. Damian abandoned all pretence of good manners and trying to communicate with the locals. "Shit!" was the only word he could muster as he backed away.

The old man continued to smile as he carefully replaced the eye as if he were just putting an egg back in an egg box. August was already twenty yards away and looking in the other direction when Damian came up level with her.

"You look like you've just seen a ghost," she said, only half interested in what his response might be: she'd seen a jewellery shop at a junction of alleyways just up ahead, and wanted to get there quickly, just in case it was a mirage.

Damian couldn't think what to say. Had he overreacted? "Didn't you see?" he began.

After he'd told August about the Hammer horror scene he'd just witnessed he felt much better: he'd turned it into an anecdote. An anecdote he realised he'd get a lot of mileage out of in the years to come. Maybe he'd even embellish it a little; have the man grab his arm or something. He felt better already, although he couldn't completely dispel the sense of foreboding this incident, along with the angry boy earlier, had left him with.

"He's probably played the same trick on half a dozen other tourists this morning already," said August, peering into the interior of the jewellery shop. "Maybe it was past its sell-by date, even to the locals, and he just wanted to get some entertainment value out of it with some prissy tourist. Are those real emeralds, do you think? No, of course they're not – not for that price."

"Who are you calling prissy! But yeah, maybe,." said Damian.

August changed the subject. "I've been thinking about what Malika and his virtual friends were going on about. It's got to be something to do with chance and numbers. Pushing the KUU, or as Malika wrote, at least a couple of times – "*tempting* the KUU".

August tugged at the hem of Damian's shirt, alerting him to the fact he was standing directly in the path of a scuffed and scarred donkey with half a dozen mattresses strapped to its back. It was August's turn to look away as the donkey's owner, an orthodox Jew in a green robe and black skullcap, whipped the donkey with disturbing ferocity. She was ridiculously sentimental about donkeys. "Enough!" said Damian, rubbing his eyes free of the dust, which had flown up from the donkey's coat where the whip had landed. "Let's get back to civilisation." Civilisation was relative in this world. Only two days ago, the Djemaa el-Fna had seemed like the most intimidating, disorientating, place on Earth. Now it seemed safe and welcoming compared to the less predictable, real life of the back streets. All you had to do here was avoid eye contact and you could walk freely amongst the crowds. They found themselves a ringside seat in a salmon-pink café overlooking the square and ordered cokes. Damian gulped down the sweet fizzy liquid as if he needed it to restore his equilibrium; half a litre of the West, with ice – so reassuring in its unchanging platonic perfection. Coke was coke, even if coke was the Unreal Thing.

By mid-afternoon the heat was unbearable, and so they shuffled back to their stone-cool riad for a siesta and shower. Later, they reconvened for a pre-dinner drink in August's room.

"As I was saying…" began August.

"But you weren't saying anything," interrupted Damian.

"This afternoon."

"Ah, yes." Damian was enjoying the rapport developing between them.

"Pushing the KUU. Taking a chance with chance."

"I'm not sure I follow you."

"You're not the only one. When I work out what I'm getting at, you'll be the first to know."

★

Having experienced a couple of dull restaurant meals where the couscous tasted like soapy bath water, they returned to the full-on eating experience of the Djema el-Fna for their evening meal.

"Do you know what they used to do in this square?" asked Damian, sensing a lull in the conversation August hadn't been aware of.

"No, but I'm sure you're going to tell me. And I'm sure I'll wish I hadn't let you, if your expression is anything to go by."

Damian laughed. "Well, it's not that bad. Well it is I suppose. But it was a long time ago. It was what got the crowds here in the first place."

"So?"

"Well, they used to bring the decapitated heads of executed criminals here, until the French arrived and put a stop to it, but then the people continued coming here, out of force of habit I suppose. And so, in a way, that's why we're sitting here today enjoying ourselves."

"Thanks for that."

"My pleasure."

Imagining an awkward silence was about to descend, Damian changed the subject again. "You haven't told me if you have a favourite KUU-incidence."

"Doesn't everyone?" August put another mouthful of food into her mouth, teasing Damian with her apparent unwillingness to elaborate, but Damian was learning. This time he let the silence between them expand until she was ready to continue. "A friend of mine, Claire, owns a quirky knickknacks shop in Shoreditch. Anyway, one day these three teenage girls, Americans blondes, big smiles, wide innocent eyes, came into the shop. They were born-again Christians and keen to spread the word. Claire's one of those widely travelled backpacking types, so she couldn't resist taking the piss out of them a bit. She told the girls she'd seen more evidence of the existence of the Islamic prophet Mohammed than she had of Jesus – which was perfectly reasonable as there is more evidence of his existence. But it's a trap of course, and these girls fall right in. 'What proof?' they ask. Some curly beard hair in a museum in Istanbul, Claire said. Then came Claire's punch line: she asks the girls if, for example, they knew the whereabouts of Jesus's foreskin? Their mouths apparently hung open in horror, but then they were literally saved by the bell; the shop phone rang and they took the opportunity to escape."

"Sorry, you've lost me. Where's the Cosmic Nudge in all this?"

"Well, when Claire emailed me this story it was the first time I'd ever heard about Jesus's foreskin."

"Didn't she just say that for shock value?"

"No, not at all. Think about it."

"I am, but it's not helping."

"Anyway, I'll get back to that in a minute. That night I was reading *Choke* by Chuck Palahniuk – he's the guy who wrote *Fight Club*. I was about halfway through. This guy has also been trying to solve the mystery of who his father is. I get to the page where he finds his mum's diary. Can you see what's coming?"

"No, not really."

"To cut a long and very farfetched story short, this guy finds out he was genetically engineered from DNA from Jesus's foreskin. I couldn't believe it! I'd never even heard of the idea of Jesus's foreskin before. And then there it was, twice in one day..."

"Staring you in the face, so to speak. So what is the idea?"

"Jesus was a Jew."

"I'm with you so far."

"And so he would have been circumcised. If the rest of him ascended to Heaven, as the Good Book tells us, the only bit left on Earth would have been... that bit. Anyway, I found loads of stuff on the Internet which told me this... er... relic wasn't just the invention of my friend Claire, and an American writer with a disturbed imagination. I found references to a dozen or so foreskins from the twelfth to the eighteenth century..."

"All claiming to be the Holy Snippet."

"Exactly. In the sixteenth century, Pope Clement VII even sanctioned one of the things as the Real Thing. Then it was stolen and didn't reappear until the nineteenth century when it was found hidden inside a church wall somewhere. Then another church was specially constructed just to house the Divine Unpleasantness. Some sanity was eventually restored

129

around 1900 when the Vatican suggested that 'irreverent curiosity' was being encouraged by this object."

Damian laughed. "KUU, who'd have thought it! Have you emailed it to the KUU Foundation archives? You could make the Top Eleven with that one."

"Not really my thing. For some reason I don't feel the need to share my Cosmic Nudges. I have a very personal relationship with the KUU."

"Fair enough." Damian thought for a moment. "Although I do think that KUUists have a responsibility to share their mini-miracles. It helps draw others to the non-faith. But that's brilliant. It's as if the KUU was pointing out how ludicrous the idea of needing concrete proof is."

"I agree. The history of religion is littered with the skulls, bones and hair of saints; the Virgin Mary's milk, St Joseph's breath. Relics were big business, still are."

"And the Knowing Unknowable Universe was telling you it's all bullshit."

August changed the subject. "Why do you think KUUism has so captured people's imagination, Damian?"

Damian looked around at all the organised chaos of the square as if seeking inspiration. "Magic. It's that simple. There's no magic to life without some kind of spiritual dimension. People may tire of dictatorial belief systems, but they never tire of magic."

"And everyone relates to the enigma of the unlikely coincidence."

"Absolutely. When I was a kid—"

A boy, perhaps twelve-years-old, fell sideways into Damian, almost knocking him off his bench. His forkful of food landed in the lap of a plump middle-aged American woman seated beside him. She struggled to her feet, chastising Damian as she frantically brushed at her skirt. The boy, without even a backward glance, disappeared into the crowd. The American woman's husband was about to make something more of the incident when Damian issued a moan of discomfort and also, rather precariously, got to his feet.

Once standing, he looked down at himself in dismay. This led August to follow his gaze, which had fallen on a patch of wet-red that was rapidly expanding on his pale pink T-shirt. If August had been in a movie she would have screamed. But she wasn't in a movie, she was in a lucid dream, and she felt correspondingly distanced from what she was seeing, although she did compose herself enough to call out to one of the waiters. The American couple, oblivious to Damian's plight, got up and left in disgust, perhaps assuming he was drunk.

Two waiters appeared. One spoke English. "I know a doctor. Wait." He ran off. The other waiter, at August's urgent request, got hot water and towels.

"Damian, Damian! Stay with us!" Her voice, not her own, seemed to lack resonance. Her clichéd lines were those of a soldier in a war movie, and like that soldier she cradled Damian's head in her lap and lightly stroked his milk-white face. There was shouting all around her. The waiter returned with the hot water and towels. If only her mother was here, she'd know what to do.

Extract from *The KUU Hypothesis* by Zachary Bekele

2. YOU CAN DOUBT

Scepticism is the Route of All Good

Make of the KUU what you will, but please don't blindly believe in it. It's just a bunch of ideas. Because doubt is poison to a trad-god it is celebrated in KUUism. The religions of the past made one fundamental error. They said, or had God say:

"This is the way it is. Take it or leave it, but if you leave it, you're in big trouble"

What kind of way is that to start a relationship with your Maker? Were I to put words into the mouth of the KUU, I would have it say:

"Here are some suggestions on how to live a more fulfilling life while also getting the occasional glimpse that there could be more to that life than meets the eye. Let those glimpses enrich your daily existence but don't let them go to your head. Be aware and creative, pursue wisdom knowing it can't be attained, and find someone to love and have a good time with."

You can doubt – don't doubt it. But don't let doubt stop you entertaining the possibility with all your imagination.

Maybe All Inspiration is Divine

The Eleven Non-Commandments were not passed down to me by a scary being in a haze of golden light. If divine inspiration was involved then all inspiration is divine. Maybe all inspiration *is* divine? Where do ideas come from? Why do they seem to come fully formed so one has to scramble to write them down before they escape back into the ether? Is it any wonder that the writers of the great religious texts believed they had a hotline to God?

The Prayer Pudding

Prayer reinforces in the powerless the notion that they are powerless. The proof is in the prayer pudding: how many times is a prayer answered? But the KUU doesn't need your prayers, why should it? Yet most religions insist on some kind of demeaning bowing-down. The old gods didn't even want you worshipping other gods, gods which, according to them, didn't exist anyway.

At One With The One

Individuality is buried by the kneeling down, the bowing of the head and the denial of dignity and the self. If you must do something for your god, why not dance? Euphoric rhythmic movement promotes transcendental feelings and is far more likely to make you at one with the One. It is also the second most enjoyable way of uniting the physical self with the mental self. Dance is body and soul as a celebration rather than a sublimation of what it is to be human.

So, get up off a your knees! Don't pray, Dance!

Extract from
The Life and Death of Zachary B
by Paul Coleridge

You Wouldn't Hear the Bullet That Killed You Anyway
August 1975

Pulse
Pressure

Pulse
Quickens

Pulse
Deadens

Pulse
Weakens

Pulse
Fading

I never managed to establish whether the fractured experimentation of *Pulse* was a deliberate attempt to follow in Bowie's arch and arty footsteps, or if it was just another by-product of Zac's cerebral meltdown. But he'd certainly given up on the teen demographic: they'd become fixated on some stick-thin Scots who were making the most banal records the world had ever known. But, occasionally, Zac was still capable of moments of musical and lyrical brilliance such as in the sublime *Earthbound*:

> *I've read about the movie*
> *And I've seen the book*
> *All news is good news*
> *From the comfort of your room*
>
> *Now the house burns bright*
> *Like a tortured soul*
> *And we're skin-trapped tight*
> *With no faith or rules*
>
> *Earthbound*
> *Where are my wings?*
> *Earthbound*
> *Where are my wings?*

Did Zachary mean 'earthbound in the sense of returning to earth after some kind of trip (LSD or BOAC) or did he mean earthbound as in bound to this earth as a soulless flesh and blood creature?

In August 1975 I interviewed Zac for the Dutch weekly *Glamuzik*. He was producing another band at the time – something he'd told me he'd never do. But the Dog Stars were part of New York's burgeoning CBGB's scene, so that intrigued him. Miles Dresden at AMT heard the band's demo and agreed with them that they were – like thousands of bands before them – The Future of Rock 'n' Roll. Record companies never like to see their artists at a loose end (they know where that leads), so Dresden asked Zac to produce them (AMT could bring in a real producer later if Zac couldn't hack it). Zac listened to the demo (a more tuneful Stooges with a dash of social awareness) and said yes. It certainly helped that the band had said they dug Zac's far-out English pop.

The interview took place at Eye Studios in Berwick Street, a few weeks into *The Deep End* sessions. The only reason Zac tolerated the Dog Stars stumbling in at two-thirty in the afternoon for a session meant to start at ten in the morning, was that it was an endearing manifestation of authentic American rock star behaviour. He worked like a dog (no pun intended) for three months on that album.

"That bass sound sucks, man. Is that all you've got?" It was the first time the gangly leather-clad Joey had spoken all day.

"No it's not all I've got, Joey. Just be patient," replied Zac, tweaking a few knobs on the mixing desk.

"Jesus, how hard can it be? It's only a bass guitar. Just whack up the fucking bass!"

"It's not that simple, Joey. I want to get a bit of definition in the sound too."

"*Definition* – what the fuck are you on, man?"

"Look, am I producing this or are you?"

"You are, dude."

"Well let me just do my job then… dude."

"Okay, cool… But can you just make the bass a bit *bassier*?"

And so it went on. Most of the time with Zac showing uncharacteristic self-control.

"Rock is raaaak – the word was meant to be said with an American accent," Zac proclaimed while waiting for at least one Dog Star to regain consciousness so he could do something. "When we Brits say 'rock' it just sounds like a lump of stone; it's stone dead."

"It's the place names too," I said. "The cities, the streets, the endless dusty freeways of America – they belong in songs."

We turned in unison as a Dog Star stirred, but it was a false alarm; he was simply making himself more comfortable in his stoned stupor. Zac warmed to his theme. "English rock works when it's fanciful, surreal or sci-fi; when it doesn't try to be real by mentioning Deptford High Street or the M11. Okay, so Ray Davis pulled it off with *Waterloo Sunset*, but that's about it."

"So what about *your* new album?" I asked, sipping cold coffee from a plastic cup I'd forgotten I was still holding.

"It's called *Swimming the River of the Soul* and it should be out early next year."

"Where was it recorded?"

"A better question might be – *why* was it recorded. Because it had to be. It's my most personal statement to date. It's about my own spiritual rebirth as a born-again questioner. Did you know that when an earthquake struck in ancient China, everyone would rush to their musical instruments to check their tuning – in case there was a misalignment between earthly music and its cosmic equivalent?"

"Heavy, man," I replied jokily. But Zac wasn't smiling.

"No, light actually. A burden has been lifted." Zac pretended he was bored by the subject he'd raised, as he listened to the bass line just one more time to see if he could make it, well… bassier.

But I wanted to hear more. "A burden?"

"I'm free now. I've sussed it all out. Religious belief is the most overrated and dangerous of all human inventions."

"More dangerous than the nuclear bomb?"

"The nuclear bomb is dangerous because we have religion. The faithful don't need this life because they have the next life. That's what's dangerous."

"But you're a Christian aren't you? You've got that painting – the St George with the monk…"

"Yes, and it's very beautiful, but it no longer means anything to me beyond the fact it depicts a black man in a position of power."

For the next hour, until a drowsy Dog Star was together enough to lay down some power chords, Zac railed against God. And man for still being under God's spell. Where had all this come from? Perhaps it was a side effect of the vast amount of cocaine he was getting through. Three weeks after my *Glamuzik* piece was published, extracts appeared in the *Daily Mirror*, various American publications, and for all I know, elsewhere. Parts of the interview ended up being compared to Lennon's throwaway Jesus comment, but it was more subversive than that: Lennon was having a joke; Zac was angry. Zac thought mankind had got things horribly wrong and it was going to be the death of all of us. That interview marked the end of any hope Zac had of cracking the States. The damage was less obvious in the UK, but he'd stopped caring anyway. I think it would be fair to say Zac was thrilled rather than disturbed by the effect his anti-religion rant ended up having. It may not have helped with record sales, but it raised his profile. And profile had sadly becoming everything by this point in his career. Zac's addiction to various substances had resulted in a dramatic drop in the quality of his music. In fact, for a while, he actually stopped composing all together. At least scribbling down esoteric thoughts on the meaning of life had given him something new to get excited about.

During 1975 and 1976, Zac's coke and cognac habit gathered further momentum. His growing paranoia and insecurity meant that he did nothing musically without trying to anticipate how it would be received.

Throughout 1976 he produced a string of singles of mind-blowing, but mannered eclecticism. *Black is Gold* utilised a gospel choir from Soweto; *Silver Soul Jetstream* sounded like Isaac Hayes at 78 rpm, and *Here We Come, Come, Come* was John Lee Hooker meets the Velvets.

And so we get to *Pulse*, released in August 1975. It was little more than its title suggests: a low-slung industrial drone anchored by the repetition of a subsonic one-note throb. Allegedly, at the time of its release, a hi-fi company threatened to sue Zac because the song physically damaged one of their speakers. As part of an out of court settlement, Zac agreed to do a TV ad for them.

When *Ride to Saturn* and *Black is Gold* failed to go Top Ten, Zac was devastated. Things had started to go wrong with 1974's self-mythologizing *The Slim-Hipped Hipster*. It was a great album if you took its tongue-in-cheek strutting arrogance with a pinch of salt, but teenage girls aren't good on irony. And even if it had been a masterpiece, once the fans have moved on, they've moved on. Although the three months holed-up with the Dog Stars did Zachary the world of good, back in the real world none of his problems had gone away. Jody was still voicing her disappointment and anger at his promiscuity. But more pertinently, Helen Wheeler was still frazzling his nerves just by the fact of her existence. Zac would start physically shaking at just the muted clunk of one of her letters dropping through the letterbox. On one occasion, Jody flung the door wide open and screamed abuse at the girl, throwing her envelope back in her face. But after a week she was back again, and her next letter suggested she had actually taken solace in the fact Zachary was married to such a rude and ill-tempered woman: surely it was only a matter of time before he left her for Helen? They could meet for dinner, Helen wrote. She'd bring a couple of bottles of his favourite wine. Helen even seemed to have a sixth sense for whenever Zac called the police. She'd vanish just before they turned up. However, they did catch her once. Zac and I watched through the slightly parted curtains of an upstairs window as they quizzed her. She smiled at them politely. They smiled back. They talked. She listened. She replied: Yes, Officer; No, Officer; Of course not, Officer. And then they left, satisfied they'd done their job. She was back outside the house three days later.

But it was Brian the keyboard player who, one afternoon, put all of these other headaches into perspective. Zac was working on the final mixes of the Dog Stars album. When the pub closed after lunch, Chris and Tom of the Dog Stars stumbled back into the studio with Brian in tow. They'd bumped into him at the pub. Brian suddenly produced a gun from somewhere and started waving it about, shouting, "Give me my fucking money, arsehole! Now!" at Zac. To my astonishment, Chris and Tom just turned around and walked back out again, apparently more embarrassed than scared, but Zac was terrified. Fortunately in his drunken gunman rage, Brian didn't notice Joey crashed-out on the floor by his feet. Joey, woken by Brian's shouting, grabbed at his ankles, and managed to get a grip on the third attempt. This gave me time to push a swivel chair spinning across the floor towards Brian. The edge of the seat caught him just below his left knee, causing his skinny rock musician's legs to buckle. But not before he'd pointed the gun at Zachary's head and pulled the trigger.

Zac's hands flew to his face as he stumbled backwards. He told me later that although everything happened in a split second, it had seemed like sluggish minutes passing: he had time to study Brian's anger-distorted face; he saw the gun lifted and pointed shakily in his direction, and he felt warm rivulets of liquid running down his face. He didn't hear a bang, but he remembered reading somewhere that a bullet travels faster than sound, so you wouldn't hear the bullet that killed you anyway. It's funny how you remember such trivial details in the slowed-down seconds before your death, Zac had thought, his eyes screwed shut, deafened by his own protracted scream. And perhaps when you're shot in the head you don't *feel* anything either. But before he could ruminate on his own mortality in even greater detail, he blacked out.

A few seconds later, he regained consciousness only to see the cinematic cliché of a perfect circle of concerned faces looking down at him. But then the concerned faces turned to smiling and laughing faces, and Zac freaked out for the second time.

"What the fuck!" He struggled to his shaky feet.

Brian waved the plastic gun in front of Zac's baffled face. "It's only fucking water, man. It's a water pistol, you stupid bugger."

Realising he'd caused more of a scene than he'd planned to, Brian rapidly sobered up. Zac once again put his hands to his wet face, examined them, and then screamed at Brian, "You cunt! You absolute fucking, fucking cunt!"

Two Dog Stars stood between Zac and the only semi-repentant keyboard player, keeping them apart. "At least I got your attention this time," shouted Brian, over a Dog Stars' shoulder. "You really thought I'd shot you. That's hilarious! You're not fucking Kennedy, you know. Did you *pray*? I wouldn't waste my time if I was you, mate. I think you've blown it in that department. God was probably cheering me on!"

Despite Brian's protestations that it had all just been a practical joke (no harm meant), he'd obviously intended on giving Zachary a good scare, and it had worked spectacularly well. He'd given up reasoning with the man in regard to getting co-writing credits on some songs, and the royalties that would bring, and so desperate measures had been called for.

Once Zac had recovered, he became even more determined to hold onto every penny of his easily-earned money. And as Brian was only on a meagre fifty pounds a week, he couldn't afford to take Zac to court. Finishing *Swimming the River of the Soul* became unbearably tense. Brian realised the only power he had over Zac was to withdraw his creative input. So one day he just didn't turn up. When the delayed album was eventually released in May 1976, *Melody Maker* called it, "an overproduced, over-portentous and over-not-nearly-soon-enough mess". The only thing worth remarking upon here was the LP's cover. It featured a Magritte-like painting of a gigantic turquoise tripod rising out of the sea against the bloodiest of sunsets. Seagulls flew around its globe-topped apex and all manner of sea creatures, mythical and real, frolicked in the waves at its three-pronged base. Zac had shown me the original acrylic months before the album's release.

"What do you think?" he'd asked.

"It's great. What's this tripod thing?"

"I just wanted a simple but iconic symbol – something enigmatic – and I woke up one morning with a tripod in my head."

"But why turquoise?"

"Why not turquoise?"

Extract from *The KUU Hypothesis* by Zachary Bekele

3. MEDITATE ON THE MYSTERY OF MUSIC

Don't Pray, Dance!

When you lose yourself in dance, you lose your ego and your self-consciousness. When mind and body are one, you are not only a better dancer (however eccentric your efforts might be) you are also ecstatically free. A KUU paradox: when soul and body are one, the soul and body feel most liberated from each other.

Music is Moral: Music is Maths: Music is Emotion: Music is Paradoxical

Why do notes and chord progressions move you? Why does a child who knows nothing about music become sad when they hear music in a minor key and happy when it's in a major key? True music is pure truth. Music is morality as art.

Mathematical Magic

Five centuries before the birth of Christ, Pythagoras discovered musical scales corresponded to numerical proportions. But why is this law important for grasping the spiritual significance of music? Music or sound is a by-product of vibration. A plucked string produces a note. If that length of string is halved, while keeping it just as taut, the result is a note an octave higher. A string two-thirds of the length will produce a note a perfect fifth higher. It's like magic; it is magic. Music, that irrational passion-arousing noise has a direct relationship with the rational abstract world of numbers.

The Cheering Ring of a C-major Chord

It's another KUU paradox that musical harmony – which is thought to be an invention of man – has a direct relationship to a pre-existing – for that matter, always existent – system of mathematical laws, which are as true here as they are on the other side of the universe. The cheering ring of a C major chord is both a scientific (rational) and an aesthetic (irrational) truth.

6

"This stuff really hasn't dated, has it?" Damian was sitting up in bed tentatively sipping the coffee that August had brought him. It was the morning after he'd been stabbed and they were listening to Zachary B on the laptop. All things considered, he didn't feel too bad.

"Oh, come on, Damian. *Do the Rocket!* and *I'm the Cubist Funk Master*, not dated?"

"Look, there are dozens of bands around now just doing a diluted version of what Zachary B did back then: The Lilac Tinted Octopus; Fux; Big Bad Daddy... the list is endless."

"But those bands are dated too! They're playing the same music their dads grew up listening to. It's just not healthy. They should be doing their own thing."

"And what might that be?"

"Don't ask silly questions. You know what I mean."

Zachary B's music was taking Damian's mind off his traumatic experience. But it was important to think about the incident in order to make sense of it. He was relieved that he hadn't had to stay in hospital because – even at the point he'd begun to lose consciousness – it hadn't been death that he'd feared, it had been the imagined nightmare of a Moroccan hospital.

"It was just a random attack," Damian said for the fourth or fifth time, as the opening chords of *Black is Gold* swelled into life. "That's what makes it scary. Yet what did that kid have to gain by attacking me? He didn't even try to rob me. Shit, I love this track – it's those backing vocals…"

"No, a random attack doesn't make any sense. That's just your rampant xenophobia coming to the surface again," said August, brushing some pastry crumbs from his T-shirt and bed linen. "You're the-natives-are-restless paranoia is embarrassing…"

"But…"

"Look, Damian. If someone was going to randomly attack you, why do it in the middle of a crowded square in broad daylight? They'd get you down one of those dark back streets and they'd make sure they got your wallet too. They'd only take the kind of risk that boy took if they were being paid."

"Okay, I see what you're saying. Some of those poor urchins would sell their kidney for a few hundred dirhams."

"We're talking about the KUU Foundation aren't we?"

"Shit! It's the only logical explanation." Damian winced as he leant over to get his cigarettes from the bedside table.

"Are you okay? Should you be smoking?"

"Stop fussing. It's just a flesh wound, as Bruce Willis would say. No big deal." He lit a cigarette and tilted his head back and to one side, so as to exhale the smoke away from August.

"So the Doc said you should take it easy for a day or two?" said August.

"I'm afraid so…"

August looked tired and concerned, but Damian could see that the concern wasn't just for him.

"If it's any consolation, I'm as frustrated as you are," he said. "But as they're giving us the run-around anyway, we'd be fucked even if I hadn't been temporarily invalided. But you've got to go to Merrick's talk this morning. Maybe you can corner him afterwards – have another go at rescheduling the interview with The-Big-Cheese Who-Is-Not-A-Big-Cheese."

"Okay."

"That okay didn't sound very okay to me."

"What do you want me to say? It's been good having you around. Not just at the Tripod, also on the streets. Much less hassle."

Damian tried to console August. "Look, if I take it easy today maybe I'll be okay for tomorrow. Do you think I *wanted* to miss Merrick's talk? The guy's a genius…"

August gave Damian one of her *are you mad* looks. "Did I just hear you right? If anyone was a genius it was Zachary Bekele. Merrick's just a charismatic showman – no different from a Southern Baptist preacher, just a little subtler. And in some ways that makes him even scarier."

Damian fell silent as he mournfully stubbed out his cigarette. August carried on talking. "He's up to something. Why won't he let us see the Leader Who Is Not A Leader? If he doesn't come up with some answers soon, the media will be all over him like flies."

"Flies? What flies? Sorry, did you say something?"

"Fuck you!"

"Now, now. Language."

★

August's map was only occasionally useful given that the often unnamed streets seemed like a malevolent maze determined to lead her astray. The trick of keeping the Tripod's glinting apex in her field of vision at all times was good in theory, but less successful in practice. So when she heard the familiar words, "American? English?" for once she answered. But the long-limbed youth with the soulful eyes was determined to show her his cousin's leather goods shop before he would put her back on track to the Tripod. Because he promised her it would only take two minutes, and that it was on the way to the Tripod, she agreed to go. Needless to say neither statement was true. Ten minutes later she cursed the boy and ran back the way they had come.

Eventually, she encountered two women, perhaps mother and daughter. She drew the shape of the Tripod in the air in front of their surprised faces and they put her back on track.

Women were now a rare sight in the busier parts of the old city and, as a rule, seemed unapproachable. There were modern Moroccan women who dressed like Westerners, but August had seen very few of them in Marrakech. As had happened in London, many Muslim women had returned to a traditional style of dress, presumably as an act of solidarity in the face of increasing anti-Muslim sentiments in the streets and in the media, post 9/11. She wondered abstractly whether the street or the media, the chicken or the egg came first as she passed breathless and perspiring through Security. August disrupted two-thirds of Row 7 getting to her seat. She was fifteen minutes late, out of sorts, and this city of men was seriously getting her down. But she hadn't missed anything, Merrick was still busy shaking hands, slowly making his way up the central aisle towards the podium.

The palpable sense of expectation in the Tripod reminded August of a boy-band gig she'd been dragged to by a friend when she was fifteen. Hidden speakers on the Tripod's facade were poised to broadcast Merrick's welcome speech to a sizable crowd outside who hadn't made it into the building. All would eventually get their chance to experience the pleasures the Tripod had to offer, but for security and safety reasons there was a limit to how many could be in the auditorium for Merrick's speech.

The triangular floor-space meant that the number of seats in each row diminished the nearer you got to the stage, with the front row having a mere six seats bisected by the central aisle. The stage itself was also, by necessity, a triangle, just large enough for three turquoise lecterns. To the left of the lecterns August noticed a white plinth on the top of which was a glass-domed display case. Inside the case was a red velvet cushion, but she couldn't quite see what was displayed on the cushion. She turned to the woman sitting next to her to ask if she knew.

"It's *the* guitar string," the woman replied in a tamed South African accent, as if this were common knowledge. "Jesus, that's sick," muttered August to herself

"That's a bit harsh isn't it?" replied the woman, clearly readying herself for a confrontational discussion.

August ignored her. The woman gave August a quick, sharp look before returning her gaze to the stage, which Merrick had just reached. Two hundred conversations abruptly stopped as his resonant voice filled the auditorium.

"Thank you everyone, and welcome. Some of you may have been to one of these talks before. They are very informal affairs so do interrupt whenever you have a question. It's just an opportunity for me to officially welcome you to the KUU Tripod – hopefully the first of many KUU Tripods around the world..." A burst of applause drowned out Merrick's next few words. He smiled and then raised a hand for silence. "Some of you will already know that many of the facilities here are free and accommodation is as cheap as we can make it. You should also be reminded that in order for supply to meet demand, paying guests can only stay two nights at the Tripod, so we recommend that you sort yourselves out a hotel if you are intending to spend any more time than that in Marrakech. There are exceptions to this rule if you are in particularly dire straights. For example, only last week we had a Mormon family from Bainbridge, New York, fleeing their gun-toting papa. They needed serious counselling before we could even think of asking them to leave, so they spent over a week with us. But..." Several people were already trying to catch Merrick's eye to ask questions, so he relented, letting his talk took a more informal route. "Yes? The woman at the back?"

A small, chunky woman with cropped hair and a stud in her bottom lip, stood up. "Why all this?" She cast her eyes around the auditorium. "Is this really what Zachary would have wanted? It freaks me out. It's unreal."

Merrick smiled the smile of the kindly teacher. "It's the next step, my dear. We have to move forward. Zachary's ideas have the potential to change the world but we still have a long way to go. The Tripod is an advertisement for those ideas."

"But KUUism was supposed to be about *us*, doing it for ourselves, like," said lip-stud's skin-and-bone boyfriend.

"It still is, my friend." Merrick's hands gripped the edge of his turquoise lectern. "But I understand where you're coming from." August was amused that Merrick was clearly unaware that his use of contemporary youth vernacular didn't ring true delivered in a public school accent. He continued on a different tack. "Yes, the KUU Tripod may seem a little imposing. And, yes, we did upset elements of the local community by building it here. But this is about the greater good. We KUUists are philosophically obliged to entertain the possibility that our local Muslim friends' god is as valid a hypothesis as our hypothesis. If only they could be as open-minded. We are already planning further Tripods in London and just outside Amsterdam. The latter being an ideal location considering what a bastion of freethinkers and free spirits there has always been in that city."

This got a few isolated whoops of approval from the audience. Some shouts for the Leader Who Is Not A Leader eventually forced Merrick to address the issue of his absence. But all he said was that there was a problem with ill health, causing the audience to collectively murmur their sympathy. August noticed that the face of the South African woman sitting next to her had acquired the set expression of the happily lobotomised. It therefore came as a surprise when the woman raised her hand. Merrick took her question.

"You say the KUU is an active force in our lives, yet you don't want us to believe in it. And why don't you like to be called a cult?"

"Two very interesting questions. Thank you."

The woman turned to August with a tight-lipped smile of self-satisfaction. August pretended not to notice.

Merrick continued. "In English the word cult has always had negative connotations. However, by definition, a cult is just an attachment to a group of ideas – or an individual – shared by a small group of people. But the media has successfully convinced us that the word cult is a byword for brainwashing, human sacrifice and countless other kinds of extreme behaviour. A group of people obsessed with footwear in soap operas would be considered a cult. But, I'm sure if you leave them alone they'll leave you alone." Merrick revelled in the laughter his wisecrack engendered. He followed it up with another crowd-pleaser. "You can laugh!"

There was more laughter, this time of the self-congratulatory variety. Merrick gave a theatrical bow. August winced.

"We are living in an age of cults," he continued. "Anyone who sets up a website devoted to their passion is a cult of one – with potential." Merrick paused in order to savour the crowd's murmur of knowing approval. "But unfortunately an idea gains more credibility in direct relation to the number of people that know about it. This leaves us in the first decade of the twenty-first century with Starbucks and Primark as our new places of worship." Although there was an auditorium full of raised hands, they could wait. Merrick continued. "We are a planet of cheaply dressed, caffeine-charged, hamburger-chompers. Can so many people be wrong? Well, yes – *the Sun* is the most popular 'newspaper' in the UK. I rest my case. We can therefore ask, in relation to The KUU – can so few people be right? Again the answer is yes. But we are growing, and growing rapidly. And you won't find Starbucks, Primark or McDonalds here – we have thrown off our chains!"

More cheering, laughter, and applause. Like everyone else in the auditorium August found herself reluctantly agreeing with most of what Merrick was saying. But that wasn't the point. The point was that euphoric group cohesion made her nervous. And she simply didn't like the man. She hated to think what her mother would have made of all this.

A young woman in Muslim dress stood up. "This is not easy, what you ask of us." The audience went quiet. August notice two security men lose their glazed expression as they tensed for action. Merrick signalled to them that there wasn't a problem and gestured to the now wary woman to continue.

"I am sorry," she said, bowing her head slightly. "I should have waited to be invited to speak."

"Not at all," said Merrick, manifesting his warmest smile from his small collection of set smiles. "Please continue."

"It is not easy. You expect us to stop being who we are. You expect too much. We were born…"

"Okay, I make this point every time. We expect nothing of you, my dear. It's what you expect of yourself that's important. That's the beauty of KUUism. That's what separates us from every other religion, cult, or whatever, of course we don't expect you to go cold turkey, as we say. As a matter of principle, if you become an entertainer of the possibility you can also continue to entertain the possibility that the stories in your Koran are true and that your god is the one true god; there is no denying that this is a possibility. You just need to let go of the crutch of *faith*. It is faith that's dangerous. If your god does exist – and if he is the merciful god you think he is – then he will understand that you are the person you are – the person he made you. He will therefore also understand that that person got to a point in their life when they had to go their own way; follow their own path. Does that make any sense?"

"Yes. Yes it does." The woman had tears in her eyes. "Thank you, thank you. You are a good man"

God, he's good, thought August, glancing back at the Muslim woman who had clearly been relieved of a huge psychological burden. A huge white Rasta with hair like strips of carpet underlay had wrapped his burly arm around her narrow shoulders. She was clearly disconcerted by this while simultaneously seeing it as part of the new touchy-feely world she would have to get used to.

"How do current ideas about evolution, natural selection, and the Human Genome Project, fit into the KUU?" asked a short, balding man with a red **Fence-Sitters Unite!** T-shirt. "Does KUUism have anything in common with creationism and intelligent design?"

"Certainly not," said Merrick with mock outrage. "Creationism and intelligent design are easier to dismiss than Islam or Christianity, because they make claims to scientific objectivity. As for the Human Genome Project, KUUists should embrace every scientific advancement in the knowledge that we may get closer to unravelling the mysteries of creation. However, the closer we get, the more marvellous the world and universe seem. Always remember that the first U in KUU stands for unknowable. Every other faith and cult emphasises knowing even in the face of the most ambiguous religious texts." Merrick took a long gulp from the bottle of water on his lectern before continuing. "Those with a deity-specific religion seem much more concerned about not letting go of what they think they have, than moving towards a more ambiguous, but ultimately more intellectually and morally truthful position. Yes, we entertain the possibility that our KUU is the Omniscient Practical Joker. But that suggests the KUU just enjoys pleasantly surprising us, rather than using its omnipotence to refashion fossil evidence and DNA sequences just to lead us up the garden path. What a preposterous notion."

Another warm cheer erupted. For the next forty minutes, Merrick dealt with every single question, however predictable, petty, presumptuous or boorish, with the same mix of charm, good humour and tempered evangelism. An old Muslim gentleman with a beard like Father Christmas was honoured with the last question of the morning. His English was precise and clear. "It's the belief issue. Why are you so against it? You are building up this vast database of extraordinary KUU-incidences from around the world which are surely a testament to God's power, and yet..."

"Over three-and-a-half million at the last count," interrupted Merrick, proudly. "Obviously we have no way of factually verifying them. But one develops an instinct for the fake Cosmic Nudge story."

"That is indeed marvellous," continued the Muslim gentleman. "But it's surely only human nature that some people should want or need to believe rather than just 'entertain the possibility' as you put it."

"So why are you here then?" asked Merrick, letting just a hint of irritation seep through into his voice.

"Because Allah commanded us to seek knowledge, not to run from it, or get angry at its inconvenient truths."

The old man received an enthusiastic round of applause, so Merrick discretely pulled them back into line. "That's all very commendable but, *commanded?* You won't find any commanding going on around here." Murmurs of agreement. "And as for being 'only human' – we can now decide exactly what being human means. We can *choose* our nature. Evolution for human beings has become intellectual as well as biological." Merrick leant forward as if he were relaying a confidence to just a select few in the room. His voice became quieter, but his microphone technique guaranteed that no one missed his carefully enunciated words. "Zachary Bekele was no saint. Nevertheless, that great man knew the truth when he found it. He wrote about the unfortunate human need for dualities, opposing viewpoints. Our predisposition to take an 'either, or' view on everything: you either believe or you don't believe; you either want this team to win or that team to win. It seems to be our default setting: pick your tribe. Occasionally I find myself introducing the idea of the Cosmic Nudge to someone who eventually says, 'I find that hard to believe.' It unnerves them when I respond that I find it hard to believe too! They're flummoxed because they're unable to set themselves up in opposition to me. Sadly, we human beings love to be able to disagree. It really throws us when we can't."

There was some light laughter and appreciative chatter. Merrick had delivered his last sentence with precisely the right tone to convey that the show was over. August felt queasy. The audience gave Merrick a standing ovation while she gathered up her things and made her way towards the stage. She noticed a flicker of annoyance on Merrick's face when he saw her approaching. "My dear, so glad you could make it. What did you think? Was I too hard on that charming Muslim lady? It's for her own good, you know. Anyway, I imagine you wish to speak to me in private. Take the lift up to Level 11. Here's my apartment key. Make yourself at home and I'll be up in a jiffy."

August didn't even get a chance to speak. She'd once again had control taken from her. The key was in her hand and Merrick had disappeared through a door to the right of the stage. At Level 9 she had to get out of the lift she was in, and into a second, smaller lift which, due to diminished space, catered for the remaining two levels. She'd imagined that the rooms at the top of the Tripod would have had claustrophobically diverging walls, but Merrick's apartment stubbornly refused to reflect the brutal dictates of the architecture around it. It was an oak panelled, book-lined space, which made her believe it was late afternoon in autumnal Hampstead rather than midday in Marrakech.

She gave a squeal of alarm when she noticed Zachary B standing in the corner, partly hidden by the coat rack. How come she hadn't noticed the grotesquely gold-suited waxwork the second she'd entered the room? But Zachary would never have worn anything so unforgivably Las Vegas. The waxwork's outstretched arm theatrically gestured towards Merrick's fake fireplace. Its soulless face was part Richard E. Grant and part Bob Marley, but not at all Zachary Bekele.

"It used to point visitors towards the lifts. Sorry, did I startle you?" Merrick had entered through the door she'd left ajar. He brushed imagined dust from the waxwork's shoulder. "But bits of it kept going missing. You know how it is, a finger here, a lock of hair there. He's safer in here with me." He turned back to August, giving her a look she wasn't sure what to make of. "We met briefly when you were a child. Did you know that? Scotch?"

"Why is it always Scotch with you people?" asked August, ignoring Merrick's mention of their previous encounter. "I sometimes think that half the world thinks they're in a movie. An orange juice would be fine."

"I'm afraid the only soft drink I've got is tonic water. Don't you want to know about when we first met?"

Merrick handed August her water before sitting down on the leather armchair behind his desk. August sat opposite him. Merrick feigned indifference to the personal digital recorder she placed on the desk between them by nonchalantly flicking through his desk diary.

"My mother told me when I told her I was coming here. I was two at the time, so you didn't make much of an impression on me."

"You were a little menace, as I recall."

"Mum also said you never even liked his music."

"No, I can't say I did. But I was the only person your mother could think of who had the editorial skills to turn all those notebooks into something publishable. His handwriting was obsessively tidy, as I recall. I had expected manic scribblings; cosmic doodles; stains of unknown provenance. You can imagine." August noticed a paperweight on Merrick's desk that looked like a snow shaker she'd had as a child.

"I just had to have it," said Merrick, noticing the line of her gaze. "I got it in an auction in the late 80's. Seventy pounds, as I recall. It'd fetch a fortune now."

"May I?"

August leant forward to pick up the object.

"I'm afraid it's screwed down," said Merrick. One can't be too careful these days."

The aspic made the cigarette butt appear to change size depending on the angle August looked at it from. She thought of saliva, DNA, and *Jurassic Park*, so was glad to be snapped back from this escalating fantasy by the fact that Merrick was telling her a story.

"Tamale, Ghana, nineteen-ninety-five. I'll never forget the state Alain was in when I met up with him. Alain was a fellow world music journo – French, lovely chap, if a bit highly strung. He looked like he'd seen a ghost or a whole army of them. He'd run out of cash in Bamako having been ripped off by a bank. And then couldn't get money from any other bank. He'd also been involved in some black magic mumbo-jumbo, which he wouldn't talk about. So when he got to Tamale he was in a terrible state. He went straight to the first bank he set eyes on, to see if he could get any money there."

Despite the fact that August stared at Merrick in impatient disbelief for going off on this irrelevant tangent, Merrick remained unfazed and continued his anecdote.

"So, Alain handed over his passport to prove his ID. When the cashier handed it back to him a few moments later, the picture in it was of himself but having aged twenty-five years! The poor bugger went doolally, screaming at the cashier. He ended up on his knees weeping in the street. Eventually, when bank staff calmed him down, it was discovered that the passport he'd been handed back actually belonged to the customer at the next till along. This gentleman happened to have exactly the same name as Alain as well as looking like Alain might look a couple of decades in the future. It turned out the older gentleman at the next till was in fact a distant cousin of Alain's, even though Alain had never met him. Priceless eh? I just wanted to share that with your lovely readers back in Blighty. The KUU moves in hilarious ways."

"Indeed." August decided to humour Merrick and then come at him from a different angle when the time was right. "Was the KUU trying to tell your friend not to dabble in black magic then?"

"No, not at all. As Zachary said, the KUU – being the opposite of every other religion on Earth – does not judge, punish, advise or lecture. It just says 'hi' once in a while, amusing us and itself in the process. Poor Alain may have been terrified at the time, but he's dined out on that story ever since."

"So what was he like then, my dad?" August was annoyed that she'd failed to suppress a slight tremor in her voice. She didn't want to give Merrick any power over her, but she also desperately needed a different perspective on her father. One that didn't come filtered through books, magazine articles, fans, disciples or her mother.

For a moment Merrick's face registered genuine empathy. "I'm sorry my dear, but the simple truth is, I never actually met him. Paul Coleridge covered all that glam rock nonsense. Although in retrospect, some of his tunes aren't too bad."

August regained her composure. She hoped Merrick hadn't noticed she'd momentarily lost it. "According to Mum, Dad wasn't all there when he wrote half that stuff. In fact she says it's a miracle that…"

"Or mini-miracle…"

"Yes, or mini-miracle – that *The KUU Hypothesis* makes as much sense as it does. So how can we take any of it at face value?"

Merrick opened a desk drawer and withdrew a battered paperback. "Zachary himself mentions divine inspiration in Chapter 2, the section headed…"

"Yes, but what if he was out of his box, or just being ironic? You have to be so exact with language. Maybe when he wrote 'You can doubt,' he actually meant, 'you *should* doubt.' Mum says he hated the very idea of belief and organised religion. What you're doing here is… is…" August was beginning to get upset. This was exactly what she'd wanted to avoid. She took a deep breath and changed her angle of attack. "Then there's all this Leader Who Is Not A Leader, crap. We all know who's up there, in the fucking bell tower, so to speak. So why all the subterfuge?"

"It's show business, August. You have to understand that your dear departed father is still in show business. People forget all the details anyway. Or rather, they remember only what they want to. Did you know the Mormon religion was founded by a convicted illiterate fraudster? And look at how well they've done. Are you sure you wouldn't like a Scotch? Look my dear, if we're talking semantics, the word 'can' as in 'You can doubt' is clearly meant as just an option.

That's what 'can' means. If individual KUUists want to move beyond that, it's up to them…"

August couldn't believe her father's precious life-enhancing ideas were in the hands of this slick spin doctor and opportunist. She leant across Merrick's desk in order to face him eye to eye. "Don't you mean, regress back to that? You're turning the KUU Foundation into everything my dad despised." August cast her eyes round the room. "This creepy place says it all. You're stuck in the past, Barney. The KUU means nothing to you. Jesus! "

"Jesus, indeed. He died for our…"

"I hope you're not serious…"

"No, no. Just kidding."

August was speechless. She had grown up as a KUUist as other children grow up as Catholics or Muslims. She felt she knew exactly what her father had dreamed of. But belief was always going to be better for business than non-belief; fanaticism not scepticism sold T-shirts and Tripod paperweights.

Merrick tried to distract August from her rising anger by telling her how he had ended up in a giant turquoise tripod in Marrakech. After *Rock On* had folded he had scraped a living as a freelance writer for a year or so. There was a year at medical school, but his heart wasn't in it. Then, out of the blue, Jody got in touch.

"Jody – your mother – said she had finally reached an emotional place where she was able to go through Zachary's old notebooks and papers. She removed some personal stuff, unfinished song lyrics and the like, and gave me the rest to put in some kind of order. The money she offered made it impossible to refuse." One thing that Merrick told August made her smile. He remembered Jody telling him that Zachary would have loved the fact that Merrick (who had despised everything that pop ponce stood for) was obliged to lovingly transcribe four years worth of his stoned ramblings. "Not written in stone, but written *when* stoned," Zachary had been fond of saying.

Merrick met Jody twice. The first time she had served tea and carrot cake while he went down on his hands and knees to be a camel for the two-year-old August. After tea she handed him the supermarket bag full of notebooks and a cheque covering half his fee, asking him to contact her when he'd produced something publishable. The second time they met was eighteen months later when Merrick handed her the hundred-and-eighty page manuscript. The first edition of *The KUU Hypothesis* – Zachary B's dreamt-of alternative bible – was published by Valentine Books as a limited edition of two-thousand in the autumn of 1985. "Jody told me that Zachary had wanted to call it *The Quite Good Book* as an irreverent dig at The Good Book," continued Merrick. "But Valentine deemed such a self-deprecating title commercial suicide. And it also didn't have the pseudoscientific gravitas necessary to sell a book of this nature." Merrick went on to relate how the first edition sold out to die-hard fans in less than a week. A second run of ten-thousand didn't sell as quickly, but it still sold out in the end. Valentine Books produced limited edition runs of this initially slim volume at every conceivable anniversary of Zachary's death (1 year, 5 years, 10 years) with an appendix consisting of the best tales of coincidences sent by readers, gradually being added. By the mid 1990's the book was beginning to take on – at least in its physical proportions – the formidable dimensions of other religious texts.

"Then the Internet came along," concluded Merrick, topping up his whisky. "From that point onwards, we began acquiring Entertainers of the Possibility from all corners of the globe at an ever-increasing rate."

August flinched as Merrick placed his disturbingly hot hand over hers, which was resting on the desk. "Look, my dear. Zachary believed that people should think for themselves, yes? So if the Coup KUUists want to believe that Zachary ignored the call to revolution by taking the fence-sitting route, or if some kid in Texas decides to blow his own brains out because he decided to push the KUU a little too far, then that's people for you. There's always going to be fools putting their own absurd spin on things, whatever wise words you put under their sheep-like noses."

"What did you just say?"

"Nothing. What?"

"The kid in Texas; one of the suicides. You said something about them pushing the KUU. You *know* something."

Merrick's smile vanished from his face. He leant forward to turn off August's recording device. There was a lengthy pause before he spoke. "Look, Ms Bekele, we never asked you to come here…" Having produced his pipe from somewhere, he began to fill it with tobacco.

"Oh it's Miss Bekele now is it. Never mind all the 'we only use first names here' bullshit. You need to tell me what's going on, Mister Merrick."

August leant forward to switch her recorder back on, but the machine was snatched from under her hand.

"I don't need to tell you anything, Miss Bekele." Merrick drew deeply on the pipe. Its embers glowed briefly then faded. "As I said, you weren't invited here. But now that you are here, since you're a direct relative of Zachary's, and since you are a very tenacious woman, you could make things very difficult for us…"

"So what are going to do, kill me?" laughed August. However, she was disconcerted to notice how cold Merrick's eyes had become.

"A rhetorical question I presume, but nevertheless not beyond the realms of possibility…"

"I'm sorry – what did you say? Are you crazy?"

"Am I crazy? That's certainly not beyond the realms of possibility either. But it's very hard to be objective about one's own mental health, wouldn't you say? Apparently if you think you might be crazy, you're probably not. It's the people who haven't a clue they're losing their marbles who are the ones to keep an eye on. But to get back to your original question: tourists often get lost in the Atlas Mountains, Miss Bekele. Some of them are never seen again. Your mobile, please."

"You are kidding, aren't you? Tell me you're kidding."

Extract from *The KUU Hypothesis*
by Zachary Bekele

4. ENTERTAIN THE POSSIBILITY, AND THE POSSIBILITY WILL ENTERTAIN YOU

Part 1

The Fun of Infinity

In an infinite universe there are, logically, infinite possibilities. This allows KUUists to look charitably on the beliefs of others. In a universe of infinite dimensions (with possible parallel universes on the sidelines) no hypothesis regarding invisible unknowns is any less valid than another. Therefore KUUism entertains the possibility that any one of the other faiths may have got it right. Handily, this could help prevent confrontations with other belief systems.

Why We Think the Way We Think, and Why We Should Think About Distrusting the Way We Think!

Thanks to Descartes, we are taught that the best way to grasp reality is to be objective and empirical. Consequently, events that are not easily assimilated or explained confuse and irritate us, so they need to be dismissed or forgotten about as soon as possible: a coincidence is just a coincidence – otherwise we are in deeply uncharted depths.

He Thought Therefore He Was Mistaken

Descartes divided thought and experience into two categories: the objective, scientific truth and the subjective unscientific emotions and imagination. Mankind has been crippled by this reductive tribal-binary division ever since. Descartes thought therefore he was. This proposition turned out to be his only certainty. Through logic he convinced himself that the rest of the world – which we accept as a given – had to be doubted: the table he drank at; the walls that surrounded him, all the sumptuous, tactile reality that makes life worth living – it could all just be a lucid dream as far as this king of the doubters was concerned. Proof if proof were needed, that you can take doubting too far.

A Little Doubting Does You Good

Doubt should be a consideration not a prerequisite. A little doubting does you good, but too much can result in intellectual constipation. Descartes became a victim of his own subjectivity and in the process invented Scientific Method, KUU help us. The mind had won and the heart was made redundant. Man began to focus on the areas where he knew progress could be made. To be focused, you need to be blinkered. And what better way to be blinkered than by looking down a microscope?

Extract from
The Life and Death of Zachary B
by Paul Coleridge

Pigment-pricked into the Dead Meat of his Wrist

March 1976

It's time to meet Zac's dealer, Mozart, but first a bit of catching up. I didn't see Zac and Jody for much of the tail end of 1975. When he got back from an abortive tour of the States in February 1976, Jody was still away promoting her burgeoning fashion business. He seemed lost without her, so I ended up going over to Zachary Mansions a fair amount during the winter and spring of that year. It was during one such visit that I met Mozart, although met is the wrong word. Whenever our paths crossed he'd either be leaving as I arrived, or his arrival would be my cue to leave. Mozart was a furtive, twitchy hippy from hell. His small talk consisted of utterances of no more than three words at a time, the last of which was usually "man". His verbal diptychs and triptychs included: Cool, man; Nice one, man; Later, man; Bullshit, man; and Maybe Friday, man.

With Zac sitting opposite him as if for a game of chess, Mozart would open his incongruously expensive-looking briefcase. By the light of the sluggishly undulating lava lamp, he would lay out a pick 'n' mix of uppers, downers, fliers, cruisers – you name it – for Zac to peruse. Alongside these multicoloured delights, he'd place the more prosaic lumps of hash and bags of coke. The only thing Zac didn't need from

Mozart was LSD: years ago a friend had sold him a bottle of pure lysergic acid he'd acquired from a bona fide chemist in Switzerland. Zac told me that a single drop from this bottle would send you into orbit. It was years before I found out from some Zac hackography how Mozart got his name. Tim Mellors was the first kid in his class to pick up *Chopsticks* on the piano, but then he wouldn't let any of the other kids near the piano, thus acquiring the nickname Mozart. Three years later, Mozart was selling magic mushrooms outside the school gates. But I didn't even *know* his name was Mozart (Zac never addressed him by name) until I noticed the tattoo encircling his wrist. It mimicked a soldier's ID bracelet and had the words MOZART WAS HERE written on the tag.

This same Zacography reproduced parts of a *Daily Mirror* interview in which Mozart was charmed enough by some young blonde reporter to confess that he'd once begun an Open University philosophy course. He'd probably always been an existential anarchist but discovering there were these impressive-sounding words to describe his nature, thrilled him. The tattoo was his bleakly humorous way of commenting on his eventual (and given his lifestyle, probably sooner rather than later) demise.

MOZART WAS HERE was also an ironic echo of the territory-marking scribbles on council estate walls by Kilroy and his ilk. But most importantly, said Mozart in his *Daily Mirror* interview, it represented his living-dangerously drug dealer's sense of his own mortality. When his dead body is found by the pigs, some day, down some South London side street, they would find he'd left the building, so to speak.

MOZART WAS HERE – or rather, Mozart *was* here – would inform the pigs that he'd escaped – into oblivion or Hell. Either way, his trompe l'oeil tattoo would only then take on its full, literal meaning. It was his final definitive statement on life, the human soul, and his mortal coil – pigment-pricked into the dead meat of his wrist: MOZART WAS HERE but they'd just missed him. And there was no point in calling back another day.

But back to the deal.

After a brief exchange about what bollocks the new Stones album was, or how the Floyd had lost their way, Zac would ask Mozart if he had anything new to "fly his kite," or "rock his canoe," or whatever his latest colourful euphemism was for half killing himself. Zac by this time took his drugs more seriously than his music.

"Now, these pink and blue ones… ," Zac would begin, holding one up to the lava light for inspection.

"Well, I ain't taken any meself yet," Mozart would interrupt, "but I've heard they're not for the faint hearted. The red ones are just in from Amsterdam – they're trippy but you feel like shite afterwards. Although some cunts get off on feeling like shite afterwards, so horses for courses, I suppose. And these blue bastards just make you feel horny, so I'm told."

Zac was like a man choosing wine for an important function. "Fascinating. What did you say the psychotropic properties of these yellow ones was?"

"I didn't. They're…"

"I'm looking for a hallucinogen which still allows me to remain fairly lucid…"

"You what?"

"I want to retain a certain level of objectivity while still attaining a degree of spiritual transcendence."

Zac would stare intensely at Mozart waiting for a response. Mozart would stare blankly back at Zac, baffled as to what was required of him. Eventually, Zac would elaborate by simplifying. "I want to get all the pretty pictures, but still know what's going on?"

"Oh right. Got you. The red ones then. They're yer babies."

"Excellent. And of course, the usual."

Amusing as these scenes could be, it was distressing to see Zac become a slave to all the usual shit that decadent rock stars end up slave to: drink, drugs and sex. Couldn't he at least have found a less clichéd way of destroying and demeaning himself? Are we all destined to end up lowest-common-denominator versions of ourselves? But I couldn't complain. I'd kind of dreamt of a co-dependent relationship with my idol, and by the end of 1976 there was always something he needed from me. His paranoid, sleep-deprived voice would crackle down the telephone line at some unearthly hour, either because *she* was outside the house again, or because he wanted to discuss some new master plan for grappling back his career. I became like his private doctor. The phone jarring me from sleep so often I'd be putting my clothes on automatically before I'd even answered it. Inevitably it affected my work. One morning Jake phoned. "Look, Paul, mate. I know how it is with you and Zachary B – and it's good for the paper and everything. But you've postponed three interviews this month already. They're the ones who do the postponing, not you."

"Well maybe they need a lesson in humility then," I replied, rubbing the sleep from my eyes.

After a pause, Jake responded, "Rod's people threatened to boycott *Rock On* after you cancelled last Thursday, Paul. I would have sent Barney but he refused point-blank to even consider it."

"Look, I'm sorry, Jake. It won't happen again."

"It can't happen again."

On one such emergency call-out, Zac had said he had something amazing to show me. He was always reminding me I was now his official biographer so, although our meetings were informal, I should record everything just in case he made some profound pronouncement. I felt like an idiot chasing after him, microphone outstretched, as he leapt up the spiral staircase to the loft studio.

"Keep up, keep up! It's a really clear night. Well, clear for London."

At the top of the steps, I was breathless and Zac was laughing. "You spend too much time sitting at that typewriter." He looked me up and down. "And you should invest in some decent shoes." Then that eyebrow lifted. "And what's with the *Thunderbirds* badge? How old are you, Paul?"

The drum kit had been moved to one side, and in its place were two large (by domestic standards) telescopes. It was typical of Zac to buy two antique nineteenth century telescopes for their brassy aesthetic appearance, rather than get state-of-the-art that were ten times more powerful and half the price.

"His and Hers." Zac pointed one of the elegant devices skywards. It was mild for March and so the air coming in through the open skylight felt welcoming, exciting even: part of the bigger world – or rather, universe – we were about to explore. He took a cursory glance through the lens. "No moon and no cloud. Perfect. But first things first, we need a joint."

I rolled a joint. We stood side-by-side like men at a urinal, but gazing up into space rather than down at drowned cigarette butts. "Knowing it's all out there is not the same as actually seeing it," began Zac, "and seeing it isn't the same as comprehending it. Here we are on this green and blue globe, hurtling through space, living our bullshit lives…"

"No… er… yeah."

Zac begun to warm to the thoughts his narcotically rewired synapses were feeding him. He held up a Malteser between his thumb and forefinger. "This is Earth. Doesn't it fuck with your mind that there's no other life-sustaining planet for as far as the mind can conceive, or our instruments have probed?" He popped the chocolate Earth into his mouth and crunched, emphasising the fragility of our situation.

"Yes, I see what you're saying," I replied, drawing on the joint. "Could I have one of those?"

"Yeah, take the bag," he said with slight irritation, as if I was blaspheming by even thinking about honeycomb-centred chocolates while he was putting the cosmos to rights. "We're stunned into submission by mind-blowing facts and figures, but these explanations are only *descriptive*. They describe *how* things are, not *why* they are." Zac took another draw on the joint before finally getting to some kind of point. "Here we are, in this loft, in this city, on this planet, orbiting a sun which is a star in the outer reaches of a galaxy, which is only one of a hundred billion known galaxies, with each galaxy containing millions and millions of stars – each one probably bigger than our sun. I mean, fuck! How are we supposed to respond to shit like that? So instead of responding, we just shrug our shoulders and roll another joint! Talking of which…"

This was what I loved most about Zachary. This was why I put up with the sulks, the tantrums and the two-in-the-morning phone calls. He had an unwavering childlike enthusiasm for whatever he was obsessed with at the time. Whether it was a new riff, a new drug, or the meaning of life, he'd ride that wave just to see what strange faraway beach it landed him on. When he realised he'd been hogging the joint, he apologised and held it out to me. I declined all the drugs Zac offered apart from the occasional spliff. I'd learnt my lesson the time Zac and Jody gave me some tea without telling me it was magic mushroom tea. It tasted oddly earthy, but I thought it was just some harmless herbal brew and drank it out of politeness while a smiling Zac and Jody watched me with almost parental attention. At first I felt dizzy and nauseous, as if I'd gone up in a lift too fast. But once I reached the top floor, my personal doors of perception opened wide and I became enthralled by the geometric patterns of the Moroccan rug at my feet. Its bright colours became as vivid as sunlit stained glass, and its prosaic fibrous surface gave way to infinite, inviting depths. It was the most beautiful thing I'd ever seen and it held my attention for what seemed like hours. My reverie was eventually broken by the sound of Zac and Jody's mounting giggles, which appeared to come from the top of the well I was at the bottom of. They were telling me why I was seeing what I was seeing, but I couldn't understand why they were telling me this, or why they found it so funny. Although I acclimatised to this world of heightened, distorted reality, for the rest of the evening I felt unnervingly separated from Zac and Jody's cosy little world of obscure private jokes and free-flowing banter. In fact, the more they tried to draw me in – the more they shared with me what they were laughing at – the more disconnected I felt. They weren't deliberately trying to make a fool out of me, but psychotropic drugs emphasise the frame of mind you're in when you take them. Perhaps they should have warned me in advance about the mushroom tea and then I might have had a friendlier experience.

Once I left the house things got worse. I had a nightmarish journey home, certain that every other person on the night bus was intent on doing me unspeakable harm. It was only after an hour of stroking Demis (for my benefit more than his) that the familiar world of solid immutable objects – bed, clothes-shrouded chair, records and wardrobe – all gradually returned to being protective presences rather than threateningly, monolithic threats.

Jody phoned the next day to apologise. Evangelical zeal had led them to want to show me how amazing mushrooms could be. They thought I wouldn't have drunk the tea if I'd known what was in it. How right they were. But two men sharing the universe was a definite spliff moment, so I took another drag. As I looked through the intricate arrangement of handmade lenses, I felt fractionally closer to the universe's mystery and wonderfulness one second, and cowered by its scary, infinite gratuitousness, the next.

"It's like music," continued Zac, after a few minutes of contemplative silence between us. "We can take it apart, note by note, chord by chord; this chord makes you sad, that one makes you happy – but that's missing the point. The point is, why does it make you happy or sad, and why is one song magical and another bullshit? I was reading about the Heisenberg Principle the other day. This science dude talking about... now, what did he call them? Non-linear Systems? To you and me that means What-The-Fuck's-Going-On-Systems. He was inadvertently letting us in on the secret that science is just stumbling around in the dark like the rest of us. They just hide behind bullshit like 'Non-linear Systems', as if it's all in the bag."

I'd only been half-listening because I'd spotted a cluster of stars that formed a join-the-dots smiling face, but I somehow came up with the right response anyway. "Of course, yeah. We know nothing."

"Exactly! We know nothing. The sooner we take that on board, the sooner the human race can move on. Perhaps then we'd get peace on earth."

Perhaps it was the joint, but suddenly I couldn't stop giggling.

"What's so funny? What have I said?"

"Oh come on, Zac. Peace on Earth? Isn't that a bit too John Lennon? I see where you're coming from, but ... well, you know..."

Zac didn't know. In fact he stared at me with the repressed rage of a six-year-old who'd been spectacularly misunderstood by his parents. "I'm serious," he continued. "Whether it's this or that holy book, or a bunch of men in lab coats – it's all the same – it's all fucking human arrogance, human tribal thinking. You're wrong; I'm right. The human race is fucking insane but no one seems to have noticed."

Seeing how angry he was becoming, I opted for damage limitation. "Well if you put it like that, it kind of makes sense."

"If you put it like that it kind of makes sense?" he mimicked in an ineffectual whine.

"Look, I'm sorry Zac. It's just when you get so... so... you know, pompous. When you dismiss the belief systems of billions of people. It just makes me laugh."

Zac took a long, slow drag of the spliff before continuing in a more measured tone. "The world's religions have stood in the way of every kind of progress we've ever made, moral and scientific, from the abolition of slavery to the introduction of birth control. Did you know the Vatican actually publicly condemned the electric light bulb?" For a moment Zac became distracted by his turquoise fingernails. But then, like a cat that had stopped in mid rodent-slaughter for a scratch, he continued on the same subject. "Take the

Bible. We know the names of the cats who wrote that stuff: Mark, Luke, John, and the rest of them. But that still doesn't stop Christians, Jews, and Muslims believing all those crazy schizoid words came directly from God. These books were about social control from the off. Faith: faith is just another word for certainty or hope. But the word hope sounds flimsy, fragile. Faith gives it wings. Look at it like this: if I say I'm *certain* God exists it sounds arrogant. If I say I *hope* God exists it sounds wishy-washy. But if I say I have *faith* that God exists, it sounds heroic. And it shouldn't be that way."

The dope, combined with keeping track of the tumble of words pouring from Zac's mouth, was making me queasy.

"Certainty, hope, faith – they're all variations on the same theme. It's just that the word faith has become the respectable, untouchable option. We're obliged to *respect* the Faithful. Between the wooliness of The Hopeful and the cockiness of The Certain, there lies the untouchable Faithful. Yet faith as a concept represents the worst aspects of both hope and certainty..."

"I'm going to lie down," I slurred redundantly, as if I needed to voice my plan in order to have the will to carry it out.

"The world needs to be returned to the artists," Zac continued, as the ceiling started to slide sideways away from me – *come back ceiling, come back!*

"The scientist pointing a powerful torch of perception at a subject, lights up a small area, but never sees the whole picture..."

"Is it okay if I crash on the sofa?"

"Yeah, of course. Just brush all that crap onto the floor. As I was saying, the scientist points a torch, but the artist, in darkness, can imagine the whole. And therefore intuitively get nearer to the truth. The truth being..."

Luckily I was taping all this stuff, because I wouldn't have remembered a word otherwise – the essence perhaps, but not the details, and the Devil is always in the details...

When I regained consciousness, Zac was still scrutinising Space: all that nothingness had to mean *something*. By four in the morning, we had agreed that statistics ending in long ordered queues of zeros weren't much help.

"Are there any of those Maltesers left?" asked Zac. "Sorry, no. You did say take the bag."

"I didn't mean... Oh, never mind."

Extract from *The KUU Hypothesis*
by Zachary Bekele

4. ENTERTAIN THE POSSIBILITY, AND THE POSSIBILITY WILL ENTERTAIN YOU

Part 2

The Atheist Believer

Although we suspend disbelief when watching a film or reading a novel, if we make great leaps of the imagination in our everyday life we are considered eccentric. Yet until the beginning of the nineteenth century there was no such thing as an atheist in the sense that we understand the word. If you were labelled an atheist it was a term of abuse levelled against someone who simply believed in a different god, not no god at all.

Rumination as Prayer

Resist just assimilating the next unlikely coincidence you experience, and ruminate on it for a while instead. Along with dancing, this is another thing a KUUist can do to replace the self-flagellating ritual of praying.

Take Off Your Safety Goggles

Take off those safety goggles science gave you and stand in the full glare of the reality of our precarious existence on this planet. If you start to feel dizzy just sit down and have a glass of water – you'll be fine in a minute. You've simply rediscovered your talent for subjective unmediated thought. Paradoxically, you are using your imagination to better experience your reality. Subjective contemplation is one step away from subjective conjecture. So you are now ready to...

... Entertain the Possibility!

You've already employed your talent for imaginative conjecture when, for example, you chose your partner. You didn't get them to fill out an elaborate questionnaire, you simply looked into the eyes of a perfect stranger and decided if they were too strange or just perfect, and acted accordingly.

The Evidence of Accumulation

Don't always expect others to be impressed by your KUU-incidences. The KUU-incidence is a form of personal revelation. If *you* felt a frisson of excitement at an unlikely confluence of events, that's the main thing – it was your Cosmic Nudge. Some KUU-incidences may seem banal so it's important to consider them cumulatively. Remember, the term is Cosmic Nudge not cosmic bolt of lightning. Even the seemingly insignificant KUU-incidence is a subtle reminder of the enigma of chance. The sheer improbability of your existence/our existence – and the very universe's existence – is the greatest KUU-incidence of all. Etc etc, Amen!

7

Marrakech, February 2007

"So what did you say when he asked for your phone?" asked Damian aghast, leaning forward in his chair. At August's suggestion he'd made it up the stone steps onto the roof. He'd been confined to his room for a day and a half and she felt he needed some fresh air. It was still early evening, but it was already dark. Some brass lanterns gave them enough light to see each other by. A bottle of gin and two glasses stood on the table between them.

"I just laughed at him. What did he expect? He's an old man – well, not old, old – but you know what I mean. What was he going to do?" August shrugged and sipped her gin. "And then I walked out. He just stood there with a self-satisfied smile on his face as if he'd convinced himself he'd won."

"He did kind of win though, didn't he? He got rid of you."

"Well, yes and no. He did slip up. We now know the suicides are connected specifically with pushing the KUU. If Alice – Malika's KUU counsellor – is still in Marrakech, we need to talk to her. We have to find out more about Malika's death."

"But aren't you bothered that Merrick threatened you?"

"He just made a joke out of it when I didn't respond in the way he thought I would. To be honest, maybe it was a joke. Yes, I am angry, of course I am. But I'm not going to let him, of all people, get to me – that's what he wants. Did you know they've got the guitar string up on a plinth in there?"

"Yeah, I did read that somewhere."

"Don't you think that's just a little bit not right?"

Damian considered this for a moment. "Yeah, maybe not, but—"

"But nothing."

Damian changed the subject. "The Doc gave me the once-over this afternoon. If I take it easy, I can go out tomorrow. I'm really sorry about all this, especially after what you've just been through." Damian looked down at his body as if it had betrayed him. August had put a blanket over his legs and they'd laughed at how he looked like some old wheelchair-bound guy in a movie.

"Don't be silly. You know this wasn't your fault." August shifted her chair a little nearer to the table and took Damian's free hand in hers. "Look, Damian, I've got something to tell you, but you must promise me faithfully that, whatever it is, it won't change your attitude towards me, and you won't be angry."

"Well it depends what it is doesn't it. If it's—"

"Just promise me. Please"

"Okay, okay. But now you're starting to worry me."

Damian shifted uncomfortably in his chair. He was concentrating on not letting it show in his face how much pleasure he was getting from having his hand held. He knew August was a touchy-feely kind of person, and so it meant nothing to her. But he was a repressed English bloke who saw opposite sex hand-holding as virtually first-base.

August's voice cut through his tumbling thoughts and feelings. "Just shut up and listen." She took another sip of gin. "You've never bothered to ask me what my other name is – no reason you should have really – but I suppose I would have told you if you had…"

"Isn't that just a cop out – that whole 'but you didn't ask me' crap?"

"Damian. Please."

"Sorry."

August's fearful yet imploring facial expression conveyed the fact that she was willing Damian to take the news she was about to impart calmly. The words were simple and direct when they eventually rushed from her mouth. "My full name is August Bekele. Those crazy parents I mentioned were Zachary and Jody Bekele."

Damian did two things simultaneously. He extricated his hand from hers, and carefully put down his drink. He then slumped back in his chair and for a full minute stared morosely at his drink, saying nothing.

August lowered her head and tilted it slightly to see if she could re-establish eye-contact. "Damian? Hello?"

"Fuck me! I mean, why? Why didn't you tell me this before? And don't say 'you didn't ask.'"

"But you didn't ask!" August slapped the table with the palm of her hand. "Damn! I knew you'd make a big deal out of it."

"This is a big deal, August. It's a huge deal." Damian stared at August as if she were a ghost, or an angel, or a bit of both. "Shit! I knew they had a kid," he said, more to himself than to her, "or at least there were rumours that Jody had been pregnant when Zachary, when your father..."

"Mum – Jody – was actually pregnant with me when they left London. I was part of the reason they left – all that madness and a child on the way too..."

"But didn't Jody Bekele just disappear?"

"That's just the media's dramatic spin on it. She didn't disappear, she just changed her name for a few years and didn't court the press. We were just another black one-parent family living in London – you can't get much more anonymous than that. Damian, please stop looking at me like that! My dad was just a musician, nothing more, nothing less. All this madness has nothing to do with him, or me."

"But what does it feel like? This is the man who wrote *The KUU Hypothesis.*"

"Is it?" said August. "Mum says she doesn't really hear Zac's voice in 'that bloody book,' as she calls it. She thinks it's too cold and over intellectualised. She's been trying to get the notebooks back from Merrick for years. She even tried to take him to court, but because he's out here in Morocco, it's not easy."

"But did she actually read the notebooks when she did have them?" Damian was now leaning forward, intensely focused. The rug had slipped from his lap, but neither of them had noticed. The clatter and cry of cyclical drumming and snaking Berber horns coming from the square seemed to be getting louder. Damian felt a growing unease as if the swelling cacophony were some ferocious enemy about to engulf them. When a cascade of car horns seemed to join in for a few bars, the noise became so overwhelming they had to stop talking.

Eventually August spoke. "She's embarrassed about it now, but no, not really. She glanced at them once in a while, but I think she feared what might be in them – personal stuff maybe, or stuff which showed he was losing it even more than she'd feared. And Dad didn't invite her to read them either. Then, after he'd gone, they became even more untouchable; the whole Pandora's Box thing, but eventually she decided Zac would have wanted his ideas made public, and so that was that."

"So why have you suddenly decided to tell me all this?"

"Because I think I trust you? Look, I don't know what I'm trying to say, but I'm sure Dad wouldn't have approved of all this."

They both stared at the apex of KUU Tripod. Its revolving globe now had the moon for company, to its left and a little higher in the clear night sky, the two spheres appeared almost identical in size. Inexplicably, their juxtaposition made Damian feel slightly nauseous. His knife wound throbbed. He shifted his attention back to what August was saying.

"It was just a bunch of Dad's stoned scribblings – his improvisations on a theme. Who knows what Merrick read into them, or how much he elaborated on them. I read bits in my teens. I even remember Xeroxing a couple of pages I liked. But I can't remember any of it now."

Damian wanted to get up and walk about, but he resisted the impulse. Instead his right hand beat involuntarily on the arm of his chair as he spoke. "I just can't believe any of this. It's like, it's like… It's like being a Christian and meeting the Virgin Mary or something. You're Zachary Bekele's—"

"Enough! This is why I didn't tell you all this in the first place! It's this kind of nonsense that I find so hard to take!" August was on her feet, gesticulating so violently that Damian feared she might strike him. He couldn't believe how quickly she'd become angry. "What's wrong with people? I'm nothing. I'm no one! All I am is a bloody prisoner of my family's past, thanks to shit-for-brains idiots like you!"

"Hey, fuck you." Damian's response was sulky rather than angry, and half just to himself. August didn't even appear to hear him. She continued, but with her anger under control.

"We all know Dad – Zachary – loved all that shit, the fame, the adoration – that was what he fed on. He probably would have loved the idea that he's ended up being worshipped like a god – God help him. But for Mum and me it's always been a nightmare: six different schools, three different countries – trying to keep out of the limelight. Now do you understand why I didn't tell you? You're *one of them*, don't you see? You're the enemy – the enemy who wants to make our lives a misery with all their fucking love and adoration!"

The lamplight revealed silvery tears on August's face as she silently paced. Damian didn't know what to say or do. He couldn't see the jet passing overhead, but he imagined it was slowly sheering the sky in two. Eventually, he found the right words.

"Look, sit down August, please. I'm sorry. I'm really, really sorry. I promise I'll stop seeing you as the Glam Virgin Mary, or whatever. Really I will."

Instead of replying, August walked over to the edge of the roof. The view of the lights and smoke of the Djemaa el-

Fna had a calming effect on her. She'd said all the things she needed to say, and she just hoped Damian wouldn't speak anymore for a while. He didn't. He lit another cigarette, painfully aware that even the scrape of match on a matchbox might disturb August's necessary period of post-tantrum meditation. He found himself covertly studying her: the splay of neat dreadlocks tied up on top of her head, arcing this way and that like a freeze-framed firework display in negative against the city's glow; the shapelessness of her white cotton dress which nevertheless accentuated the architecture of her hips. Of course, she was just a woman! She'd been just a woman ten minutes ago, and now she was just a woman again – a very beautiful woman too. He smiled to himself at the fact that he could even put a sexual spin on a moment like this. *Get a grip, you sad perv – think about something else.*

Five minutes later, August sat back down at the table. Damian hid his amusement at the fact that she just continued their conversation from a point just before it went off the rails.

"I'm not as sceptical as Mum though. She thought that even the title was wrong. I've tried not to care all these years. I've tried to keep my distance. But it was an itch I knew I'd have to scratch one day."

This is interesting, thought Damian: if two people behave as if something bad hasn't just happened between them, then it might as well have not have happened. And somehow this unspoken agreement creates a new bond of understanding. Who'd have thought it! Because the atmosphere was now definitely more relaxed. Damian had crossed over into a more adult world in which the right thing to do was to join August in her pretence that they hadn't just had a heated argument.

"Now I understand why it was so important to you to get this story," began Damian. "But what do you expect to achieve?

August topped up their glasses. "I've no idea. But what Merrick has done – what the KUU Foundation is doing – is wrong. End of story. And all these suicides, it's just really creepy. I felt defensive about the KUU as Dad had envisioned it. It was supposed to be about personal revelation not big business." Damian was surprised to see August suddenly fold in on herself with a fit of the giggles. "Sorry, sorry. It's just that... It probably won't seem funny now, but obviously I grew up a KUUist, but for a while I was a lapsed KUUist. The only decent schools Mum could ever find for me were Catholic schools, so I had to play at being the Good Catholic Girl for a few years, and some of it inevitably stuck. Mum would try to deprogram me when I got home from school, but I was like any other kid – I needed to rebel. Except for me it was backwards rebelling, I suppose." August wiped a tear or two of mirth from her eyes. "I remember kneeling nervously by my bedside praying, knowing it would make Mummy cross, but also knowing that if I didn't pray then that would make my teacher, Mrs Trew cross, so I couldn't win really. But then I worked out that if God was watching – as he surely was – obviously God would be on Mrs Trew side rather than Mummy's, so praying seemed my best bet. I'd turned the sound down on MTV when I spoke to God because it was only polite. But one time *Man in the Mirror* came on, and I loved *Man in the Mirror* despite finding the strange white man who sang it, a little disturbing." August gave Damian a knowing smile. "So there I was, my eyes shut and the music blaring, unaware that Mummy had come into my bedroom. In one graceful movement she gently parted my praying hands and lifted me up by them. 'Don't pray, dance. You remember,' she said, smiling at me. Then we danced around my bedroom. *Man in the Mirror* segued into George Michael's *Faith*, and I made her laugh by imitating the way George Michael was wiggling his bottom on the screen. I loved to make Mummy laugh. This became a bit of a private ritual between us and sometimes I would just pretend to pray so that Mum would dance with me. It drove her nuts."

Damian wasn't sure if August's tears were still tears of mirth, but he guessed they were more ambiguous tears generated by a complex mix of memories and emotions. Uncertain as to what to say, he launched into a story his grandfather had been fond of telling him. "During the Second World War, my granddad joined the navy and his brother joined the army. Towards the end of the war, Granddad found himself stationed in Delhi. It was his twenty-first birthday, he had some leave, and so he decided to do some sightseeing. He was walking down a side street when, to his amazement, he saw his brother coming towards him. Can you image? They had not seen each other for nearly five years. They embraced, went for a beer, and then went their own separate ways. It turned out the brother had been chosen from five hundred men to go and pick up a truck from Delhi. The truck hadn't been ready, so he went for a walk around town. These two men could have been stationed anywhere in the world, yet they ended up on the same street of the same huge bustling city on the twenty-first birthday of one of them. Brilliant eh?

August wasn't quite sure what to make of Damian's rapidly imparted, second-hand anecdote. But he'd figured that if he kept talking, he might not have to ask her about why she'd become so upset.

"That's quite a story..." she began.

The crisis point seemed to have passed.

"You've got your dad's eyes," he risked,. "And his mouth too, kind of..."

August smiled. "Have I? Thanks."

Damian relaxed. "You're welcome."

Extract from *The KUU Hypothesis* by Zachary Bekele

5. REJECT ORGANISED RELIGIONS, AND IF YOU'RE AN ATHEIST, REJECT THAT TOO!

Part 1

If I could write in flames across the sky, one short statement to the billions of god-fearing people on this planet, it would be:

"LET GO OF YOUR BELIEF. IT'S MORE TROUBLE THAN IT'S WORTH!"

FACT: Most believers' faith is the faith they were arbitrarily born into. It is one of the few things in life, along with our name, that we take for granted and make no personal choice about

FACT: Many have died, and will die, and are still dying as you read this – fighting over the small print from the undeniably ambiguous texts of their holy books.

Belief is an End not a Beginning

There is no point in denying the validity of the religious or spiritual experience and the expansive and transcendental feelings it can generate, but the problem lies in the need to label it.

Cow Knowledge

Suppose we imagine we can see the complete picture. This implies the intelligence we humans possess is sufficient. How much intelligence is that? Twice as much as a cow? A hundred times more than a goldfish? Isn't it more reasonable to assume we are only slightly less limited in our understanding of this world and universe than these two co-inhabitants? What does observation and experience teach the goldfish about the world beyond its bowl? Almost as little as we know about life on and beyond the goldfish bowl that is Earth.

We Know Nothing

FACT: We know nothing about what happens to us after death.

FACT: We know nothing beyond what is filtered through our sensory organs to our brains.

FACT: Making a choice with regards to a theological position is patently absurd. Because... We. Know. Nothing.

Extract from
The Life and Death of Zachary B
by Paul Coleridge

Baby Powder and Fruit Pastilles
August 1976

"Nice one, Paul. You're a star," Colin shouted from the other side of the stage.

"No, *you're* a star," I had just enough wind to quip back, as I unburdened myself of a heavy case of effects pedals. Getting the thumbs-up from Colin, or my hair ruffled by Brian, was what made playing at being a roadie such fun. Of course it was also indescribably thrilling to casually rest your hand on the textured cladding of a Marshall amp, or stand with one foot up on a wedge monitor looking out on a soon-to-be-filled concert hall, or to lovingly remove Spike's bass from the scarlet bedding of its velvet-lined case, and let's not forget the pleasure of admiring the beauty contest of Zac's guitars lined up across the stage: the utilitarian simplicity of the Telecaster; the Audrey Hepburn elegance of the white Stratocaster; the Platonic perfection of the maple-finish Les Paul, and last but not least, the Rubenesque curves of the Martin acoustic. It didn't matter that I had no more status than a tea boy: I was plectrum boy, drumsticks boy and joint-assembling boy (Brian told me he so admired the sleek design of my six-paper spliffs he'd kept one as a souvenir). The fact was, I needed to be a part of the world I reported on. After all, what kind of job description is reporter? It's so passive; so contingent on there being something to report. Yet the war correspondent who is held hostage or loses an eye or an arm – now you're talking! So I needed to get in with the band and become part of the story, rather than just an adjunct to it.

It was while I was playing at being a roadie, during the heat wave of 1976, that I bumped into Helen Wheeler again. Or rather, she nearly tripped over me. Zac was playing an Anti-Nazi League gig in a South London park. Satisfyingly fatigued from helping the band set-up, I decided to find a good spot on the yellowed grass in front of the stage before it got too busy. I loved London in the summer. Once you were at one of those free weekend festivals, you became part of a temporary alternative society for the event's duration. There'd be the young hippy families, the disenfranchised youths, the grungy unemployed and – always in possession of the same park benches – the corned-beef-faced tramps struggling to discuss the meaning of life with booze-scrambled brains. The other London was reduced to something on the horizon, grey and hushed by distance, its characterless tower blocks made wobbly and insubstantial by the rising heat haze.

Lying belly-down on the itchy grass, reading Martin Amis's *Success*, I recall being irritatingly semi-alert with the thought that at any moment some gambolling child would trip and land his Softwhip smack in the middle of my naked back. And then there were the ladybirds – so charming in the singular – but that summer there was a plague of them. There was a water shortage so the little buggers would bite you just to get a drink.

Anyway, I was so preoccupied with such anticipated discomforts, that I failed to notice the pair of pale feet in aqua-blue flip-flops that had stopped directly in front of me. My eyes moved up past faded pink flares to a white gingham smock-top and then, above the top, a familiar smiling mouth painted the colour of seaside rock. Shielding my eyes from the sun, I confirmed her identity. Her hair was now short, like Mia Farrow's in *Rosemary's Baby*.

"Hi," she said, nervously stroking the back of her head (maybe the hairstyle was new to her too, and she feared it was misbehaving).

"Hi," I replied, with feigned neutrality. I wasn't sure whether to put the book down (which would lead her to assume I thought she was stopping) or keep it held to attention (indicating I wasn't interested in continuing the conversation beyond these initial pleasantries). So rather absurdly, I fanned myself with it.

Helen and I had seen each other several times since that first encounter at Wembley in 1973, but eye contact was always broken as soon as it was made.

And now here we were in the strangest of social situations: we knew each other and yet we didn't know each other; we had the most important thing in our lives in common, and yet she seemed as wary of me as I was of her. And the damned sun just kept beating down, making even the slightest frisson of anxiety turn into a film of sweat on my forehead, which, once wiped away, instantly returned. I resorted to complaining about the heat in the traditional British manner, but she immediately broke the rules of such small talk by disagreeing.

"I think it's great that they've got such a lovely day for it."

"Yeah, I suppose so. But these bloody ladybirds."

"They don't seem to like me," she shrugged. "Or rather, maybe they do like me, and that's why I've not been bitten once. Can I join you?" She conjured a purple towel from her denim shoulder bag and, with a deft flap, spread it on the ground next to me.

"Be my guest," I replied redundantly.

"Do you think there was a Zachary A?"

"Sorry?"

"It's always made me smile. The idea that there was an even more perfect Zachary: Zachary A, and Zachary B is just the second-rate copy."

I caught on, and offered my own tangential notion. "But surely if Zachary A was a robot or clone, Zachary B would be the upgrade; the improved model. "

"Yes, that makes more sense."

Makes more sense? Nothing made sense in conversations with this girl.

Zac was headlining so we had to tolerate a clutch of one-hit-wonders, no-hit-hopefuls, and ubiquitous festival regulars, before our man came on, dressed-down (for Zachary anyway) in a salmon-pink T-shirt and billowing yellow loons. The Now got the few hundred fans who were massed around the stage, dancing and swaying to a string of hits and favourite album tracks. Although Helen and I agreed it was a shame they didn't play any new material, to my surprise, she also agreed we should stay where we were, rather than get involved in the sweat-bath down at the front. But the biggest surprise was that she didn't even hint or suggest that I could use my influence to get us backstage to meet Zac after the performance. It had been worrying me all afternoon. I mean, can you imagine it? What would I have said: "Hi Zac. Meet Helen. She's the obsessed fan who's been giving you sleepless nights for the past three years, but she's a nice girl really". How could it not have all ended in tears? But Helen was cool. Not cool as in hip, but cool as in calm and inscrutable. Whether her disconcerting ability to constantly surprise was affected or innate, I couldn't say, but she didn't strike me as someone putting on an act. As a park full of misfits gradually took on board the fact that the day was over, Helen caught me off guard again. With childlike glee she said, "Would you like to see my Zachary B scrapbooks?" I could tell from her expression she was aware of the innuendo implicit in her question (the oh-so-obvious echo of an invitation to view etchings), but she was also adept at conveying that no flirtatious euphemism had been intended. Before I had time to decline, she added, "It's only ten minutes walk."

Saying no would have been an act of profound cowardice, so I said, "Yes, why not?"

Helen's first words as we entered the three-bedroom terrace house were, "Don't worry, my parents are away." She registered my brief look of panic and added, "I just meant you won't have to meet them, silly." She shrugged a one-shoulder shrug, and looking around, exasperated. "I really need my own place. But you know how it is."

I did indeed know how it was. I was still in the same ghastly bedsit I'd been in since moving to London. I suppose I could have moved, but money was always tight. Suddenly she brightened. "I'll put some music on. Would you like an orange barley water?"

I had expected Helen's potpourri-scented bedroom to be completely plastered with pictures of Zachary B. So I was almost disappointed that the peach-coloured walls were home to only two Zachary images: a tour poster from 1973, and a still from the *Strange Camille* promo. So again she'd confounded my expectations (or rather, disappointed me, by not being a generic psychopath). While she was making our drinks, I sat on the edge of the bed and took everything in: some dust-coated dried flowers in a school-made vase sat on the windowsill; a red Dansette on the floor was flanked by two orange LP cases and a matching singles case; on a green wicker chair, a couple of plump-bellied teddies sat with their heads inclined toward each other and their startled eyes fixed on the ceiling.

When Helen returned she put on *Silver Soul Jetstream*. Its familiar sound relaxed me. Leafing through one of her scrappy scrapbooks, I began giggling.

"What's so funny?" She asked.

"It's just some of these pictures. Look at this one." It was a glossy centre-spread, the surface of which was badly dimpled due to the fact Helen must have used a water-based paste to stick it in. Against a sea-green backdrop complete with cartoon bubbles, a pouting Zac (mutilated by a staple scar in the middle of his smooth, bare chest) stood astride a stuffed shark. Other members of the Now were larking about in the background in frogman suits. We smiled at other ludicrously posed pictures involving unlikely props, all done, presumably, with the idea of making Zac appealing

191

to pre-teens. "Do you know something?" I said, as Helen sat down next to me on the bed. "I used to buy *Jackie* and *Mirabelle*. I was happy to face the newsagent's withering look just to get stupid pictures like this."

"He's such a chameleon, don't you think?" said Helen, pressing her ice-filled glass to her cheek.

"Er, yeah, I suppose so."

"That's why I take so many of my own. I've only got two or three decent shots, but they're so much more *real* than magazine photos. It's like having a souvenir of a little bit of your own memory – something you *saw* rather than something someone else saw. Do you know what I mean?"

I wasn't sure I did, but nodded anyway. She leant over to open a dainty drawer in her dainty dressing table. It was crammed with those brightly coloured photo envelopes Boots give you.

"It's so expensive getting pictures developed so I've started doing my own," she continued. "Mum and Dad paid for all the developing fluid and stuff. They were just relieved I'd found a hobby. Black and white photos are coolest. Though sometimes I still take colour ones. It depends on my mood." Then it registered what I'd just said to her. "I think it's brave of you to admit to buying girls' magazines. You're not a nancy-boy are you?"

"Do I look like a nancy-boy?" I prayed the answer was no.

"Not really. But would looking like a poof be *that* bad? Zac looks poofy, but it just makes him more sexy, don't you think?"

I'd never been expected to have an opinion on so many different things in one day. "Well, yes, I suppose so. I mean, no, it wouldn't be so bad."

Again she'd thrown me. Even though I was older than Helen, I felt like Dustin Hoffman to her Mrs Robinson, stumbling around in the dark for the appropriate response and the words to express it in. But as we've just touched on the topic, perhaps it's time to briefly address the subject of Zachary B's sexuality. There were rumours he was bisexual, but I never saw any evidence of it. Today we talk of men being in touch with their feminine side, but Zac wasn't just in touch with his feminine side, he was in love with his feminine side. Zac and his feminine side were inseparable; they were seen everywhere together. But – as the man himself put it; "I'm only interested in having sex with people as beautiful as I am – which narrows it down to just a tiny percentage of the female population". But back to the inaction with dear, sweet Helen...

"Oh yes, I nearly forgot." She picked up a small porcelain trinket box from behind a forest of perfume and hairspray bottles on her dressing table, before sitting back down next to me and carefully opening the lid. Inside were three little parcels of pastel tissue paper in the softest blue, pink, and yellow. She unfolded the blue paper parcel with an archaeologist's practised care, to reveal... a single cigarette butt.

"Zachary's," she said, as if that were explanation enough. She then added, "The other two are Brian's and Spike's – I think." She anticipated my next question. "Cambridge Corn Exchange, March the nineteenth, 1972. There was a coach trip to see the band. After the gig, a bunch of us followed the car back to the hotel. The band were in this roped-off area, but you could still get pretty close."

"I'm astonished you even got into the hotel."

"Zac must have told the security people to let a few of us in. Maybe it gave him a kick that he could give a little wave from behind the rope, and a bunch of girls would scream back in reply."

"But not you."

"No, not me. I'm not the screaming type. Anyway, after wine and crisps and stuff, everyone left or went to their rooms and the rope was taken down. We then had a couple of minutes to swoop before the hotel staff cleared up. We were like locusts – it was so funny! But I'd kept track of which ashtrays each of them had used. Zac had stayed in one place talking to these three women, so I knew exactly which ashtray to go for. Then I just took one of the butts that didn't have lipstick on it. Simple!" She picked up the other two parcels. "I'm not *absolutely* sure these were Brian's and Spike's, but I'm not that bothered, really. This is my prize exhibit." She held out the fag end of a fag, pillowed in its nest of blue tissue, for me to inspect.

"Yes it's … er… great. You must be very proud"

"Now you're making fun of me." She seemed genuinely hurt. I didn't know what else to say. But I did find the keeping of this grimy souvenir a little odd, distasteful even. I confess I also needed to bring the power balance back in my favour. This seemed the right time to ask her something I'd wanted to ask her all along. "So why do you do it?"

She responded as if it had never occurred to her to question her own behaviour. "Why do I do it? Now why *do* I do it?" She lovingly re-wrapped her treasured butt. "I don't know really. I suppose it's like bird watching. Aren't bird watchers obsessive, spending days and nights hoping for a sighting of a red-throated warbler? " She was playing with me again. "But surely there's more to it than that? I mean – come on, Helen. You're outside his house almost every night. And then there's the letters, and—"

"Well, yes. Obviously." She became flustered for a moment. "Obviously I'd die for Zac. I don't imagine many tweedy old gents would die for a lesser speckled…" she giggled at her own extended metaphor. But seeing that I wasn't amused, she changed tack yet again. "You can talk, Paul Coleridge. What's the difference between us, when it really comes down to it? It's just that you get paid to pester Zac." Her argument was absurd so I just laughed. This did something to dissipate the tension. Perhaps it was cruel of me to press her. I tried to make amends. "Fair point. Journalists can be complete arseholes, but that's not my style. And I don't stitch people up either. If Zac doesn't want something in print, it doesn't appear in print."

"Like what! Like what!" She bounced up and down causing the bedsprings to squeak in protest. "Please tell me!"

"Now come on, Helen. If I've not betrayed Zac's trust in print, I'm not going to betray it to you now, am I? He trusts me. That's why he doesn't do interviews with anyone else."

She gave me a resigned smile and wiped her forehead with the heel of her hand. It was now evening, but still oppressively hot. "Do you enjoy writing?"

"Yeah, I suppose so."

"Is it hard?"

"Kind of, but words are magical. Certain words have an inner light – they connect with readers in a very direct way."

"How do you mean?"

"Well, the reader does half the work without realising it; they complete the picture. Words unlock their memories and imagination."

She gave me a puzzled look, which briefly manifested itself in cute little hieroglyphs on her forehead. "How do you mean?"

I was enjoying this safer, less personal direction the conversation had taken. "Oh, I don't know. How about 'Marrakech' or 'harbour'? Each of those words will conjure up a different image or world for each reader. A world within a word."

"And 'world' and 'word' are the same apart from the 'L'. In the beginning was the world!"

"Yes, exactly. Hey, you're right. Even if you've never been to Marrakech you have an impression of what it's like in your head, from a TV program, a novel, or even *Encyclopaedia Britannica*. That impression might be completely wrong, but it'll be as vivid for you as a memory of that place. I suppose the hard bit is putting all the duller, less emotive words around the firework words. What I'd really like to do is write a novel."

"Fireworks – there's another one!"

"Er, yeah…"

"Water. Dog. Ball," said Helen, excitedly. "Now I'm thinking about the *Ladybird* books I grew up with. 'Jane threw the ball. The dog chased the ball.'"

We both laughed. The sun had deserted the room apart from a bright rhomboid of intense pink by the bedroom door. It became the focus of my attention as our conversation began to falter. I closed the last of the scrapbooks.

"I'd better be making a move, Helen."

"When you've gotta go, you've gotta go," she replied cheerily.

"Yeah, it's been nice."

"Yes, hasn't it."

"Great."

"So?"

We were back to one-syllable words like the "hi"s our conversation had begun with in the park and it made me feel inexplicably sad. Our eyes met as she opened the front door, and I realised how little I'd looked at her directly during the whole time we'd spent together. I could smell her endearingly cheap perfume – not cheap as in tart-cheap, but cheap as in affordable but rather two dimensional: baby powder and fruit pastilles came to mind.

I leant forward to kiss her, but her index finger came up between her mouth and mine, and delicately planted itself on my lips as if she were shushing me. It was a gentle but effective deterrent. She wasn't shocked or annoyed. Perhaps she simply wasn't ready. I buried my hands deep in the pockets of my jeans (absurd behaviour given it was such a hot evening) and trotted off towards Brixton tube station. And that was that. I could have phoned her I suppose, but the whole situation was just too weird. For one thing I would have felt disloyal to Zac, and for another, the girl *really* unnerved me. I did bump into her once more, a week or two before... but we'll come to that later. For now let's just get back to the Now.

After the disastrous tour of the States, Zac needed a way out. However, he was in a no-win situation. In retrospect, he should have just walked – got into films or TV, written a book or something – anything rather than try to win back his fans. He had his head in the clouds – and his arse on the fence of his homegrown religion. Even if Zac had suddenly found he could walk on water, it wouldn't have helped.

Supertramp, 10CC, The Rubettes, Gentle Giant are, for me, band names that conjure that Angel Delight era – all vacuous, yet all filling the musical vacuum between the last sexually-charged throb of glam and the first bar-chord clumsily struck by an Iggy-loving punk rocker. Although fashion had been the wind beneath Zachary B's wings, it was soon to become the sun melting the wax that held them in place. Sadly, punk rock would make an Icarus out of Zachary B.

Extract from *The KUU Hypothesis*
by Zachary Bekele

5. REJECT ORGANISED RELIGIONS, AND IF YOU'RE AN ATHEIST, REJECT THAT TOO

Part 2

Closed Books

Belief is an end not a beginning. Because they are all focused on blinkered certainty, Christians are spiritually closed, Jews are spiritually closed, Muslims are spiritually closed and atheists are spiritually closed. Becoming a dedicated non-believer is as ridiculous as blindly believing, when there is no conclusive evidence for either position.

The Power to Control the Sun

The big questions for the first men must have been – Who am I? Where am I going? And when will it all end with an axe in the back of the skull? The only place to look was up, as only death and dust lay at their feet. The Sun blinded, but it also warmed. It burned, but it also chased away the darkness with its concealed dangers, both real and imagined. It destroyed crops, but it also helped them grow. How could something so paradoxical and powerful not invite worship? Mankind wasted no time in anthropomorphising the gratuitous Sun, seeing it as a cruel entity that would give and then take away at whim. What could be more natural than to start asking, and then praying to the Sun to act more justly and kindly? Perhaps during periods when each day arrived without a hitch, and the crops grew green and strong, man began to believe, like hungry pigeons in a food-earning experiment, that their Sun-worshipping rituals had brought about this fortuitous outcome

The Neurotic Cycle of Worship

The birth of a sense that the pious individual who prayed had control over his own destiny lead to people believing that they could gain a slice of the omnipotence and power of the almighty Sun through prayer. After all, the Sun's daily appearance was surely indisputable evidence of the power of prayer, and therefore man's capacity to influence the behaviour of the cosmos: the illusion that one is in control is better than not being in control at all. And so the neurotic faux-symbiotic relationship with our gods began.

PART TWO

Whoever fights monsters should see to it that in the process he does not become a monster. And when you look into the abyss the abyss also looks into you.

Friedrich Nietzsche

1

Marrakech, February 2007

"OUT! OUT!!" Paul Coleridge hurled one of Jamila's shoes across the room at her. She scrambled to pick it up, while simultaneously cowering at the possibility of further missiles, and trying to put her clothes back on. "YOU FUCKING WHORE!" Tears streamed down Coleridge's face, spittle and snot glistened around his mouth and chin. Jamila actually was a whore, so Coleridge's reiteration of her job description made little impact on her as an insult. But she was also the only real friend Coleridge had, although he didn't seem to realise it. Her English was good, but that was what got her into so much trouble.

"You state the obvious, Mr Coleridge."

"FUCK YOU!" Coleridge launched the headless torso of Darth Vadar at Jamila. It broke some more as it hit the window-wall just to the right of her head. Having found her shoe, she turned to her ankle-length jalaba and headscarf, which were carefully folded on a chair (Coleridge insisted she wore traditional clothing whenever she visited him; she found this weird but it wasn't a big deal).

"This reminds me. You owe me for these fucks that you speak of," said Jamila, standing upright again. "It's been three weeks since I have had any money from you."

She put on her jalaba in jerky, violent movements, apparently not caring if she tore it. Coleridge felt the shift of power between them move in her favour and so he put down the vintage 1966 Dalek he'd been about to throw at her.

"Okay, okay, credit card. Wallet's in my jacket pocket – the one on the floor by the computer," he said, before adding in a pitiful whine, "Why do you do this to me, Jamila?"

"You do this to yourself, Mr Coleridge."

"And why the fuck won't you call me Paul? I pay you twice the going rate and you still won't call me Paul!"

"I am sorry Paul. I forget."

Remorse hit Coleridge, as it always did after arguments with Jamila, and he began sobbing uncontrollably. She had been visiting him at the Tripod once a week for over a year now, and he sort of loved her. He could have had a younger woman – he could have had a ten-year-old if he'd wanted – but that would have been sick. And anyway, he needed someone he could talk to. He wasn't sure what age Jamila was, perhaps late thirties? It was hard to tell with her dark, flawless skin. What he did know was that, aged sixteen, she had been raped, and the resulting child caused her family to disown her. He propped himself up on his pillow and watched her vigorously brushing her hair before a compact mirror. Coleridge had no mirrors in his apartment: he got more then enough of his fat lumbering self thrown back at him from the three tapered glass walls which delineated his world at the apex of the Tripod.

"Stay?" he said, almost inaudibly.

"You want me to stay now?" She turned to face him, hands on hips. "I'll stay, but only if you pay me three-time going rate and stop throwing your toys at me."

"Fuck you."

"We back to 'fuck you'? Okay, I go."

"I'll get some breakfast sent up. Whatever you want. I'll…"

But the glass doors had silently closed behind her. Coleridge briefly thought about how he missed the slamming door option, living in this modern monstrosity. Had Jamila missed it too? Do Muslim women even slam doors? Do they dare? He was sure Jamila did whenever she got the chance. Where was his whisky? The bottle had somehow rolled under the bed. Barney had started him drinking whisky. The bottle retrieved, he slumped back exhausted on his pillows. Once he'd got his breath back, he unleashed a good five minutes of expletives, whispered, screamed and hissed. Then he put his shoes on, just so that he could stamp his Tracy Island into a thousand pieces.

He got onto his recliner, grabbed the TV remote and aimed it at the single-bed-sized screen.

(*Zap!*) Well I never: a cut 'n' paste Zachary B documentary. There's some grainy home-movie footage of a three-year-old Helen running across the greenest of lawns towards the camera in that haphazard, forward-rolling way of the newly erect. She falls, then, undaunted, gets up again, continuing her progress towards the camera until her laughing out-of-focus face fills the whole screen. A quarter-smile created a comma at the corner of Coleridge's spittle-dappled mouth. How sweet Helen was as a child! How sweet we all are. Then she was gone, replaced by footage of Zachary's funeral. The great and the mediocre clambering from limos, trying hard to remember – given the solemnity of the occasion – not to smile or wave at the camera. The banal hillocks of flowers, and the fans clumped like emperor penguins against the cold, clutching hankies and comforting each other.

Coleridge shifted his weight, groaned, and fell asleep. Consequently, he missed most of a review programme on which three cultural pundits were seated at a TV-table working themselves up into a state of self-righteous indignation about *The Life and Death of Zachary B* all over again, simply because of a new made-for-TV adaptation of it. The discussion hastily moved on from the risible TV mini-series back to the book itself.

"It's not a work of fiction so why did he write it in the style of a novel? It's an insult to Zachary Bekele's family" began the pundit with letterbox-shaped glasses.

"Absolutely," interjected the one with the goatee.

"Most of the people in that… that… excuse for a book are still with us. It was an outrageous breach of their privacy," continued letterbox-shaped glasses.

"The whole sordid thing was unforgivably voyeuristic and exploitative," began the chinless blonde with the long-neck. "I remember feeling quite nauseous by the end."

"Yes, the degree of visceral detail in the final chapters was particularly unpleasant and unnecessary, as I recall," said letterbox-shaped glasses.

Coleridge had never understood why the novelistic style of his memoir upset people so much. That was simply how he'd remembered everything: the conversations with Zac; Helen's bedroom; *that* night - so that was how he'd reported it. True Crime was the biggest growth area in publishing, his agent had told him in order to persuade him to finish his once-abandoned work.

Because the call for the book to be banned had never gone away, neither had the demand for it.

Coleridge's eyes flickered open for just long enough for him to see the critic with the goatee pick up the DVD of the TV mini series from the table and wave it in the air with histrionic outrage. Coleridge stabbed at his remote.

(*Zap!*) There was the English television presenter Bill Grundy, still goading the Sex Pistols (as he would do forever in this world of constantly recycled and reassessed cultural titbits). Coleridge plunged down the lift-shaft of his own mortality as it dawned on him he was now more like the corpulent, sweaty Grundy than the delinquent schoolboy, Rotten. Three decades separated him from this farcical non-interview that had somehow become History. And look at Siouxsie - she'd seemed scarily sexy back then. Now she just looked like some sweet silent-movie angel to his jaded eyes, the lids of which were slowly lowering again like malfunctioning garage doors. What kind of fate was this to befall the little boy who used to linger for an age over which boiled sweets to choose from all those gigantic jars? Then, as he drifted once more into sleep, his fragmenting sideways-slipping mind began to create its own entertainment.

The fish with the cow-like face stared neutrally at Coleridge from the murky depths of Mozart's fish tank. It's funny the things your subconscious remembers, and then uses to furnish your dreams, he thought – in his dream. The fish's petrol-spectrumed scales had been replaced by corpselike grey-white flesh, as if it had been skinned alive. At a couple of feet in length, the cow-fish was much bigger than the fish he remembered from Mozart's tank. It noticed Coleridge and began swimming towards him, leaving fuzzy bits of its rotting body in its wake. These flakes hung briefly in the water before being darted upon and consumed by the ever-vigilant smaller fry. The cow-fish reached the tank's glass, facing Coleridge. Its tragically soulful eyes (yes – soulful, not soulless as you might expect) seemed to be imploring him to do something to help it. Its dumb mouth slowly opened and shut, opened and shut. Coleridge heard the fish's voice in his head: '*Break the glass, break the glass...*' Sweat-soaked, Coleridge shuddered awake. The remote was still in his meaty fist, so everything was okay. He tried to replace the phantoms of his nightmare with the garishly smiling faces of the outside world.

(***Zap!***) "*Families and couples will love the gorgeous golden beaches. Prices start at an amazing £159 per person, so why not ...*"

(***Zap!***) A fake blonde selling fake jewels with a fake smile.

(***Zap!***) The square-jawed action hero told Coleridge all about his latest generic blockbuster.

(***Zap!***) What a miracle Satellite TV was, thought Coleridge. As a child he remembered having to turn a stubbornly stiff dial – clunck, clunck, clunck – between just three channels. Yet even in this baking, backward city the roofs were festooned with the concave mouths of skyward-pointing satellite dishes, like just-born chicks silently screaming for sustenance. When the end of the world came, he hoped it would happen in a flash – instant oblivion – just so the fucking media wouldn't get a chance to put their spin on it!

Befuddled by whisky, he looked down at his remote, like a drowsy, baffled ape. He considered it's egalitarian power, literally at his fingertips. An involuntary shiver followed another swig from the bottle – did he even like this stuff? And then he was asleep again. Nightmares are cunning. They root us in the familiar: a room or house we know well, people we know or people who are as convincing as any we know. Every detail and texture is in place as if conjured by state-of-the-art CGI software. But once the nightmare knows we have been hooked, it dims the lights and ushers in the horror.

Coleridge calmly reached for the hammer his dream had conveniently placed on the coffee table a few feet from the tank. He did a bowler's run-up and then swung it at the wide expanse of glass. He knew the cow-fish would die rather than escape, but he had to stop the pleading voice in his head. A great slab of water hit him and carried him across the room, smacking him against the far wall. But then the water kept coming. *He* was now the feeble creature in danger. His head was bent sideways, only inches from the ceiling, straining to get at the last wedge of air which was rapidly being pushed out by the rising water level. The water closed over his head. Below him, Mozart's black leather furniture issued dense clouds of panic-stricken bubbles. *Please don't let the cow-fish see me, please don't let the cow fish see me.* But of course it saw him and slowly turned his way, like a ship coming into dock. With his lungs fit to explode, he backed himself into a corner of the ceiling, as the sorrowful faced cow-fish closed in, as if for an intimate kiss. His scream released the last of his air.

Coleridge gasped awake. "Fuck, fuck, fuck! Barney, Barney!" he shouted into his TV remote. "Idiot!" he shouted at himself, hurling the remote across the room, and locating the phone. "Barney! Paints! I need some paints. No, not *pants*! Paints! No, hang on – make-up. Make that make-up. And I need some coke too!"

Barney had a lot to answer for: Coleridge was now slave to all the bad habits he had resisted for half a lifetime. He simply needed something to help him cope with the pressure of being The Leader Who Is Not A Leader – whatever the fuck that meant. In fact, about the only illicit substance he hadn't acquired a taste for, was Barney's own particular favourite, heroin. He was too squeamish to inject, and although chasing the dragon had sounded exotically appealing, the lorry-exhaust fumes coming off the tin foil repelled him. "That stuff can't be doing you any good," he'd once said to Barney, without a trace of irony. But cocaine made everything brighter, sharper and gloriously harder. It lifted him out of his self-made morass and sent him off on all-night virtual adventures, leading him by the mouse to whatever the Internet wanted to show him or sell him. With his coke-filled asthma inhaler by his side, he was primed for anything.

Coleridge's door buzzer buzzed. He wrapped his grimy bathrobe around himself and stumbled over to the small monitor by the door. Barney's sickeningly concerned face filled the screen.

"We need to talk, Paul."

"Have you got the coke?"

"Yes, I've got the coke." Merrick never felt comfortable in the spacious light-filled apartment that Coleridge had turned into a squalid student hovel. Here, at the apex of the Tripod, the three converged steel legs dictated the shape of Coleridge's living space. There was no ceiling, no verticals to restore equilibrium, just three triangular glass walls tilting inwards, giving the impression of a large glass tepee. Sometimes he would lie under the bed just to be in a stable rectangular space – how we take for granted our verticals and horizontals! But it was Coleridge's escalating addiction to eBay which unnerved Merrick more than the smell and the untidiness. TV and movie collectibles littered the floor: a Captain Scarlet with a missing arm (so much for being indestructible) lay trapped under the green hulk of a Thunderbird Two; several generations of PlayStation consoles lay like a pile of ancient bones in one corner. And every inch of the floor was carpeted with newspapers, magazines and books.

Merrick waited patiently while Coleridge shakily poured some whisky into a tea-stained mug for him. Then he got straight to the point.

"As you know, Paul, you're here for a reason." Coleridge laughed, coughed and then laughed some more.

"What, you mean 'a reason' as in, a higher purpose? Or 'a reason' as in, to do your bidding? I suspect the latter."

Merrick had never seen anyone literally speak between clenched teeth before, but Coleridge had managed it with those last four words. It was time to adopt the tone of the patient but firm headmaster. "You know exactly what I mean, Paul: We have an agreement. You've got to become more actively involved again; start pulling your weight. I've been very, very patient. You need to remember that I… well, I did effectively save you."

"So that's what you did!" Coleridge's tone was theatrically sarcastic. "Oh, that's funny. Very funny…" But Coleridge wasn't laughing. He was vigorously scratching his left arm, just below the shoulder. "Because I certainly don't *feel* saved, I feel cursed. I feel like I'm in… in purgatory." He turned back to Merrick, forcing close proximity eye contact in an attempt to call the bluff of his irritatingly calm gaze. He continued with quiet intensity. "You're all fucking crazy, you know that don't you? Although I'm not sure what that makes me."

Merrick, repelled by Coleridge's blowtorch breath, took a step back and looked around for a surface to put his mug down on. "Paul, dear fellow, aren't we being just a little overdramatic? Let me be blunt, as you've been so direct with me. You have simply got to start earning your keep again."

Paul knew exactly what this meant. It meant going back to those interminable weekly meet-the-bloody-public sessions: smile; grasp shoulders reassuringly; listen to – more often than not – banal tales of coincidences (other people's KUU-incidences can be as dull as other people's dreams) and say a few words ('but keep it short and non-specific – we don't want you saying the wrong thing. Be like the Queen,' Barney had advised). Apart from that, there were interminable book signings and the occasional request for Zachary B rock star anecdotes from a small contingent who weren't interested in Zachary's posthumous career as the new messiah. Everyday the queues were enormous. He couldn't believe how understanding and even loving these people were. It just felt wrong. In fact it felt totally fucked up, as he'd said to Barney at the end of his first very long day. 'You've just got to look at the bigger picture,' Barney had responded, placing a reassuring arm around Paul's shoulder and giving him a chummy squeeze. Paul remembered that chummy squeeze because the only other person who had ever given him a chummy squeeze had been Zachary. In retrospect, in a moment of uncharacteristic self-awareness, Paul had realised that that moment of casual body contact had influenced his complicity far more than all of Barney's carefully structured arguments. As he'd squeezed, Barney had said, 'These people need Zachary's story to make sense. You're their main living connection to the great man himself. That's why you're here; you're meant to be here'. How strange it was to be hearing Barney-past in his head while Barney-present was still waffling on at him now. With some effort, he refocused his attention on Barney-present. "I didn't hear any of that, Barney. But whatever it was, I'm not interested. So if you wouldn't mind…"

"For once, Paul, I think this will interest you. You remember the reporter I told you about?"

"Yes, yes. And please don't talk to me as if I'm a child. I told you I didn't want to see her. Nothing's changed."

Merrick looked skyward, exasperated. There was nothing to do but come straight out with it. "The reporter is August Bekele – Zachary and Jody's daughter. I didn't tell you before because I didn't want to freak you out, but you've left me no option…" As he spoke, Merrick had turned to look out at the violet and salmon sky, and at the sun that appeared to be speeding up its descent the nearer it got to disappearing behind the Koutoubia Mosque. He waited a while for Coleridge to respond, but eventually the man's silence compelled him to turn around. Coleridge had assumed the foetus position on the bed, his back to Merrick. He'd come back later.

Once it was dark, Coleridge felt calmer. Earlier, he'd found a small package on his bedside table which Jamila must have put there for him before she stormed out. Although he knew what it was, folding back the tissue paper to reveal and smell what was inside still gave him pleasure: the small reddish-brown clumps of myrrh looked like dry clay. The first time Jamila had brought him myrrh she had solemnly informed him that this sweet-smelling substance 'calmed restless spirits'. When he googled myrrh he found out that it was the dried sap of trees that only grew in Somalia and parts of Ethiopia. Ethiopia – where Zachary's father came from. KUU, who'd have thought it! He had felt instantly reconnected to Zac. The next time he saw Jamila he hugged her and thanked her. Since then she'd occasionally brought him some more. When it had been one of Jesus's birthday presents from the three wise men, it had cost more than pure gold. Now it could be bought cheaply from any spice merchant. He put some in the incense burner Jamila had also given to him, and lit the candle beneath it. Then he ordered himself another Tracy Island on eBay (his fourth, not including the one he'd had when he was five) and everything, for the moment, was right with the world.

Eventually, after hours of playing computer games and watching TV, he slumped into sleep, his remote control flaccid in his hand. At some point during the eternal, infernal night he found himself gazing up through his three slivers of window at the paint-spray of stars – at Zachary's knowing, unknowable universe. It prompted him to shut his eyes tightly and take solace in his own velvety, starless universe. The outer universe seemed more unknowable and less knowing with each day, hour, and minute, that passed. He would call Jamila and apologise – not now, but in the morning. *No, now.* He needed to do it now. He needed to *see her now.* He heaved himself out of bed and searched for her number in his wallet. He was immediately distracted by a yellowing scrap of paper, which he carefully unfolded. It was a cutting from a newspaper he'd picked up from the seat next to him on the train, the day he'd left England for Morocco. To Coleridge, the story reported on this scrap of paper was part prayer and part exquisite mathematical puzzle. Contemplating its dizzying infeasibility always cheered him up.

A ten-year-old girl called Laura Buxton released a helium balloon with her name and address on it, from her garden in Blurton, Staffordshire. The balloon landed, a hundred and forty miles away, in Pewsey, Wiltshire, in the garden of another ten-year-old girl called Laura Buxton. Both girls owned a black Labrador, a guinea pig, and a rabbit.

He read the story twice, then carefully put the cutting back. The only other things in his wallet were his credit card, a photograph of Phil, aged 21, smiling behind his decks, and an ancient library card. Having forgotten his need to call Jamila, he slouched back down in front of his always-alert computer and clicked on the 'buy now' option on an original 1960's Tracy Island (it had to be an original) for the bargain price of two hundred and eighty six dollars. Even the box was a work of art with its yellow lightning-flash graphics. A sudden jolt of shame made him wish he'd tidied up before Barney had visited. Barney must have noticed the porn DVDs scattered about, as brightly packaged as the sci-fi merchandise they shared floor space with. While his heart still conspired to pump blood to his penis, Coleridge would remain in lust with every female generous enough to put her naked body in front of a camera – no strings attached – for his virtual consumption.

PLAY: the girl on the screen took a nonplussed nipple between each thumb and forefinger and teased it into life. She looked at Coleridge to see if he approved. He did approve. He preferred to see girls flying solo – pleasuring themselves while looking him shamelessly in the eye, giving every impression that they were delighted by his focused animal attention. He would therefore curse profusely whenever some jumbo-sized penis loomed into frame like a veiny 1950's sci-fi monster, spoiling everything. It baffled him that other men delighted in seeing women's orifices plugged by organs which were – not only not theirs – but presumably put theirs spectacularly to shame. He paused the encroaching sci-fi penis and rewound to those enchanting nipples. It was just beginning to get light.

Extract from *The KUU Hypothesis*
by Zachary Bekele

6. EMBRACE AND DELIGHT IN THE COSMIC NUDGE

The Cosmic Nudge is the KUU Saying Hello

It is the KUU acknowledging your existence while hinting at its own existence. The more you delight in the notion of the Cosmic Nudge, the more you will be nudged.

A Semi-interventionist KUU

Most of us either believe in an interventionist god or a non-interventionist god. The KUUist of course should consider the third option: that the KUU is semi-interventionist. If you accept – as experience tells you – that prayers go unanswered, you get back your dignity and independence. You will have evolved, intellectually speaking, from the belief-cursed human race.

We Are Not Persecuted or Favoured.
We Are Free

If we accept we are neither favoured nor persecuted by a higher being, we become responsible and ennobled. Cosmic Nudges don't reward or punish, they just gently tease. The Cosmic Nudge is the light of infinity glimpsed through a tiny rent in the opaque curtain of everydayness.

Awe-inspiring but Not Fear-inspiring

Cosmic nudges are playful rather than frightening in their effect. The KUU doesn't have an Old Testament bone in its omniscient body.

The Quiet Solace of the Mini-Miracle

Another name for the Cosmic Nudge is the mini-miracle. The mini-miracle isn't like the miracles of other religions, because it isn't a kick in the teeth to those it didn't encompass. The man who walks away from the burning building will speak of his escape as a miracle. But what of those who died? Look, a cripple walks again! But what of all the other cripples? This is why the KUU only deals in mini-miracles: they have no victims, their only purpose is to generate a frisson of wonder and a questioning spirit.

Extract from
The Life and Death of Zachary B
by Paul Coleridge

The Battle of Trafalgar
August 1978

"I honestly can't do it, Jody. Remember when we went up the Eiffel Tower? I was terrified!"

"You weren't terrified, Zac. You were just a little nervous,"

"A little nervous! I was a lot nervous."

"You need to face up to your fears then. You're doing this, you know that don't you?"

"Yes, Jody. I know that." Zac shrugged. He never minded people seeing Jody was usually in charge. In fact, he seemed to enjoy having decisions he couldn't face making, made for him. Some granddad of a councillor had filled me in: the column of solid granite was 181 feet tall. If you added the 18 foot statue of Nelson... All I could think was: rather him than me.

The stage had been erected in front of the National Gallery. After several British engineering companies had told Valentine he was asking for the impossible, he found a Swiss company who jumped at the challenge of creating a way Zac could be lowered from Nelson's shoulder onto the stage below. Because of the steep gradient, the problem wasn't getting him down as much as making sure he didn't come down too fast. And now it was five in the morning on the big day itself.

"You've got to laugh," I said to no one in particular. "Turning a monument to a great British Naval hero into a glorified prop for a rock star."

"Bloody hilarious," said Zac grumpily, burying his hands further into the pockets of his purple crushed-velvet jacket, before continuing his restless pacing.

"Oh the irony and campness of it all," Brian said as he rolled himself another cigarette.

"Since the GLC realised the event would promote London as much as Zac, they've been so helpful," Jody said, diplomatically changing the subject.

When Zac had first been told the full details of the stunt he responded with unusual bravado: rock stars were meant to die young and it would boost record sales. But as the reality of the undertaking dawned on him, he backtracked somewhat. During a four-in-the-morning anxious phone call, I pointed out that whenever anyone in the future looked up at Nelson's Column they'd think of Zachary B.

"Do you think?" he replied.

Then I played my trump card. "Didn't your parents meet in Trafalgar Square? It would be a great way to honour them." I could tell that the silence on the other end of the phone was a good silence. Jody came on the line to thank me. When she gave the phone back to Zac he was already making plans.

"It's perfect" he said, thinking aloud. "I could wear an eye patch…"

'Bowie's already been there," I replied, instantly regretting it. "*Diamond Dogs* – publicity shots," I added, as ever the compulsive anorak.

"Bollocks," said Zac, deflated.

"Don't worry, sweetheart, we'll come up with something for you to wear," I heard Jody say in the background.

"I just don't want to look camp, or at least not too camp, but I've always rather fancied epaulettes…"

It was time to hang up. He was thinking about his stage gear, so we had him.

There was only one notable incident in the run-up to Trafalgar. Dwindling funds had caused Valentine to fire most of his staff, so we'd all become involved in helping out. Even Brian sat in the storeroom, solemnly putting together publicity packs and sticking stamps on them. Zac had said to Brian, "Once this is all over we'll sit down and sort out all this money business." He was probably bullshitting but it galvanised Brian (and therefore the rest of the band) into helping out. Brian said to me, "If Horatio thinks I'm going to forget what he said, he's got another thing coming. " He wasn't going to let Zac backtrack.

Late one afternoon, when everyone except Zac and I had called it a day, the doorbell rang. Mozart's voice crackled over the speaker demanding entry.

"I'm not here!" Zac hissed at me, as if he believed it was true.

"He's not here," I said to the entry phone. "Bollocks he's not there," came the muffled reply. "Let me in *now*. I ain't gonna hurt no one. I just want a word with the big guy."

He rang again, then he rang some more, and then the ringing became continuous. I cursed the fact that the receptionist had gone the same way as everyone else, and went to let Mozart in. Zac, in the meantime, found a person-sized space under Valentine's desk and secreted himself there. Mozart marched past me without even acknowledging my existence (nothing new there), and threw open the office door.

I hadn't seen Mozart in over a year, and hardly recognised the biro-blue suited man who took just three seconds to find Zac, and another three seconds to drag him from beneath Valentine's desk. The skunk-addled hippy had been replaced by an amphetamine-fuelled businessman. Mozart was now both a physical and a mental presence in the room, and he was no longer short of words.

"Zachary, me old mate. It's been six months. I can't do business like this, you know I can't."

"Look, Mozart… er… mate. It's a bit tricky right now. It's a cash-flow problem, but if you could see your way to letting go of my throat I'll make a couple of phone calls and—"

"Oh, *please*. I've heard it all before, Zac, *old boy*. It's over eighteen grand now, and my patience – as you can see – is running out. This. Just. Won't. Do!" Each word was accompanied by Mozart's fist landing hard on Valentine's desk. I had no idea things had gotten this bad. I tentatively handed Mozart one of the publicity leaflets we'd been sending out to the press. He seemed surprised there was actually someone else in the room, but took it anyway. After holding it very close to his eyes for longer than I imagined it would take anyone to read it, he returned his attention to Zac. "So we're back in the big time then are we, Mr B?"

"Yes. Yes we are, Mozart. Isn't that right, Paul?"

"One week!" Mozart banged the table one last extra hard time, and finished his short percussion solo by slamming the door behind him as he left. Zac wept like a baby. When he realised I was staring at him, he ran to the loo where I could hear him being histrionically sick. Five minutes later, and a few shades paler, he returned. Sitting at Valentine's desk he looked up at me with hopeless, bloodshot eyes.

"What am I going do, Paul?"

"Can't you pay him in instalments? I know things have been a bit quiet lately, but you must have enough…" I stopped in mid-sentence because Zac's face clearly told me he didn't have enough.

"The man's a psycho. I've heard stories…" Zac's eyes welled-up again as he thought of those stories. No happy endings, I suspected.

"Look, Zac," I began in a reassuring tone, not knowing how I was going to finish the sentence. "Trafalgar will turn things around. The BBC are expecting the biggest audience they've ever had for a live event – bar royal weddings and stuff. So how can it not turn things around? And then you'll be able to pay off that creep."

Over the years, Zac's drug habit seemed to have increased in direct proportion to his inability to pay for it. Clearly Mozart had only let Zac become so in debt because he couldn't comprehend that an upper-middle class pop star wouldn't eventually have the cash. He was probably also reluctant to turn away someone who'd been such a good customer for so long. So this mess was Mozart's fault as much as Zac's – which must have made Mozart even angrier, despising himself for falling for Zac's lord-of-the-manor act in the first place. But back to Trafalgar Square. Brian and I sat down between the paws of one of the lions at the foot of Nelson's Column. I was amused by how much pleasure Brian was deriving from seeing Zac so nervous.

"The cunt's shitting himself." He said as he shook out a cigarette and we stared up at the indecisive sky.

"Hopefully it'll brighten up later," I said, changing the subject.

"Yeah, hopefully." Brian clearly didn't care one way or the other.

"So, you and Zac still haven't sorted out your differences?"

"Look, Paul, mate, I know you think the world of Mr B. But we're still on fifty quid a week: the same as *five years ago*. We're getting two hundred each for today, which is nice. But imagine how much his Lordship and Valentine will make! Colin's talking about leaving after today. He's got a two-year-old girl now, you know." He waited for me to respond, but I couldn't think of anything to say, so he continued. "I was thinking about becoming a postman, but the hours wouldn't suit me. Zac takes the piss, end of discussion. And now his excuse is that the records aren't selling like they used to. Well, fuck that."

Valentine's Bentley purred to a halt in front of us. He informed us with much coke-fuelled glee that he'd finally sorted out a helicopter by calling up an old pal from the Marines who 'owed him one.' Standing over us in a ridiculous canary-yellow suit, he looked like he was about to fish some coins from his pocket and drop them in our laps. Awkward in our company after only thirty seconds, he said, "They're going to need a hand with the backdrop.".

"We'll need some grub before we can do anything," replied Brian.

"There's a Wimpy by Charing Cross Station, or egg rolls backstage," were Valentine's parting words, as he headed off towards the stage.

"An egg roll it is then," said Brian, loudly. "I'd rather have a cheeseburger but *I can't fucking afford it,*" he shouted after Valentine's receding yellow back.

Zac had wanted the stage design to harmonise with the facade of the National Gallery behind it, but the budget wouldn't stretch to fake Corinthian columns, so trompe l'oeil painted columns were being quickly produced by set-designer friends of Jody's.

As we made our way across the square, I was awed by the amount of people, vehicles and equipment everywhere. The police and Red Cross had set up camp over by the Mall and the BBC had three equipment-laden vans parked to the left of the National Portrait Gallery. And Charing Cross Road was choked with vehicles of every description. The Square itself was already roped off. A smattering of police officers stoically ignored the flirtatious behaviour of some early-bird arrivals. The huge Geneva Cable Car Company truck rumbled out of the Square – their work was done as they'd set up the bespoke pulley system the previous day. The control booth was situated in the cordoned off stretch of road between the stage and the National Gallery.

A blank-faced technician informed me they were using the funicular method, which involved having a counterweight for Zac. In other words, it would work like a chair-lift, but without the chair. All Zac had to do was call the guy in the control booth on his miniature walkie-talkie (attached to his prop microphone) when he was ready to descend. Zac was disappointed he couldn't do a live vocal, but it was technically impossible. He would have to lip-synch to a tape of his voice played alongside the band's live performance.

No wonder Zac was apprehensive. Firstly, he was to be lowered by helicopter on to Horatio's epauletted sandstone shoulder (according to Jody it was just wide enough to accommodate his 'skinny little ass'), and secondly, there had been no opportunity to rehearse this procedure. Zac's only reassurance was a laminated card a GCCC technician had handed him with a rather-you-than-me grin. It looked like one of those in-case-of-emergency instruction sheets you get on an aeroplane. Once Zac had been lowered onto Horatio, he had to attach one set of harnesses to the pulley system before he disengaged himself from the other set, which were attached to the helicopter. As I returned to the Square with Wimpy meals for Brian and myself, the sight of the right-angle triangle created by the vertical of Nelson's Column, the horizontal of the ground, and the dizzying diagonal of sturdy steel cables, took my breath away. Who'd have thought such a ridiculous idea could be turned into reality? After eating, we helped get the backdrop in place and then returned to our favourite spot between Leo's huge bronze paws. It was at this point, that a battered old van covered in generic punk script grumbled to a halt directly behind Valentine's Bentley. A gaggle of drunken punks stumbled out onto the pavement.

"Well, look what the cat's dragged in," said Brian, more loudly than was wise.

"You what?" came the response from the punk I recognised to be the Spurned's lead singer, Razor. But the challenge was only half-hearted: punks were all front. Lacking the will to get any further, the Spurned cracked open some Red Stripes and slumped down on the curb a few feet from us. Brian took this as his cue to join the rest of the Now on stage for the sound-check. In a spirit of camaraderie I joined Razor on the curb.

"So what's your part in all this, mate?" he asked, proffering his Players Number 6. A thicket of lager-yellow hair crowned a head, which was home to a decidedly feral set of closely grouped features.

"Oh, I'm just a writer," I replied (I didn't want to say critic, for fear of criticism).

"So what you written then?"

"Oh, you know; books, some journalism."

"Murder mysteries? I love a good murder mystery."

"Er… yeah, I have done," I lied.

He looked me up and down, registering with some distaste, the flared jeans and wide-lapelled corduroy jacket. But perhaps because it was going to be a long day, he gave me the benefit of the doubt.

"So who did it then?" he asked.

"Who did what?"

"In your book."

"Oh, you mean the murder. You'll have to wait and see."

"What read it? Fuck off." His speed-fried brain channel-hopped to another subject. "We didn't even wanna do this gig, but Valentino – or whatever his fucking name is – offered us a wad we couldn't afford to turn down." He shrugged his narrow shoulders. "And who can say no to a TV audience of 7 million?"

I nodded understandingly. Zac's one-two, one-two-ing reverberated between the buildings. Razor's hand was a blur as he vigorously scratched the back of his head.

"Zac B's alright. If it wasn't for him, half this lot (he pointed at the row of button badges on his jacket lapel) would never have even picked up a guitar. It's all just music, innit."

"Absolutely. Zachary B is just passing on the baton."

"What's a baton when it's at home?"

I ignored Razor's question because I knew there was no genuine curiosity behind it. Each of his badges was a tiny masterpiece of incisive graphic design: a tin medal of honour; a message to the rest of the world of his alliances. The Jam, Buzzcocks, XTC, The Clash. I patted him on the back and wished him luck (which seemed to worry and confuse him) before making my way over to the stage, accompanied by the repetitive thwack of a lone snare drum echoing endlessly between Canada House and South Africa House. By 2 p.m., people were flooding in through Admiralty Arch. Perhaps a third were punks, but the rest were a diverse mix of curious Londoners and out-of-town day-trippers who weren't sure what they'd stumbled upon.

As the Spurned scruffed themselves up, ready to go on stage, Zac told me – in the same tone one might announce the death of a parent – that the Spurned's debut album *Growing Pains* had just entered the charts at number eight. At 3:05 p.m., the Spurned took to the stage to a roar of approval from the still-expanding crowd. They played their set of already short songs at twice their normal speed and so finished at 3:25 p.m. They encored with half their original set, but still the audience wanted more. By the time they'd backed off the stage for the final time (with uncharacteristically broad grins on their smug, smudgy faces) they had played their set two-and-a-half times. It was painfully obvious that much of this audience were trying to put off the moment when the Now would put a downer on their afternoon.

At 4:35 p.m., after half-an-hour of trouser-vibrating dub reggae from the hippest sound-system Valentine could afford for thirty quid, Brian, Colin and Spike – along with Basingstoke session guitarist Ricky Jade and Detroit backing vocalist Fountain Penn – stepped onto the stage with all the false bravado they could muster. Brian's opening synth chords to *An Eye for an Eye* sounded particularly thin after the molar-loosening bass throb of King Tubby, but at least it received a nostalgic cheer from a cluster of die-hard fans. Moments later, the phased clatter of a helicopter's rotary blades drowned out the band. Everyone looked up as the metallic fabric of Zac's futuristic take on Horatio Nelson's uniform scattered the afternoon sunlight in a hundred different directions. After much manoeuvring of the helicopter, Zac's posterior finally touched down on the cold stone of Nelson's guano-encrusted shoulder at 4:40 p.m. – five minutes after the Now had begun *An Eye for an Eye*. But

Zac hadn't given up yet. He raised his right arm high, and his slightly-out-of-sync voice filled the air.

> *"An eye for an eye.*
> *Revenge fills the sky.*
> *If I die then you die.*
> *An eye for an eye!"*

What a defining moment in the history of popular music and London! Or at least it would have been if it hadn't all gone horribly wrong from that moment onwards. Punk rock's unwritten manifesto stated that, firstly, songs should be no longer than three minutes in length. Secondly, that they should be fast and furious. And thirdly, that there should be no – I repeat no – self-indulgent soloing. At 4:44 p.m., *An Eye for an Eye* ended with the obligatory sustained bar-chord and a staggered splash of cymbals. The GCCC's pulley system creaked into gear, and began to lower Zac. After twenty seconds it stopped, stranding him a third of the way along his diagonal path to the stage. A chill breeze of discontent went through the crowd. Then at 4:48 p.m., the Now sealed their fate: they started jamming. They'd been playing the opening to *Waves Crashing* for five minutes (chosen as the second number because its extended intro gave Zac plenty of time to reach the stage). But when the band realised the pulley system had stalled, it was either jam or leave the stage defeated. And they were enjoying themselves: jamming is fun – for the musicians doing it. But oh how I prayed that Zac would deliver them from self-indulgence (for thine is the kingdom) sooner rather than later. Because they were oblivious to how restless the audience were getting, they had become purveyors of that misnomer, progressive rock, which was a red rag to this bullshit-loathing mob of pissed and pissed off punks. A crowd innately desires to be of one mind – it just needs directing. And every shrewd troublemaker, from the pugnacious football thug to Adolf Hitler, knows this. Unfortunately that one mind is rarely wise, and rarely has good intentions. And so the hissing, swearing, booing chill breeze rapidly turned into a disconcertingly forceful wind, and the first of many missiles began to rain down on the stage. A furious, tearful Fountain delivered a torrent of Detroit-style verbal abuse at the audience, but that only incensed them more. By 5:02 p.m. (some five guitar solos, two drum solos and one bass solo later), The Now were dealing with a life-threatening tornado. Empty cans (that once contained Red Stripe) rained down on their heads, and punks (who now contained Red Stripe) vented their anger on a rock group who had inadvertently exposed these lovers of musical directness to some of the most self-indulgent drivel they'd ever heard.

For a while the Now had been torn between dropping their instruments and running, or staying loyal to Zac. But at 5:05 p. m, they ran.

"Jesus, they're going mental!" shouted Spike as he reached the backstage area. Brian and Colin were right behind him. Colin had a cut on his temple, and Spike was hugging his bass like a security blanket. Fountain had already cornered Valentine and was hectoring him to triple her session fee. A couple of St John's ambulance men attended to the shocked and wounded.

"What the fucks happening with Zac?" asked Spike, who seemed the most together.

"I'll check out the control booth," I shouted back. I scrambled down the short aluminium stepladder that led from the stage to the tiny orange prefab, and flung open the door.

The Geneva Cable Car engineer turned and said in precise, brittle English, "The clamps are clamping too hard. It won't move."

"I can see that," I replied. "Maybe if you back it up a bit, and then try again?"

"Back it up a bit? Yes, I will try that now." He pulled on a lever and then pressed an absurdly large metal button. Eureka! Zac began to jerkily descending again. I patted the

Swiss gentleman on the back and ran back up the steps to the stage. From behind the massive Marshall stacks I watched the audience. Because there was no one left on stage, they'd begun to turn on each other. Zac, a look of abject terror on his face, was now more than halfway down. He told me later that while chaos had been reigning below, he had felt unnaturally calm. His fear of heights had been replaced by a delicious sensation of omniscience generated by his crane-shot view of the matchbox-sized stage below and plenty of self-medication. He only panicked a little when a pigeon flapped past his ear and continued upwards to the summit of Horatio's hat, reminding him that he was somewhere only winged creatures had any right to be. However, his woozy sense of wellbeing instantly evaporated when one of his platform-booted feet awkwardly and painfully misconnected with the stage, at the exact same moment as half a cheeseburger greased and ketchuped his face. Zachary B had been returned to earth, both physically and metaphorically, with a bump. Spike and I immediately rushed on stage to help a limping, disorientated Zac to reach safety, just as a new wave of cans and the harmless shrapnel of half-eaten sandwiches, rained down. Eventually, Valentine sent the Spurned back out to placate the crowd. Razor was reluctant at first, but a couple of extra twenties were snatched at – as a dog snatches at a flying stick – and the Spurned motored through their set one last time.

★

The Sun went with 'THE GLAM WHO FELL TO EARTH'. A grainy photograph showed poor Zac at just the moment his foot twisted and his face distorted in agony. Six and a half million TV viewers shared in his humiliation. It was official: The Now had become The Then. And the Spurned were anything but. I didn't call the office for weeks. For one thing, I didn't believe anyone would have the heart to be there. I imagined passports being grabbed or handfuls of barbiturates swallowed. There'd been an atmosphere of last-ditch despair even at the planning stages of Trafalgar. At a record company meeting in December of the previous year, I'd noticed Zac was unshaven and dressed in an old tweed jacket, jeans and an off-white T-shirt. Only a single diamond-eyed Aztec god earring gave any indication of his once glamorous persona. His hands were shaking so much that even lighting a cigarette was intensely demanding. This was doubly humiliating for the man, given that all he did at that meeting was light cigarettes.

Extract from *The KUU Hypothesis* by Zachary Bekele

7. FORGET ABOUT LOVE, EMPATHY AND RESPECT ARE THE REAL DEAL

Too Many Loves

I love the Rolling Stones, I love pizza, I love you, I love my mother, I love this jacket, I love God: one word meaning so many different things. But let's forget about pizzas and God for a moment. Even 'people love' has its ambiguities. There's the unconditional love of the exasperated parent for the wayward teenager, the blind love of 'love at first sight,' the sweaty palms of 'first love,' the black eye of 'jealous love,' the heartbreak of 'unrequited love,' the house-watching of 'obsessive love.' And sometimes we don't even *like* the person we're supposedly in love with.

A Scientific Equation of the Heart

As it's hard to even love on a one-to-one basis, how can we love our neighbour, our country or even our god in the way we're expected to?

'The Lord — and the Lord alone — is our God. Love the Lord your God with all your heart, with all your soul, and with all your strength. Never forget these commandments I am giving you today.'
Deuteronomy 6. 4-9

Commandments? How would you respond if your mother or lover *commanded* you to love them? Even if you did choose to obey them, how would you view them from that moment on? However, the problem also resides in God's need for exclusivity. Surely love is one of the few things there is an unlimited supply of? The more of it you give out, the more of it is created. This is not sentimentality — it's a scientific equation of the heart: love generates more love, expanding exponentially. God may get away with demanding love but He couldn't do the same with respect.

Respect is All You Need!

Respect is rarely blind, stupid, jealous or crazy because it requires prior thought, and — by definition — has to be earned. Respect is all you need! Without it there is no real love, only the kind we have for pizza or a favourite pop group. Respect is also less draining than love. Who has the energy to hand out love, flower-power style, to complete strangers? Most of us barely have enough of the stuff to keep a family together.

2

Marrakech, February 2007

It was three in the morning and Coleridge felt like shit. Perhaps he should he go for a swim? The only time he ever left his Tripod apartment was to go swimming, but it had to be when no one else was around. Once he'd gone down too early, only to hear the metronomic bass thuds, like a giant's urgent pulse, still issuing from the adjacent dance floor. He immediately panicked and trotted back the way he had come. Perhaps because it was an experience no computer game could simulate, swimming meant everything to him. As the warm water buoyed him up, and the smell of chlorine filled his nostrils, he felt ten years old again. But today it was just too much effort. In fact, everything was too much effort and everything irritated him. He couldn't get the light in his apartment right; when he adjusted the dimmer switch to the luminosity he wanted, the lights flickered erratically. Then there was his blue suede recliner; because he'd put on so much weight lately, its chunky arms seemed to aggressively press in on his upper body as if trying to eject him.

And then there was this tooth. It wasn't loose, but it didn't feel like a part of him anymore either. Involuntarily he stroked the small raised scar on the underside of his chin. It felt inorganically hard as if there was a shirt button buried just beneath the skin. He wanted to rip at it with his fingernails. Occasionally it was dully painful – the ghost of a far greater remembered pain... but he didn't want to think about all that. He reached for his TV remote.

"Zap!" he said aloud, like a kid with a toy laser gun. Why didn't remote controls *really* make a zapping noise, or maybe fire an ice-blue zigzag of light at the TV? he wondered. Then we wouldn't take for granted the miraculous way they instantly transport us from one discrete world to the next at the press of a button.

(*Zap!*) Fast-changing images simultaneously reflecting off all the surrounding glass.

(*Zap!*) A lycra-lacquered bottom jiggled like an overloaded spin-dryer to some boorish and leaden hip-hop. No. Next.

(*Zap!*) A glistening chicken breast lowered with loving exactitude onto a basil-flecked knoll of mashed potatoes.

No. Next (*Zap!*) A monochrome couple tentatively kissed goodbye on a steam-submerged station.

No. Next. This was the job he'd given himself: to check each channel for life – for signs of intelligence – and then move on to the next one.

(*Zap!*) A mercurial ripple of squirrel jumped from branch, to thinner branch, to thinner branch still, and then...

(*Zap!*) A model turned towards the camera, her slow-motion hair catching up with her a full second later. *Why doesn't she just go away and leave me alone!* He realised he'd hissed the words aloud, even though he'd planned to just say them in his head; he was always doing that. He thought about calling Barney, or someone else on Level 10, but decided against it. There was nothing they could do. If he didn't agree to see her, others would come.

(*Zap!*) Heartbreakingly young soldiers clambered from trenches, half obscured by the double veil of flying shrapnel and time-ravaged film-stock.

(*Zap!*) *'Text A, B, or C to...'*

(*Zap!*) Chandler had upset Monica, again.

(*Zap!*) Another bloody Zachary B documentary! It must be because it's coming up to the anniversary, thought

Coleridge. Was it *Top of the Pops* or its German equivalent? He wasn't sure at first, but then the camera swung round to the lifeless rag-doll dancing of the tank-topped audience; it was clearly *Top of the Pops*. Zac scything the air with his guitar as if it were a conduit of considerable power – a chainsaw or something – rather than just a slab of wood with strings attached. A close-up of Zachary B's face seemed to make eye contact with Coleridge across the aching decades. In an often-practised move, he rolled sideways and vomited into a red plastic bowl at his side. Then he continued to channel hop, eyes dead, mouth lolling open.

Coleridge had only gone out once since Merrick brought him to Marrakech in 2005. He got as far as the Djemaa el-Fna before running screaming back to his Tripod tree-house. He hadn't realised that the amount of attention the average tourist received in Marrakech could be compared to the amount of attention Posh and Becks received at a Leicester Square movie premier. In other words, it wasn't personal – it wasn't because he was the main living representative of the man who had invented the fastest growing religion of the twenty-first century – it was just the way the locals treated every moneyed (or potentially moneyed) Westerner. But even if the locals had had any interest in KUUism, Coleridge hadn't been photographed since 1982 and so it was unlikely they'd have even recognised the shuffling overweight man who came blinking into the sunlight. After this terrifying experience, Merrick saw to it that everything Coleridge needed was delivered to him at the Tripod.

Coleridge was done with the real world – he'd always thought it was overrated anyway.

Aim... steady... and... fire.

(**Zap!**) A young mum force-fed her tearful child carrot-sticks under the watchful eye of a patronising dietician.

(**Zap!**) Ross told Rachel he still has feelings for her.

(**Zap!**) *'Effective, protective relief, with...'*

(**Zap!**) Everything beamed down to us from balletically drifting satellites. Coleridge stabbed at that button and moved on, always moved on. By jump-cutting away from these rictus-grin messages he turned their desire to sell him everything into a decontextualised moving collage of beautiful people and meaningless graphics: he made their relentless attempts to fill his life with stuff he didn't need and didn't want cubist. In a moment of uncharacteristic altruism, Coleridge wished he could do this channel-hopping job for the whole planet, not just himself. He must remember to suggest the idea of a KUU TV channel to Barney in the morning: *'We do the hopping for you! Mosaic TV, 24 hours a day! 24 different channels a minute! Enjoy the chaos!'*

(**Zap!**) *'Who Wants To Be A Millionaire.'* Jesus! Again, Coleridge was surprised to hear aloud words he'd meant to keep in his head. The young female contestant was at the crucial stage where she'd won £8,000. If she answered the next question wrong she'd drop to a shameful £1,000. If she got it right, her prize money would swell to £16,000. The host, Chris Tarrant, milked the moment by pausing for an eternity before asking her the next question:

"Where in the human body is the tibia located?: 1 – in the arm, 2 – in the leg, 3 – in the head, or 4 – in the back?"

"That's really weird," the girl said. "I was asking my sister that same question this morning?"

Chris Tarrant looked perplexed. "What, you mean you were preparing for tonight's show?"

"Yes, I suppose so."

"So what's the answer then?"

"Well, my sister didn't know."

Audience laughter. Tarrant continued to look bemused. The girl gambled anyway, and won herself £16,000.

Coleridge smiled to himself and zapped to the next channel. The girl could have asked her sister any general knowledge question in the world. And, of course, there are an infinite number of those, with an infinite number of new ones being added every second, as the world keeps adding exponentially to its stockpile of trivia. But she gambled anyway, perhaps subconsciously appreciating the KUUness of the chain of events she had just experienced. The more Coleridge thought about this, the more remarkable the KUU-incidence seemed. Not just because of the events which he'd just seen unfold on the screen, but also because he had never watched *Who Wants To Be A Millionaire* before. Something had just made him pause in his zapping for long enough to be Cosmic Nudged. He picked up the phone.

"Barney?... Sorry I didn't realise that was the time... Look, is August Bekele still around?... Good. I'll see her tomorrow... No, too early. Make it around three. I need time to prepare... Yes, prepare... Don't panic, I'll be on my very best behaviour."

As soon as he'd made the decision he knew it was the right thing to do. He'd always seen August's mother, Jody, as a kind of angel. This was partly because, since his teens, he'd seen all black women as angels. It was black women who poured every last drop of their hurt and love into many of his favourite songs. And as they sung, they seemed so beautiful in their pain, their open and proud faces making manifest their generous but betrayed hearts. Then there was the inner glow of their skin, so different from the uncooked-chicken unpleasantness of his own. Even the black nurse who sometimes used to take him to his sessions with Dr Sanderson always had a smile for him. All the other mean-lipped harridans rarely even granted him eye contact. He knew his love of black women was based on stereotyping, but was stereotyping still bad if it was positive rather than negative? Probably. But anyway, he had to meet August. He *wanted* to meet August. He needed to have another kind, black woman's face look upon him with compassion and goodwill in his hour of need.

★

August was in a carpet shop the size of an aircraft hanger when she got Merrick's call. Her guidebook's suggestion was to call the seller's bluff and walk away if they wouldn't bring their price down. But because she hadn't managed to suppress her enthusiasm for the rug she desired, the salesman was standing his ground. Damian, who found this whole bargaining thing embarrassing and demeaning, had remained outside. He was trying to discretely photograph authentic Moroccan life, but unfortunately that authentic Moroccan life would usually see what he was up to and demand some kind of authentic Moroccan currency in return for being so picturesque.

"We're in!" said August, running from the shop towards Damian. The disgruntled salesman followed close behind, confused by her sudden loss of interest; perhaps she was trying to secure a better deal with her swift exit. "Merrick just called," she continued, ignoring the salesman whose price was dropping fifty dirhams at a time. "The Leader Who Is Paul Bloody Coleridge will see us tomorrow afternoon. We need to see Alice Cooper today so we'll hopefully have something to fire at him."

The previous night, after saying goodnight to August, Damian had borrowed her laptop to see if he could find out a bit more about Alice Cooper, particularly whether she was still living in Marrakech. From Facebook and one or two other sites, he pieced together the skeleton of a biography. She was born in India but had white, English parents. Her family moved back to the UK when she was ten. She graduated from Exeter University in 1972, and almost immediately became a professor of Arabic and Islamic studies there before giving up her post in 1989 to become Professor of Comparative Religion at the California State University where she remained until 2006. In the summer of 2006 she became a lecturer and councillor-in-residence at the KUU Tripod. He then ascertained, via private message on the KUU Foundation forum, that she was still living in Marrakech. He wrote to her asking if she would meet a couple of born-again questioners from England? She responded almost immediately with her address.

"Yes! School's out!" Damian punched the air. How did detectives manage before the invention of the Internet? he asked himself.

★

Was it Malika's death that made you leave?" August asked Alice. The three of them were seated at a grubby white plastic table, on grubby white plastic chairs, in the enclosed courtyard of Alice Cooper's residential riad. The place had none of the picturesque trimmings of August and Damian's riad, just lines of washing and a long neglected water fountain with a forlorn-looking ram tethered to it. The ram seemed to stare at them with both fear and hope. Damian thought that Alice, a small make-up-less woman in her late fifties, looked like the kind of woman he saw at anti-this and anti-that marches on the evening news.

Alice considered the question for a moment or two. "Not entirely. I'd been thinking about it for months. Things were changing there."

"How do you mean?"

Alice took off her horn-rimmed glasses and placed them with unnecessary exactitude on the table in front of her. Again she took her time responding. When she finally spoke it was with the gravity of a world-weary theologian. "To me, KUUism is not just about mini-miracles. Even when Zachary used that term I don't think he was entirely serious. It was just a bit of throwaway alliteration, if you will. The wise KUUist should take both Paul's sordid little memoir and Barney's 'editing' of Zachary's words, with a heaped tablespoon of salt."

"So what's gone wrong in your opinion, Ms Cooper?" asked Damian, as he considered whether to take another sip of the body-temperature orange squash in front of him. Since their big argument that never was, Damian had felt confident that August wouldn't object if he interjected with questions.

"Plain 'miss' will do, young man. I can't be doing with that ridiculous modern invention 'Ms' with its silly buzzzzzz at the end – who needs equality if you're going to sound like a bee every time you tell someone your name?" She chuckled to herself, but instantly became serious again. "Barney started to push the whole Cosmic Nudge side of things. It was really rather sinister."

"Sinister? How so?" asked August, leaning forward. "It's just a return to praying and wishful thinking, don't you think? If a KUUist doesn't get Cosmic Nudged for a while, or gets nudged but his fellow KUUists don't think it's a credible Cosmic Nudge, then…"

"Like what? What isn't a credible Cosmic Nudge?" asked Damian.

"Oh, you know: your mother or best friend phones just when you're thinking about them. One thinks about one's mother a hundred times a day, it's just that one conveniently forgets about all the other times. But of course you remember thinking about her the one time the phone rings. It's just not really a mini-miracle is it? And if someone is clutching at straws like that, it can be quite upsetting if their fellow KUUists point it out."

"So was Malika one of these kids?"

"Curiously enough, no. That's what's so strange. In fact he told me he'd been in the KUU Foundation's Top Eleven KUU-incidences on more than one occasion." Alice chuckled. "That boy was being nudged so often he was in danger of becoming a believer!" Damian got up to photograph the courtyard. Its lack of obvious charm charmed him. August just let Alice talk. "Do you know what I think? I think the modern Muslim is a little bit in awe – even in love with – The American Dream. That's the problem, you see. They don't know if they're coming or going. There's the exciting new spell of shiny, sparkling capitalism, and the older, deeper spell of Islam. So they have to end up hating us, to stop themselves from loving us. Our world is their new devil."

"Do you really believe that?" asked August.

"Absolutely. I recently read that a new translation of the Koran revealed that it's a handful of raisins not a harem full of virgins that awaits martyrs in paradise. What a let-down for all those poor young men who've thrown their lives away. Isn't that hilarious?"

"Or tragic," said August.

"Tragic – hilarious, what's the difference?"

"Sorry, Alice, but could we get back to Malika?"

"Yes, of course. Now where was I?"

"He was getting nudged a lot."

"Yes, yes. It was the usual kind of thing, you know: unusual words cropping up twice in an hour; bumping into someone in the street who he'd been to school with back in England..."

"Was he well educated?"

"Why do you ask? I suppose you think only the naïve and the brain-dead fall for all this?"

"Not at all. I was just..."

"You'd be surprised. Faith refugees come in many shapes and sizes. We've had a Secretary of State trying to pull away from his Catholic upbringing; a Nigerian brain surgeon whose family walked out on him when he turned his back on Islam and came to the Tripod for support..."

"Of course you have. I really wasn't trying to... So what was Malika's problem then?"

"I alluded to it before. He was what we call a borderline believer. Some KUUists need a lot of intellectual discipline to tread that fine line between healthy scepticism and total open-mindedness. For others, it's the most natural thing in the world. It's a Zen thing, you see. That boy Malika was dizzy with it all. He loved the world that had suddenly opened up for him, which seemed so full of wonder and surprises. But about a month before he died he got quite angry with me for insisting that – from an ideological standpoint – it was important to remain sceptical; to accept that all the Cosmic Nudges he'd been experiencing *could* just be the product of blind chance. He was on a downward spiral – although he saw it as an upward spiral – towards the curse of faith. In other words, he had turned his back on what Milan Kundera once called – in relation to the novel – the wisdom of uncertainty. Or to put it another way, the poor boy had gone full circle. Having kicked away the crutch of Islam he'd fashioned KUUism into a new crutch, just as other Coup KUUists had done before him. Zachary's emphasis was on *maybe*. The Coup KUUists decided to reinterpret this to mean *probably*, before eventually distorting it even more until they arrived at *most certainly*."

"They've gone from being faith refugees back to being faithful; they've turned KUUism into a faith. That's truly fucked up," said Damian.

"You could say that," said Alice, smiling. "Even by being a KUUist you are being unKUUist, given that Zachary wanted us all to go and make up our own non-religions rather than just accept his take on things. This makes the Coup KUUists the complete antithesis of everything Zachary stood for. However, if you want my honest opinion, even The KUU Foundation itself now has a Coup KUUist agenda. Paul is their martyr, and Barney their equivalent to an American TV evangelist. This was one of the reason I felt I had to leave."

August and Damian remained silent.

"Do you disagree?" added Alice.

"Unfortunately not," said August. "Do you think all the other suicide victims came from a similar place to Malika? Were they also Coup KUUists?"

"Sorry? Coming from the same place?" A nervous tic caused Alice's eyelids to flutter rapidly. "Oh yes, got you. Yes, I do believe they were. There was a forum topic on the old www..."

"To push or not to push?" said August.

"That was it," said Alice.

"Yes it was taken down. We did get some fragments of it, from Malika's computer," said Damian.

"I'd like to see them if that's at all possible," said Alice.

Damian produced the disc from his bag. The three of them went inside.

Alice's apartment was almost completely devoid of personal effects, apart from the precarious mini-skyscrapers of books on the floor, and a small garish painting of an Arab leading a camel which hung slightly askew on one white wall. August and Damian stood behind Alice as she sat at her desk scrolling through the pages of dialogue they'd already combed for clues.

"Don't you just loathe all this computer-speak," said Alice, her pained face unnaturally close to the screen. "Do we know what this Final Affirmation business is?"

"Not yet," said Damian, discreetly tipping the rest of his drink into a nearby plant pot. "But it doesn't sound good."

"The Coup KUUists can be as scary as any religious extremists," continued Alice. "They've read all kinds of nonsense into Paul's memoir. You know the kind of thing: Zachary's baptism by water pistol; the descent from Nelson's Column; the neon cross; the scrabble game spelling out Zachary's destiny. You can read something into dogs' doo-doo if that's your prerogative."

"Have Merrick or Coleridge ever issued any kind of statement to try to put a stop to it?" asked August.

"Of course not. It's all power to the cause. They love it. Or at least Barney loves it. I think the KUU is just one big intellectual joke to that old soak, or one big social experiment. He's just along for the ride – and the money and power, of course." "But what about Paul Coleridge?" asked Damian, getting more interested in the turn the conversation had taken. Again, Alice paused before answering. "Obviously Paul's a very damaged man. I only met him a couple of times when I was working at the Tripod. The first time he was charming and jokey; the second time he was on another planet. Maybe Barney keeps him drugged or something – I'm not sure who needs who more in that relationship. The last straw was the new introduction Barney wrote for the 2006 edition of *The*

KUU Hypothesis. Previously, he'd been happy with just an 'edited by' credit, but this stepped over the line."

"How so?" asked August.

"It was a lot of contemporary science guff – bringing in the Human Genome Project, String Theory, Dark Matter and the like. And do we really need to be told all about Schrödinger's Cat again?" Damian thought, yes, he did. But he said nothing. "It may be a delightful notion to contemplate – that there are thousands of universes somewhere where Zachary, The KUU Foundation and the Tripod never existed, but…"

"And where *Telegram Sam* rather than *Put Your Glam Rags On* went to number one in 1972, interjected Damian. Both women ignored him. "Well, I need to be told about Schrödinger's Cat. What the fuck is Schrödinger's Cat?" he added, sulkily.

"The point I'm trying to make," continued Alice, a little stuffily, "…is that Barney was offering up these scientific theories as some kind of proof. But it's just scientists daydreaming in the same way it used to be mystics daydreaming. Just because maths has been thrown into the equation – no pun intended – it doesn't make their daydreams any more credible. It's just not what Zachary would have wanted."

"Are you sure about that?" asked August, put out by the possessive tone this eccentric woman was using when she spoke of Zac. As if he had been *her* father.

Alice sighed. "It's all very well these boffins talking about how the physical evolution of mankind can now be manipulated through our DNA, but Zachary was more concerned about our emotional and intellectual evolution. Would anyone like some tea?"

"Yeah, cool," said Damian. "But I'm still not clear what your problem with Merrick's new introduction is? What's he say in it anyway? I've got an early Nineties edition."

"Oh, you know, all the usual stuff about how life couldn't be this mind-bogglingly complex without there being a designer. It's all completely outside the spirit of KUUism. Zachary scoffed at so-called proofs…"

"But what about The Three Near Proofs?" interrupted August. "Don't you see, my dear? They were just another one of Zachary's paradoxical jokes; his way of playing with our preconceptions. Even just putting the words 'near' and 'proof' together is a self-evident contradiction." Alice was clearly disappointed that her guests didn't appear to be as intellectually astute as her. "Zachary knew the Near Proofs were tantalising in the way they seemed to offer insights into the mathematics of chance. But he also knew they were a long way from being proof of anything. And then of course there's the added tantalising tease of the Third Near Proof…"

"I knew Zachary was fucking with us with all that Near Proof bullshit," said Damian.

"Now we're on the same wavelength, young man," said Alice. "KUUism isn't about proof it's about wonder! If the Knowing Unknowable Universe is the creator of all things then it's outside the realm of physical laws anyway. Thus scientific objections are as invalid as mystical hypotheses!" As Alice talked, she rummaged in a cupboard for cups and saucers, or rather, the right cups and saucers. When the kettle began its urgent whistling she poured the water into a huge brown teapot. "The Omniscient Practical Joker is always moving the goalposts – that's what Zachary said. Isn't it a hoot that scientists have ended up with the Heisenberg Uncertainty Principle – a complete admission that they haven't got a bloody clue what's going on?" With an absurd theatrical flourish, Alice opened a biscuit tin and placed it in front of August and Damian. It contained a half-empty packet of custard creams. "You wouldn't believe how much these cost. Specially imported, you know." She held out the packet. "I only get them out for special guests."

"Not for me, thanks," said Damian, with a little too much conviction.

"I'm on a diet I'm afraid – since New Year," said August.

"Diet? But you're nothing but skin and bone. I insist."

August took a custard cream. She gave Damian a sharp look, and so he took one too. "Now where was I?" continued Alice. "Oh yes, Rutherford's dictum; Occam's Razor states that the simplest explanation is usually going to be the right explanation when it comes to the intricate workings of the universe. And what's the simplest explanation for all this?" Alice didn't wait for an answer. "Why, the KUU of course!"

August and Damian raised their half-eaten custard creams in a parody of a toast.

"But to return to Malika's suicide," began August, with a note of barely veiled impatience in her voice. "Can you think of anything else that might connect Malika to the other victims, Alice?"

"Only his tender age," said Alice. "Perhaps we need to ask ourselves why all of the victims have been so young. I sense we are dealing with the issue of the malleability of the barely matured human spirit here. But more than that, I'm afraid I'm as much in the dark as you are."

August was about to ask Alice whether she had any thoughts on the guns of the suicide victims having two rather than just one spent-cartridge, but she knew in her heart that she'd be wasting her time and they were running late anyway.

"This has all been extremely helpful but we need to make a move," August said, carefully putting the rest of her biscuit down on the edge of her saucer as she stood up to shake Alice's hand. "We're seeing Paul, or rather, The Leader Who Is Not A Leader, this afternoon so we need to…"

"Are you now? Well I never." Alice replaced the biscuit tin lid and, straining, put the tin back on the highest shelf of her almost bare kitchen cupboard. She then turned back to them, slightly breathless. "I thought all that Leader-Who-is-Not-A-Leader business was nonsense too – Barney's input, no doubt. But at least Barney's decided to let you see Paul. They must be desperate. Anyway, do give them both my best wishes. And tell Paul he's his own worst enemy. He needs to learn to stand up to Barney a bit more."

August opened her mouth to speak, but no words came out.

Extract from *The KUU Hypothesis*
by Zachary Bekele

8. THE PARADOX IS
THE PANDORA'S BOX

If You Can't See Ambiguity, Keep Looking

Paradoxes are common in religious writings. You will certainly find plenty of them here – some intentional, some unintentional, some between the lines and others staring you in the face. Even the dictionary definition of paradox teems with its own paradoxes:

"A seemingly absurd or self-contradictory statement that may or may not be true"

– it seems to be absurd, it may or may not be true, it contradicts itself. What a slippery creature the paradox is. But what is the paradox's relevance to KUUism?

1. The paradox suggests that nothing is black and white and we are never on firm ground.

2. The paradox may indicate humour where none before was apparent. It is the grinning sidekick of irony.

3. The paradox suggests new tangents of thought, helping us escape a rigid mind-set.

4. The paradox may expose a nugget of wisdom, a thousand more questions or an unnerving dead-end.

5. What we most value can be unquantifiable and indescribable: beauty, genius, the taste of mussels, the feeling of looking out to sea, the face of a loved one.

6. The truth or falsehood of the Big Idea is irrelevant. An idea can be beneficial regardless of its grounding in reality: most truths have a limited shelf life anyway — as the constantly changing mind of science demonstrates. The KUU is a new version of an old idea. New ideas have the potential to free us from old ideas. As soon as just one person has this idea alive in their head, it's alive in the world.

7. A life without a spiritual dimension is two dimensional, but a life dominated by religion and a sense of reward or punishment in the next life, is tragic. So don't jump in at the deep end of belief, just splash around in the shallows as a born-again-questioner. All KUUism requires from you is an open mind and a pleasant disposition.

Extract from

The Life and Death of Zachary B
by Paul Coleridge

We Are 99.9% Empty Space, Man
January 1981

Rock On's features editor, Jake Golding had been in a bad mood for weeks, thanks to one of Barney's little escapades. In November 1980, Barney absconded to the States for an MTV audition. Although we partied on his return a mere four days later ("They said I was too English. How can you be *too* English!"). An atmosphere of unspoken resentment lingered, but because Jake was intimidated by Barney (it was a class thing) he took his frustrations out on me by refusing to commission a Zachary B comeback feature. However, luckily *Glamuzik* (astonishingly still going strong at the time) commissioned the piece. Otherwise I might never have found out what cemented Zac's ideas about KUUism.

★

My heart sunk when I saw the strobing crucifix on its fibreglass mound. Zac had either spent too much time looking at the creepy drawings Helen was always sending him or he was hell-bent on further upsetting his Christian fans. It was also immediately clear that the video for *Straightjacket Disco* was going to be one of those videos where 'artistic vision' far exceeded budgetary constraints with excruciatingly embarrassing results.

I poked my head round the tiny doorway of Zac's trailer. A peach-faced girl stood on either side of him, powdering, brushing and blushing him back to life – or an approximation of life. At first he didn't notice me in the peripheral vision of his bulb-framed mirror, but eventually that eyebrow shot up in recognition.

"Paul, my man, how delightful! What do you think of the set? I wanted a kind of *Close Encounters* meets Ten Commandments feel."

"You've certainly got some kind of biblical sci-fi thing going on there," I replied.

What an interminable day it turned out to be on that chilly outdoor set: extras gave that little bit extra, dancers massaged aching limbs, cameras dipped, swooped and panned, and it was gone midnight by the time everyone gathered around Zac for the final shots of him up on that strobing cross. The Australian director (who's name now escapes me, but he clearly believed he was meant for better things) had a hard time of it trying to coax a performance out of an increasingly disgruntled Zachary.

"You okay up there, Zac mate?"

"Do I look like I'm okay?"

"We need a couple of low angle shots. Could you turn towards the arc light on your right?"

"Like this?"

"No, that's *my* right. And can you look like you're suffering a bit more?"

"I don't look like I'm suffering?"

"Er, no, not really. You just look bored or maybe constipated."

"Great. Okay, I can do suffering. Not a problem at all."

"And we're releasing the doves in a tick, so when we do, could you manage awe-struck? Then we can call it a wrap."

Yes, the 'climactic' dove scene. The anoraked dove man had been standing around all day with his hands wrapped around a succession of steaming drinks. He'd occasionally 'coo' reassuringly to his boxed feathered friends before returning to his dog-eared *Daily Mirror*. Eventually, his

– and the doves' – moment arrived. The director shouted "Action" and the dove man lifted the lid… Not a bird stirred. Because of a day of cramped incarceration, the doves were either asleep, sulking or terrified. The dove man tipped up the box until eventually the birds fluttered and flapped pathetically out. It seemed cornily prophetic that none of them took gracefully and symbolically to the sky. At two a.m., a much relieved Zachary was untied from the cross he'd had to bear for more than three hours. While he scrubbed off his make-up (the two girls had gone home hours ago) I asked him about the video's meaning. Realising my question was sincere, he gave a considered response.

"At the risk of stating the obvious, it's about how important iconography is to the staying power of religion." He paused to attend to a stubborn patch of eye shadow. "After all, why does Christianity concentrate on images of Jesus as a baby or Jesus nailed to a cross? Why not some pictures of him knocking together a table or chair – he was a carpenter after all, wasn't he? Or was that just his dad? Anyway, I wanted to get the idea across that even Jesus had his twelve-man PR team working out what image would work best for him. In fact, the Big J's image was still being fine-tuned hundreds of years after his death."

"Cool." I said, not knowing what else to say.

"Yes, cool," Zac replied coolly.

I changed the subject – slightly. "So how's your own bespoke religion coming along? I couldn't tell, last time, if this was something you were wholly serious about."

"Serious? Serious is a word I've banished from my vocabulary. I'm not *serious* about it, I'm *humorous* about it. The gift we humans have for humour is greatly underrated. However, it's a non-religion not a religion. Or if you prefer; a *non*-belief system."

"But aren't you asking for trouble? I read you were physically attacked in Atlanta by some born-again Christian."

"Oh, that was just a one-off. And she was American, so what do you expect? Fuck the States. It was never going to happen for me there anyway. Even Bowie didn't crack it there until he made a bloody Philly-soul record. You couldn't drive me home now could you, Paul? I don't want to bother any of these film guys…"

It was gone four when we got back to Swiss Cottage. Zac abandoned his telescope ("too cloudy") and began walking slowly around the loft, caressing surfaces as if he was acknowledging their existence for the first time. "Take this table. It's made from these tiny building blocks – so tiny, yet so big in their potential for destruction. One of God's little Jokes."

"Sorry?"

"Well, it's crazy isn't it? The idea of something so small being so powerful."

He spun one of the telescopes round so vigorously that I thought it was going to topple over. I had no idea what he was on.

"It's the blackest of black jokes: the black hole of black jokes. Theologians go on about free will, but the atom is the biggest test of free will. Has it always been there, waiting for us to discover its secrets? Waiting for us to decide what use to make of it?"

He moved in closer for one of his conspiratorial moments.

"Do you know what I think? The world wasn't made in six days, *it's still being made*. Everyday it's being added to and changed in fundamental ways by God – for want of a better name. Every time those clever-dick scientists think they've got it all figured out, God teasingly re-sharpens the picture, re-tunes reality, and once again the ultimate structure of things becomes just out of reach. I mean – take these damned atoms…" Zac pretended to hold one up between thumb and forefinger for inspection. "We thought we'd got a handle on the atom by the end of the nineteenth century. We thought that was it. That was the ultimate building block of the universe – God's little Lego bricks."

"But how wrong we were," I said, encouragingly.

Despite the manic glint in his eyes, Zac was still lucid. His shitty day was forgotten thanks to whatever he'd shoved up his nose or down his throat.

"And did you know atoms are mostly empty space?"

"I can't say I did."

"Yep, there's just a tiny nucleus floating around in there. And inside that nucleus there's a bunch of protons and neutrons being held in their orbits by a force stronger than Earth's gravity. We are 99.9% empty space, man. Made from atoms as old as the universe itself. In fact we're effectively immortal ghosts. Did you know about these little blighters called quarks, which are not only invisible, but can be in more than one place at a time? These quarks actually *change* when they're being examined – as if they know they're being looked at. I'd say all this shit makes my humble homemade religion seem fairly sane by comparison."

"Have you been reading *The Boy's Own Guide to Science* or something?"

Zac laughed. "You kill me, man!" The Americanism sounded absurd delivered in his upper-middle class accent.

"You keep mentioning God. I thought you didn't believe in God anymore?"

"I don't. Or rather, I don't believe in God. I entertain the possibility of God. Now, roll another spliff, old boy."

"Can you elaborate?"

"If I must," said Zac, feigning exasperation. He was clearly bursting to tell me more. "It comes back to that tribal-binary thing I was talking about," continued Zac. "Even in something as mysterious and unknowable as the spiritual, we are pressurised into stating a definitive position. I take my tripod's third option and say, 'I entertain the possibility'. I've even named my possibly non-existent God – the Omniscient Practical Joker, if you will – and it's not a he or even a she, it's an *it*. It's The Knowing Unknowable Universe – or the KUU, for short. I'm very much in the early stages of thinking all this stuff through – giving it shape – but I'm getting there. There may even be a concept album in it."

"The KUU. I like it. It has a nice sinister ring to it. But you can't seriously be saying that this KUU is 'the answer' and that the answers believed by countless millions of people for thousands of years are wrong?"

"Oh absolutely I can! The KUU is so much more *wholesome* than all of that other twisted shit. Really it is."

I laughed. "But how can so many people, for so long, have been wrong? Because that's what you're saying isn't it?"

Zac shrugged. "Firstly, all those old gods and sods have had millennia to establish themselves. Secondly, since when were the masses right about anything? And thirdly, most of them have to be wrong, coz only one of them can be right – it's only logical, as Mr Spock would say. And anyway, the three big ones have only been around for a couple of thousand years, maximum. And that's a blink of an eye in evolutionary terms or even in human terms. You have to ask yourself why God would wait so long to fill us in? Do you read the tabloids, Paul?"

"Well, I…"

"They sell millions more than *The Times* or the *Telegraph*. Does that mean they're more likely to be right? Does it fuck. Do you want to know what started me on all this?"

"Well, yeah. Of course."

Zachary settled back in his armchair, taking on the air of a man about to tell an epic adventure story. "I'd booked myself into this drugs recovery program – a sort of meditation centre in Fulham run by this Malaysian guy. A few weeks earlier, I'd shortened the name to The KUU because I was tired of writing 'The Knowing Unknowable Universe' all the time in my notebook. I'd become completely obsessed with the KUU. I suppose it took my mind off the fact that I'd not been able to write a new song for months. So anyway, I've just completed my first meditation session, and nature called. I'm on the loo and directly in my line of vision, hanging on the toilet door opposite me, was this flipbook of naff abstract paintings with snippets of wisdom written underneath them. The words under the picture that happened to be exposed read… hang on, I need my notebook. Yes, here we are…" Zac read from his notebook:

"KUU (VOID) DOES NOT MEAN NON-EXISTENCE BUT EXISTENCE (all things undergo constant change)."

Pretty cool, eh?" he continued. "I almost freaked out in this guy's toilet. I had to cover my mouth to stifle a mixture of laughter and cries of astonishment. The words were from a book called *The 31 Passages of Egolessness* by some cat called The Very Reverend Ryuho Okawa. He was the President of The Institute for Research and Happiness. So here was my acronym, 'KUU', not only already out there in the world, but also having a similar meaning. I researched this Japanese dude and found out that – unlike all the other religions – he was interested in happiness rather than guilt and misery, which was in keeping with my 'you can laugh' non-commandment. I then looked for the word 'KUU' in other languages. It was great to have something other than my own fucked-up head to think about for a change. But to cut to the chase, the only other language I found the word in was Swahili in which KUU means: **Head/Chief/Great/Important/Major/Elder/Old.**"

Zac finally took a breath, which gave me the chance to interject. "So there was this word you thought you'd made up, meaning more or less what you'd defined it to mean – in two other languages?"

"What are the chances, eh? Anyway, when I told Jody, she said, 'Coo, who'd have thought it!'" Zac paused, clearly expecting a response from me. "Don't you see? 'KUU, who'd have thought it? The word 'coo' – or 'KUU' – in this context is a polite non-blaspheming substitute for the word 'God' as in 'God, who'd have thought it!' It was yet another connection. Then Jody pointed out that 'KUU' also sounds like 'coup' which the dictionary defines as '*The overthrowing of the established system by illegal or violent methods*.' What a lovely idea that was! That my throwaway deity had the potential to replace established religions while also saving the world with its irreverence, vagueness and good humour! Such a weird and unlikely chain of coincidences had to mean I was onto something. Especially given that I'd built the idea of KUUism around coincidence even before any of this shit had happened."

Although Zac's eyes were half closed and he was visibly deflating in his chair, there was no stopping his mouth. So I just lay back on the sofa, looking up at the rectangle of universe visible through the skylight. It was very late – or perhaps it was very early the next morning – when I noticed Zac had stopped talking. I looked over and saw the touching sight of Zac cradling Charlie the greyhound's head in his hands. The sleepy dog's unconditional adoration made me think of the fans of a few years ago. Appreciative of this audience of one, Zac attempted to start up a dialogue with the dog. "So, what do you know, pal?" he asked Charlie. "Do you know things I don't know? Because you can certainly smell things I can't smell. Are you the one that's got it all sussed out?" I didn't think he was aware I was watching him, but then he turned towards me and smiled.

"We can't know what this fella's thinking. He's just another enigma to add to the endless list of enigmas…"

"Is there anything left in that?" I pointed at a knocked-over wine bottle by Zachary's feet.

"No. But there's some Southern Comfort under the mixing desk. Now where was I?"

"Enigmas."

"Yes, of course. I mean, we're even enigmas to ourselves. Would you jump into a fast-flowing river to save a stranger's life?"

"Well, actually I can't swim, but—"

"Are you capable of murder?"

"It would depend on—"

"Could you take your own life?"

"I'm not—"

"Exactly. How can we know unless we're put in a particular situation? And so most of us will never find out if we're courageous, evil or just intolerably, banally average. So if we're even a mystery to ourselves, what hope do we have of figuring out everything else. What do you say, Charlie?"

Charlie's forlorn dog face offered Zac neither agreement nor disagreement, it just carried on adoring him. Maybe dogs do have it sussed out; maybe the meaning of life is simply to find something or somebody to love unconditionally, and so all those dumb pop songs were right after all. I liked the fact that, despite Zac's rampant egotism, he thought we humans might be no more significant than the rest of the planet's crawling, eating, fucking, fighting creatures. But as usual, my focus on Zac's words soon began to drift.

"… no boffin or spaced-out mystic has even touched the surface…" Ink-blue sky pin-pricked by lights. "… after all, our capacity to understand is limited by our intelligence as human beings, isn't it?" The pin-prick lights dissolved. The last thing I heard was Zac telling me his previous question had been rhetorical and so he wasn't offended I hadn't answered it. When I regained consciousness, I looked at my watch and was surprised to find I'd only been asleep an hour. Had something woken me? Yes, there was an unnaturally loud scratching sound coming from somewhere. I sat up and looked around. I hadn't noticed the state of the place when we'd gotten back from the video shoot. The floor of the studio was littered with dog-ravaged pizza boxes, splayed music magazines and Chinese takeaway tins spilling their noodle entrails. I realised the scratching was coming from the studio monitors. Then Zac's voice issued from the speakers.

"Good boy, good boy. Well done, boy!" Zac appeared in the mixing room with Charlie trotting close behind. "I think we got it this time." The bruise-blue areas under his eyes looked like inverted eye shadow.

"Got what exactly?"

"A decent scratching sound from old Charlie here," he said by way of explanation, as if he were stating the obvious to a senile old aunt. "Could you press Rewind and then Start, please Paul?"

What issued from the monitors sounded like the sonic no-man's-land between radio stations: ghostly voices, moments of howling static – and in there somewhere – Charlie's arrhythmic scratching.

"Well done, boy!" Zac said, patting the dog's long, lean back. Charlie's look was still the look of love, but perhaps tempered slightly by confusion or even fear – probably because of the din his sensitive dog ears were being subjected to.

"What *is* this?" I asked.

Either Zac thought the question irrelevant or he didn't hear it, because all I got as a response was, "Shush! I love this bit. Listen…"

At last something reassuringly musical pushed through the fog of noise – a squiggle of jazzy sax that warmed the dissonant sonic landscape like a smattering of poppies in a Monet field. Eventually, the piece darkened again before building to an end-of-the-world crescendo which Zac emphasised by pushing up the stereo faders.

By now, Charlie was cowering under the mixing desk. I was certain he was trying to cover his ears with his paws. Finally, there was an eerie scream that seemed to get sucked backwards into silence. The only sound remaining was Charlie's plaintive whining from beneath he desk. Zac adopted his usual camply-challenging hands-on-hips pose. "So what do you think?"

"What do I think? I think you've got one talented dog there…"

"Seriously, Paul. Give me some feedback."

"I think there was enough feedback on the track…"

"Ha bloody ha. But it wasn't a *track* anyway. It was *a movement*; The Final Movement, to be precise."

"I see."

"I believe it's my masterpiece," he concluded with as much histrionic bravado as he could muster. "Obviously it's far from finished: there's going to be a dubby section in the Second Movement in which I'll be breaking some eggs into a tin bucket while piling on the reverb. You see, I want that dry, brittle sound followed by that liquid slop you can only get by breaking eggs into a tin bucket."

"So you are the egg man then, Zac?"

But Zac's sense of humour had deserted him. "The egg man? Sorry you've lost me. Are you taking the piss?"

"I thought you were the one taking the piss. It was a joke. The Beatles? *Magical Mystery Tour*?" There's nothing worse than trying to explain a joke that's fallen flat, so I became as irritated at Zac as he was at me. But I counted to ten and located the diplomat in me. "So what else is left to do to it then?" For once it was the right thing to say. Zac sat down and calmed down. He had many plans for *Laughter in the Dark* (named after his favourite Nabokov novel). For the first movement, he planned to record the manic polyrhythmic clatter of the rattling windows of the top deck of the 159 bus he remembered from childhood. Then there was the hollow dong you got from hitting a gas radiator pipe with a biro; you could apparently almost taste the metal in that sound. And so on. I took a deep breath. "It's certainly a brave departure. I take it you're no longer concerned about giving the kids what they want?"

Zac laughed. "Look, the kids don't give a shit about me anymore, so why should I give a shit about them? And this is a journey *I* need to go on."

That italicised '*I*' is pure Zachary B. The way it nonchalantly leans to one side, striking a pose.

"It'll certainly give the press something to write about."

This too was the right thing to say. Zac smiled. "I've arrived at my ninth symphony without having to write the first eight. Neat eh?"

What an absurd trumpet blast of self-aggrandisement, counterweighted by a twinkle in the eye to indicate he was at least partly making fun of himself. How good it was great to hear the old Zac again. *Laughter in the Dark* achieved posthumous notoriety in 1991 when the "long thought lost or destroyed" (isn't that always the way?) recordings were released on V Records. Barney Merrick – God bless his 100% Egyptian cotton socks – even gave it a rave review in the left-field music magazine *Organised Noise*. Get this:

'*Shifting plains of ephemeral, fugacious textures are postulated and then abandoned, as pure sound metamorphoses into music through systematic repetition and restatement. Fractal, apparently self-replicating sounds spin off into infinity creating both a macrocosm and a microcosm of infinite depth and variety. In this living, breathing urban symphony, Bekele has created an hermetically sealed universe which warps and confounds our sense of what music is, and can be.* Laughter in the Dark *is exactly that — a challenging post, postmodern manifesto which is somehow both chillingly devoid of emotion yet also effusively, extravagantly polyphonic. This is a soundtrack to pre-millennial angst, nine years before the fact, written nineteen years before the fact. A fitting testament to a man of late-blooming genius.'*

After I'd endured *Laughter in the Dark*, Zac shared his other new obsession with me. He'd been working on some paintings. Or rather, he *hadn't* been working on some paintings. Leaning against the back wall of the studio were three blank canvases. Zac shifted one of the canvases a couple of inches to the left, and then looked to me for a response. Art wasn't really my field, but I knew a blank canvas when I saw one. I thought nothing, so I said nothing.

"They're about possibility," Zac said, unfazed by my silence. He stepped back to better admire his own absence of work. "In that sense they're very optimistic. They're also about elevating the concept of fence-sitting to a higher plain."

"A higher fence then."

Zachary continued, with stretched patience. "Art's not really your thing is it, Paul, but I shall endeavour to explain. The idea is that I will never get off the fence regarding these works: they could have become portraits, battle scenes, landscapes, masturbatory fantasies, orgies of bloody violence..."

"But aren't they abstracts? Minimalist abstracts?" I interjected: I did know a bit about art and felt compelled to prove it.

"No, no, of course not. You've got hold of quite the wrong end of the paintbrush there, my friend.

"It's you who has got hold of the wrong end of the paintbrush."

"Very droll. But yes, I can see why you might think they're abstracts. They do look like abstracts, but they're more paintings-in-waiting. They're the pure, unadulterated expression of my refusal to make a definitive statement. I have decided to pause on the threshold of something great… and leave it at that."

"Fantastic," I offered, unconvinced.

"I'm glad you think so, because I intend to do more."

It was definitely time to go. I left Zac to his world of hypothetical masterpieces and went downstairs. I was surprised to find Jody pacing in the hallway as if waiting for bad news from the operating room.

"Well?" said Jody. She seemed to think I'd know what she was referring to.

"Well what?"

"He's out of his mind, isn't he?"

"I wouldn't say that. He's just being Zac. Perhaps a little wired, but I've seen him much worse."

"The video shoot was the first time he's been out of that loft for a month. And all he'll eat is porridge. It's like being married to some mad professor. We don't even talk anymore…"

I tried to reassure her. "At least he's not smearing shit on the walls. I even caught a glimpse of the old Zac. You know: tongue-in-cheek cocky; unapologetically pretentious."

"He's a fucking junky. There, I've said it." Jody's face contorted in disgust. "I said I'd leave him if he ever did smack. And now he's doing smack and I'm still here, God damn it!"

I was out of my depth again. "Can't you just cut off his supply? Tell that creep Mozart not to come here anymore?" I expected my mind-numbingly obvious suggestion to be met with derision, but Jody gave me a hug, kissed me on both cheeks, and ran into the room she used as an office.

"Brilliant, Paul." She frantically leafed through her Filofax. "What kind of damned stupid name is Mozart anyway. Ah, here we are."

There's nothing more frustrating than hearing only one side of a conversation, but whatever Mozart was saying to Jody agitated her further.

"Why are you laughing?… No, I'm serious… How dare you!… Since when?… He owes you what!" She slammed down the phone and turned her tear-filled eyes to the ceiling. "Zac, Zac, *Zac* – why do you do these things to me!" For a moment she seemed defeated, barely aware I was in the room. Then she gathered together some things and threw them into a bag.

My chivalrous alter-ego once again manifested itself. "Look Jody, give me Mozart's number. Maybe if it came from a bloke…"

"Paul, you're very sweet. But a man-to-man chat isn't going to sort this out."

"So are you going there now?"

"To see Mozart? Yes. But really, I can deal with this." Her words said one thing, but her flustered hands said another. She could barely fasten the catch on her handbag.

"I'm coming with you," I said firmly. "Okay, come with me then. Thank you," she replied, with some relief.

Extract from *The KUU Hypothesis*
by Zachary Bekele

9. THE THIRD WAY LEADS TO THE KUU TRIPOD

Middle Ground Radicalism

The KUU needed a visual symbol. The cross and the star were already taken, the square seemed too square and the circle too self-contained. The tripod was perfect in its iconic simplicity – anyone could draw it with just three strokes of a pen. Yet, only after landing on it for aesthetic reasons did its deeper resonances dawn on me. The tripod gave my anti-binary middle ground radicalism the visual representation it needed. Once erected, its arbitrariness seemed far from arbitrary and it's KUUness glaringly obvious. A tripod is the strongest self-supporting structure. Take one leg away and it's a tribal-binary disaster.

The Lure of Opposites

We are programmed to make decisions between this and that, between good and bad, between the Apollonian and the Dionysian, between the red team and the blue team. Grey areas are avoided, ambiguities ignored. Our culture has us believe we live in an age of certainty and indisputable progress, marching blissfully blinkered into a perfect future. Even our greatest thinkers only seem to pose either/or questions or definitive statements. Is there a God or isn't there? Is the table real or isn't it? To be or not to be, I think therefore I am. Everything is reduced to the taking of sides while the truths remain ambivalent and overlooked. The third leg of the tripod represents the fact the overlooked is often the answer.

The View From the Fence

Because of our YES/NO mindset, we dismiss the idea that sitting on the fence might actually give us the best view. Like other phrases that cover this middle ground of perceived lack of commitment, it has negative, wishy-washy connotations. But the view from up on that fence gives you an unbeatable 360-degree panorama. And if you take sandwiches, you're laughing.

The Way Out of the Tribal-Binary Prison

The Tripod is the way out of the tribal-binary prison. The tribal binary prison is where you are forced, by implicit cultural pressure, to make an either/or decision rather than maintain an often far more reasonable position of remaining undecided. The third leg of the tripod symbolises this third choice that need not be a choice. 3D is always better than 2D! You don't have to be certain. You don't have to be single-minded. You don't have to take sides. Once you have achieved this shift of perspective, you escape the confrontational essence of the Yes/No, Good/Evil, Atheist/Believer tribal-binary mindset.

3

Marrakech, February 2007

Because so little light filtered through the small stained-glass window of her courtyard-facing room, August didn't wake until her alarm clock jolted her out of a night of a thousand dreams. Well, not dreams exactly, more like short scenes that lurched and melted into each other, populated by both familiar and unfamiliar people all with bad intentions. Her dreams these past few days felt more like challenges: she was a child, a teenager, her adult self; she argued, screamed and sobbed at personal injustices, lost loves and lost luggage. Then those beep-beep-beeps would mercifully haul her back into the real world and leave her relieved, exhausted and discombobulated. Despite the fact she plugged herself straight into Kool and the Gang on her iPod, the last of August's dreams refused to dissipate.

She had dreamt that her mother was in Marrakech and had decided to come along with her to meet Paul Coleridge. Jody and Coleridge had not seen each other for nearly a quarter of a century. As soon as Coleridge (who August wrongly dreamt of as a cross between William Burroughs and Freddie from *Nightmare on Elm Street*) set eyes on Jody, he shot her dead. August saw the neat red hole appear in the centre of her mother's forehead, before she sunk to her knees and then fell forward onto her face. "It was the will of the KUU," Coleridge calmly stated as he held fast to August's wrists to stop her from clawing at his waxy, mottled face.

August's dream-world struggle continued even on waking, as Coleridge's phantom grip became the pink polyester sheet that had wrapped itself around her during the night. She wriggled and kicked herself free before finally stamping the malevolent thing into the floor, as if to prevent it from ever playing the same trick on her again. It was only then that the imagined challenges of the night gave way to thoughts of the real challenges of the day ahead. She still had no idea how she was going to react when she met this man. She knew herself fairly well, but not when it came to big stuff like this. Having mentally gone through the scenario of meeting Coleridge many times, she'd come up with nothing: her mind simply didn't want to go there until it had to for real. She'd spent most of her life thinking about Zachary Bekele: her father; this man she loved but had never met. She disapproved of the millions of people who had no right to love him, while accepting that she didn't know him any better than they did.

Jody had talked to August about Zachary on many occasions over the years, and this did help August somewhat to add substance to the person behind the austere words of *The KUU Hypothesis* and the schizophrenically sycophantic/sarcastic words of Paul Coleridge's memoir. However, Zachary still seemed more like a fragmented work of fiction to August – a man made up of his own and other people's words – rather than a fully rounded human being. August remembered Coleridge's book distressed Jody for many reasons, but mainly – oddly enough – because it depicted Zachary as shallow and self-obsessed. This was just "the switched-on, spaced-out Zachary" not the Zachary she knew. What moved August most about her parents' story was that her mother had been a Methodist before Zachary came along and "cured her", as she put it. As a teenager growing up in Georgia, Jody became increasingly confused by the knowledge that she'd been born into a religion which had, in God's name – for hundreds of years – put her people into slavery and killed untold millions in the process. Yet "her people" (as she'd begun to refer to them, under the thrall of the black power movement of the 1960's) continued to worship the blue-eyed saviour with the sad upturned face, with more fervour than any white folks she'd ever met. How could that be? Having broken free from slavery, how could they continue to bow down and abase themselves before yet another white man, even if he did have a halo? Why didn't they find out who their own gods were *before* they'd been snatched from their homeland? She eventually concluded that the only explanation was that their lives were so damned hard they had to have something to look forward to: a next life in Heaven – at God's white right hand – was better than nothing at all.

"But wouldn't all the white folk be there too? How could that be Heaven?" a baffled ten-year-old Jody had asked her parents. But she got a slap round the head for her trouble. When her folks put on their Sunday best for church, she would refuse to go, but she'd be dragged there anyway, crying and screaming, until the disapproving stares of other churchgoers shamed her into behaving herself before they reached the church doors.

When Jody finally left for college in Atlanta she still didn't know what to do with her frustrated spiritual yearnings. She'd anticipated finding enlightened tutors, or even fellow students, with whom she could share her doubts and frustrations. But almost everyone suffered from Christianity in one form or another. Even when she investigated African religions she just found more Christianity, and Islam of course (which also had Christ in there somewhere, along with the Old Testament at its judgmental core). Most heartbreakingly of all, she felt no connection to the multitude of African gods with their Picassoesque faces and their potions and curses.

One day she read about the Anuta tribe who lived on a tiny island in the South Pacific. They'd had their own perfectly adequate gods, but Christian missionaries saw them off before refusing to let this tiny isolated community have a health clinic because – as they put it – it undermined the power of prayer. She was also horrified to learn of many African tribes in which female circumcision was so brutally absolute that the genital area ended up Barbie doll-smooth except for the two necessary holes. Whatever she read about religion just made her more angry, hurt and frustrated. And then she met Zachary who freed her from the guilt of not worshipping her master's god. August remembered her mother proudly explaining that it was she who first told Zachary to write down all his thoughts. "Otherwise he would have just let them blow away on the wind," she'd said.

Thinking about all this was upsetting August, and she knew that getting upset was counter-productive if she was going to retain any kind of objectivity – never mind control her temper – during her meeting with Coleridge. It was still early, and she could hear the tinkle and clatter of breakfast things from the courtyard. She resisted the superstitious impulse to phone her mother and make sure she was okay. However, she needed to do something to clear her head. For the first time since arriving in Marrakech she put on lipstick and mascara. But five minutes later she washed it off again: it didn't seem appropriate. Then she remembered that she hadn't bought any earrings yet; she bought earrings in every city she visited. So she knocked on Damian's door and told him to meet her at midday in a cafe they'd noticed but hadn't been in yet: Zachary Tea was a squat café on route to the Tripod. It had a crude homemade wooden tripod on the roof and was always busy.

As soon as August had gone, Damian opened her laptop. He wasn't sure where to begin – or how many YouTube videos would distract him along the way – but he knew there was work to be done. It was only just after nine, but it already felt hotter than the previous day. Up until this morning, his room had been comfortingly dark and cool, like the nave of a church (the vague smell of incense added to this impression), but today the breeze that had flowed under his ill-fitting door was absent, and the air he moved through was disconcertingly dry and dense. He'd been out briefly yesterday, but on returning he had to drink a litre of water before he felt himself again. He should have listened to the doctor and stayed in at least one more day. However, Damian's blinkered philosophy in relation to illness was "ignore it and it'll go away". Unfortunately, such bravado didn't work when it came to knife wounds, however shallow.

So, where should he start? He got nowhere trying to find out about who was really in control of the KUU Foundation, behind the figureheads of Merrick and Coleridge. However, he did stumble across a feature in *The Times* on the connections between Nick Valentine and the KUU Foundation. Valentine had done everything he could to play down his involvement with the KUU. It was still a highly controversial organisation, particularly in America where Valentine did a lot of business. Damian found a *Time Magazine* interview in which Valentine said that he couldn't deny being Zac's manager during the 1970's, or being the publisher of both *The Life and Death of Zachary B* and *The KUU Hypothesis*. But they're just books, Valentine protested: "If you published murder mysteries it doesn't make you a murderer. I don't share Zachary's world view but, you know, I had to make *The KUU Hypothesis* available to the fans." *Time Magazine* claimed Valentine completely financed the KUU Tripod.

On another site, Damian filled in some gaps in his knowledge of *VMedia*. In 1984, Valentine Records branched out into home videos, changing its name to Valentine Media. In 1990 it became *VMedia* (always italicised for extra diagonal dynamism). Damian learnt from the company's own website that *VMedia* sold just about everything to just about everyone: from train tickets to trainers; from mobile phones to immobile homes; from real estate to the unreal states induced by the most sophisticated computer games on the market, and, no doubt – as soon as they became legal – the most sophisticated drugs on the market. But what about music? Damian found a recent quote from Valentine:

"Who gives a shit about music? I've got a bunch of rappers on my books who sell millions, and all I've got to do is pay for their videos. All kids want these days is a new mobile every other week, an MP3 player that's too small to operate."

Damian wondered how had this second-division music manager become one of the most successful businessmen on the planet. Wikipedia offered some answers. Valentine didn't get off to a great start. Two weeks after Zachary B's funeral, he made himself the fans' Public Enemy Number One by putting out a substandard and incomplete Greatest Hits album. He added insult to injury by releasing an album of very lo-fi demos, recordings which Zachary B would undoubtedly have preferred left in the vaults. But, to his credit, Valentine responded to the outcry from fans by withdrawing the album almost immediately. After a rethink, he contacted Zac's favourite producer, Justin Hammond, and persuaded him to turn these works-in-progress into the posthumous solo album *Light the Way*. Original members of the Now and a string section were brought in to flesh-out the recordings. Damian jumped to a YouTube clip of a sober-suited Valentine explaining to chat show host, Russell Harty, that the album had been put together with loving care to honour Zachary's memory. The bastard even persuaded Jody Bekele to write the sleeve notes. The title track was originally no more than a vocals-and-piano sketch, but with added orchestration it captured the public's lack of imagination like nothing else Zachary had done, ending up as much a part of Christmas as *White Christmas*. Obviously its huge international success was partly a result of Zachary's tragic fate. But *Light the Way* was also the kind of sickly sweet medicine the public love to lap up as the year rolls to a sentimental close.

Damian clicked on a link to the original demo and listened to the song with new ears. Presumably Zachary B adlibbed the vocals, because the lyrics creaked with non sequiturs and clichés. But it was probably these very ambiguities – the way the God idea and the love idea (the universal and the personal) accidentally intertwined – that resulted in *Light the Way* selling more copies than the rest of Zachary B's back catalogue put together. When you also consider it was released on Valentine's own label (after AMT dropped Zachary following the controversial crucifix video) the irony becomes even more apparent. Essentially, *Light the Way* was the main catalyst for Zachary B's fame growing exponentially with each passing, posthumous year, which, in turn, has led to increased interest in his book. So, although it took Christianity a couple of thousand years to spread its gospel by bloody deed and thunderous voice to every corner of the planet, thanks to a vacuous Christmas song and the power of the Internet, Zachary Bekele's scriptures of doubt, laughter and coincidence took a mere twenty years.

As Damian knew most of this stuff already, he moved on to Wikipedia for information on Valentine's post-Zachary B career. By the mid 1990s, *VAirways* was dominating the skies with its chubby cut-price passenger jets. This helped finance Valentine's controversial power building in Brussels. But why Brussels? Because even cities are brands these days. London had spruced itself up by the turn of the millennium with its gherkin and giant Ferris wheel. But Brussels was still hanging low with just a picturesque but hardly iconic church steeple or two plaintively saying, "look at me". A city's global image depends on its silhouette, rather than on its girth and sprawl, because an iconic skyline can be graphically represented on letterheads, brochures, and coffee mugs. Belgian architect Tomas De Smet's design barely strayed from the napkin sketch a drunken Valentine had handed to him at their first restaurant meeting in December 2000. The *VMedia* Building was constructed within eighteen months and achieved instant notoriety. On the plus side, it was architecturally daring in its gracefully angled, 270-metre-tall twin towers which inclined, at a steady gradient, away from each other from a single base. But on the minus side, by unquestioningly recreating Valentine's V-logo writ large (without realising the unambiguous message it would send out to the rest of the world), De Smet made the biggest mistake of his career. So, just as London's elegant new landmark got crudely renamed The Gherkin, Valentine and Brussels got stuck with The Fuck You Building; a fitting name for a structure representing a huge multinational that exploited third-world labour like there was no tomorrow. Damian was about to click on a link to some satirical cartoons in *The New Yorker* reacting to The Fuck You Building, when he realised the time. Shit! Computers were evil! He quickly brushed his teeth, threw on a T-shirt, realised the T-shirt was on back-to-front, and in one deft movement borne of experience, sorted himself out. Written on his chest, white on sky blue, were the words: **Entertain the possibility, and the possibility will entertain you** – his favourite Zachary Bekele quote. He stood before the full-length mirror and ran a cursory hand through his hair. He was still running late, but not that late.

Extract from *The KUU Hypothesis* by Zachary Bekele

THE KUU MULTI-SYMBOL TRIPOD
Part 1

The tripod is a multi-symbol for all occasions. Each version helps us to escape the tribal-binary cul-de-sac. As soon as the tripod's metaphorical legs are firmly planted in your imagination, you'll realise there is no occasion when the KUU Tripod template isn't useful.

1. The KUU Maybe Tripod

The KUU Tripod represents the idea that human thoughts, ideas and opinions cannot only be supported by the 'YES' and 'NO' polarity. MAYBE is the third leg. It is an equal to the apparently sturdier YES and NO. If it wasn't there, then the whole metaphorical structure would collapse. The Uncertainty Principle is a constant in KUUism.

2. The Entertaining the Possibility Tripod

Entertaining the possibility lies between being subjective and being objective, between being sceptical and gullible. The KUUist may lean more towards the subjective (the underdog in our post enlightenment age), but should also learn to distinguish between open-minded conjecture on what *could* be possible and mere whimsy. Honorary KUUist, Wordsworth, called this kind of creative consciousness a "wise passiveness" – an apt description for the KUUist's receptiveness of heart and mind.

3. The KUU Name Tripod

The number three is already a favourite with religions: The Holy Trinity and the Hindus with their divine trilogy of Trimurti, for example. Further three-for-the-price-of-one gods can be found in Peru, Egypt, Greece, India, and Mexico. In this respect, KUUism has ended up conforming to the norm. But the KUU Name Trinity is unique in that it's a non-personifying acronym of three elements, which needs to be taken a word at a time yet understood as a whole.

Extract from
The Life and Death of Zachary B
by Paul Coleridge

You Shouldn't Have Come Here;
You Know That, Don't You?

October 1981

"Beer? Cognac?"

Even this simple invitation of Mozart's had an undertone of implicit threat. He circled Jody and I – sizing us up – his purple/blue two-tone suit seemed metallic in the subdued lighting of his high-rise apartment. And then the phone rang in another room and Mozart left us to answer it. I looked around his Bermondsey version of a gangster's paradise: his gaudy gaff full of tasteless but expensive furnishings. Do all drug dealers have a fish tank running right along the length of one wall, and a black leather three-piece-suite? I'd like to think so. Of course I'd had no previous experience of how such people lived, but I'd seen enough films. Mozart had obviously seen those films too, and he knew his clients had seen those films. And so presumably, out of a sense of duty, he became their worst nightmare; he had an archetype to live up to.

"I'm glad you find this all so amusing, Paul," said Jody, giving an involuntary shudder. "The bastard is playing with us!"

The two walls of his lounge not taken up by the fish tank consisted of a continuous strip of window. Outside, a thousand other windows gave pointillist definition to the otherwise barely visible cityscape. Five minutes crawled past. Because the situation seemed so unreal, I wasn't as unsettled as I should have been. And so I idled over to the sombrely lit fish tank as if it were an exhibit in an art gallery. The water had the semi-opaque consistency of minestrone soup. Flecks of silver, ruby and orange changed their minds every half-second about where they were going. A larger fish with a face like a depressed cow, languidly cruised amongst these smaller fry. I wondered why smaller fish always moved in that fast, nervy way. Was it an illusion created by their size? Or was it because they really were nervous because any second they might be eaten alive? The cow-fish cruised right up to the glass. It seemed to be trying to tell me something with its slow-motion mouth. A moment later, Mozart reappeared cradling a large glass of Cognac.

"My ears are burning. I hope you've not been saying bad things about me. Come through. I'd like you to meet a couple of business associates of mine."

In a smaller, even darker room, two men sat at a small round table in silent communion. One was tall and thin, the other was grossly overweight. They looked like a kind of Laurel and Hardy from the dark side.. I'd always thought poker was the game of choice for the criminal fraternity, but these two were hunched over a Scrabble board. A Victorian standard lamp with a tasselled shade provided the only illumination in the room. My surreal notion that these two hoodlums were silent movie refugees was enhanced by the fact that the thin one ruffled his hair with nervy frequency, and the fat one could barely get his short, thick legs under the tiny table; if he sneezed the whole lot would go flying. The two men looked up at us with an air of glazed indifference. A mere four monosyllabic words had so far blossomed in their game: A horizontal WON had ONE dropping down from its middle. ONE had END branching out from its end. And END had DEAD dangling from its D.

276

Hardy looked up at Mozart. "So who are these friends of yours then?"

Friends was said as if the word was being held at arms length. We were introduced, but as this was a Mozart introduction, no names were exchanged or hands shaken: mute head nods had to pass for good manners. Mozart rejoined Laurel and Hardy at the table.

"I hope you lowlifes haven't been cheating while I've been gone." He studied the board for an inordinate length of time.

Eventually, he plucked three fresh letters from the box.

"Fuck! Almost..." Mozart stared at his new letters. He had the M and U, but only one R and no E. Otherwise he could have opened out the game a little. "I almost got MURDER. Bollocks!"

With a sweep of his hand, Mozart brushed all the letters onto the floor before striding back into the main lounge area. Jody and I hesitantly followed him.

You know how it is when you know you shouldn't laugh, but you can't stop yourself? First there'd been Mozart's foppish affectation of swilling his Cognac around, and then this childish tantrum over a dim-witted game of Scrabble.

"What's so funny, my friend?" Mozart's unblinking eyes locked onto mine. His neck jutted pigeon-like as he came towards me.

"Nothing, it's just ... No, nothing."

"Do you always find *nothing* funny, cunt?"

Jody interrupted. "Look, Mozart, leave him out of it. He just came with me for... well, company really." Jody steeled herself before continuing. "I need you to stop supplying Zac with whatever you're supplying him with. I mean *everything*. I don't even want him smoking weed."

Mozart's laugh was wheezy and joyless. "And is this what *he* wants? Does he even know you're here? And does he know you're treating him like a fucking six-year-old – no more sweeties?"

"I didn't come here for an argument. This isn't open for discussion, I—" Jody continued.

Unwisely, I interjected. "Look, Mozart, Zac's in no position to make decisions for himself at the moment. He's not well. Jody's just trying to help him. If that makes you a customer down, then that's unfortunate but..."

Mozart began pacing his generously proportioned lounge as if it were a West End stage, stopping occasionally to fire words and accompanying spittle into our faces. I could see Laurel and Hardy through the open door to the other room, still crawling around looking for Scrabble pieces.

"A customer down. Shit, you people make me laugh! I'm to stop supplying him and that's a cross I'm going to have to bear? Sure, up until a few weeks ago I was still letting him have stuff. I felt sorry for him. And what with him being a rock star an' all, I thought the money would come through eventually. But nothing. Nothing!"

"Yes, well..." Jody began stiffly, "when we have the money you'll be sent a cheque for all that we owe you. But, until then, I don't want you anywhere near us, or—"

"I hope you're not about to threaten me, Mrs B, or whatever your stupid fucking name is. I don't respond well to threats, bitch."

As Mozart was still churning out the clichés, I thought I'd join in. "Hey, that's no way to speak to a lady!" I was immediately aware that there had been no conviction in my voice, and that my words didn't even measure up to Mozart's tired, recycled material. Consequently, I found myself instantly pinned to the wall with one of Mozart's waxy hands locked around my throat.

"Nihew wey to speak to a leedy, nihew wey to speak to a leedy," he sneered. "Who do you think you are – David fucking Niven?"

Laurel and Hardy had given up looking for Scrabble pieces and had joined us in the lounge. They seemed at a dangerously loose end. Mozart realised this.

"Okay, grab him boys," said Mozart, sounding almost bored.

I could smell Hardy's luncheon meat breath, as with practised ease he got me in a headlock under his huge arm. Jody started beating his vast back with her fists but he didn't even seem to notice.

"Naughty, naughty," said Laurel, grabbing both of Jody's arms and pulling her away from Hardy. She managed a backward kick to Laurel's calf, which caused him to yelp and hurl abuse at her, but he didn't loosen his grip. Hardy pulled me upright and then brutally yanked my head back so that it was angled as if for dental surgery. Dental surgery! This was just one grisly scenario that went through my mind in those few long seconds. It was my death – not my life – that flashed before my eyes. Or at least a dozen different scenarios heading in that direction: the claustrophobia of the pitch-black boot of a car as it flies off a bridge into a river; watching and screaming as my fingernails were pulled off one by one; feeling the bullets tear through my flesh, the knife slowly drawing across my throat... Then I realised Mozart was talking again, levelly but firmly.

"You shouldn't have come here; you know that, don't you? It was un-be-lieeevably stupid of you."

"Yes, yes, we know that. *I know that*."

Mozart looked past me, at Hardy. "So what do you think we should do with this loser? Bag him up and drop him in the Thames? Or just cut up his face, so his girlfriend won't be able to look at him anymore?"

"Let's cut him up *and* drop him in the Thames," volunteered Hardy, scarily excited, mopping sweat from his tandoori-red brow.

Then Mozart's tone lightened. "Can I offer you a light?" he asked, with mock geniality, producing a cheap BIC lighter from his jacket pocket.

"A light for what? I don't have a cigarette," I replied, nervously.

"A light to guide you through life, my young friend. A light that will always remind you of Mozart." He gently stroked the underside of my chin with his index finger, as if I were a cat. He addressed his next words to Hardy rather than me. "So *smooth*. I don't think our young friend here has even started shaving yet. Chin up now!"

Jody, seeing what was about to happen, struggled harder to free herself from Laurel's grip. But he viciously twisted her arm, forcing her to stop.

Hardy pulled my head slightly back, as Mozart flicked on the BIC and held it steadily under my chin. Warmth turned to heat, which turned to unimaginable pain and the ghastly stench of burning flesh, as I screamed for mercy. It felt like a hole was actually being drilled through my skin, my flesh, and right into my mouth. Tears streamed from my eyes as Mozart continued to look gleefully into them, holding the lighter steady. But I could no longer hold his gaze. As I lost control of my bladder, I realised I'd crossed over into a different realm of being, where even the next second of existence could no longer be taken for granted, and each of those unwanted seconds lasted an eternity. Then, out of the corner of one tear-blurred eye, I saw Mozart give a head nod – like the singer signalling to the drummer to end the song. Simultaneously, Mozart backed off, Hardy released me, and Laurel let go of Jody. I collapsed to the floor, moaning. But I was immediately hauled to my feet again by Hardy, and shoved out into the communal hallway. Jody, pushed forward by Mozart, stumbled out right behind me. We clung to each other while Mozart delivered his final ultimatum.

"Here's how it works. I want my money – in full – by this time next week. One. Fucking. Week."

Jody kept her composure, even managing to appear defiant in the way she strode off towards the lift. The pain emanating from the underside of my jaw was so intense I couldn't even focus on the lift buttons: Ground, we want Ground – did I say it aloud or just in my head? When we got back to the car, I glanced nervously back to check Mozart wasn't following us.

"I'm sorry," I said to Jody from the passenger seat. Deep shame was a useful distraction from the pain.

She seemed genuinely baffled. "What do you mean, you're sorry?"

"Well, I'm sorry I didn't do or say anything more to... well, you know... help."

"Cut the macho bullshit, Paul." She handed me some Kleenex from the glove compartment to apply to my wound. "Only an idiot would have put up a fight. I had no idea Mozart was so *serious* these days. You met him back in the day? He was just this spaced-out hippy. But that was one hard-assed hippy we just had a run-in with."

"To be honest, I just thought it was all some kind of act," I said, fastening my seatbelt with shaking hands. "I even laughed in his face. What was I thinking?"

"Don't be too hard on yourself." Jody put the key in the ignition. "It's the actors you've got to watch: they created themselves from the ground up; give themselves some flash nickname, and then they learn how to believe in... not themselves exactly, but the person they've turned themselves into."

"You seem to know a lot about all this..." Jody smiled stiffly. "I've known a few *brothers* in my time, just like Mozart. If you don't buy into their act, you're their biggest threat. Laughter's their Achilles' heel, it really is. He had to teach you a lesson not because of what you *said* but because of what he sensed you were thinking. He saw in your face. You didn't *believe in him*."

"So what are you going to do?"

"There's nothing I can do at the moment, but when the next royalty cheque drops through the letterbox we'll pay the creep off. You're still shaking."

"Yes I'm still shaking! I thought I was going to fucking die in there."

"Hey cool it now, Paul. It wasn't me who made you piss your pants." Jody coped remarkably well with Mozart. It's funny, but women don't have the same sense of what their place is in the world as men do. Men modify their behaviour depending on who they are with, and are always aware of where the balance of power lies. So although Mozart had money and therefore power, Jody didn't measure herself against his sense of his own self-importance, she simply saw someone who had to be stopped from killing her husband.

★

Two weeks after the Mozart incident, Zac and Jody left London for good. Jody found a newly renovated seventeenth century farmhouse in a small village on the South Downs called Shoreford. Zac didn't even bother to go and see the place – he either trusted Jody's judgement or he was past caring. For his own inscrutable reasons, Zac wanted to travel by train to his new home, and so we said our goodbyes at Waterloo Station. Jody was a bit tearful, but Zac seemed peculiarly detached (perhaps due to some medication or self-medication). He looked around at all the people on the concourse and seemed disgruntled that no one was inclined to mob him. Whenever I tried to start a conversation he responded with a multipurpose grunt

"For goodness sake, Zac, cheer up," Jody said, giving him one of her playful shoves

"Nobody asked *him* to come anyway," replied Zac, sulkily, rummaging in his pocket for something.

"Zac! Don't be so rude! It's nothing personal, Paul. He's been like this all week. He's always been in two minds about leaving London."

Zac didn't even respond with his usual grumble to us talking about him as if he wasn't there. He just stared into the middle-distance, making sure we got the full message of his indifference from his stiff posture. I noticed how soberly dressed he was: powdery-purple suede jacket, black denims and a wide-brimmed fedora that left half his face in shadow. It suddenly dawned on me that perhaps, for once, he didn't want to be recognised by anyone. For, since Trafalgar, in the eyes of the public, he'd come to represent the more farcical, cartoon-like aspects of the rock world: he'd become lumped in with Gary Glitter rather than David Bowie, and it must have hurt like hell.

He looked like an invalid as Jody led him to their platform. I followed a couple of steps behind. As they boarded the train, Jody turned with a resigned smile.

"Thanks for everything, Paul. We did all we could. And you did all you could. But sometimes all you can do is move on." She probably uttered some other warming and meaningless words, but I'd stopped listening. I was now the one staring into the middle-distance, feeling curiously weightless in the ambient cacophony of the busy station. "You'll come and visit us won't you?" she continued. "I'm sure Zac would like that."

But Zac was already in first class with his back to us, facing the front of the train, and the direction his future lay in. Jody kissed my cheek, and that was that.

That evening I switched on the TV and let its flickering images wash over me. Eventually, I made myself spaghetti on toast and then got back to my book, this book. Surely, this wasn't the end of the Zachary B story? It wasn't a very upbeat ending if it was. In fact Zac's story had been going steadily downhill for the past five years or more. Were the public going to be interested in reading such a story? I began to wonder if there'd be a single reader left out there for this biography I'd put so much time and energy into. But then I bumped into Helen again.

Extract from *The KUU Hypothesis* by Zachary Bekele

THE KUU MULTI-SYMBOL TRIPOD
Part 2

4. The KUU Peace Tripod

If every religion entertained the possibility that the others might also be on to something, then what would there be to fight over? The great holy books should be admired not died for. It's only stories; it's only art. It's not loved ones, laughter, music, or food. If we see Judaism, Christianity and Islam as the three legs of our KUU Peace Tripod prior to assembly – each leg pointing skyward but parallel, reaching for a heaven of its own making – it is unstable and precarious. Yet, if understanding grew between these belief systems, these legs would gradually lean in towards each other, eventually meeting at a single point: the apex of the KUU Peace Tripod.

5. The KUU Morality Tripod

Give a man a holy text and he'll beat another man around the head with it.

Most of us respond in a knee-jerk way to moral dilemmas, assuming that our initial gut response is the correct one. Yet the wisest solution often lies between the tribal-binary human faculties for feeling and thinking, and between the perceived tribal-binary absolutes of right and wrong. Right and wrong are in fact the tribal-binary world's most unreliable absolutes, mired as they are in the individual's prejudices, religious beliefs, biological imperatives, misplaced loyalties and amount of background knowledge he or she has access to. In regard to religious beliefs, most of us really don't need the threat of unspeakable punishment in the afterlife to behave ourselves. Yet, we've been lead to believe that our societies would degenerate into anarchy if it weren't for God's instruction manuals. However, if anything *was* permitted, an innate instinct, and desire to retain the status quo, would prevent the vast majority from immoral or destructive behaviour.

It's Not Important to be Right, But it is Important to Admit When You're Wrong

The KUU Morality Tripod is concerned with the dissipation of tensions between previously irreconcilable opposites. The third leg should always be offered as a stimulus for discussion rather than a definitive answer. Answers are not the business of The KUU. Another honorary KUUist, Aristotle, described a virtue as a mean between two extremes. Etc etc, Amen!

4

Marrakech, February 2007

Merrick's favourite place in Marrakech to down a dry Martini was the Churchill Piano Bar. The clash of Art Deco and eighties kitsch – along with the ban on backpackers and shorts-wearers – made it the ideal location for him to play the colonial overlord while getting drunk with Ramadi and some of his fellow lapsed Muslim chums. They would lounge around in the racing-green leather armchairs, letting the sleepy pianist fill in the gaps in their conversation with his jazzy meanderings. But drinking at lunchtime always made Merrick feel terrible for the rest of the day, so why was he doing it now? Simply because he needed to get away from Paul and the Tripod. He'd had three Martinis already, and was building up to confronting Ramadi and his mates about their constant insinuations that he and Paul were in a gay relationship. Okay, so Ramadi probably thought all Englishmen were gay (apart from perhaps Tom Jones and a few Premier League footballers), but that didn't make him feel any better. He hated the very idea that he had anything in common with the pathetic shadow of a man Paul had become, never mind the idea that he was close to him in *that* way. He'd been married, for Christ's sake! Merrick's wife, Mary, had died eight years previously of Churg-Strauss syndrome, a rare disease she would have survived had her doctor not misdiagnosed her condition. Barney took little consolation in Zachary's prescribed view that the KUU is powerless in regard to the Gratuitous. If it had been cancer he could have coped, because cancer is always on the cards. However, the odds against getting this disease, and dying from it, were astronomical. He therefore decided that the Gratuitous had it in for him – even if this self-destructive superstition was in direct opposition to Zachary's conception of the Gratuitous. Zachary had written that the Gratuitous doesn't have it in for anyone; it's just an impartial fact of life… and death. But Merrick had come to believe that the Gratuitous was just the Devil in sheep's clothing. There was no other way he could make sense of Mary's death. She was only thirty-two.

"How is your friend upstairs, Barney?" asked Ramadi, downing half a glass of red wine in one gulp. Because of the metaphysical drift of his thoughts, Barney thought Ramadi meant God – or rather the KUU – but he replayed Ramadi's question in his alcohol-fogged head, and this time heard the note of mischief in his voice: the bastard meant Paul *upstairs* at the Tripod. So Barney continued studying the painted montage of legendary jazz musicians on the wall behind the pianist, as if he'd not heard Ramadi. But Ramadi wasn't going to be deterred. "Your friend, how is he?"

Why pretend, thought Barney, on his fourth generous Martini. "Out of his fucking mind," he replied, louder then he'd meant to.

Ramadi and his friends laughed. Barney bought his fifth consecutive round, and then suggested they catch some belly dancing at the Comptoir. He liked to think that Hell would have the same blood-red walls, black furniture and deep-sea lighting as this basement bar. But Ramadi reminded him it wasn't even two yet, so it was unlikely there'd be dancers. So while Ramadi and his hirsute gang got louder around him, Barney conjured up the Comptoir dancers in his mind's eye. Then he imagined their lascivious, voluptuous counterparts in Hell's hotel bars; how they'd drip with sensuality – and you probably wouldn't even have to tip them. Then it was two-thirty and he had to get back to the Tripod. Fuck Paul fucking Coleridge! Fuck him!

★

"What's the matter with you? Like the album cover, I said!" said Coleridge waving the *Aladdin Sane* CD case in Jamila's face. "What you've done just looks like a Frankenstein scar or something."

"You know this is costing you double, Mr Coleridge," said Jamila. "I was with a client and he was not happy when I—."

"Paul. *Call me Paul.*"

Sitting on the edge of the bath, Coleridge studied himself in the mirror. Jamila had already shaved off his hair and eyebrows, so he looked like an oversized baby in an off-white T-shirt and yellow shorts: it wasn't exactly the look he was aiming for. Jamila sat on a stool opposite him, a make-up box on her lap and a brush in her hand. She took the *Aladdin Sane* CD box from him, as a mother might gently take scissors back from a child, and propped it back up on the washbasin. Today she was in a pink blouse and jeans rather than traditional Muslim clothes. She was trying to smile but there was a tightness around her mouth. Coleridge scowled at his reflection, and then rubbed at the clumsy zig over his left eye and the wobbly zag across his right cheek.

"Stop it!" Jamila lightly slapped his hand away. This produced a faint smile from Coleridge that manifested itself against his will.

"It's all wrong," he whined.

"That is why you must not fuss with it. Let me do it." Jamila touched the underside of Coleridge's chin.

"What is this scar, Mr Paul?"

"It's nothing."

"Obviously it's something."

"It's nothing." Coleridge changed the subject. "Do you know who's visiting me this afternoon?"

"You have told me, Paul. You tell me many times. The daughter of your... your—"

"Yes, correct. So I'm making a bit of an effort."

"Who is this man to you? He is a god, yes?"

"Who, Zachary? No of course he's not a god. You just don't get it do you. We've moved beyond all that. Zac was just a philosopher. A thinker."

"It is God that you need, Mr Coleridge, not a thinker. And you think too much."

"I *think*, Jamila, it would be better if you kept your opinions to yourself. What good has your God done you?"

Jamila treated this question as both rhetorical and unanswerable, and so remained silent. She only had the black line between the wide red zig and the narrower blue zag, left to do, and she needed a steady hand. She hoped she'd be allowed to go home once she had finished.

"That's more like it!" Paul leant towards his reflection. "I think we're nearly there. You see, I knew you could do it." After a silence of some minutes, Paul managed to catch Jamila's eye in the mirror. "What are you scared of, Jamila?" he asked, with genuine curiosity.

"I think it is you who are scared, Paul. What are you scared of?"

For a moment Jamila thought she'd gone too far. Coleridge's reflection glared back at her from the mirror with terrifying ferocity, but by the time he'd turned to face her, and clasped both her hands in his, he was addressing her gently, as a father might address a confused child.

"Yes, once I was scared, Jamila, but not anymore. You couldn't possibly understand. Your God is there to instil fear. Mine is there to instil wonder and laughter. But very soon now, you and all your people – the whole human race in fact – will be free from the shackles of faith and belief. No more guilt, no more shame, just knowledge and…"

Jamila was able to slowly withdraw her hands from Coleridge's as he became caught up in his speech. "Is that all, Paul? I have somewhere else I must be. I wish you luck with your—"

"Luck doesn't come in to it – well, actually it does, but that's another story. Why don't you come along? You wouldn't regret it."

"It is not possible."

"It is not possible," mimicked Coleridge, cruelly. "Have a nice day," he added in a vowel-stretched parody of an American accent. The door slid shut and Coleridge was again alone. It was an hour before she arrived. What should he wear to go with his splendid lightning bolt? Jamila really had done a fine job in the end. He didn't want to look ridiculous, so in the end he opted for a black cotton shirt and his favourite vintage Levis. Not vintage because he'd paid an absurdly inflated price for them, but vintage because he'd had them for thirty years. Unfortunately their 42-inch waist meant he could no longer button them up, or even raise the fly higher than half-mast, but his belt would keep them up. He'd just have to wear his shirt untucked.

★

The Tripod was busier than ever when August and Damian arrived an hour before their appointment with Coleridge. The tourist season was gradually getting underway and this had added somewhat to the numbers pouring through Security. According to Ramadi, The Tripod was increasingly attracting people who had no interest in KUUism, but just wanted somewhere to hang out, shop, and generally take advantage of the facilities. Merrick had mentioned to August that they might be introducing a stricter door policy, which would require visitors to fill out a questionnaire to prove their commitment to KUUism before they'd be allowed in. August had just glared at him in disbelief.

It took them half an hour to get through Security, and so it was something of a relief when they finally sat down at a faux-French café on Level 6. But they'd only been settled for five minutes when, across the concourse at an organic burger bar, trouble started brewing between three biker-types and a plaid-shirted redneck and his family.

"God-damn-it! You aint even got no drinks nor nothin'!" the redneck shouted. Weighed down by a tray of food and drinks, he was outraged that these refreshment-less lowlifes were occupying one of only two tables outside the burger bar. His mood was further aggravated by the fact they were focused on making roll-ups and studying a map they'd spread out on the table, rather than paying him the slighted bit of attention. The biker-type, August and Damian assumed to be the alpha-male (if his piercings-count and tattoo-tally were anything to go by), eventually acknowledged the redneck in a Glaswegian accent.

"So what brings you to these parts anyway, my Yankee buddy?"

The Redneck couldn't believe that this freak, having ignored his protestations, was now trying to engage him in small talk. One of Alpha's two smirking mates shrugged his shoulders at the American in a parody of sympathy. The other shamelessly let his eyes follow two ankle-socked Japanese girls who were walking past.

"Is that your school uniform?" he shouted after them.

They giggled and quickened their pace. Customers at surrounding eateries tried to conceal their interest in the unfolding drama.

"I told you we shouldn't have come in here," the redneck's wife whined, glaring at the three men as if they were sewer rats. One of their two children started crying.

"And why's that then, exactly?" asked Alpha, head tilted to one side, grinning.

"I wasn't talking to you," redneck's wife fired back.

Redneck upped the stakes. "Do I need to speak to the manager?"

Alpha, bored with the lack of any real challenge this showdown offered, slowly got to his feet. "We were just leaving anyway."

His mates also got up and gathered their stuff together. It looked like a fight had been avoided, but Redneck couldn't resist an under-his-breath parting shot.

"Fucking Satan-worshipping KUUists."

Alpha turned (leather squeaked, metal rattled) and his two companions, like slightly out-of-sync dancers, and followed suit. Alpha and Redneck squared-up to each other. Mouths stopped chewing and chatting. A waiter became a statue halfway through wiping a glass.

"What's Satanism got to do with KUUism?" asked Alpha.

"You're all gonna burn in Hell. The Lord's sword will strike you down! Sodomite fucking faggots! Look at yourselves – you're filth! You're the lowest of the low, you're..." Spittle spraying from Redneck's mouth, but because he couldn't find words venomous enough to convey the depths of his loathing, he eventually spluttered into silence like a faulty lawnmower.

Redneck's wife squashed her two sobbing children to her vast bosom. Her accusing eyes said, 'Now look what you've done,' to the three men. August and Damian were silent during all of this, waiting to see how the biker-hippies would respond to Redneck's rant. But Alpha was just staring at the Redneck and his family as if they were some kind of hyper-realist pop art exhibit. Baffled by Alpha's lack of response, Redneck looked around himself for the first time. Suddenly aware that he had an audience spurred him on.

"Home-oh-sexuals, fucking home-oh-sexuals! Goddamn, motherfucking—"

"What is it with you hardcore Christians and anal sex?" Alpha also rose to the challenge of an audience. "In fact, any kind of sex. This, this... sickness these people have..." He gestured at Redneck, but spoke to the onlookers. "This is what we're trying to get away from here, isn't it? This is what we all were once. This is what traditional religions turn us into. It's pathetic. But also very, very scary." He turned back to Redneck who was wiping sweat from his face and neck with a handkerchief, muttering obscenities under his breath. "What's wrong with you, dude?" Alpha continued. "So much fucking hate in the name of your turn-the-other-cheek Jesus. Where does it all come from, buddy, coz it's poisoned your wee soul. I feel sorry for your kids. Maybe they'll come back here one day. Hey kids, come back when you're older. Just don't bring your mummy and daddy with you!" Alpha continued to berate the American family as they made their way to the lift. The children's heads remained buried in their mother's bosom. Eventually, a security guard placed a gentle hand on Alpha's shoulder, presumably as a hint that he'd said enough. Alpha gave a jaunty bow and then sat back down with his mates. The concourse re-established its noisy ambience.

"Fuck," said Damian. "Perhaps Merrick's got the right idea about keeping this place for KUUists only."

August drew the last of her smoothie into her mouth before answering. "Dad would have wanted these doors open to everyone. If you put up walls it's just a provocation for others to come and try to knock them down."

"Yeah, I suppose you're right." Damian consulted a leaflet he'd picked up at some point. "How about some table-football? Or a surreal therapy session? We've still got half an hour to kill."

"Surreal therapy, I think."

They took the lift up one level. The difference in atmosphere was startling. Although there was an outlet selling coffee and pastries, the rest of the space was taken up by easels and other work surfaces. A Rubenesque woman reclined on a chaise longue, red fabric cascading from her lap in a sufficiently complex way to provide a pictorial challenge for the circle of artists around her. All August and Damian could hear was the brittle scratching of charcoal on paper, and the hushed voice of the female tutor giving one-to-one advice to students. They carefully made their way between the easels to where the tutor was standing. The young Muslim woman greeted them with a warm handshake.

"Would you like to join us?" she asked.

"Shouldn't there be a surrealist therapy session on now?" enquired August.

"Unfortunately it had to be cancelled. Another suicide I'm afraid"

"You're joking!" exclaimed Damian.

"This would not be the kind of thing I would joke about, sir. Andrew was a friend of mine."

"Figure of speech. Sorry." Damian put his head in his hands. "When did this happen?"

The woman had either forgotten she still had August's hand clasped in hers, or she needed the physical connection to give her the strength to speak. August suspected it was both, and so resisted withdrawing it.

"Only last week. We are still in shock. It happened here, after a class. Andrew was a resident here; a counsellor as well as an art teacher. He helped me to un-believe. But now I am thinking I need to believe again. I need to know Andrew has gone somewhere better. Somewhere good."

"Nowhere is better," said Damian, flatly. "Hopefully he is nowhere – just as he was before he was born. Can I ask you how he did it? As if we don't know already." August and the Muslim woman stared at Damian in horror. "What? What did I say?" Damian was genuinely baffled. "Look, I'm sorry, but Zachary was very clear on the evils of believing in an afterlife. There really is nothing wrong with Nothing."

"What are you on!" hissed August in his ear. Damian ignored her. This was no time for sentimentality as far as he was concerned – particularly in the light of KUUist philosophy in this area. They were meeting Coleridge in a few minutes and needed all the inside information they could get.

"We can't regress to all that afterlife bullshit every time a friend or relative, you know – passes over," he continued, embarrassed, but passionately sure he was right. "You see. You can't even escape it in the language: 'passes over', 'rest in peace' – vague cop-out euphemisms. So was it a gun? A Smith and Wesson?"

The woman looked down at her shoes. "Yes. Yes it was a gun. But I couldn't tell you what kind."

Damian was on a roll. "Which begs the question: how did this guy get a Smith and Wesson past security? They're more thorough here than at JFK Airport. He'd either have to know someone at Security, or—"

"Damian! Enough! We'll have this conversation later. We are very sorry for your loss... er?

"Tahira."

"Tahira. Thank you, Tahira. We will find out why your friend did this. But for now we've got to go. What was your friend's other name?"

"His name was Andrew Barden. God bless you."

"I entertain that possibility," replied Damian, giving the KUUist's response to this well-meaning believer's antiquated expression. They were back in the lift.

"What were you thinking in there?" said August.

"I was *thinking* that we're running out of time. Look, you're the bloody journalist. I'd have thought you'd have learnt by now not to get emotionally involved."

August's voice trembled with repressed emotion. "My father's non-religion is killing people and I'm about to meet Paul Coleridge... so, you know, don't tell me not to get emotionally involved!"

"Okay, yeah. Sorry."

August took a deep breath, and decided she'd been too hard on Damian. "I'm sorry too. You did good."

"Thanks. Hey, stop the lift at 8. We need to talk about all this before we see Merrick and Coleridge. We've still got ten minutes."

Level 8 was mostly staff accommodation and appeared to be deserted. The majority of the live-in staff were at work and those that worked nights were asleep. The smell of disinfectant hung in the air. August followed Damian's lead and joined him cross-legged on the floor of the corridor.

"Why didn't Merrick mention this latest suicide?" whispered August. "It must have happened just a day or so before we got here. There was nothing in the press about it."

"It's about the gun, I know it is. And you can bet your bottom fucking dollar that there were two spent cartridges."

"But we don't even know if that two-spent-cartridges stuff is true."

"As I said before, it's too arbitrary to make up. It means *something*, I know it does."

August checked her watch. "That lunatic will probably refuse to see us if we're as much as a minute late."

"Are you sure you can go through with this?"

"I have to go through with this."

A flushed Merrick was waiting for them outside Coleridge's apartment. "I need to warn you about Paul," he began.

Extract from *The KUU Hypothesis* by Zachary Bekele

Morality is Mammalian

Our morality is a synthesis of our animal instincts and our self-awareness as human beings. As things stand, animals are the civilised inhabitants of this planet and we are the out-of-control beasts.

1. We are unique in our capacity and desire for singular and mass murder of our own species.

2. We are unique in our capacity and desire to kill other species for fun and greed rather than survival.

3. We are unique in our desire to stockpile wealth, possessions and land far in excess of our needs while others of our own species are dying in their millions.

Morals are the Human Articulation of Instincts

Once a child has worked out the cause-and-effect rules that get it food and hugs, it's halfway to understanding what it is to be human being in society. Smile and you'll get a smile back. Reach out and something pretty, fun or edible might be put in your hand. Reaching and smiling are instincts. Morals are therefore the articulation of instincts.

1. Selfish behaviour isolates you.

2. Altruism makes you liked, accepted and respected.

3. Forming alliances strengthens your position. As one, you are alone. As two or more you are a partnership, a team, or even a superpower.

All moral codes stem from these basic concerns: a paradoxical blend of selfishness and altruism. Even the most simple-minded individual manipulates others with a mixture of Machiavellian cunning and innocent good will, often without even knowing they're doing it. KUUism is about responsibility, rather than the handing over of that responsibility to a higher authority, be it human or supernatural.

Extract from
The Life and Death of Zachary B
by Paul Coleridge

The Keeper of the Cigarette Butt
February 1982

Literary critics sometimes give authors a hard time if their fiction is liberally scattered with unlikely coincidences. They suggest that such coincidences stretch credibility to breaking point while oiling the creaking mechanisms of lazy or contrived plots. Even poor old Dostoyevsky and Thomas Hardy have come in for some stick on this front. I say, leave these fiction writers alone! They speak a truth that few have yet to recognise, because doesn't life throw up the most unlikely coincidences all the time?

It was about six months after Zac left London. I was in a Swiss Cottage greasy spoon, following the slow-motion progress of snow through the steamed-up window, when Helen's precious cigarette butt crossed my mind. This got me thinking about the holy relics of saints and the like. Zac was no saint, but how different was the experience of his fans from the religious awe previous generations have felt before gold-leaf-framed figures on church walls? It's all just theatre: alchemy to manifest ecstasy. It's light, colour and music fused together to generate a transcendental experience. Was Helen just thinking ahead when she became, so to speak, The Keeper of the Cigarette Butt? Obviously, she looked at it with disproportionate wonder, as a reminder of a special time, a place, and a person. She'd probably have rather died than part with the grubby little thing. That butt was her piece of Zachary B, because it had been Zachary B's butt. These thoughts preoccupied me as I stabbed at my yolk with a blunt chip and stared out at the dancing snow. So when I heard Helen's voice say, "I know where he's living," at first I thought it was just part of my reverie. But then the same voice repeated the same sentence, as if we were already in the middle of a conversation.

"Don't look so pleased to see me." Helen affected a sulky scowl as she brushed snow from the front of her big grey duffle coat.

"Wow! Hello. Sorry. I was just..."

"I didn't mean to startle you. But I do know. Where he's living, that is."

I knew who she was talking about – and she knew that I knew – but a script had to be adhered to. I put another yoke-tipped chip into my mouth. "Where who's living?"

But she was having none of it. "Do we have to play games, Paul Coleridge?"

"No. No, we don't." I was disproportionately pleased to hear her say my name: my sense of self had been slowly dissipating over the past few months. So that was who I was: Paul. Coleridge "I was miles away. How are you? Can I get you a coffee or something?"

I didn't tell Helen I'd just been thinking about her. But, actually, her appearance didn't really surprise that much. I was getting used to Zac's "Cosmic Nudges" – his name for chance events like this. And it wasn't really that much of a Cosmic Nudge. This was Zac's old neck of the woods, and so we two stray dogs were both still skulking around, irrationally hoping he'd return. So it was only a matter of time before we bumped into each other.

"A tea and an apple turnover, please." She flopped down in her tomboyish manner in the chair opposite. "No, actually I'll have the apple pie – with custard."

Her hair was longer again. The duffle coat suited her. She looked even nicer than she'd done at the Anti-Nazi

League gig. Well, when I say nicer, I mean more together. Not so flaky, not so unemployable. But she must have been thinking exactly the opposite of me: more flaky and more unemployable. I confess I'd let myself go a bit. When you spend so much time at home writing, you forget that the real world expects you to make some kind of effort whenever you go out into it. Although Helen insisted she was no longer obsessed with Zac, she still hung on my every word when I talked about him. When did I last see him? What were his last words to me? When was there going to be a new album? But tiring of Planet Zac, I changed the subject and asked about her childhood.

"Oh, you know. The usual."

But of course it wasn't the usual at all. She'd had no interest in playground gossip, boys, TV or pop stars. She spent most of her pre-teen years with her nose in a book. Reading was her first passion, and then with adolescence came her second passion: Zachary B.

"He was just so beautiful – that's what got to me first," continued Helen. "There was this poster in the window of Athena – between Van Gogh's *Starry Night* and that lady tennis player with no knickers. I had no idea who he was, but I just had to have that poster. And the funny thing was, I didn't even try to find out who he was. He was just my exotic prince. Then Mr Stewart, one of the trendier teachers, asked us all to bring in our favourite record. Obviously I was the laughing stock for bringing in Sibelius's Fifth. But Sofia Griffin got a big cheer when she strutted up to the front of the class with *Mellow Dramas of a Generous Heart*. When she held up the sleeve, I thought my heart was going to explode. There he was, my Athena prince, in a Venetian-red robe with some ivy-covered chunks of classical architecture behind him. All very Pre-Raphaelite." She smiled at the memory. "I just blushed and blushed, certain all the other girls could read my mind. And the more I thought about how red I was going, the redder I got. Sure enough, Gayle Wilson noticed first. 'Miss, Miss – look at Helen Wheeler, Miss. She's gone as red as a beetroot!' But everyone hated Gayle Wilson anyway, whereas they just thought I was weird. Sofia mumbled something about the record being better than Slade, and then she lowered the stylus. My first thought was that Sofia should look after her records better. It was so scratched up." She paused and looked into my eyes, perhaps to make sure she wasn't boring me, but I was captivated.

"You should write, you know. I can picture the whole scene. So then what?"

She seemed thrilled by my praise, but covered it well. "There's not much more to tell. It was an epiphany, simple as that. As soon as the first song *Avenue Paris* faded, my love for Zac became more complete, more three-dimensional. I'd worshipped that poster and that had been enough. But the fact he could also make this amazing other-worldly sound. It was a kind of validation of my own judgement – my own instinct about that face, which I'd known had to belong to someone with a beautiful spirit." She smiled at the memory. Then her face fell, and her eyes welled up with tears. "It's just so sad that he seems to have lost his muse. I still write to him most weeks – though not as often as I used to – trying to encourage him; recommending books and classical music – things I think he might like. I know he probably never even sees my letters, but it feels good to write them… What about your childhood?"

She had taken me by surprise again. But then I took myself by surprise, by talking about stuff I'd never talked about to anyone before. I always spoke of my brother, Phil, as if he were still alive. But he had died in a car crash coming back from some village hall disco after a gig. It happened just days after our all-night Hendrix wake. Following my confession, Helen seemed to look at me with renewed interest. I had become more substantial to her, somehow. I never told anyone about Phil, or the fact that my mum and dad weren't around anymore either – cancer and heart attack, respectively – because it just started relationships off on the wrong footing. When I moved to London, only a few weeks after Phil died, it was an opportunity to reinvent myself – to move on from both my provincial identity and my ghost family.

Helen leant back, tipping her chair onto its back legs, studying me with friendly astonishment. "Boy, you've had it rough, but you hide it well. I suppose everyone hides these things well. So who was the last person you talked to about all this?"

I'd made a pyramid of sugar on the table by tearing open several of those little paper packets and pouring out their contents. I smiled. "I almost spilt the beans to Zac a few years ago. But they all thought I was an oddball already, so I didn't want to add fuel to their perceptions. And I liked the new me. If you act the part, you eventually become the part. And that was Zac too, wasn't it? Playing a part?"

"You're talking as if he doesn't exist anymore…"

"Well, he doesn't, in a way. Don't you feel that? Who knows if he'll ever make another record?" I said, dejectedly.

"But if he's happy, that's the main thing isn't it?"

"Is it? I think the main thing is that he makes more music. That's his destiny."

"Oh don't be so pompous, Paul. He's a human being. He can do what he likes."

"Well that's rich coming from you – someone who hasn't given him a minute's peace in eight years!"

We bickered, joked, sulked and laughed for another hour or so. But I kept my cool regarding Helen's knowledge of Zac's address. For one thing I didn't want to confirm her suspicions that I wasn't privy to such information myself. Then, as Helen got up to go, she wrote something down on a used envelope she took from her bag, folded the envelope in half, and placed it on the table in front of me. She then put a fifty pence-piece on top of the folded envelope.

"To cover my teas and apple pie," she said, tapping the fifty pence piece..

I tried to protest, but she was having none of it. She briefly rested what I took to be a consoling hand on my shoulder, and then left. For a second, I felt protective of Helen as I watched her look momentarily confused about which direction to head in as she stepped back onto the high street.

I unfolded the envelope. In Helen's neat, girlish hand were her contact details, Zac's South Downs address and, for some reason, Brian's address and telephone number. I was brought back to reality by the surly waitress gathering up the tea set's worth of cups and plates that we'd accumulated.

That envelope sat on my bedside table untouched for a couple of weeks. I hated the fact that I wouldn't have had it, if it hadn't been for Helen. It symbolised a complete reversal of our roles. I'd been the one with the power – the information – now it was her. I never did find out how she got hold of the information – maybe through fan club connections. But it was another wound to my self-esteem. That envelope was the proverbial last straw that broke my bent and buckled back. I know how pathetic this is going to sound, but when Zac left London my life simply stopped. Obviously it wasn't Zac's fault that I didn't have a girlfriend or a social circle outside of his crazy little world, but that was the truth of the matter. Perhaps dear reader, you thought I had just left my friends and girlfriend out of this memoir because they weren't central to the story? Oh if only that were true! But no, my one true love was music, because music loved me back. Music gave me the benefit of the doubt. Music stuck with me through thick and thin. Music indulged my mood or rescued me from it. T. S. Eliot wrote of a life measured out in coffee spoons, but my life was measured out in platonically perfect guitar solos and majestically sublime choruses. I'm sure you understand. We've all had moments in our insignificant lives, dignified, memorialised or immortalised by a three-minute pop song. Treasured moments, banal moments; the popular song isn't fussy. That first playground crush encapsulated in a sentimental ballad. That first under-the-sweater grope pumped out as a testosterone-charged rocker. Or even the song that was playing the most during that summer you spent stacking shelves in the local supermarket.

Each forever makes its mark, for better or worse, until death do you part. I still have my first record player (a Cavalier Record Reproducer – a four-speed (16, 33, 45 and 78 rpm), mid-twentieth century design masterpiece, even though two of its speeds were already redundant when I bought it with hard-earned paper-round money). I smile a nostalgic smile every time I look at it. Unfortunately, nostalgic smiles are the only kind of smile that I can muster these days.

However, I digress. It's hard to write about what I'm going to need to write about next, but I'm getting there. Zac and Jody didn't contact me once after they moved to the country. Not even a phone call. A month or so before Helen gave me Zac's contact details I had tried calling Valentine to get Zac's new phone number. Valentine's undisguised irritation crackled down the line at me.

"Look, Paul. Zac isn't seeing or speaking to anyone at the moment." A pregnant pause. "You're part of a time he feels he's moved on from…"

I told Valentine that Jody had invited me to visit when we'd said goodbye at Waterloo Station, but perhaps because I hadn't even been convinced myself by her throwaway, 'you must come and visit us,' I wasn't going to be able to persuade Valentine of its validity. He'd never liked me anyway.

"My instructions were to give no one contact details. End of story. They're making a new life for themselves down there," Valentine continued. I thought quickly.

"I need to fill in some gaps in the biography. I'm sure if you told Zac it's me?"

"Sorry, Paul."

"There's just this section of the book which I—"

The line went dead.

That phone call had a bad effect on me. For weeks I veered between anger and a kind of ecstatic self-pity. Zac and I had never really been friends. I had been used – just like countless other poor souls who got drawn into Zac's black hole orbit. I had just about kept it together since Trafalgar, but only just. Career-wise I was getting less and less work from *Rock On*. Barney's smug smile said it all: "I was right and you were wrong – Zachary B and his ilk were just a flash in the pan." I'd been *Rock On's* way of getting to Zac, but now Zac had ridden off into the sunset they no longer needed me. The paper was now full of new young-gun writers who'd come in on the coat-tails of punk. I loathed punk, so I'd been left behind.

I got up when my body refused to let me sleep any longer. And I worked half-heartedly on this memoir that, at the time, one publisher had actually shown a passing interest in (who could blame them for cooling off on the project, given the downward trajectory of the second half of the book?) But at least that publisher's chapter deadlines stopped me from going under completely. I just focused on the words, tapped away at the keys, and only stilling my hands when Mr K shuffled passed my door (I owed him three months rent). I'd look at Demis curled up on the bed and think: you and me, Demis – we'll let the world pass us by, and only wake up when were hungry. I should have been trying to forget about Zac, but because of the book even that was impossible. In fact, as I reread my tea-stained manuscript (yes, *tea*-stained not *tear*-stained), I began to see certain events and conversations in a new and less agreeable light. It was as if he was taunting me from between the lines. I also listened to all the interview cassettes I'd accumulated again, detecting condescension in Zac's tone that I'd not been aware of at the time. Or there'd sometimes be something about the way he laughed… Eventually, it hit me. It wasn't *my* opinion he'd wanted each time he'd asked me about a song or an LP cover design, it was a generic fan's opinion – I was his generic fan. And all the shit he'd had me deal with: talking to Helen, looking after Jody, driving him to the fucking off license at three in the morning… I tried not to get angry, but trying not to get angry just makes you angrier.

And then I bumped into Helen at the café. That afternoon cheered me up no end. When I got back to the bedsit that evening, I was shocked by the sight that greeted me. I couldn't believe that the deep-pile carpet of balled-up sheets of paper – with the odd fast-food container shipwrecked on this sea of wasted words – was all my own work. But I still crunch, crunch, crunched my way across this ocean of debris, and sat down to my Airfix-kit-curry and supermarket-brand beer. And then Demis died. Or rather, Mr K had him put to sleep. "He was crapping everywhere," was the only explanation I got from the murdering bastard. That cat's murder upset me far more than it should have done. Have you ever stuck your face into a cat's furry belly? The sensation is a synesthetic orgy of the subtlest, loveliest unnameable smell and an almost intangible feathery softness. Demis never did his business in *my* room, so it was nice to know there'd been some mutual respect.

My personal crisis deepened over the next few days. I began re-examining my behaviour towards Zac. Was it something I said? Or was it because I didn't take hard drugs, so never shared that great illusory journey of intoxication – upward to some dizzy hour of laughter and heightened perceptions, and then down again to idealistic but profoundly ignorant political debate at three the following morning? We all have the Fortresses of Solitude of our own heads, but an acid trip or line of coke creates the illusion of those fortress walls coming down, doesn't it? But when Zac and Jody gave me mushrooms, it was a complete disaster, so I couldn't win. I spent hours thinking along such lines while loathing myself for doing so. Then, one morning, (or perhaps, afternoon) I decided, enough! I gathered up everything on the floor into bin bags, washed all the mugs, cutlery and plates I could find (crusty ancient pottery and strange iron-age tools beneath my paper sea), and by the time I'd finished, it was early evening.

Exhausted, I sat down to watch the six o'clock news. There was a report about a planned bypass that would obliterate the beautiful landscape near the village of… yes, you've guessed it, Shoreford. While my beans-on-toast coagulated and cooled, I stared in disbelief at the raincoated TV reporter outside the quaint village station. So now what? The answer had to be a beer. But this was the new me, so I couldn't just trudge down to the off-licence and haul a four-pack back to the cave. I had to go out.

Ten minutes later I was in my local, sipping a pint of IPA as if it were a restorative soup, waiting for my brain to enlighten me as to what to do next. It's interesting how alcohol simultaneously defuses thought and focuses it. By the time I'd finished my second pint, I knew I had to speak to Zac. It was that simple. I had to find out if Zac's rejection of me was just a fiction Valentine had invented, a fiction I had invented, or if there was some other more mundane reason for Zac and Jody's silence.

I looked around the pub at the hapless, the hopeless and the dying, and realised how easy it would be (as easy as falling off a bar stool) to end up like them: drinking as though my life depended on it, when in fact it was my death that depended on it. I grabbed my coat and left. The damp, cold air fired me up, and informed me of what to do next. I remembered Brian's address was also on the envelope Helen had given me. I'd not seen Brian for years, and East Dulwich was only half a mile down the road. Maybe he'd like to go with me to visit Zac? For some reason, I was nervous about going on my own. I went back to the pub to give him a ring.

★

Merrywood Estate was a dump. Needless to say, the piss-perfumed lift wasn't working, so I climbed the three flights of concrete steps, carefully avoiding eye contact with the ashen-faced youth who barged past me just before I reached Brian's door. I was touched that he seemed pleased to see me, but he looked like he would have been pleased to see anyone.

"Well timed, mate. I only just got back meself."

His low-ceilinged flat smelt of fried onions with a base note of overcooked sprouts. The lumpy sofa looked like a Henry Moore reclining nude with a sofa cover thrown over it. I opted for the only other seating – a wooden kitchen chair – and watched Brian through the kitchen door as he fished a couple of mugs from the sink and wiped them half-heartedly with a paper towel. His Ziggy hairstyle had retreated and greyed, combats and a T-shirt had replaced loons and a silk jacket, and a burgeoning beer gut swelled incongruously above legs that were still pipe-cleaner thin. Poor old Brian: still clearly without the money he was entitled to, and back on the dole. He handed me my tea and sat down as comfortably as his sofa would allow.

"So what do you want to see that cunt for anyway?" I felt acutely embarrassed.

"I've not had much work lately and I thought I might be able to get a piece out of it…"

"Jammie Dodger?" Brian passed me the packet. He looked more than tired – like a punctured and stamped-on football. Brian read my thoughts. "You're thinking, how could he have sunk so low?" He took out a pouch of tobacco and made the skinniest roll-up I'd ever seen. "Don't worry, I'm used to it. Look, I walked out after Trafalgar, and I've not seen him since. I can't afford to take him to court, so…"

"I'm sorry…"

"*You're* sorry. Look, take your fucking WH Smiths notebook and go and see your precious Zachary B-for-buggering-bastard, but I ain't going to be keeping you company."

"Are you sure I can't buy you a pint before I go?" I said, after an hour or so of directionless chatter.

"Nah, you're all right. The local's a shit-hole anyway," replied Brian. But I could see that a light had gone on behind his eyes at the thought of a beer.

"Oh come on, Brian. You look like you could do with a pint. It's on me."

I knew I was putting off what I needed to do, but the two pints I'd had earlier were pining for company. We sat at a table by the deceased fruit machine. Brian was soon venting.

"Valentine's a tight-fisted fucker too. I blame him as much as Zac. He trained Zac. We did this short tour of

France in '76; went over on the ferry and used the support band's gear. I had to insist the band got cash – English notes, no fifties – coz otherwise the money would have been swallowed up by the band's overdraft. But guess who flew first class and stayed in a five-star?"

"Jesus…"

"Have a second guess."

"No, I mean…"

"Yeah, I know what you mean. Let me tell you something else: when the band finally split – about four months after I walked out – we got together for a kind of celebratory drink, minus Zac of course. It was a way of dealing with it all, I suppose. But it was hardly a celebration. It was late, they'd called last orders, and suddenly we all went really quiet. It was weird because it seemed to hit us all at the same moment – what fucking dummies we'd been. We had fuck all to show for five years work. We'd been too busy getting laid and shovelling shit up our noses to even think about the future. And now Colin's back with his mum in Balham, Spike is back to the flat-share he had with some old art school mates, and I'm…" Brian's shoulders sagged wearily, and he lost focus for a moment. Then he continued on a different tract. "Valentine should have given up on Zac after Trafalgar. But he never liked to admit defeat. He was so pissed off he couldn't look Zac in the eye for weeks. But that vulture… it is a vulture isn't it?"

"Yeah, I think so. If that's what you mean."

"But that vulture thought there still might be some meat left in Zac. But Zac had become like his… now what are those other big bastard birds called?"

"Albatross?"

"Yeah, albatross. He should have bailed out, rather than get in even deeper, trying to launch the cunt's solo career. What a fucking farce that turned out to be!"

We both laughed. I told Brian about the video shoot, the useless doves and everything; we laughed some more. Brian rummaged in his jeans pocket for some cash to buy the next round – it was agonising to watch.

"No, really, Brian. This is on me." I waved a pound note in front of his face. "Just one more and then I'll leave you in peace. This stuff could end up in my book. And you'd have got a darn sight more from the *Sunday Mirror* than just a couple of pints." This argument seemed to satisfy him. He chuckled and relaxed.

"Remember that shot of him on the cover of *High Profile*? What a pillock!" He rolled another three-strands-of-tobacco cigarette. "He looked like a cross between Simon Le Bon and Farrah Fawcett-Majors. I look at it whenever I need cheering up. The bleached mullet, the pink suit with the mile-wide shoulders. And trying to make some crusty Thames tug look like a classy Mediterranean yacht. Priceless!"

"That was when everything *really* went pear-shaped."

"Including his hairstyle." Brian laughed.

"I always thought it was a wig." I replied. But Brian had become distracted by the barmaid clearing our table.

"What became of that stalker girl? Did you ever give her one?"

"No, Brian, I never 'gave her one' but I've seen her a few times over the years. She's actually quite nice. But, you know, we never…"

"Yeah, well. They often *seem* nice. But that one spelt danger. Zac told me that after Lennon was shot, Jody started intercepting all her letters and destroying them."

"But what kind of 'dangerous person' would give their victim a home address and telephone number?" I asked, in Helen's defence.

"A bonkers one?" offered Brian.

When Brian's attention almost immediately returned to the barmaid, I realised the novelty of my company had worn off.

"I'm going to have to get going, Brian."

"No problem, mate. Good luck and all that."

★

With the long ribbon of the motorway rushing smoothly beneath me, I felt better than I'd felt in months. I'd drunk more than I should have, but I knew that if I put off the trip until tomorrow I probably wouldn't go. It had to be tonight. It was still relatively early and I'd be there before ten if I didn't get lost. Everything would be fine once I'd spoken to Zac. We'd laugh at how Valentine had got it all wrong, and that of course he was delighted to see me. And would I like to hear some new tracks he was working on? The thought of new tracks took me back to 1968 and the first time I ever heard a Zachary B song. I remember slipping *Niagara Falls Again* from its white paper sleeve, studying the vivid red fly agaric mushroom logo on the label, and then lowering the weighty stylus onto its spinning surface. Even my record player seemed to love that single! I would stare at it, hypnotised, as the slight warp of the vinyl caused the player's arm to appear to bop in time to the beat. One revisionist critic recently described *Niagara Falls Again* as "a taut slice of proto-punk." But even I concede that its lo-fi credentials were more an accidental by-product of a cheap four-track studio, than Zachary anticipating the punk sound of the late 1970s.

Back in the present, I had a pleasing moment of lateral perception. The dark glistening tarmac beneath my wheels became the record, and my car, the stylus; I was the stationary stylus as the road rushed beneath me at a steady 45 rpm. Oh to be a stylus! You can't get closer to the music than that! As the miles from London clocked-up, I found myself feeling surprisingly buoyant. Whatever the outcome of my visit was, I would accept it. It was time to move on and grow up.

It's been said, over the years, by the usual suspects, that my relationship with Zachary Bekele was unrequited love, but I would emphatically deny that. It was hero worship, plain and simple. Previous generations of young men needing male role models had looked to army generals, cricketers, film and TV stars. But for someone of my generation it was the sexually ambiguous, otherworldly pop stars that changed how we saw the world and ourselves. Cultural historians still haven't had much to say on the life-changing influence of glam rock's most glamorous male stars. We're talking about a major overthrowing of a tribal-binary (to use Zac's own terminology) division here: men and women. Suddenly sexuality-as-persona became a spectrum rather than just the dead duality it had been for centuries. Perhaps the reason for this dearth of serious analysis is that glam rock is still viewed as something of a cultural joke, thanks to the curse of the bandwagon jumpers: those "builders dressed as princesses" (as Zac put it) with their stubble and acne-pocked jaw lines making a mockery of their meticulously glossed lips. In essence, there were two glam rocks: the mutton dressed as lamb Second Division, and the gods dressed as goddesses, First Division. The latter changed lives, the former merely provided video footage for look-at-how-funny-the-70s-were TV clip shows. As I pulled into the long gravel drive, I told myself I'd be calm and friendly, regardless of my temperamental pop star friend's mood. But that didn't stop me being somewhat crestfallen when, after two protracted rings of the doorbell, I found myself facing a frowning Zachary Bekele, already in his kimono silk dressing gown (it was only ten-thirty), theatrically consulting his watch.

"What on earth are you doing here?" he asked, with a quite unnecessary amount of undisguised distaste.

Extract from *The KUU Hypothesis* by Zachary Bekele

10. DON'T WORRY ABOUT DEATH – IT'S NOTHING

If you need something to anchor you in this slippery world of KUUism here are two facts I encourage you to accept as gospel:

1. The sun will come up tomorrow (regardless of what our sun-worshipping ancestors may have thought).

2. One day your precious dream of a life will end.

We'd all like to know what happens after 2, but the desire to know won't deliver the answer. It's either not useful for us to know, or there is nothing to know because Nothing is all that awaits us. Answers have been offered in authoritative tones for as long as the question has been asked. In fact, anyone with the merest inkling of an idea as to what's in store after death is guaranteed an attentive, hopeful audience hanging on their every word. That's why organised religions are so successful, death keeps their fires burning. But death is Nothing and because it's Nothing (or Nothingness) it's nothing to worry about.

Let's Calm Down About Death

If you watch an old black and white film of a cityscape teeming with people, it doesn't fill you with dread because it depicts a world in which you didn't exist. So try to imagine future footage of a hectic world of humans going about their business which, once again, you are not a part of. It's not that painful is it? Death as Nothing is surely better than death as eternal torment – the alternative offered up to sinners (therefore, all of us) by other religions? Perhaps our deep-rooted fear of death stems from a fear of the afterlife punishments our judgmental religions have lined up for us? Yet death is the end of debt, responsibility and toothache.

A More Cheering KUU Hypothesis in Regard to Death

But if nothingness still fills you with dread, as a KUUist you can entertain the possibility that whatever you personally want for your post-corporeal existence could actually be yours. As previously suggested, in an infinite universe there are, logically, infinite possibilities. So I propose that all KUUists might get the afterlife they desire for being such unswerving entertainers of possibilities.

5

London, December 2005

Paul Coleridge didn't think the Future was futuristic enough. In fact, on that dishwater December morning in 2005, it was no more futuristic than the gaudy yet grimy fabric of his train seat.

"Yeah-yeah-yeah. Okay... hello... hello? I got bad reception, innit – the train and shit. Phone me when you get home. Yeah... no... cool."

"You know, I rang him, and he was like, you know. So fuck 'im – jer-get-me?"

The conversations that erupted all around him like firecrackers had been eviscerated of substance and content. Everyone was telling everyone else... absolutely nothing. This future seemed devoid of forward momentum, sheen or optimism. It was only two hours since Coleridge had been thrust back into the churning chaos of London, but already he couldn't wait to escape it. Nothing he'd seen on TV could have prepared him for how much things had changed and yet hadn't changed.

On the surface, the change wasn't obvious: the music the kids were listening to was just a diluted, sanitised version of what Zachary, Bolan and Bowie had done. And London was just as sunless and prosaically satanic as he remembered it. But there were a couple of big differences. Firstly, the LED screens everywhere, even at the bus stops; even on the buses.

317

And secondly... well, at first he had thought half the city had gone insane when he saw so many people on the streets apparently talking to themselves. Then he realised they were on mobile phones, but they were on mobile phones *all the time*, so maybe they had gone insane? Of course he'd seen mobiles on TV. But TV hadn't informed him that people constantly needed to communicate where they were, which shop they were passing, how many minutes it would be before they got home, or got to the office – or that they were: on the bus, on the way home, or on the way to the office. And *everyone* had a mobile, even the tramp outside the tube station. Who was the tramp phoning? His mum? Other homeless people?

When they got to Victoria, Merrick bought Coleridge a coffee and a crayfish and rocket sandwich. Rocket? What was rocket? The sandwich was so chilled it tasted of nothing. Rocket turned out to be lettuce, and although the coffee was stronger than he was used to, it was all froth. But at least these irritating distractions stopped him from shaking for a while.

At Coleridge's request, they had gone for a pint (he so needed a pint) before beginning their journey to Gatwick to catch their flight to Marrakech. He was shocked to discover that pubs were still chocolate-brown caves with mustard-yellow ceilings (or maybe they'd just become so again?) and still played *Jeepster* and *White Riot* loud enough to make everyone talk more loudly, but not loud enough for the music to be heard above the hubbub. But at least the London Pride hit the spot, and put him in a better frame of mind for travelling.

On the Gatwick train, Coleridge watched but didn't watch the receding city mutely sparkling below an ominous El Greco sky. As it got darker, a billion twinkling windows were left behind, making his own reflection suddenly visible in the train window. The train's brutal overhead lighting made a coarse landscape of his face; how old he'd become – not that this information hadn't been available to him before, it was just that now, on this train – with Barney snoring volcanically in the seat next to him – there was no escaping his ghostly, ghastly self. With a detached objectivity borne of exhaustion, he realised that he looked both sad beyond words and blankly emotionless: a lost soul in this world from which he'd been snatched nearly a quarter of a century earlier. He didn't fight Barney's will, because he no longer had a will left to fight with. Marrakech was as good a solution as any to help him deal with the new kind of Time that was suddenly opening out before him. *The Life and Death of Zachary B* had been published in 1990. It had generated a considerable amount of money, which Barney promised him access to once they got to Morocco, but he couldn't imagine what use this money would be to him.

Marrakech, February 2007

Merrick addressed August and Damian with the bedside manner of a village doctor. "I need to warn you about Paul. As you know, he's been through a lot. And he's still a little fragile."

Damian stared at Merrick, aghast. "Now why doesn't that surprise me? The guy was already fucked up, even before you made him the king of the fucking castle..."

Merrick ignored him. "So it might be in your best interests, as well as his, if, for security reasons, I remain in the room with you."

"Plus, of course, you want to keep an eye on us," said Damian.

"Whatever you think is best," said August, trying to keep the anxiety out of her voice.

While they stood on the threshold of Coleridge's apartment, August could only smell new carpet. But, as soon as the door slid open, she was hit by a sour fug of stale clothes, cheese and onion crisps and other unnameable, unthinkable odours.

"You'll acclimatise," said Merrick, making the universal hand gesture of 'ladies first.'

August tentatively entered the apartment, with Damian and Merrick close behind. Damian immediately began to take pictures of a living space that looked like it had been turned over by a drunk, angry, and possibly blind burglar. Apart from the lightning bolt, shaved head, black shirt and jeans, Coleridge had made one other gesture of goodwill towards his guests. He had adjusted the angle of his recliner to a more upright position. He occupied it with the strained poise of an enthroned king, a bottle of gin held before him like a sceptre. When he spoke it was similarly awkward and formal.

"It's a pleasure to meet you at last, August. You look so much like your mother... and father for that matter. I was hoping we could talk privately, but from the look on Barney's face I can see that's not to be. Please, do sit down."

Even Merrick lost some of his studied calm when he saw Coleridge. "Where's your hair? You look like a glam rock Mussolini!"

"Thanks for the vote of confidence, Barney."

Remembering that it was imperative Coleridge wasn't upset, Merrick quickly made amends. "Actually you look... interesting. Is it all your own work?"

"No, of course not. Jamila did it. She's a real artist."

Merrick scrutinised Coleridge's *Aladdin Sane* lightning bolt. "She's done a fine job. But you're not switching alliances I hope?"

"Don't be ridiculous, it's just a look."

"And a very striking one, if I may say so."

Coleridge narrowed his eyes at Merrick in an attempt to ascertain if he was being made fun of. Merrick's smile was as inscrutable as ever, so he let it go. As the interview – for want of a better word – progressed, August felt like she was a reluctant relative waiting for this man to die, as he attempted to make peace with the world. She was surprised to discover that Coleridge had the fragmented air of someone in their eighties rather than fifties. He ignored questions, went off on tangents and laughed at inappropriate moments. More than once, Merrick indicated to August and Damian by facial expression that it was best just to let him do this thing his way.

"Dr Sanderson, dear Dr Sanderson, she never would tell me her first name – but I respected that. She said I needed to finish my book on Zachary as truthfully as I could; put some demons to rest. I had to embrace the child in me. Yes, I had a rapport with Dr Sanderson. Her hair was always pulled tightly back in a bun. It seemed to open her eyes wider, make her look more attentive..." Coleridge lost focus for a moment, so August took the opportunity to interrupt with a question. She hadn't exactly acclimatised yet, but at least she'd stopped shaking.

"I read somewhere that you underwent some kind of regression therapy..."

"Yes, it scared the shit out of me. We'd tried the hypnotism route a couple of times before, but no joy. But this time I went under. I was back there – in the house, Zac's house. But did any of what I remembered actually happen?" Coleridge gave an exaggerated shrug. "Who can say? But the person who stared back at me from the bathroom mirror was covered in blood. I mean, *really* covered in blood. At first I didn't even recognise myself. I was red from head to foot – an absolute mess!" Coleridge checked his audience for reactions, perhaps expecting to see shock or revulsion, but all he saw was studied calm and concerned attention. He took a long gulp of gin and signalled to Merrick for a cigarette, which was quickly produced.

August became more focused when she realised that Coleridge seemed to be covering ground he'd not been over countless times before in previous interviews.

He leant forward and spoke in an excited, yet hushed tone. "The truth is I felt newly born. I ran my fingers through my blood-drenched hair, staring at my reflection, trying to work out what I was feeling. Then it hit me: this was the blood of birth not death. *My* birth. My rebirth! A baptism if you like. I was petrified and elated at the same time. The man in the mirror was a total stranger yet also a perfect, platonic manifestation of myself. I no longer felt fragmented and vague as a person. I had *become*. Do you understand?" Clearly no one in the room did understand. This momentarily fazed Coleridge, draining him of the will to continue. So again, August took advantage of the break in his monologue.

"So how did you deal with this excavated memory, if that's what it was?"

"It was hard to get my head around it," continued Coleridge, after a couple of deep, wheezy breaths. "But Dr Sanderson explained that this was 'an edge I was now free to step back from'. I'd focused a lifetime's worth of repressed anger, envy and resentment into a single beam of being in control. Do you know *Death Vampire* from *Put Your Glam Rags On*? The last track on Side 1? There's a rumour that Mick Ronson played on it. I was Zac's death vampire."

August had been coping well, but suddenly tears of anger began to well up, threatening to let her down. She discreetly took a few deep breaths, trying to fight the nausea. It was important to stay calm and keep Coleridge talking.

"Are you okay, August?" asked Merrick. "We can stop there if you wish?"

Registering his tactlessness, Coleridge punched the arm of his recliner in exasperation, his face red. "Oh dear, I'm so sorry. Why can't I keep my big mouth shut."

Seeing the interview potentially slipping away, August composed herself. "Calm down, Paul. I'm fine, really. Keep going." She summoned an empathic smile and Coleridge fell for it.

"You really do have Zac's eyes," he said dreamily. "Do you know what *really* cracks me up? I read an interview with your mother in which she said that they just never got around to inviting me to the farmhouse. Can you believe that? *Never got around to it.* Your mother *knew* I wasn't going to be sneaking him bags of smack like the rest of their London circle, and yet… You see, if they had *got around* to calling, he'd be alive today. So that big *why?* that everyone from the psychiatrists to the tabloid hacks have been asking for decades has a very simple answer: *because that's how things panned out.* Maybe Jody was going to phone me but the doorbell rang and the impulse was forgotten; so it was the village postman's fault. There's no more a single answer to their stupid *why* than there was to all the cosmic *why* questions Zac used to bore me shitless with. No offence."

"None taken," August said, reflexively.

"The Knowing Unknowable Universe needed Zac dead so that Zac's philosophy could be communicated to the world. That's why I'm here. *I* was the instrument the KUU used to bring about the necessary death of the great Zachary Bekele."

Now a sobbing Paul Coleridge had ownership of that italicised 'I'. Merrick gripped Paul's shoulder consolingly while simultaneously addressing August and Damian. "I think we need to call it a day, folks."

But Coleridge hadn't finished. Through a soggy paper tissue he continued. "I'm sorry but it just does my head in. They *respect* me here – how sick is that? I'm their living link to a legend. *I'm* a legend – by proxy anyway. It's fucked up, that's what it is." August was about to interrupt, but Coleridge raised his hand to indicate his need to continue. "Your mother Jody was – *is* – a very perceptive and giving person, August. She told me I had a masochistic streak to my personality – a need to be the victim. I sulked at the time, but she was right. I've always been perversely drawn to my tormentors, always coming back for more, rather than walking away. People become frightened by my need – no one wants that kind of responsibility. And now..." Coleridge looked around his ramshackle kingdom. "And now people queue for hours to pay their respects to me. Aren't I courageous to have gone through all this? How gracious I've been in accepting my responsibility to spread the wisdom of Zachary Bekele. It's really, really scary."

"Oh I see. So you're the victim?" August tried to keep the edge out of her voice, but her widening eyes indicated her agitation. Coleridge had become distracted by his reflection in the window. He'd been constantly, nervously touching his face, so his lightning bolt now looked like a huge, hideous bruise. "If only I'd been cuddled more as a child," he said to his reflection.

"Enough!" said August, rising to her feet.

"Please hear me out, August. And not just as a child – I've never, ever had any of that." August reluctantly sat down again. "I've never held someone else's hand or got lost in someone else's eyes across a restaurant table." Coleridge laughed. "Jesus, I'll be singing *Light the Way* next! But I'm not just being a big softie, it's the truth. And it's a hard truth, not a soft truth."

For a moment everyone was speechless. Then Merrick said, "Maybe we should move on?"

For another hour Coleridge drank gin, smoked Merrick's cigarettes and surrendered to his fragmented memory as it jumped backwards and forwards in time. When he mentioned seeing Zachary's funeral on TV for the first time, years after the event, and how it made him realise the vast black-hole gravity of what he'd done, August interrupted with the inevitable question – how could he live with himself? Coleridge looked faintly exasperated, as if he'd expected better from her.

"You people never tire of asking me that one. As if you think I'm suddenly going to say, 'good point,' and spontaneously raise a gun to my head and blow my brains out. I live with myself because that's all I've got, and because there's so much more to me than the person who did that terrible thing. Zac may have said that death is nothing, but the other side of the coin is that life is *everything.*"

"Talking of blowing one's brain out, Paul," began August, sitting forward. "Do you have any thoughts on all these gun-related suicides?"

Coleridge spent so long looking down at his blue and red smudged hands that August thought he'd slumped forward into sleep. Then he raised his head and repeated his De Niro shrug. "Search me. We've got nutters just like every religion's got nutters. There are KUUists who want the KUU to be something more than it is. They want proof, or hope, or forgiveness – all the bullshit all the other religions dish out. Maybe their disappointment led them to do what they did?"

Damian paused in his picture-taking. "Isn't it just a little a bit of a coincidence that all the suicides were shots to the head with the same kind of gun? And what about rumours that in every case there were two spent cartridges rather than just the expected one?"

"Coincidence? You want to talk about coincidence?" Coleridge began, laughing uncontrollably. "Coincidence

325

is what it's all about, my young friend!" Coleridge clearly resented this interjection from a mere photographer. He fired a look of spoilt-child aggression at Damian before continuing.

"Conspiracy theories and nothing more. Sometimes I wonder who thinks that stuff up." He went off on another tangent. "Is it a coincidence that Zac's posthumous careers as both anti-guru and rock star symbiotically perpetuate each other?" Again Coleridge rocked with laughter. "I like that: 'symbiotically perpetuate each other'. I should write that down." A worm of snot peaked out of one nostril and then retreated again. "Lennon said the Beatles were bigger than Jesus, but Zac – bless him – is actually a serious contender! He's jumped right to the front of the adored dead rock stars queue. Good for you, Zac!" Coleridge raised his bottle of gin. It looked like he was about to stand up, but then he presumably decided it wasn't worth the effort and slumped back again. August thought of a doomed turtle that had been rolled onto its back. "Yeah, once you're up there, that's it! A dead rock star – just like a new puppy – is forever, or at least forever immune from cultural re-eval... re-val..."

"Re-evaluation," August interjected flatly.

"Yeah, that. Imagine if someone suddenly said Bob Marley, Kurt Cobain or John Lennon were actually fairly average? It just couldn't happen. And now we have Zachary Bekele the Self-fulfilling Prophet. You've got to laugh, haven't you? Everything in his little non-belief system fed into his own myth-making. Remember how the music press obituaries quickly re-calibrated their position on him? That's what dying does for you in show business. As for being murdered? Even better! So much more romantic than just drowning in your swimming pool or choking on your own vomit. And then he even did the whole death and resurrection shtick! It's just that he only did it in a virtual sense. Yet his image is still everywhere. And image, of course, is everything. And virtual reality is as real as real reality these days, isn't it? I certainly feel like I'm in a bloody computer game in this bloody place..." More laughter led to more coughing, which in turn led to more gin. "Think about it – I do all the fucking time. Firstly, if Zac hadn't died then his crap demo of *Light the Way* wouldn't have been turned into the world's new anthem for peace and mutual understanding – and whatever other bullshit you want to read into it. Secondly... fuck secondly! But the KUU is what we'd all been waiting for – people, I mean. You know, the fucking *common* people. We're sick of hate, and guilt, and not eating pork or prawns on Wednesdays or whatever. Everyone *loves* a coincidence. And everyone loves to laugh and needs to doubt. And *I* love prawns and pork. Fancy not being allowed to eat prawns! What's that all about? I FUCKING LOVE PRAWNS!"

Seeing that Coleridge seemed about to hyperventilate, Merrick gently interrupted. "I think what Paul is trying to say is that Zachary Bekele gave us back a sense of wonder, mystery and spirituality without all the moral and instructional baggage that usually comes with the territory. Zachary tuned into a need that the world's non-believers and disillusioned believers alike didn't even know they had. All that spiritual stuff's in our genes. We're predisposed towards spirituality – sometimes against our better judgement."

"Hey, hold your horses there, mate," interjected Damian. "We didn't come here for a KUU sermon...."

Coleridge jumped back into the ring. "Barney, you don't need to tell them what I'm 'trying to say' because I'm fucking saying it! The old doctrines may not cut it anymore, but that god-shaped space in people's hearts still needs filling. Zac's detractors have said he only provided half answers to ill-defined questions, but he never claimed otherwise! That was the point. Look, read this..." Coleridge was suddenly on his hands and knees, rummaging around under his bed. Eventually, he reappeared with a bulging scrapbook of photos and press clippings. He must have looked through it many times because despite his inebriated state he was able to locate the page he wanted almost immediately. "Here. This is what some Cambridge don said about the KUU back in '88. Before it had all taken off."

August took the scrapbook from Coleridge and read the clipping his chubby finger indicated. It was written by the Cambridge academic/celebrity philosopher and serial adulterer, Clinton Ashbury:

> *'The deceptive simplicity of Zachary Bekele's charming and profoundly logical argument for a move away from spiritual diatribe to a more primal yet questioning matrix, has to be seen as representing a seismic shift in theological thinking in the rationalist, science-blinkered Western world we live in. The subversive genius of the man lies in his refusal to actually make refutable points. He has turned fence-sitting into a noble and positive stance... '*

Before August could get any further with the essay, Coleridge broke her concentration with further babbling. "You see, KUUism puts the ball straight back into your court, leaving you to decide to what extent you entertain the possibility." Coleridge's face dropped into a drunkard's caricature of melancholy. "It's just a pity he's not around to see all this. But then if he was, it wouldn't be here to be experienced! Ha! It fucks with your head." Finding the gin bottle empty, he sucked on his inhaler. "I hated *Laughter in the Dark* when Zac first played it to me; I just thought it was a joke, but I listen to it a lot now... Did you know that the sound at the end is Zac screaming but played backwards?"

"Everyone knows that, don't they?" Damian interjected.

Coleridge ignored him. "The silence that follows that scream is actually the silence that, in reality, preceded it. Brilliant eh? It's a scary silence because the scream sounds like it's being sucked away. Barney, stick it on for me would you?"

"Yes, your majesty," said Barney, as he smiled stiffly and walked over to the CD player. August was relieved that something had finally shut Coleridge up. She found the album self-consciously avant-garde which, paradoxically, made it sound all the more dated now. Coleridge tilted back his recliner to watch the darkening sky. He remained silent for the entire length of the piece, so no one else spoke. After the CD finished it was discovered Coleridge was unconscious, so that was the end of the interview. August and Damian knew no more than they had when they'd gone in. Merrick looked relieved. August was grateful for the barely audible insect-like whirr that the CD player made as it switched itself off. Anything was better than the eerie silence preceding Zac's sucked-away scream. It was as if he had known what was to come.

Extract from *The KUU Hypothesis* by Zachary Bekele

THE GRATUITOUS

In keeping with KUUism's contrariness in regard to the doctrines of other religions, evil as a supernatural force had to go, and be replaced by the Gratuitous. Evil is an emotive and provocatively meaningless word. The Gratuitous is that which is without order or purpose. In other words, the neutrally destructive forces outside the KUU's field of influence such as earthquakes, disease, decay, car crashes, cancer and the malicious, egotistical spirit of mankind. There is no battle between Good and The Gratuitous. The Knowing Unknowable Universe is either disinterested, accepting or impotent in regards to the atrophying and sometimes plain destructive influence of the Gratuitous. Therefore, the Gratuitous just keeps on raining down.

The Line Versus the Circle

The KUU is the outwardly spiralling circle of fecundity. The Gratuitous is the razor-sharp straight line with no presence or personality, despite its unarguable directness. It's the unexpected drought that destroys the expected bountiful harvest. The Gratuitous is linear shit hitting the cyclical fan.

The Blinkered Egos of the Saved

But on the positive side (for this is KUUism), the concept of the Gratuitous does away with the notion of the saved or the unsaved. It firmly challenges the blinkered egotism of the solipsistic religious fanatic who walks away from the front-page-news disaster in which many others died, shouting, "God saved me!" We need to accept that the semi-interventionist KUU has no power (or inclination to power?) over our earthly lifespans and so the Gratuitous rains down fire and rubble on innocent babies and convicted rapists alike. There is no 'saved' with the Knowing Unknowable Universe. There is only the lucky and the unlucky. What real sense can be made of a god who saves one individual but lets another thousand individuals die? However, if there is life after death it will be of a kind we can't possibly conceive of. So use the notion of the Gratuitous to keep you grounded and appreciative of every precious moment of your fragile physical existence.

The Gratuitous delivers us from evil (or rather, ego), etc etc, Amen.

Magic Versus Decay

The process of birth and renewal is magical and is the work of the KUU. It is balanced by the certainty of the process of decay leading to death — which may seem persecutory, evil, cruel and meaningless — but is simply the Gratuitous trying to reclaim the natural living universe just as air will try to reclaim a vacuum.

Extract from

The Life and Death of Zachary B
by Paul Coleridge

Zac's Powerless Guardian Angel
February 24th, 1982

Helen became so much a part of the night-time landscape around the Shoreford farmhouse that a family of foxes went about their business around her as if she were just a bush or fence post. If we are to believe Helen's police statement, one of them even brushed against her leg on one occasion. She wrote that the foxes acceptance of her (for that was how she saw it) added to her feeling that this was the place she truly belonged, and that the alternative "real life" she'd begun to make for herself in London was just a dull compromise. This made her feel both happy and sad at the same time – an emotional state she appeared to luxuriate in. The obsessed and delusional will find symbolic significance in even the most mundane of events, so tears sprang to Helen's eyes when that fox brushed past her leg. She interpreted the event as the animal silently informing her that she truly was Zac's guardian angel, because even his terrain and its wildlife embraced her. When she had first written to Zac, Helen had thought of her words as passing from her best Parker fountain pen straight into his head – becoming part of him – just as the words of his songs were a part of her, in her head. She knew he got hundreds of letters a week, which he probably never opened, but that wasn't the point. Denial of reality was a fact of life for Helen. And there was always a higher plain her obsession could rise to – a deeper level of imagined intimacy to aim for.

Watching Zac's house from his picturesquely overgrown backgarden for hours on end was like meditating upon a huge, banal art installation. She would stare up at those bright rectangles of yellow light, waiting for the thrilling moment a shadowy profile passed, or linger for a moment. Or when one rectangle would vanish and another appear a moment later, as Zac or Jody moved from bedroom to bathroom, or kitchen to lounge. Helen said in her statement that she felt like God one minute, and a privileged worshipper of her very own God, the next – alternately omniscient and insignificant. How many deity worshippers get to see and be near the focus of their worship? Yet there was Zac putting the kettle on, Zac boiling an egg, Zac drawing closed the heavy midnight-blue curtains.

When she started taking her camera along, it not only gave her vigils more of a sense of purpose, it also it also gave her something to get excited about when she wasn't at Zac's house: getting home as quickly as possible to develop her pictures. She became the creator of her own Zachary Bekele relics. For, in the mysterious world of art and collectibles, original photos have greater intrinsic value. They are perceived as far more aura-rich than mass-produced photos in magazines. But Helen *was* getting better. Her visits to the farmhouse had become much less frequent. Her first proper boyfriend, Adam – who gave her stuffed animals and helped her see, for the first time, her true worth in his love-struck eyes – was saving her from all this. Thanks to Adam, and the weekly therapy sessions he'd booked her into, she'd even gained some insight into the fact her behaviour was a little unusual. Despite this progress, she still occasionally drove down to the farmhouse for old time's sake. Needless to say, Adam didn't know about these lapses. After all, she didn't want to hurt his feelings when he thought she was doing so well. But this is what was really funny. She decided, for Adam's sake, that this night, February 24th, 1982, was going to be the very last time she drove the 43 miles to Shoreford. She had an interview the next day, which she should have been preparing for, but the nature of her addiction meant she simply told herself this one last visit would bring her luck in the interview. And once she'd decided this was to be the last time, it became even more important that she went.

After phoning Adam to say she was too busy preparing for the interview to see him, she threw the books she wouldn't get a chance to study into the back of the car, and drove to the farmhouse faster than was necessary or legal. She smiled to herself as the endless yellow dotted line got sucked beneath her wheels. She might even say hello to Zachary this time – wouldn't that be something! Yes, suddenly she could imagine saying hello! Zac's power over her was lessening minute by minute – he was slowly becoming Earthly and mortal – she could envisage actually saying hello. But then as the thought of saying hello took hold, her heart-rate increased, and Zac was once again re-imagined as perfect and unreachable. Such was the paradoxical seesaw workings of Helen Wheeler's mind when it came to her exotic prince.

Her unnecessarily detailed police statement went on to describe how she went to her usual spot (at the mulchy roots of a comfortingly large oak tree about twenty yards from the house) and got out her binoculars and camera. She thought she'd take a few photos, drive back to London, and then set up her makeshift darkroom in the bathroom, for the last time, to develop her pictures. They would probably just have been shots of the back or Zac's head, but if she was lucky, Zac might take the dogs for an evening walk, or maybe she'd catch him at a window, alerted by his sixth sense to squint out into the darkness suddenly; willing himself to see what he most feared was out there...

It was at about nine-thirty – just as Helen was about to give up and go home – that she noticed almost every light in the house had been switched on. This was unusual in itself, but she also thought she'd heard a car pulling into the front drive. Normally, she kept what she called, "a respectful distance" from the house (such was her warped logic regarding respect), but tonight was different, tonight was her Last Night. So she walked briskly down the side passageway, following the sound of muffled voices that were just discernable through the dense flint. It sounded like arguing, but she couldn't hear what was being said.

Although it had been dark for hours, Zac still hadn't drawn the curtains. As she edged along the damp walls, she experienced a new frisson of excitement at the notion she could so easily get caught. The first window she reached must have still had the original glass in it, because everything she could see through it rippled slightly if she moved her head at all. Facing each other in the book-lined room were two armchairs separated by a squat oak table. On the table sat a single half-empty beer glass and an ashtray so full it appeared to have erupted cigarette butts. Helen thought of her cigarette butt, back in London, snugly wrapped up in its tissue. A large glowing fireplace made the whole scene almost cornily cosy. This was probably the room where he sat and read her letters! Were any of the books that she had recommended to him on the shelves? She peered in, like a wonder-struck child at a bauble-burdened Christmas tree, trying to make sure she remembered every intimate domestic detail. There was an atmosphere of something having been interrupted, but there was no sign of Zac or anyone else. Then she remembered her camera. She had momentarily forgotten the reason she'd moved closer in the first place. She took several pictures before moving further down the side of the house.

How different the kitchen's chrome and white interior was from the cosy sitting room she'd just been studying. Chrome appliances stood like a platoon of miniature robots along the white marble work surface, awaiting orders. She pointed and clicked twice more; she was getting into the swing of this. But then she heard the voices again – two or more men – disconcertingly nearer this time. Some banging and crashing noises followed. They must have come into the kitchen!

She heard shouting and screaming. Through the camera's viewfinder, she saw a head crack against the inside of the window, only inches from her face. It left a syrupy red smear as it slid down the glass. Helen reflexively jumped back. But, perhaps made fearless by shock and adrenaline, she resumed her position and aimed the camera back into the room. Presumably the lens distanced her from what she was witnessing (as it apparently does for war photographers) because she somehow found the courage to continue on what was now a very different mission. However, she was momentarily unnerved when a man's anger-distorted face appeared to stare straight back at her through the lens. For the past ten minutes she'd relied on the fact that anyone in a well-lit room, looking out into a night unilluminated by street lamps, wouldn't be able to see very much. But, before she had a chance to see if she recognised the man, both he and his victim dropped below the line of the window sill, and out of her field of vision.

She needed to get to a high vantage point. She noticed two old tractor tyres leaning against the wall. With some effort she stacked one on top of the other and clambered up on them. Although her camera continued to control the degree to which she emotionally engaged with the events that were unfolding, what she saw next caused Helen to faint like the sensitive heroine of a Victorian melodrama. What she saw was the angry man wrapping a length of the thinnest steel wire around the neck of her precious Zachary. What she saw next was the centre of her existence having his head virtually cheese-wired from his body as his lifeblood issued forth all over the pristine-white kitchen, as if from a lawn-sprinkler.

Helen was right about me not seeing her on the other side of the window, because – despite the fact I was completely deranged at the time – I do remember freezing for a moment and looking out into the darkness and seeing nothing. Perhaps I was hesitating to question the madness of my actions, or maybe I was just hoping to be stopped or distracted. But I was no more capable of stopping than a lion is able to resist tearing to pieces the antelope it has just felled.

When Helen regained consciousness a few minutes later, like a child from an afternoon nap, she rubbed her eyes and, although disorientated, gathered up her things and walked purposefully back to her car without a backward glance. Shock had done the decent thing and made her temporarily forget what she had just witnessed. This is apparently a fairly common occurrence for trauma victims. If only I had been so blessed. But, yes, we are finally getting to the crux of what this memoir is about. As much as it's the story of the life and death of Zachary Bekele it's also a testament to the lightness of my naivety and the weight of my guilt. I was as innocent of the inexorable approach of this awful moment as you are innocent of whatever unspeakable deeds may lie ahead in your life. But of course there are still unanswered questions. For example, given that I loved and respected Zachary Bekele so much, why did it all end like this?

Extract from *The KUU Hypothesis* by Zachary Bekele

11. DON'T PUSH THE KUU

A Cosmic Nudge is Like a Surprise Gift, So...

don't ask for help, money, a change in fortune or any other material thing that requires the KUU to step-up its semi-interventionist relationship with you. Pushing, is essentially praying, which we've already established is unlikely to get results. If the KUU takes pleasure from surprising us, a prayer – or even just intensely wishing for something – would take away that pleasure. When the KUU nudges you, don't expect fireworks or life guidance: when ambiguity is sustained, your free will is respected. Mystery is essential to doubt, and doubt is essential to being a KUUist.

Be Grateful for Just a Nudge

The KUU may astonish or amuse, but you shouldn't try to control the show, or want proof of the supernatural nature of your experience. One more mini-miracle could tip you over into belief, and that's the last thing the KUU wants. Don't bore your friends with tales of your KUU-incidences. KUUists should know when to shut up; this would make them unique in the realm of the religious.

The Weeping Virgin and the Edible Elvis

For every Virgin Mary crying blood in a Mexican church there's an Elvis on a taco shell: in the warped world of KUUism either could be holy hoax or kitsch miracle. The idea that Jesus was God in human form wasn't finalised until four hundred years after his death. Man can't live with unresolved questions for very long, so Jesus' status as a deity was eventually settled upon, regardless of the fact that no further evidence was forthcoming one way or the other.

6

Marrakech, February 2007

Aladdin Pain
Joined: 24 Jan 2005
Posts: 1023
Location: undisclosed
Posted: Wed Feb 13, 2007 11:45 a.m.
Post subject: To Push or not to Push
I'm a believer, I just can't bloody help myself. The glam god Zachary was sent to us to preach non-belief just to tease us. The KUU wants us to believe, and when we believe it will give us the final affirmation.

Doubting Thomas
Joined: 01 Aug 2006
Posts: 680
Location: Bristol
Posted: Wed, Feb 13, 2007 01:55 a.m.
Post subject: To Push or not to Push
11 days to go!!! It's nearly Happy Deathday time everyone! Are we all ready?

Navelgazer
Joined: 03 Sept 2005
Posts: 681
Location: Maastricht, The Netherlands
Posted: Wed, Feb 13, 2007 02:05 a.m.
Post subject: To Push or not to Push
I've heard Marrakech is awesome! I'll be there but I'm shit scared.

Aladdin Pain
Joined: 24 Jan 2005
Posts:1024
Location: undisclosed
Posted: Fri, Feb 23rd, 2007 12:17 p.m.
Post subject: To Push or not to Push
Don't be scared NG, your better than that. This will be amazing, I promise you. I still can't tell you who I am, but when you find out it will give you strength. Don't forget, if you want to be part of the Final Affirmation you need to get to the Big T party by 10. Embrace your fate. The KUU has brought us all together.

Joe the Lion
Joined: Dec 2006
Posts: 13
Location: Liverpool, England
Posted: Fri, Feb 23rd, 2007 12:42 p.m.
Post subject: To Push or not to Push
But it was the Internet that brought us all together wasn't it?! But seriously. Can't make it mate. No cash. But good luck to you all – you'll need it! ;-) That's some serious shit you're all doing!

Jane E
Joined: Jan 2007
Posts: 01
Location: Lee, Lewisham, England
Posted: Fri, Feb 23rd, 2007 13:05 p.m.
Post subject: To Push or not to Push

Hi guys! I had to tell you all what happened to me and my boyfriend. We'd just got back from one of those package cruises on the Nile in Egypt. The weekend after we were walking through Greenwich Market, and I said that I had a feeling that we were going to bump into someone from the cruise – you know how it is, you spend a week with a group of people you've never met before and it's strange when you say goodbye because you probably won't ever see them again. Anyway, my boyfriend he was like saying *yeah right* or something and looking at me like I was mad. Five minutes later I couldn't believe my eyes. A few feet away is this woman from the cruise and it was the one person we disliked on the cruise because she talked rubbish all the time in a very loud voice. So luckily she didn't see us! We stared at her for a bit because we couldn't believe it was her but we could hear her nattering on just like she'd done on the boat – it was defo her! We thought it was extra funny that the KUU made it the 1 person we least wanted to see again! My boyfriend is now a bit more interested in the KUU!!! Love Jane

Aladdin Pain
Joined: 24 Jan 2005
Posts: 1025
Location: undisclosed
Posted: Fri, Feb 23rd, 2007 12:17 p.m.
Post subject: To Push or not to Push
Great story, Jane – good for you! But could you post it in the New KUUs strand? It might even make the Top 11!!

Jane E
Joined: Jan 2008
Posts: 02
Location: Lee, Lewisham, England
Posted: Fri, Feb 13rd, 2007 13:05 p.m.
Post subject: To Push or not to Push
Sorreee!!! I'm always getting it wrong!!!

Doubting Thomas
Joined: 01 Aug 2006
Posts: 681
Location: Bristol
Posted: Fri, Feb 13, 2007 13:30 p.m.
Post subject: To Push or not to Push
The {{{vibes}}} are really kicking in! Looking forward to the big T party!!! I'll PM you later AP! See u there my KUU brother!

Damian and August had been up all night speed-reading page after page of self-obsessed posts in Malika's Word files, looking for a single crack in the cryptic curtain of chat room banter. All they'd learnt so far was that many of the contributors had a limited grasp of English (usually the English or American ones) and maybe a hundred or more cyberspace acquaintances were coming from all over the globe to meet in Marrakech this week. As to why, that was still a mystery.

Then Damian spotted something. "The Big T Party. Shit, that's it!" He turned from the laptop to face August. "The 'T' is the Tripod. 'Eleven days to go; that was posted eleven days ago. Something big is going down at the Tripod today."

"Do you think it's a Coup KUUist terrorist attack?" August asked. "Shouldn't we tell someone?"

"No and no," Damian replied, firmly. "Aladdin Pain's last post – this one here: I'll be waiting for you all – he or she is there already. They're an insider."

"But who says there's no Coup KUUists working for the Foundation? And who says they couldn't be dangerous?"

"I suppose so, but a terrorist attack? It just doesn't feel like that from reading all this stuff. All these people are looking forward to something. They're excited. We'd have noticed more anger or aggression if they were building up to some kind of attack."

Yesterday, August had emailed her newspaper's office to see if anyone could verify the Internet rumours about the two spent gun cartridges. Her laptop pinged. The email from an overworked assistant editor was typical in its brevity. It simply read:

Not two spent cartridges – one spent, one empty.

The answer was in those eight words: a lateral-thinking puzzle with a sting in its tail. When it hit August it was too much to fully grasp. She could see from Damian's stunned expression that he had simultaneously figured it out. It was all about a potentially fatal act of faith; it was about pushing the KUU. They had to get to the Tripod as soon as possible.

★

A tight-lipped Jamila finished applying a fresh lightning bolt to Coleridge's upturned face. She pulled away as Coleridge tried to kiss her forehead with beneficent condescension for her impressive effort. She said she wanted nothing more to do with the rebirth of mankind. For once, Coleridge wasn't fazed by her behaviour. He simply saw it as naivety and a failure of the imagination on her part. He believed that the Knowing Unknowable Universe was not a vengeful deity, so Jamila would benefit from the Final Affirmation whether she involved herself or not. For it was the whole world – and therefore Jamila too – that would be freed from the albatross of faith by the most mind-boggling KUU-incidence the world had ever witnessed. Because the intervention would be an act of the Knowing Unknowable Universe and *not* an act of Allah, or Jehovah, or Yahweh, or Apollo, or Brahma, or Athena, or Anubis, or Zeus - or even Venus - all religions and creeds past and present would instantly be made redundant by this single act of compassionate intervention by the deity without a face or a hidden agenda: no one would die from an almost inevitable bullet through the brain, and therefore the human race would be instantly freed from millennia of religious conflict by this act of beneficent omniscient compassion from a power that didn't want our prayers, our fear, our guilt or our subservient worship. After all – were they even to exist – would any of the notoriously angry, jealous, insecure gods of old deem to answer a call not specifically and humbly addressed to them? Coleridge knew the answer was no.

Coleridge also believed that news of the Final Affirmation would spread from the Tripod as fast as the media could carry it, which these days that was faster than the speed of sound.

But why today? Because it was the morning of February 24, 2007, the 25th anniversary of Zachary Bekele's Deathday. It was exactly 25 years since Paul Coleridge had seen to it that the Self-fulfilling Prophet met his homemade maker, and now Coleridge was going to find out what destiny the KUU had in store for him and his small tribe of Coup KUUists.

Considering the KUU Foundation had more than 11 million KUUists on its database, the number of people who began to trickle into the Tripod from 8 a.m. onwards was pitiful. After the nightshift workers and overnight guests had abandoned the building following Merrick's triggering of the fire alarm, he dismissed the baffled Security staff telling them – without a trace of irony – that the building needed to be closed for security checks. Although the staff dispersed, the guests – some still in dressing gowns – stood dazed in the early-morning sunlight, dodging donkeys and fending off offers of assistance from opportunist locals.

Coleridge stood behind the security desk, handing each nervous newcomer a brown paper parcel tied up with turquoise ribbon. Each Coup KUUist took their parcel and made their way to the seats nearest the podium. If anyone tried to speak to him, Coleridge just smiled and put his finger to his lips. Consequently, they walked away, perhaps slightly embarrassed, but nevertheless reassured that everything was being done with the appropriate degree of propriety and solemnity. He had never felt this sense of purpose before in his life, apart from when... but that was different, now he was giving rather than taking away. Although, thinking about it, even then he had given: he had given Zachary Bekele to the whole world, and had thus been awarded his own destiny in return.

No more being dragged backwards by his hair towards some arbitrary, chaotic future. He recalled the day in 2005 when Barney had been waiting for him outside Brixton Prison. He should have been grateful to be free, but how could any longer in there have been any worse? Time 'inside' was a manmade construct, dished-out in day-long chunks with each chunk identical to the last. The future had been written out of the equation, especially during the first few years when he just busied himself with *The Life and Death of Zachary B*, watching TV, and exercising. After he'd been told he was to be released (thanks to the single-mindedness of the KUU Foundation's lawyers), time became even more elastic – stretching almost to breaking point, whilst almost stretching him to breaking point. And then one day he was on the other side of that high wall, and there was a broadly grinning Barney waving a rolled-up newspaper to get his attention, as if he were a flight controller bringing in a small private plane. What would have become of him if it hadn't been for Barney? The global media had responded with affected howls of outrage when the KUU Foundation elevated his status to that of a holy man and gave him – of all people – what was affectively a luxury home in Marrakech. This of course caused sales of both *The KUU Hypothesis* and *The Life and Death of Zachary B* to increase even more: people wanted to know more about this non-religion that had trumped Christianity in the forgiveness stakes.

Coleridge remembered a press conference in which a softly spoken Merrick had explained that it was just another KUU paradox – and thus a reinforcement of the whole of Zachary's philosophy – that Zachary had needed Paul Coleridge to bring about his necessary demise. Without

Paul's actions – generated by the Shoreford bypass KUU-incidence – KUUism would never have existed and there wouldn't have even been a KUU Tripod to install Paul in as Zachary Bekele's holiest living representative. In other words, without Paul Coleridge's *love* there would have just been another ageing rock star doing his twentieth Greatest Hits tour, and a pile of notebooks stored away in a cardboard box somewhere. Coleridge found Barney's soothing, bizarrely rational explanation for the pitiful course his life had taken, at least partially consoling: yes, Love – perhaps that was what it was all about after all.

★

At exactly 10 a.m., Merrick keyed in the code to lock all the doors, and Coleridge slowly made his way to the podium, swaying slightly, both hands cradling his Smith & Wesson. He'd found its gun oil perfume curiously comforting over the past few months on the many occasions that he'd handled it, marvelling at its sleeping power (and therefore at the KUU's sleeping power). Studying the engraved image of an atom just above the handle's rubber grip, made him recall Zac's talk of atoms: so tiny and yet so potentially powerful.

★

Zachary B's greatest hits had been blaring out of the speakers for over an hour, dispelling the nerves and elevating the spirits of those entering the Tripod: there was nothing like a bit of nostalgia to help you loosen your grip on the present. But as the Final Affirmation (or 'The Big Push' as some called it) grew nearer, the final movement of Zachary B's mordent instrumental *Laughter in the Dark* swelled into life. Coleridge straightened his back and smiled at the 141 hopeful faces looking up at him, their brown paper parcels pressed to their chests like hot water bottles. He was happy. Everything was going to plan.

★

Five-hundred Smith and Wesson, Model 340s, along with some rifles and machine guns, had been stored in the secret floor beneath Level 1 since the day of the Tripod's completion. There had been a great deal of paranoia – not entirely unfounded – when the Tripod first opened its doors to the public. How were the local Muslim population going to respond to this bold architectural and philosophical encroachment on their world? Even if it was in the nicest possible way, this non-religion was laughing and doubting in their faces. So Merrick had made use of old-school-tie contacts 'back in Blighty' and got the KUU Foundation kitted up with enough weaponry to stop a small army of God-botherers, should they turn up with gnashing teeth and burning torches. When Coleridge heard about this arsenal he realised his burgeoning Russian roulette idea could be made a reality. It was the will of the KUU that this armoury had been made available to him. At least that was how he preferred to recall the sequence of events so as to glean maximum KUU resonance from them. But, in fact, it was only when Merrick told him about the guns that he came up with the idea. Our duplicitous friend, the subconscious, sometimes reshuffles the facts so we can delude ourselves to maximum effect. Coleridge had asked himself, what use had these guns been otherwise? The Tripod had experienced one inept terrorist attack in 2006, during which the van exploded just before it reached its destination, killing the driver and five innocent people. But the explosion hadn't even been heard inside the cloistered interior of the iron and glass fortress.

★

Once Merrick had instigated the evacuation of the Tripod, he went to the CCTV surveillance room on Level 10 to watch events unfold. Settling down to a smoked salmon and cream cheese bagel, he congratulated himself on having the forethought to order breakfast before setting off the fire alarm. Because he found it far more edifying than any of the other facilities the Tripod offered, Merrick spent many idle hours in the surveillance room: this was real reality TV! He could watch the swimmers and the dancers, and then… but never mind all that. Today his voyeurism was taking on a far richer dimension. He leaned in closer to the monitors, like a man about to watch a favourite sports event. Out of twenty screens only three were of concern to him: the first was showing the small stage of the auditorium; the second was showing a crowd gathering in front of the stage; and a third showing the view out from the front entrance.. This last screen, Merrick was pleased to note, currently just showed robed and sandaled locals going about their business as usual, as if the Tripod were invisible to them. Some distance away, he noticed around thirty people in animated discussion. There were agitated guests wondering why they couldn't get back into the Tripod, and deeply distressed Coup KUUists who had missed the 10 a.m. deadline. Occasionally, one or two of them would come up to the entrance to peer in, before returning, dejected, to the main group.

Merrick's hand froze before it could deliver the last morsel of bagel to his mouth. August Bekele and her brattish photographer sidekick had appeared at the main entrance. At least the camera's aerial view made them look reassuringly insignificant. Their faces were pressed to the glass to minimise reflections and shade their eyes as they peered in. Although they couldn't possibly gain entrance, Merrick was disconcerted by the fact that they'd clearly figured out what was going on. He checked his watch; ten minutes to go. Paul would be starting his speech at any moment. He thought of Voltaire's last words '*I go in search of the Big Perhaps.*' There was something KUUish about the Big Perhaps. Might Zachary have read Voltaire? He doubted it.

Merrick turned his attention back to the stage monitor: Paul had jumbled up the notes for his speech and was shakily sorting them out. A smiling, long-haired Coup KUUist in a caftan handed back a sheet of A4 that had drifted to the floor. Merrick repeatedly pressed a button until Paul's absurdly painted face filled the screen. Was the man insane? Merrick wasn't sure. Paul had his lucid days – and he'd been totally focused and single-minded about today. And what if he was right? What if mankind *was* about to enter a new age in which faith and belief were no longer an issue? What if the KUU *was* going to finally treat us as equals by confirming its existence during an event that – as Paul had put it – would make the loaves and fishes look like a suburban barbecue? And Paul's inversion of Russian roulette was brilliant in the way it flipped over that most notorious of fatalist's gambles so as to turn it into a reckless counter-intuitive leap of faith: if you fired a gun at your own head with only one live cartridge in it, you were a brave but foolish man. But if you fired a gun with *five* bullets and only one empty chamber, you were a true Coup KUUist. How could the Knowing Unknowable Universe not respect such a blackly comic devil-may-care gesture of abyss-tempting fatalism? There was a cosmic logic to it, Merrick thought: spiritual need and wishful thinking, holding the KUU to ransom, obliging it to cause the cylinder of every revolver in the auditorium to spin round to its one empty chamber. Halleluiah! There would be a chorus of dull clicks and the human race would enter a new era in which belief and faith were both redundant because the Truth was finally out. The truth being that the world would finally know for sure that there was an omniscient higher intelligence acting as a benign if mischievous force in their lives. Some days Merrick found himself sharing Paul's excitement, but on others he felt sure the man had lost it completely. Paul hadn't even been fazed when the 'suicide' victims began to be reported.

"Why couldn't they have just waited one more month? One more fucking month!" he had screamed at Merrick, throwing the newspaper across the room. "It needs to be all of us, together! The KUU has no respect for impatience. If we behave like children it will treat us like children."

"Isn't that just a little Old Testament, old boy?" Merrick had responded, resting a hand on Paul's shoulder. "Death for being impatient is a little harsh, isn't it? Most of those kids weren't even out of their teens. And in a way you did rather put temptation their way with private-messages telling them where they could get hold of the right kind of gun. If you ask me, I think you wanted to have a few of them test-run this experiment before…"

"Don't be ridiculous! And don't call it an experiment! The KUU didn't kill them, they killed themselves. Or if you prefer, the Gratuitous killed them. The KUU just stepped aside, so to speak – as is its prerogative as a semi-interventionist deity."

Merrick had said nothing more. He was unnerved that Coleridge had become so certain about everything. This wasn't how a KUUist was meant to be. He finished his bagel while continuing to alternate his attention between August and Damian, and the sweat-slicked face of the man who was now slowly and methodically removing his Smith and Wesson from its wrapping and putting it on the lectern in front of him. He had no idea who Coleridge was anymore.

The gathering of Coup KUUists didn't know who Paul Coleridge was either, but it was enough that he was a flesh-and-blood connection to Zachary Bekele. August and Damian would have been interested to learn that the Coup KUUists had never actually been a threat to KUUism. Realising there was always more money to be made from belief than non-belief, Merrick had welcomed them with open arms as soon as he had been made aware of their existence, thus both baffling them and neutralising them as a possible disruptive force in the future.

★

August and Damian could see very little from the front entrance, but they could hear the maudlin din of *Laughter in the Dark* issuing from the Tripod's exterior speakers. Damian paced up and down, talking to himself as much as to August.

"So the 'suicides' were just the sad bastards who couldn't wait. The extra missing cartridge was due to the fact that one cartridge had been removed in the first place. Jesus, this

353

is sick! You know what? Zachary shouldn't have gone on about death meaning nothing. You can't fucking win with this religious shit. Either the unthinking zealots will kill themselves because of some promise of a bunch of nubile virgins waiting for them on the other side, or they'll kill themselves because they think they'll be saved by the power of some motherfucking almighty KUU-incidence. I mean, who in their right mind would indulge in an act of faith that required their god to stop them from killing themselves? And even if they're not saved by the Knowing Unknowable Universe, Zac has told them that death was nothing to get uptight about anyway, so in their minds it's a win-win situation. Fucking idiots"

"But the Near Proofs might have been a factor too," interjected August. "Although, to be honest, I think Merrick put the first two of those in. They're just not open-minded enough for my dad."

"I disagree. As Alice said, 'Near proofs – that's a paradox'. Zachary loved paradoxes, especially funny ones. Look, the whole point is that KUUism was supposed to be the world's first *casual* religion. All this dissection of it is pointless bullshit."

August and Damian were filling in time with idle chatter. They were helpless unless the police turned up. A couple of Coup KUUists, probably Eastern European, came over to ask them if they knew another way in. Further disgruntled guests and Coup KUUists joined their group.

"People take what they want and ignore the rest," said Damian. "Near proof is near enough for borderline believers. Then there's the ultimate tease of the third missing proof. Surely all that dice and Lego stuff is just pseudoscientific slight of hand anyway."

"I think that's a little unfair," interrupted August, not sure if she was defending her father or defending a philosophical standpoint. But whatever she said next was lost in the din of multiple sirens as two police cars and an ambulance threw up a dust storm as they vied for the same limited parking space in front of the Tripod. One car disgorged three officers who immediately began redirecting pedestrians and traffic so as to create more space for other emergency-service vehicles. The sight of the uniformed officialdom of disasters dissolved August's interest in further philosophical debate. But despite the fact that her father's love and common sense had been turned into nihilism and death, she still had one dumb, innocent question left in her, although she didn't imagine Damian would have the answer. "Why is he doing this?"

"Who, Coleridge?" Damian gave a hollow laugh. "Fuck knows. The man's a lunatic, so why even try to explain his actions? We need to find another way in – a fire exit or something."

Damian's words drew the attention of some of the disheartened Coup KUUists. An intense young man with unblinking eyes patted Damian on the back, but then awkwardly stepped back, unwilling to take the lead in whatever happened next. A thick-set man in his late thirties, whose wraparound shades suggested he thought he was Bono, proposed dividing into two groups, but his voice was drowned out by a woman whose whimpering had turned into wailing. So August, Damian, the Bono clone and a few other Coup KUUists decided to check the building for other ways in. Halfway down the west side of the Tripod they found a fire exit, but it was as impenetrable as the entrance. When they reached the far corner of the Tripod, they realised they had at least found a vantage point from which they had a side-on view of Coleridge and his attentive audience in the main auditorium. The final movement of *Laughter in the Dark* was the soundtrack to Coleridge's shaky voice as he began his speech. He'd been tempted to call it his Final Speech, but that might have been tempting fate. He placed both hands firmly on the lectern; partly because he'd seen other important speakers do this, but mainly because he needed to steady himself.

"Hello, my people. I was hoping there'd be more of you, but well done anyway. What you have decided to do takes great courage, so perhaps it's not surprising that many have dropped by the wayside." Murmured exchanges stopped the instant Coleridge continued. "So give yourselves a round of applause." There was a smattering of hesitant handclaps. "Don't look so worried, this is a happy day, a joyous day. We may be in the hands of the Omniscient Practical Joker, but we can trust that he will see the joke and honour our recklessness, our bravery, and our... I won't call it faith, but I will call it bravado. It's time for a showdown!"

"That's fucking beautiful. I love this guy," the Bono clone said to Damian. Damian responded with a stiff smile. Coleridge paused to consult his notes. Someone sneezed. "KUU bless you," responded Coleridge.

The audience found temporary release in laugher. Coleridge, finding his confidence boosted by this mood shift, straightened up a little before continuing.

"We are moving forward today – whatever happens. The Final Affirmation will either bring nothingness or joy. As Zachary said: death is nothingness; so what's to be afraid of? But if the KUU honours us – as I entertain the possibility it will – with the most mind-boggling KUU-incidence in the history of mankind, we will know there is a Knowing Unknowable Universe. In fact it will become the Knowing Knowable Universe, and a new age of *true* enlightenment will begin."

"Shit, I wish I was in there, dude. This sucks," said the Bono clone to Damian.

Damian found the man's shades deeply disconcerting. Without eye contact he couldn't tell if those eyes were alive with evangelical zeal or half dead from drug abuse. He was reminded of those black rectangles used by newspapers to hide the identity of the famous and the infamous. But with his wraparound black rectangle, this jerk wasn't so much hiding his identity as assuming the identity of another.

"So you're a U2 fan then?" asked Damian, attempting to get a handle on the Bono clone's state of mind while simultaneously taking the piss out of him. Bono clone opened his mouth to answer just as Coleridge's tone became more officious and urgent, drawing everyone back to the reality of the approaching storm.

"Okay, everybody. Count down the final four bars of *Laughter in the Dark* with me. Then we will be joined together, either in ecstasy or the big bang of nothingness! Sixteen... fifteen... fourteen... thirteen..."

The tempo of *Laughter in the Dark* was deathly slow, so it was a painfully protracted countdown. "Seven... six... five... Spin your chambers!" The whirling rattle of more than a hundred revolvers having their chambers spun, reverberated around the auditorium. "Four...three... two..."

As Coleridge lifted his gun to his temple he was delighted to see everyone in front of him do the same in perfect synchronisation, as if they were saluting him as he saluted them. Everything was going to be okay. Zachary B's backward scream. "One...Zero."

THE THREE NEAR PROOFS

The Pseudo Science of Time, Space and Freewill

How do we analyse the likelihood of a specific KUU-incidence in a meaningful, rational way? Just as the KUU is a non-religion, it is also unapologetically unscientific. Yet even a scientist would find it impossible to collate all the confluences of time, space and freewill that are needed to orchestrate a remarkable coincidence.

THE FIRST NEAR PROOF
Russian Roulette

The object we most use to play with chance is the humble dice. The dice is so ubiquitous that we have the expression 'to dice with death'. Is it a coincidence that the revolver used in the genuine dice-with-death game of Russian roulette also offers the player a one-in-six chance?

The Six Dice Throws

Is a KUU-incidence the equivalent of throwing six sixes on your first try? Or is it the equivalent of throwing it a hundred times and getting a six every time? It's impossible to say. A KUU-incidence cannot be measured by a specific benchmark, and that's what makes it a KUU-incidence. But to return to the dice for a moment, there's actually only a 1 in a 1000 chance of you throwing six sixes in sequence. These odds become near to infinite for a mere 50 sixes, one after the other. Yet this is not the world of infinite variables in which KUU-incidences occur, this is just chance operating on six numbers. Yet by limiting the variables, it's easier to see how astonishingly unlikely chains of coincidence in the real world are. However, we still might shout 'YES!' after throwing a pair of sixes. This isn't because we are more likely to be astonished if we know what the boundaries are, it's because KUU-incidences are just too remarkable to grasp and assess. Our logical minds prefer order to mystery and therefore turn away from unexpected fissures in our everyday reality. As I wrote that last sentence I came to the word 'fissures' and realised I didn't know how to spell it. It was on the first page my 1015-page dictionary fell open at.

THE SECOND NEAR PROOF
The Six Lego Bricks

Like the dice, the Lego brick is another small, simple geometric object capable of revealing something interesting about chance. Pick up six standard bricks and put them together in a way that pleases you. The chances of me now recreating your little Lego sculpture without seeing it are 102,981,500 to 1. Again, within extremely limited parameters, we get surprisingly high statistical odds against even the simplest coincidence occurring.

Divine Mischievous Intervention

The question I am asking in relation to the dice and lego bricks is this: if the mathematical improbability of something as simple as the throwing of six sixes is so high, how much more mathematically improbable is a KUU-incidence involving many, many more variables? The fact is, all of us have a few such stories of coincidence that were so mind-bogglingly unlikely to occur, that it's not unreasonable to suspect divine if mischievous intervention took place.

THE THIRD NEAR PROOF

Editor's note: at this point pages have been torn from Zachary Bekele's notebook. The next few pages contained song lyrics, poems and drawings but at no point does Bekele return to the subject of The Third Near Proof. If these missing pages are ever recovered they will be included in future editions of The KUU Hypothesis.

Extract from
The Life and Death of Zachary B
by Paul Coleridge

As Bad Luck Would Have It
February 24th, 1982

While watching the eternal sameness of the road stretching before me, and listening to the sub-bass rumble-and-roar of the traffic, my mind created several scenarios of how things would pan out once I got to Zac's. But even the most negative of these wasn't as banally deflating as that look, and those words. But it was the tone as much as the words. And that italicised *you* that singled me out as the last person on Earth he wanted to see standing on his doorstep.

"What on earth are *you* doing here?"

It took me a couple of seconds to find my voice. "I was going to phone first, but... you know, it was an impulse thing..."

He wrapped his kimono a little more tightly around himself, scrutinising me through narrowed eyes. "Look, Paul, this really isn't on. Do you know what time it is?"

It was ten-thirty; hardly late by Zac's standards. Or at least, the old Zac's standards, for this seemed to be a very new Zac standing before me. I was completely thrown. In fact, I was so shocked at being greeted so dismissively – rather than with backslapping, high-fiving enthusiasm – that it all just tumbled out.

"I needed to see that you were okay," I mumbled, looking anywhere but directly at him.

"Why wouldn't I be okay? I'm great," came back the perfectly reasonable response.

"Well, I... you know, I..." And then I started to cry, which wasn't a great idea. "My life's just fallen apart. I've got nothing now you and Jody and the band have..." Through a blur of tears I saw that a little compassion had appeared in Zac's eyes.

"Look, Paul. You don't even know me, not really. That was then, this is now. Jody and I have a new life here. I've packed in the smack. I've packed in all that shit. I've rediscovered my core being, so I really don't need all this.... this... negativity. If the KUU wanted us to meet again it would have happened..."

"Exactly! Exactly!" I suddenly saw a way in. "It *did* want us to meet again, Zac. I saw Helen. You know Helen – well, you don't know her, but she was... she's... well... she's your stalker, remember? We met by chance, by KUU-incidence, and she..."

"My stalker?" One step forward became two steps back. Now I'd really lost him. Zac started to retreat into the hallway.

"Forget I said that. Forget the stalker stuff. Anyway, she's really nice. And I bumped into her – by chance – but more importantly there was this news report – this evening, on the news. It was a Cosmic Nudge, don't you see? She gave me your address. And the bypass. The Shoreford bypass?"

I was flushed from this rush of words but Zac wasn't convinced. As I watched him backing away – as if from a rabid dog – Mozart's fish tank, of all things, came to mind. I was one of those busy little fish industriously picking the food from the impervious bigger fish's teeth. That was what I'd been for all these years – one of Zac's bloody cleaner fish!

Zac was talking to me. "Paul. This is a little embarrassing to be honest. I don't know why you're here, I really don't. And the fact you got my address from that... that... girl. What's got into you?"

"You've got into me. And she's not crazy…" I whimpered.

"Look, this is silly. You need to get a life, man."

"But I had a life, Zac. Don't do this to me…" Somehow I found myself in the hall. Zac had continued to back away, repelled by my self-pity, and I just kept advancing on him, weeping, pleading. He may have tried to shut the door on me, I don't remember.

"Just go home, Paul. Please."

Then he made his fatal mistake. He turned his back on me and started to walk away down the hall. I had been dismissed. In a variation on that philosophical conundrum of the tree falling in the woods – I no longer existed because Mr Zachary Bekele no longer observed me. I was a harmless little cleaner fish. Obviously I didn't articulate all this to myself at the time, it just manifested itself as a painful tightening in my stomach and a rising, almost joyful anger, blasting away all the noise and clutter that had filled my head for months. What happened next was absurd, comical even. I ran up behind him and jumped on his back, simultaneously wrapping my legs round his waist, like a child forcing an adult to give them a piggyback. Maybe, subconsciously, I was intent on some kind of embrace, however grotesque. At last I was actually physically close to this person who had never even seemed corporeally real to me before that moment. We stumbled around like that for several minutes. He swore loudly as an Art Deco lamp crashed to the hall floor. He twisted this way and that as we staggered into the over-bright kitchen, banging me up against the Aga one minute, the fridge the next. But I clung on tight. I think I was even laughing. Eventually, he dislodged me by repeatedly banging my right thigh against the sharp edge of the fridge door handle. And then he was the one laughing – mocking me, taunting me. I started screaming – he screamed back. I felt light-headed with it all! At last I was getting the *real* Zachary Bekele: this was real rage, and real loathing. That was when I pushed him backwards with all my strength and his head hit the window. I wasn't sure if the sickening crack was the glass or his skull, until I saw the blood on the windowpane. He slid to the floor, dazed but still conscious. I sat astride his chest, pinning both his arms to the tiled floor with my legs. He continued to hurl abuse at me. He even spat at me – can you believe it? I hadn't planned to use the guitar string. I mean, my God, I hadn't planned any of this. But, as bad luck would have it, my arms were free, and a long coil of broken guitar string lay within arm's reach (an Ernie Ball E-string – the thinnest – Zachary always used Ernie Ball). If Jody had been there it wouldn't have still been lying in the middle of the kitchen floor, where Zac must have lazily dropped it, but there you are. As Zac continued to tell me what he really thought of me, I realised I couldn't bear to listen to him rewriting the previous ten years of my life for a moment longer. I looked, for one last time, into those black-hole eyes for just a glimmer of empathy, sympathy or humanity, but there was nothing but bile and repulsive animal terror, so I carefully looped the thin strand of steel wire under his thrashing head, crossed the two ends over each other, and pulled.

"Aaah!! Shit!" I yelped.

I'd wrapped the string around my hands for extra purchase and obviously it bit into them horribly. I quickly pulled my driving gloves from my coat pockets, wriggled them on, and then, to Zac's dismay, continued the job I had started. I pulled and pulled, my eyes tightly shut, my mind purified and calmed by bright white light and a scream, which wasn't backwards.

Later – I don't know how much later – I found myself curled up in a ball, naked on the kitchen floor. The first thing I noticed on opening my eyes was the neat pile of blood-sodden clothes a couple of feet away by the fridge. I grasped what I had done, but immediately banished it from my mind so that I could work out what to do next. I went into the ground floor bathroom which led directly from the kitchen, avoiding the sticky footprints that my other self had left, and filled the bath with hot soapy water. I then went to the fridge where I was relieved to find a bottle of vodka; I took a generous swig. With a Flash-saturated cloth I tackled any areas I'd left sticky hand or footprints on. A tiled and wipe-clean surface throughout meant cleaning up wasn't as big a chore as it might have been. The hardest thing was avoiding seeing what my other self had done. That is, keeping Zachary nothing more than a dark-red lump in my peripheral vision. When it eventually came to dealing with the body, I threw a bucket of hot water over the whole area and attacked it at arms-length with a mop. Then I put my blood-soaked clothes and shoes into a wicker wash basket. I managed to stop myself from vomiting until I'd finished.

I returned to the bathroom to take a shower, sighing with relief as the last of the pinkish-red water swirled anticlockwise down the bath's plughole. Finally, I threw everything, including the wicker basket, on to the log fire in the sitting room. I suppose it was the shock, but I felt serenely calm during all of this: towels, water, blood… death, cleansing. Afterwards, I warmed myself in front of that fire, staring into its crackling depths for God knows how long. When it eventually died down, and my trancelike state dissipated, I threw water over it. It hissed back at me reproachfully. I shovelled the sodden ashes into a bin bag. Zac's walk-in wardrobe furnished me with a relatively sober bottle-green suit (a little tight across the shoulders) and a brand new pair of brown Church brogues (symbols of the new country squire Zac, I presumed), and then I drove back to London. And that's about it. I'm ashamed to say that when I got back to Peckham, I slept like a baby. The next morning I even woke with a fully-formed cover story for myself if the police happened to find a stray fingerprint: I'd say I'd visited Zac the previous day. Hopefully, Jody had been away all weekend so there would be no witnesses to contradict me. After driving for miles without any real plan, I handed over the suit and brogues to a shrunken old lady in an Oxfam shop in Beckenham who, reassuringly, couldn't see much further than the end of her nose. If I sound detached about all this it's because I'm trying to convey how I felt at the time. I could barely remember the event itself, and the practical matter of clearing up dominated the aftermath. Yes, I had bouts of crying, shaking and puking later, but that night I was driven only by an instinct to get past it all; to survive it. Perhaps this initial calm was also down to the fact I thought I'd freed myself: Zac's spell had been broken, but of course the spell is never broken, if anything it becomes unbreakable. If you extinguish a life, that life just takes over your life – unless of course you're a psychopath hardwired to separate actions from consequences. But whatever you might think of me, I'm no Mark Chapman. I *felt* emotion. I *felt* anger. Chapman wasn't even a big Lennon fan. His favourite rock star was Todd Rundgren, for Christ's sake!

Now, if you're the kind of reader who goes back over all you've just read looking for clues as to why things panned out as they did, don't bother with *The Life and Death of Zachary B*. Most of it was written during the twelve-year period in which the events took place, with only occasional interjections from me as a contemporary, editorial presence. So this is the gospel according to Paul, before Paul knew his destiny or, if you prefer, this was the tale of my innocence before my guilt. It's therefore a truer portrait of me than, say, Giles Brown's spiteful narrow-minded effort. Brown never even met Zachary (or me for that matter), yet he painted me as a sad, twisted freak from the beginning. Before Brown's book came out in 1988, I was pitied. Then his version of me became every hack's template. Every dirt-digging article used the same grim picture (an unused passport photo – unused for good reason) to support their most-evil-man-on-the-planet angle. So I can only thank God for the KUU (if you'll excuse the tautology) for my reinvention as the more-or-less good guy. So what else is there to say about my three parts who-done-it to one part I-did-it, memoir? Well firstly, yes, I really did do it – even though there are conspiracy theorists out there that have tetchily informed me I didn't. And secondly, I would have got away with it too, what with the police's Stone Age detection techniques on my side. To be nabbed back in those days you'd have to leave your driving licence at the scene of the crime. Plus this memoir would have made a perfect smoke screen with its I. D. parade of archetypally perfect suspects: the crooked manager; the greedy keyboard player; the crazy stalker; the jealous wife and the unpaid drug dealer (death by unpaid drug dealer isn't exactly unheard of.),

Oh Helen my less evil twin, why did you go and spoil everything? It's funny if you think about it. She must have wasted thousands of hours over the years spying on Zac. She was Zac's powerless guardian angel. And then, on what she'd planned as her very last night as his stalker, all that wasted time ended up meaning something. She was, as they say, in the right place at the right time to take three blurred snaps of my moment of weakness (and my moment of limitless strength and freedom) that became the evidence to support her police statement. I really didn't see that one coming.

But to return to those pesky conspiracy theorists for a moment. Their favourite crackpot notion is that some right-wing religious extremist did it, hoping for his fifteen minutes. Plenty of them thought Zac was the Antichrist (check out Dominic Barker's laugh-a-minute *Sects & Drugs & Rock & Roll*), and maybe he *was* the Antichrist. Like most God-fearing Christians, I never read the Bible. Perhaps because I feared I wouldn't find my God in there after all. But Zac had read it, and found plenty of ammunition in its gold-edged pages to chip away at my fragile faith. Perhaps, if I'd argued with him more, I might have rediscovered my own convictions – or discovered if I even had convictions. But, by force of habit, I was always the interviewer; we didn't have discussions, I just let Zac talk. I just let Zac chip away at my God until, effectively, he took His place.

Extract from *The KUU Hypothesis* by Zachary Bekele

THE KUU CREATION MYTH

Paradoxes of the Big Bang

As we come to the end of my attempt to rehabilitate the human imagination, let's free-fall back to The Beginning of All Things.

BANG!

Nothing became everything, as everything fled from nothing as fast as it could.

BANG!

There's nothing more singular than the indivisible, invisible needle-prick in the vastness of space from which all matter rushed into being.

KUUism's Take on the Big Bang

A few days after reading that scientists are close to knowing the complete history of the Universe apart for the first second preceding the Big Bang, I read an analysis of the Bible which pointed out that although all of creation took place in six days, '... *a day to God is a thousand years to mankind*'. If this timescale is applied to the Creation it means that those six hectic days of God either equal 6000 years (God Time) or that the act of creation was completed in 1. 42 seconds (Man Time). The 1. 42 seconds answer tallies nicely with that first second of the universe, which remains a mystery to scientists. So, give or take half a second, Bible and boffins agree. Given that both the laws of physics and time only pose a limitation upon us physical beings, it might have amused the KUU to summon a universe of matter from its metaphorical sleeve in the blink of an eye, for an audience 15 billion years in the future to mull over. And a rest of 0.2367th of a second on the seventh 'day' would have been perfectly adequate for the Mighty KUU.

BANG!

Everything from nothing in an instant; just as death is everything *to* nothing in an instant. Each man is a universe that comes into being in an instant and disappears in an instant. The universe of our cerebral cortex is our own personal universe; our own dark glimpse of infinity. Etc etc, Amen.

7

Marrakech, February 2007

The second of silence following the backward scream that ends *Laughter in the Dark* seemed infinite to Damian. Then came a curiously muted cascade of bangs, like exploding firecrackers. He recoiled as three discrete drops of blood appeared at eye level on the other side of the Tripod's glass wall. His eyes and brain automatically connecting them, like a join-the-dots puzzle, into a perfect triangle: triangle; tripod – meaning was everywhere. But then he cursed his own simple-mindedness: of course they formed a perfect triangle – any three dots would if you imagined three straight lines connecting them (which the eye – egged on by the order-seeking brain – is inclined to do). He was reminded of the inexplicably depressing fact that if you threw six dice they're just as likely to all land on six, as any other arbitrary mix of numbers. We just place more significance on a throw of six sixes. A couple more seconds elapsed while these inappropriately measured and abstract thoughts danced around in the personal universe of Damian's brain. But after those two elastically stretched seconds, the full horror of what those three red drops signified hit home, and he stumbled backwards away from the glass. His peripheral vision informed him there was a lot more blood, but he wanted to be spared the details; he wanted to be spared visual memories he knew that he would never be free of. But

Damian was the only person moving *away* from the Tripod. He had to push through a surge of wide-eyed people intent on witnessing whatever there was to be witnessed. As soon as he had retreated twenty yards, he sat by the roadside and focussed on the comforting banality of the dirt at his feet. He thought he might start crying or screaming or something, but nothing. Perhaps if he just stared at the ground in front of him forever (a couple of Christmas-bright bottle-tops and a hank of animal hair provided handy additional diversion) he could forget about what had just happened and what was still unfolding all around him. But it was so hot. He could feel the pink sting of sunburn on his forehead, particularly along his hairline; he hated being so fair-skinned. Police whistles and car horns seemed to be playing something by Schoenberg. Then his shoulders were being shaken and August's concerned conker-brown eyes were looking urgently into his.

"Are you okay? Where's your camera? Come on now, Damian, get a grip."

"Yes, yes, my camera. Shit! Okay, yes… I've still got it."

August had a journalist's talent for detached objectivity that made her a focussed, if reluctant, witness to what Damian had needed to flee from. But even she had despaired at one point, just before she had to look away. It was the moment all those guns were raised and placed against soft, vulnerable temples. She had banged on the thick glass, but her fist had just made a dull useless sound. She was as powerless as everyone else to stop this gruesome titbit of history from unfolding. The thing she'd unfortunately always remember was the left-handed man who ruined the whole gruesome choreography of the event by jerking grotesquely to the right, as everyone else buckled and fell to the left. Damian's hands were shaking too much, so August grabbed the camera, ruffled his hair reassuringly, and left him contemplating the bottle tops and dirt while she went back to get whatever pictures she could. When word reached her that a number of people in the Tripod had seen sense at the last moment, she found herself thanking God (or at least using that expression in her head and half meaning it) for this small mercy. For this wasn't a bunch of brainwashed Jonestown co-dependents. This was a disparate unconnected group of individuals who'd been seduced by an idea on the Internet. That idea had enthralled many of them right up until the very last second. But then their instinct for survival had stopped them from squeezing the trigger. For a moment, when August saw all the survivors running about, she couldn't stop herself from entertaining the possibly that the KUU *had* intervened and had made all those guns spin round to their one empty chamber. But the faces of the people pounding mutely on the glass definitely hadn't witnessed a miracle; they'd witnessed a fall back into blind faith and now desperately wanted out.

★

Merrick was a man waking from a dream. He had wanted to be able to handle it, but couldn't. He wasn't as sadistically voyeuristic as he would have liked to have been. He too had looked away. When it came down to the nitty-gritty, he'd had neither the stomach nor the nerve to join Coleridge and the meagre few who'd joined him in his ludicrous fantasy. Maybe if more people had turned up he would have embraced the dream, but it would have had to have been an awful lot more people, a few thousand at least. But, no, who was he trying to kid? He wasn't cut out for acts of faith.

After checking the monitors to see which emergency exits were receiving the least attention from the crowds and authorities, he called British Airways and booked an early afternoon flight to London. It had all been a blast but the party was over. If only he'd had the Machiavellian genius of a James Bond villain then he could have taken more advantage of this whole ridiculous business. But realistically he was just an opportunist without a conscience. He looked around his office, at the chunky first editions, the collection of single malts and of course Helen's butt – it all had to be left behind. This was no time for sentimentality. But, no, he had to take the butt. He found a sturdy paper knife and prised the prize free, ruining his Edwardian desk in the process. Then he tapped in the code for unlocking Exit 4 and took the lift down.

★

It took the authorities nearly an hour to get into the Tripod. Eventually, a police officer commandeered a 4x4 and reversed it repeatedly into the entrance until the doors caved in. By this time, the survivors had gone up to the accommodation levels and found duvets and sheets to cover the dead. August got a few shots of the auditorium before she was ushered back behind the ineffectual barrier of road cones the police had put in place.

Damian sufficiently composed himself to help August attend to survivors. A middle-aged French woman, repeatedly flicking a sickle of dyed-black hair from her eyes, reported that dozens of people had dropped their guns in horror as soon as the first shots were fired. August noticed the Bono clone was sitting by the roadside with an acoustic guitar, flatly crooning *I Still Haven't Found What I'm Looking For* to a group of student types who had gratefully shrugged off rucksacks, opened beer cans, and assuming the cross-legged position associated with such occasions.

"All I can hear is people saying, 'suicide cult', 'suicide cult'," said Damian, exasperated. "But it wasn't. It was just wishful thinking taken to the extreme. These weren't people wanting to die so they could go to a better life. The better life was going to be here and now when the KUU had saved them... What? What have I said?"

August stared disbelievingly at Damian. How could he be defending KUUism after all this? She paused before she spoke.

"People are sick, sick, sick – and that includes you. I really can't discuss this with you now, Damian."

The Bono clone had moved on to croaking *In The Name of Love*. More people joined in each time he reached the chorus. Damian sulkily turned his attention to this impromptu concert. He found himself reluctantly impressed that the Bono clone and his audience seemed to be in their own little world, oblivious to the surrounding chaos and noise. With TV crews unloading equipment, thereby obstructing the exit routes of furious ambulance crews, Damian thought this shaky rendering of U2's greatest hits by a would-be X-Factor contestant seemed quite poignant, and even heroic. And what's more, the Bono clone was becoming more Bono-like with each passing anthemic song. He was clearly gaining energy and confidence from what was probably his first ever, fully attentive audience. As he began *Where the Streets Have No Name* a Bono-like smirk even played around his mouth.

"I can't take much more of this. He's so *flat*," said August.

"Don't be horrible," replied Damian. "Although how he can wear that leather coat in this heat, beats me. Some people will do anything to look cool."

"But it doesn't look cool. It's too small for him. Look at the sleeves."

The Bono clone looked momentarily thrown as he stumbled over a chord change in *Sunday, Bloody Sunday*. The fact his audience seemed equally unsettled by this mistake, further unnerved him. The protective bubble he'd created was going to burst unless he quickly regained his footing. But, rather than continue as if the miss-fingered chord hadn't occurred, the Bono clone made the mistake of going back to the beginning of the second verse and starting it again. Almost inevitably, when he reached the same chord change, his hands betrayed him for the second time. August and Damian stopped talking. The feeling of unease that was growing in the Bono clone's bubble had rippled out and reached them.

When the Bono clone got the chord change wrong for the third time, he swore loudly, threw his guitar to the ground and stamped on it repeatedly until he could comfortably stand in its wreckage. The silence that followed was relative, but still palpable. August and Damian, without speaking, moved in closer.

The Bono clone addressed his audience. "The fucking boat went without us, man!' There was a murmur of agreement.

"Look, it's over, Geoff. Don't make a scene, love," said someone with a Manchester accent who must have been the Bono clone/Geoff's girlfriend "Our plane was delayed, it's nobody's fault."

"Fucking *VAirways*! Fucking cheapskate bastards!"

August found herself experiencing another dreamlike moment, like the one she'd had when Damian was stabbed: what her eyes could see, her brain retreated from. Geoff – who somehow seemed more real now that he was 'Geoff' rather than just the Bono clone – had produced from the pocket of his too-small coat, the familiar Smith & Wesson revolver. He studied it as if it were some ancient artefact he'd just dug up from the dust at his feet. He smoothed back his hair and grinned his Bono-ish grin.

"Who cares if things went tits-up in there? Maybe this isn't about *in there*. Maybe it's about me. Maybe it's about us."

August wasn't sure if by "us" he meant his new audience or just his girlfriend. But then he pointed the gun at his girlfriend. Even though he pointed it in a stylised James Bond fashion, her cry of alarm, which she partially stifled with a raised hand, was real enough.

"Sweetheart, put the gun away," Geoff's girlfriend pleaded.

"But I thought you wanted what I wanted – what we all wanted. The KUU will take care of us."

"Please, Geoff. Don't do this!"

"But I want to set us free. You believe don't you? You said you did. Fuck, how can you not believe? There's no evidence for Jesus Christ coming back from the dead like some kind of holy fucking zombie, but everyday we're being *rained on* by Cosmic Nudges."

Geoff became fully focused on addressing the crowd. "Just before we came here to Marrakech – this is Jade by the way – we were in Edinburgh visiting a friend. She was one of the twins in that 90s band Soho. Remember them? *Hippychick*? No? Oh well. Anyway, we had an hour to kill before we were expected at Pauline's – one of the twins – flat, so we went to the first pub we stumbled across. Because the place was so tiny it was impossible not to hear what the group of old blokes standing at the bar were talking about. Four of the group had turned out to be two pairs of twins. These two pairs of twins had never been into this pub before and didn't know each other. One of the two regulars shouted across to the other, 'You're a gamblin' man Jack. What do you think the odds of that are?' And I thought, yeah, what are the odds? And what's more – what are the odds of encountering two sets of twins on the way to meeting half of a third set?"

Geoff waved the gun around as he tried to make his fevered brain remember another mini-miracle or two – as much for himself as for his audience. "Yeah-yeah. Only last month we were in Mexico City – weren't we sweetheart? And I met an old mate waiting for the same coach we were. I hadn't seen him for five years, yet there he was. We used to go to the game together. Then a week later – you remember – we saw him again in some other part of the city. And this is the biggest city in the fucking world." Again he waved the gun at his girlfriend. "Tell them about that new friend of yours, sweetheart… Okay, I'll tell them. Jade finds out that her friend took the Eurostar to Paris for her birthday. So Jade asks her when her birthday was, as you do, and she says February. When in February? The tenth. Anyway, it turns out they both went to Paris to celebrate their twenty-fourth on the same day. They were even born the same fucking hour. I'd like to know what the odds of that are. And Zachary, KUU bless him, expects us *not* to believe. What's that about? I mean, this is the guy who actually told his killer that he was going to kill him – at least a year before it actually happened! He said, 'You kill me, man.' It's in Paul Coleridge's book." Andy became bent double with laughter. "You can laugh: you've gotta fucking laugh, haven't you?"

But before anyone could find the courage to take advantage of Geoff's lapse of focus, he was upright again and sufficiently composed to adjust the upturned collar of his coat to the precise angle he preferred it. Sweating profusely, he clearly would have liked to take it off, but it was part of his very being.

Damian felt he'd been watching this drama unfold for days. But then Geoff raised his game. It was as if he suddenly remembered what this was all about. He slowly raised the gun to his sweat-beaded temple. Unfortunately, his girlfriend's sharp cry of horror drew Geoff's attention back to her.

"Sorry, love," he said, shaking his head. "But you said we'd do this *together*. You said you'd push the KUU too." Geoff briefly aimed the gun at his tearful, terrified girlfriend, then back at his own temple. "I can push the KUU for both of us. It's as if the Knowing Unknowable Universe is saying to me, 'Trust your instincts, Geoff – what have you got to lose?' And I've decided I've got nothing to lose. I no longer fear death because, worse case scenario, it's nothingness, according to Zachary. But I'm not worrying about death anyway, because this gun will *not* end my life. I'll spin the chamber round and it will land on its one empty chamber, and then I'll know that the KUU loves me with a love like no other love. For fuck's sake, man. Bono still hasn't found what he's looking for, but I have! You can laugh, man! You can laugh!"

The crowd did not laugh.

"Okay, so don't laugh. But you *could* laugh - you have my permission, my friends," continued Geoff. "And you can doubt, if that's your thing. But I'm done with doubting. Doubting's for losers. The Knowing Unknowable Universe wants my faith, *needs* my faith, I know it does. Zachary's 11th Non-Commandment was, don't push the KUU. But isn't it obvious that Zachary meant that as a challenge – that the Knowing Unknowable Universe has laid that down as a challenge? It's just another KUU fucking paradox. It's an invitation to go against the advice of the KUU in order to earn the KUU's respect. And I respect that! Fuck, yes!"

Geoff was becoming increasingly agitated and manic. The next time he pointed the gun at his girlfriend, she froze but remained silent, perhaps fearing that saying or doing anything might bring about the wrong result.

Again, Damian cursed those stupid mirror shades. Geoff's eyes might have given a better indication of his state of mind – was he drug or sun crazed? Scary or just scared? How *serious* was this jerk? He was clearly an attention-seeker, but was he also an intention seeker who had lost his marbles to the Knowing Unknowable Universe?

The gun went back from his temple to his girlfriend, from his girlfriend to his temple. He rambled on about what his bespoke heaven would be like if the Knowing Unknowable Universe didn't choose to save him (spit and sawdust pubs on every street corner, a whore house peopled by supermodels, a widescreen TV the size of a football pitch…) and the faith-free future ahead if the Knowing Unknowable Universe did choose to save him (how proud his mum, his girlfriend's mum, and even Bono himself were going to be of him).

Then Geoff began to calm down. He seemed numbly detached – as if distractedly torn between takeaway menus – in regard to whose life he was going to put at the mercy of KUU Russian roulette.

It suddenly struck Damian that this man really had lost the plot. He really was going to go through with this. But because he couldn't bear the idea of leaving his girlfriend behind if things went wrong: this idiot was going to pull the trigger on her first.

Damian didn't *decide* to do anything, he just found himself wrestling Geoff to the ground. Moments later, he realised he might have made a big mistake. Geoff wasn't as tall as Damian but he was physically heavier, and, by nature, much more aggressive. An arm the size of a shoulder of beef, pressing down hard on Damian's windpipe, stopped him from breathing. Although he could feel no pain, he could see from a bloom of red on his T-shirt that his stitches had broken. He managed a desperate but ineffectual punch to the side of Geoff's head, which at least sent those fucking wraparounds flying. Both of Damian's arms were suddenly pinned beneath Geoff's legs, as the crazed busker sat astride his chest. One of Geoff's hands went for Damian's throat, the other, seemingly with a will of its own, still couldn't decide which direction to point the gun in – although now Damian was his second option. It was pointed directly in Damian's face, then back to Geoff's temple, then back in Damian's face. Damian noticed how small the glinting stainless steel object was – perhaps only three inches long - like a toy.

Damian's last self-consoling thought was that he might choke to death before this man made a decision as to whether to shoot him or shoot himself. What was it he saw in Geoff's gaze in those last few moments? Anger? Relief? Childlike confusion?

Then came the bang that creates silence.

Damian simply couldn't process what was briefly in his field of vision. A third of Geoff's head, along with one of his eyes, simply wasn't there anymore. Geoff – whoever Geoff was – was no longer Geoff, or Bono, or anyone anymore. He was just a mess of red and an oppressive weight from under which Damian didn't have the energy to extricate himself. Then there was nothing but the intense azure sky, as he greedily drew in the hot dry air, which his lungs had so desperately missed, while hands grabbed him and pulled him from beneath Geoff's corpse. He felt intensely uncomfortable being hugged and kissed by the strangers that crowded in on him. He wanted August to come over and join him, but she seemed to be deliberately standing back, making sure she didn't catch his eye.

Someone gave him water (Highland Spring?!), someone else gave him a large sticking plaster – a temporary solution for his reopened knife wound. And a third person produced a clean T-shirt from their bag and handed it to him. This led him to look down and see what was wrong with the one he was wearing. Horrified, he tore it off and gratefully took the replacement. The words now written across his chest, white on dark blue, seemed to mock him with their singsong levity – **KUU, who'd have thought it!** Yet they also made him smile: KUU, who'd have thought it, indeed. He didn't feel like a hero, but that's apparently what he was. A couple of journalists told him – in the form of questions – what he'd just been through:

"So what made you risk your own life to tackle this mad gunman?"

"What was going through your mind when…"

"Did you at any time fear for your own…"

"As a KUUist yourself, do you have any message for the world?"

He gave them the kind of banal sound bites they would have filled in the gaps with themselves had he refused to play ball. He told them he'd felt compelled to save the girl; he told them he hadn't hesitated, and he told them that this lunatic fringe of KUUists in no way represented the true fence-sitting, non-dictatorial, non-belief system that he still stood by. He told them the truth and nothing but the truth. But he didn't tell them the whole truth.

★

Paul Coleridge was – yet wasn't – surprised to find he was still alive. He hadn't heard a bang, but he knew (from some vague memory he couldn't quite place) that the bullet would have entered his brain before the sound reached his ears – so not hearing the bang was no guarantee he was still alive. And he also knew there had still been some doubt (or rather, not enough faith) in his coke-buoyed brain at the moment he pressed the trigger, because he hadn't been able to stop himself from tightly shutting his eyes with instinctive dread, like a child bracing itself for a slap from an abusive parent. So when his personal mini-miracle occurred a split-second later he was momentarily ecstatic. His famous last words would have been, "Three, two, one, zero," but, as it turned out, the first words of the rest of his life were an incredulous, "I'm still here" – even if they were drowned out by the bangs

381

and screams telling him things hadn't gone so well for everyone else. Coleridge then sought refuge in everything that was still right with the world. This could be narrowed down to firstly, the fact that *he* had been saved – which was obviously the KUU's plan all along. And secondly, it had been established that Zachary's 11th Non-Commandment was right – Don't push the KUU because if you do, the KUU will fuck you up. And yet the KUU had saved him! So it must want something more from him. He sat down behind his blood-splattered lectern ruminating on what that might be. Eventually, after some indeterminate period, hands gripped both his arms and roughly hoisted him up. Two young police officers half-led and half-carried him towards the shattered main entrance.

★

August and Damian sat by the roadside exhausted, watching but not watching the continuing clean-up operation. They were at the still centre of a tornado of people shouting orders, weeping, or just desperately looking for other people. A camera crew wove past them with balletic precision. Occasionally, someone asked if they were okay. Damian was happy being ignored again, following his moment of accidental heroism.

"We're going to have to get you to a hospital," said August.

"Yeah, I suppose so," said Damian.

"You did good," August added, in her bad American accent, putting a friendly arm round Damian's shoulder.

"Did I?"

"Yes, of course you did. What's the matter with you? Something's the matter, I can tell."

Damian was saved from having to give an immediate response by the arrival of a waif-like Japanese girl in a red hoody. She handed him *The KUU Hypothesis* to sign. The flyleaf was already festooned with signatures.

"God knows why she wanted *my* autograph. If only she'd known who *you* were," Damian said to August, managing a mischievous grin. "Maybe I should run after her and tell her."

"Don't you dare! And don't change the subject."

"What was the question again? Okay, okay. It was just that I told those press vultures exactly what they wanted to hear..."

"And? So?"

"Well, it was all bollocks." Damian's eyes filled with the tears he had made every effort to suppress. "I wasn't thinking about that stupid girl who should have known better than to be with that arsehole in the first place. I was suddenly just really, really pissed off. I just had the irrepressible urge to land a punch on that crap busker's nose for thinking he was Bono; for making a mockery of the KUU; for wearing stupid sunglasses; and for being such an all-round jerk." He wiped his eyes with a dusty hand. "Maybe the heat just got to me. It's certainly getting to me now."

August's uninhibited, chiming laughter made it impossible for Damian not to laugh too. "You're being too hard on yourself," she said. "Although, having said that, you've behaved like a hero should behave; you're being self-effacing. Perhaps you're just not comfortable with the idea that you might be more of a man than you thought you were?"

Was she asking him or telling him? Damian considered the possibility that she was right. He was glad he couldn't think of a wisecrack response, as he didn't want her to think he had taken her words lightly. Perhaps he'd eventually come to appreciate the fact he'd been tested today, and passed the test. He'd always assumed that under that kind of pressure he'd have just stood back and let some other reckless fool be the hero. Yet he'd somehow become the hero, just by acting on an impulse that temporarily overrode the default coward in him. Damian was stopped from further reflection when August grabbed his arm more tightly than was strictly necessary.

"It's him. He's still alive. And he's *smiling*, for God's sake!"

Paul Coleridge's smile broadened as the sun's beneficent rays struck his face. He shut his eyes for a moment and turned his face skyward like a blissed-out cat, enjoying the fiery red universe of his own inner eyelids. The two police officers, sensing he had no intention of struggling, loosened their grip but continued to lead him towards one of the squad cars. As the three men drew level with August and Damian, Coleridge dropped to his knees and started praying. As this wasn't a direct attempt at escape, the young officers became confused as to what to do next. Embarrassment, and an acknowledgement of another's need to commune with his maker, froze them. But then one of the officers – perhaps remembering the horrors he'd just witnessed – became agitated and impatient. He bent over Coleridge and tried to prise apart the man's praying hands so he could lift him to his feet. Coleridge glared at the officer, his bottom lip trembling with spoilt-child resentment, his face red with the effort of stubbornly keeping his hands together. Eventually, with the other officer's help, Coleridge's hands were parted and his journey to the squad car resumed. August was disconcertingly reminded of when her mother had stopped her praying as a child ('don't pray, dance!'), but for Paul Coleridge it was too late for dancing.

★

Because their instinct for survival overrode their instinct for religious affirmation, 125 Coup KUUists decided at the last split-second not to push the KUU. Of the seventeen Coup KUUists who pulled the trigger, a statistically predictable three survived. There were only two women amongst these seventeen. Neither of them survived.

Extract from *The KUU Hypothesis* by Zachary Bekele

The Big Question
What About all the Suffering in the World?

KUUism could hardly avoid tackling the one question thrown at every religion by believers and unbelievers alike. Why doesn't the KUU do something more constructive than just tickle us with Cosmic Nudges?

The Devil of Choice

Why assume your deity is all-powerful? Because it makes you feel better, safer, more fearful or more humbled? Yet to make such an assumption is to fall back into the anthropomorphising, tribal-binary (God is either all-powerful or doesn't exist) trap. The Gratuitous doesn't exist as an entity it's just a concept, not the Devil in sheep's clothing. The only devil is the one that lurks in us all as a by-product of the human curse of choice. Animals just do what they do; humans can *choose* what to do. But the problem lies in the fact that bad decisions are usually the easiest ones to take, that's why they're called temptations. We, the devil, imagine the worst of acts and then – to make gods of ourselves – carry them out.

Extract from
The Life and Death of Zachary B
by Paul Coleridge

The Truth is Perhaps Even More Unnerving
23rd August 1971

I didn't fully comprehend the reality of the decision I'd made to change my life, until the Cambridge train eased into the steel-arched mouth of Liverpool Street Station, screeching and growling like a Hendrix solo. As London's smoker's breath filled my nostrils I felt simultaneously petrified and liberated. Although it's a big-city cliché, I was nevertheless surprised by the instant invisibility the place granted me: the complete absence of curiosity in the faces of the thousands of commuters flowing up and down escalators and through absurdly narrow gates, rushing to catch trains that were already departing. You had to become no more than a free-floating corpuscle in the city's sluggishly pumped bloodstream. If you didn't calibrate your tempo and rhythm to the tempo and rhythm of these channelled crowds when you joined them, you'd just get spat out or trampled underfoot. London was a place for the focused, the blinkered, the ruthless. Was that me? The alternative was life in a cardboard box under Waterloo Bridge. So perhaps the starkness of the options forced me to get my act together. I would have to change just to survive, never mind thrive.

After six months of sending samples of my work to all the music papers and hearing nothing back, doubts were creeping in. I took on-board what I knew all along – that these publications get hundreds of articles from desperate hopefuls every day. But the crux of the problem was that – just like you – I'm not some character in a film or a book; I'm not carefully delineated and stylised for the convenience of a story, a reader, or even just for the convenience of myself. Because that's the bottom line isn't it? If only we could all be shiny two-dimensional archetypes, unfazed by the shit thrown at us every day, gliding through life with whatever narrowly defined attributes our omniscient author has granted us. We could just be... oh, I don't know: charming and ruthlessly ambitious; shrewd and brave; weird and wonderful; camp and bitchy, handsome and mysterious. But instead we're all these things – but only for a couple of minutes each day, or a few times a year. I'd be grateful if I could manage "handsome and mysterious" just once in my entire life, because most of the time, my omniscient author has cursed me with "frightened and fragmented", "diffused and confused" – or on a good day – "clumsy and clueless".

Sitting in my Peckham bedsit, I'd type out album reviews, make Xerox copies, and send them off to all the music papers. But then I'd be crippled by anxiety when it came to making the follow-up phone call to the *NME*, *Rock On*, or *Melody Maker* to check they'd received my letter. I'd put off calling for days, sometimes weeks. When I eventually psyched myself up enough to phone, the singsong secretary would interrupt my mumbled monologue with, "I'm afraid Jake is in a meeting. Can I say who called?"

"So when will he be out of the meeting?"

"I couldn't say, sir."

"Is there a good time to catch him?"

"Not really, sir. Can I say who called?"

"It's okay. I'll try again later."

An innocent enough exchange you might think, but "nervous and painfully self-conscious" me would be replaced by "doubtful and paranoid" me and I'd imagine the editor of the NME, or whoever, making frantic hand signals to his secretary to get rid of this time-waster as quickly as possible, and when she'd done that, to get his number changed. Of course the more likely scenario was that he *was* in a meeting, as busy people often are, but that wouldn't even cross my mind: that's the paranoia of the powerless for you – we think the world is actively trying to avoid us, whereas the truth is even more unnerving – it doesn't even know or care that we exist. But one baking hot day in August, I'd had enough of the humid hell of my tiny bedsit, so I quickly shaved and caught a bus into town.

Extract from *The KUU Hypothesis* by Zachary Bekele

Optimistic Doubt

The Knowing Unknowable Universe blithely presides over a world in which it's not our meticulous plans that change our lives forever, it's when we act on a whim. We go in one bar rather than another, and so meet the person we will spend the rest of our lives with, or someone who offers us the job we've always wanted. So all we can do is act upon the stuff thrown at us and let life's slipstream take us where it will. Tripodic thinking, as ever, gives us the meaning of life: it has nothing to do with the traditional oppositions of free will or no free will. It's the third option of partial free will.

The Grace of Powerlessness

It is impossible to circumnavigate the KUU's apparent desire to keep us on our toes: if there are two possible doors to open, your future probably lies through a third door you've not stumbled across yet (or even a bathroom window you can only just squeeze through). But don't take my word for all this. Invent your own bespoke hypothetical deity and consider how He/She/It might be influencing or not influencing your life.

Optimistic Doubt

But do put optimistic doubt at your bespoke religion's generous heart. Optimistic doubt needs to be the new spirit of the age. It turns the whole thing around. Instead of living in constant disappointment at not receiving what you think is rightfully yours, you live for the moment and so experience pleasant surprise when good fortune – or a life-affirming Cosmic Nudge – comes your way. Dwelling on the past, or thinking only of the future, means you miss the present. Life is the Now.

The KUU pressed the START button...

...and the rest is mystery. Ultimately, perhaps questions of a metaphysical nature should remain unformulated, and then their residue – a sense of wonder – can remain like a beguiling perfume in the mind.

EPILOGUE

Helen was in a crowded room-to-hire above a pub off Piccadilly. She couldn't wait for the ban on public smoking. The fact it was only a matter of months away made her even more annoyed at having to put up it now. Everything she was wearing would have to go straight to the dry-cleaner's tomorrow. The two improbably young barmaids looked sullenly baffled as to the nature of this gathering of mostly middle-aged men: surely they couldn't all be gay? They didn't even look gay. Yet what other reason could there be for their obsession with the camp seventies pop star whose image had hijacked the TV screen above the bar? There was even one sad old bastard trying to mimic the pop star's appearance, despite being at least twice his age. And now there was this woman too. Why was she here?

Helen was beginning to wonder this herself – she didn't know anyone here. Only at the very last minute had she decided to take the plunge and go. So she hadn't even let Mark A, Glam-man or Sensimilija Sam (the three Cubist Funk Master chat room contributors she had the best rapport with) know she was coming. She squeezed through to the bar, hoping a drink would give her enough confidence to speak to someone. She'd, no doubt, had on-line discussions with any number of these men, but what made her think she'd recognise any of them when she got here? How stupid was that? As she finished her first half of cider she wondered what Adam would say if he knew what she was getting up to while he was away. Probably something like, "I can't leave you alone for five minutes." But it had been a long five minutes. He'd been on a documentary shoot in Tanzania for nearly two months. What did he expect her to do – sit at home twiddling her thumbs? She no longer had the twins to worry about: Katie had moved in with her boyfriend and Molly was at sixth form. These days she found most of their shared friends (who were essentially Adam's friends) deadly dull: they complained about the dumbing down of culture, and yet they discussed gastro-pubs and Nigella recipes with the same gravitas they used to apply to art-house movies and exhibitions. So suddenly there was this hole in her life and Zachary B just crept back in. The first time she dragged her old LP cases down from the loft and unclipped their rusty catches, she was dizzy with excitement. It was scary really. There were songs in these boxes that she'd not heard for more than a quarter of a century. All Adam had to say on the matter was that all this vinyl was worth something now, especially as she'd looked after her albums so well. She'd replied that they couldn't be worth more than they were worth to her. Initially, she'd just studied the covers and lyric sheets – she'd wait until he was out of the house before she'd play anything. Obviously, he was concerned about her "raking up old memories" as he put it, but she knew it would be okay. She'd lived a whole lifetime since then: briefly had a career, then the children. She could honestly say she'd more or less forgotten about Zachary B...more of less... obviously when there was a track on the radio, her pulse would start to race. But then Elton would be on next, and she'd be back to normal. Even when the whole KUU thing hit the headlines she'd remained unmoved. Her therapist had advised her not to read either Zachary or Paul's book as they might trigger a relapse, so she didn't. And as the years went by she found she was no longer even curious about them. Zachary B was someone – no, *something* – which belonged well and truly in the past – a past that, only now, she felt a burgeoning nostalgia for.

But what did all these men in this smoke-filled room feel? Eventually, the would-be Zachary B look-alike came over to speak to her.

"So who do we have here then?"

"Helen. Helen Friel," said Helen. She saw no reason to lie about her name. Her married surname – and the fact she'd almost doubled in size – would probably prevent anyone from realising she was *that* Helen.

"I'm Zachary C. No, really. Changed it by deed poll back in '84. I front a Zachary B tribute band called the New Now. We're at the Half Moon in Brixton, next Thursday night."

"Don't you mean the Half Moon in Herne Hill?"

"It's *nearly* Brixton. And Brixton just sounds better, doesn't it?"

"If you say so."

This was the only response Helen could muster. She was too busy trying to make sure her face didn't reveal how repelled she was by the sight of this Anti-Zachary. His permed-to-death hair was a black cloud, out of which his fake-tanned face emerged. Absurdly white teeth only served to emphasise the shabbiness of the rest of this ghost-of-glam-past.

Helen remembered a whimsical conversation she'd had with Paul Coleridge a lifetime ago, about a hypothetical Zachary A. But this Zachary C didn't fit in anywhere in their fantasy factory line of Zachary clones. Realistically, this Zachary C should have called himself Zachary D-minus, or even Zachary F-for-Fail.

Zachary C interrupted her drifting thoughts. "Would you believe the fans sometimes talk to me as if I really am Zachary B?"

"No, not really."

Zachary C cackled. "At least you're honest. But it's the truth. The rest of the lads wear wigs, so they can just go to the bar after the gig without getting recognised. But this…" He ran his fingers through his scary fuzz. "This is real. So I get pestered. Comes with the territory."

"I see."

"They talk to me as if I'm really him. All that KUU bollocks doesn't help. Maybe they think I'm him resurrected or something." Zachary C was obviously hurt that Helen continued to look sceptical. "They're just clutching at straws, I suppose," he said, shrugging. "Isn't everyone these days. Anyways…" He turned to one of the gawping bar girls. "Another Harp please, darling. Anything for yourself, love?"

"Cider please. Just a half. Do you make a living from this band then?"

"Yeah, no probs. Two or three gigs a week, mainly up north. Mini-tour of Europe next month, Japan in June, and it gets busy around Christmas. So what brings you here then? You don't look like a Zachary B fan."

"What does a Zachary B fan look like then?"

"Fair point. I suppose I'm the exception to the rule. So?"

"Curiosity, I suppose. And boredom. My husband's…"

"Well, good on you. Are you staying for the quiz? We need an extra team member."

"Yes, I suppose so."

"It's you and me then, sweetheart. And our friend Clive here."

A pink-faced, pot-bellied Clive threw a drunken arm round Zachary C's shoulder. His orange silk shirt clashed spectacularly with both his face and his tight turquoise trousers.

"Who's our lovely lady friend then?" he asked, peering myopically at Helen. "We've not seen you here before, have we?"

"Don't mind Clive," said Zachary C, squirming free from his embrace. "He's not usually like this. It's his birthday today. Fancy having your birthday on the same day Zachary was murdered. What a bummer. So he always gets a bit merry."

Helen tried her best to look sympathetic. "Yes, that is unfortunate. Happy birthday, Clive."

★

On the train back to North Dulwich, Helen admitted to herself that she'd had quite a good time. It had been an age since Adam had taken her out. The last time had been a gig in some converted warehouse off Brick Lane. It had been Adam's fiftieth and he clearly wanted to prove he was still up for a Proper Night Out. The headline act they had waited around half the night for were pitiful. A lank-haired youth called Ovid stood behind an Apple-Mac lectern lurching about like a puppet with its strings tangled. According to Adam, he was "triggering other people's music against sampled loops," whatever that meant.

"I thought you said there was a band?" She shouted to Adam over the floor-shaking noise.

"This *is* a band," he'd shouted back, but she could tell he was no more convinced than she was.

Her overall impression had been that nothing much had changed in thirty years: she knew at least half the songs the DJ played; denim was still the default setting for casual clothing, and students still looked like students. But she *had* changed: to the boys she was now invisible; to the girls, a curious anomaly to be furtively scrutinised and whispered about. She remembered a girl with a waist no thicker than a weightlifter's thigh, and the obligatory tattoo in the small of her back, holding her mobile outstretched in front of her so as to take a photo of herself and her boyfriend, and a porridge-pale hoody who threw up while his mates pretended they didn't know him. Blurred back-projections threw up arbitrary words and images: MONROE; WAR; HENDRIX; FASCISM; BLAIR; POLLUTION. So, that had been the last time. Which was why, she realised in retrospect, it had been important that she'd enjoyed herself this evening. She also needed something new and good to hang her memories of Zachary B on and reaffirm her own identity – her own precious era – in a world both unchanged and as alien as another planet.

Her quiz team came a respectable third. She'd even

answered three questions correctly herself (although she cursed herself for forgetting where Zachary was born). What was most shaming was that the quizmaster had slipped that absurdly easy question in especially for her (the wink gave it away). She was astonished at the depth (or should that be width?) of knowledge these men had of all things Zachary B: who played sax on *I'm The Cubist Funk Master*? Who was the third act on the bill for the 1977 Japanese tour? Who was *Bomb the Righteous* directed at? Bowie played Stylophone on *Do the Rocket* – true or false? (False, but he did give Zachary the very Stylophone Zachary himself played on the record). She knew a few B-sides, but she couldn't have said what the B-side of *Do The Rocket* was going to be, before Zachary insisted it had to be *Liza in Leather* (answer: *Don't Leave – Dance!* which Zac apparently wanted to put out later as an A-side – although that never happened).

The fact that none of these men came on to her, might have been upsetting twenty or even ten years ago, but now it was just a relief. But they were all very sweet anyway, and seemed to enjoy the novelty of having a female fan in their midst. Wives and girlfriends had dropped off one by one over the years, and female forum members rarely plucked up the courage to come and meet these men they tapped out on-line chat to almost every day of their lives. Helen was interested and pleased to learn that there was a ban on any talk about KUUism at these gatherings. The Cubist Funk Master Forum was strictly about the music. The organisers had learnt from experience that discussions about KUUism only led to fierce disagreements, which spoiled the celebratory atmosphere. And it wasn't like they needed to find anything else to disagree about: at one point during the quiz, there was a passionate argument about whether it was Bowie, Bolan or Bekele who first used black backing vocalists. When no definitive answer was arrived at after an hour, the Bolan supporter stormed out in a huff. But the most important thing for Helen was that no one guessed who she was; what a fuss that would have caused! She put on BBC News 24 while she got ready for bed. Newsworthy disasters – natural or unnatural – always looked the same. Blanket-covered bodies on stretchers, faces shocked into neutral blankness, dust rising, debris falling. Whether it was an act of God or act of God-worshippers, the end result was always the same: the endless chain of wake-up calls that never woke anyone up. And then there was the name "Paul Coleridge" rolling from left to right along the bottom of the screen. Could that bald, grossly overweight man being bundled into a police car somewhere foreign really be *that* Paul Coleridge? She was just congratulating herself on the fact that the story of his arrest, and all the horrific accompanying details, meant no more to her than if it had been a report of some remote earthquake or famine, when the phone rang. She pressed mute on the TV's remote, and picked up the phone, hoping it was Adam. It was Adam. Everything had gone well with the shoot and so he was coming back a week earlier than planned. He loved her very, very much and couldn't wait to get home. Helen switched off the TV and put a saucepan of milk on the stove. Was it a hot milk night, or a cocoa night? She decided it was a cocoa night.

AFTERWORD

My KUU non-belief system started life as what might be called a piece of conceptual art, several years before it found its natural – and it now seems inevitable – place as the stoned ramblings of a fading rock star desperate for a slice of some real adulation.

But perhaps I'm being too hard on Zachary and myself. When I first found myself trying to create the blueprint for a viable semi-sensible alternative non-religion it was with a genuine if playful passion. I wanted to see if it was possible to devise a theology which went completely against the troubling grain of all that had gone before it, yet made perfect if eccentric sense as an alternative. Once the initial name and ideas were in place, all the KUU-incidences described by Zachary did occur, but it was via emails and the Internet rather than letters and the library, that improbable connections were made. And it was my wife who saw my acronym for a new kind of god written on a toilet door in Finchley. And also, just in case you hadn't guessed by following the adage "you couldn't make this stuff up" – 99% of the KUU-incidences in this novel (Jesus' foreskin, the three-legged greyhounds, the man who got handed the wrong passport in an African bank etc.) occurred exactly as written, with only names changed to protect the paranoid. In fact, the only fictional KUU-incidence was the one involving the Shoreford bypass.

While I was writing *Etc Etc Amen* I had fun creating a discography for Zachary. It helped make him more real to me, and was also useful as a timeline reference while writing the faux biography sections. I've included it as Appendix 1 in tribute to anoraks everywhere. Especially the ones who can't even resist studying the ephemera of a rock star who never existed. Appendix 2 consists of further extracts from *The KUU Hypothesis*. Some readers of earlier drafts of the novel found *The KUU Hypothesis* sections too long, in the sense that they wanted to get back to the two narratives. However, other readers found these sections the most enjoyable part of the novel. So, on balance, it seemed sensible to put the parts least connected to the narrative outside the main body of the novel.

Howard Male. May 2012

APPENDIX 1

A Selected Discography of Zachary B

SOLO SINGLES

Niagara Falls Again/Orbit 5
1968 Mushroom Records
M1272

The Rhyme Traveller/
England, My Queen
1968 Mushroom Records
M1842

Don't Laugh At the
Messenger/Outside the
Dome
1969 Mushroom Records
M2098

Straightjacket Disco/
Straightjacket Disco Dub
Remix
1980 Valentine Records
V01

Sex Vampire/ Juice on the
Loose
1980 Valentine Records
V04

Cosmic Nudge/Bad
Habits
1980 Valentine Records
V05

Future Funk Landslide/
Scene Stealer
1981 Valentine Records
V03

Light the Way/ Light the
Way (Original Demo)
1982 Valentine Records
V16

SINGLES WITH
THE NOW

Where Are My Wings/
Monumental Days
1970 AMT Records AMT
4621

African Princess/Jody
(Double A Side)
1970 AMT Records AMT
4701

Death Jet/I Know
Nothing
1971 AMT Records AMT
4621

Brave the Spotlight/
Kensington Jam
1971 AMT Records AMT
4733

High as You Can Go/As
Far as the Mind Can See
1971 AMT Records AMT
4668

An Eye for an Eye/So
What's Your Name?
1971 AMT Records AMT
4703

Sensimilija/ Secrets of
Njarou
1972 AMT Records AMT
4739

Cosmic Blood Brothers/
I'm Outta Here!
1972 AMT Records AMT
4809

Don't Leave – Dance!/
Shadow of a Silver
Thought
1972 AMT Records AMT
4621

Put Your Glam Rags On/
Put Your Glam Rags On
Again (extended version)
1973 AMT Records AMT
4656

Do the Rocket/Liza in
Leather
1973 AMT Records AMT
4689

Black is Gold/Black is
Gold (instrumental)
1974 AMT Records AMT
4733

Ride To Saturn/I'm The
Cubist Funk Master!
1974 AMT Records AMT
4762

Here We Come, Come,
Come/Here We Come,
Come, Come. Part 2
1975 AMT Records AMT
4871

Pulse/Pulse Quickened
1975 AMT Records AMT
4941
Silver Soul Jet Stream/
Rapid Fire
1976 AMT Records AMT
4909

Galaxy Funk-Up/Cheap
Chains
1977 AMT Records AMT
4982

Who's Fooling Who?/
Faster than Light
1977 AMT Records AMT
4991

Pretending's Easy/You
2 Me
1978 AMT Records AMT
5121

SOLO ALBUMS

Mellow Dramas of a
Generous Heart
1969 Mushroom Records
M2076LP
Side One: Avenue Paris,
Treasures, Underworld,
Deep Love, The Rhyme
Traveller, Don't Laugh
at the Messenger, The
Message.
Side Two: Coat of Arms,
Planet Romance, Strange
as it May Be, Flowers
for the Free, The Cynic
Smiles.

Straightjacket Disco
1981 Valentine Records
V22A
Side One: Future Funk
Landslide, Born to
Push it, Cosmic Nudge,
Pedestal Love, De-Shock.
Side Two: Straightjacket
Disco (revisited 54 Mix),
Pretending's Easy, You
2 Me, My Fate In Your
Hands, Everybody Say
Now!, Drop Out.

Zachary Bekele. Demo
Tremors
1982 Valentine Records.
Double Album. V29A
Side One: Through the
Telescope, On that
Journey Still, I Know
Nothing. Light the Way,
You Can Laugh, Knowing
and Unknowable,
Through the Telescope
(alternative version).
Side Two: Don't Tell Me,
Boys of Gun Law, You're
Getting Warmer, The Day
You Met Me, Everything
is Amazing, KUUdos.
Side Three: Waves
Crashing, Paradox, Love
Steps In, Your Secret
Voice, She's Alright, Wise
Blood, Raising the Sun,
Raising the Sun (take 2).

Side Four: The Strangest
Thing, Heartsing,
Sadness Spills Over, Only
Moments, You Can Laugh,
Have Some Faith, A Cold
Coming (We Had of it).

Light The Way
1983 Valentine Records.
V103A
Side One: Light The Way,
On That Journey Still,
Through the Telescope,
The Enigma of Chance,
Don't Believe, The
Dreamer's Pool.
Side Two: Sadness Spills
Over, The Strangest
Thing, Shots in the Dark,
A Grain of Sand, The
Great Deflator, Belief is
an End Not a Beginning.

Laughter in The Dark
1991 V Records
VCD2897A (double
album on a single CD)
Album 1: Prelude,
Margot in Red,
Albininus's Theme, A
Cross of Pebbles, You Can
Doubt.
Album 2: Blind Luck, Tea
Rex? Margo, Come To
Me, Laughter in the Dark,
The Meaningful Void.

Laughter in the Dark
The Chelmsford
Symphony Orchestra
2001 V Records
VCD7964A
Side One: Laughter in
The Dark Part 1.
Side Two: Laughter in The
Dark Part 2, 1971 Ten
Minute Interview with
Zac Bekele.

WITH THE NOW

Magpie
1970 AMT Records AMT
4723LP
Side One: Meet Your
Maker, What Star are
You? Children Know,
Monumental Days,
Somebody Somewhere,
Where Are My Wings.
Side Two: Jazz Cafe, The
Vision, Bad Day for a
Good Time, A Fine Day,
Pictures of Invisible
Things Parts 1 & 2.

Tomorrow's Bride
1971 AMT Records AMT
4877LP
Side One. Boy Meets
Girl Meets Girl. The Eye.
Darkness Visible. Jody. I
Know Nothing.

Side Two: Crushed Velvet
Girl, Brave the Spotlight,
Death Jet, Lost For
Words, African Princess.

An Eye For An Eye
1972 AMT Records AMT
5001LP
Side One: Sensimilija,
Make Her Go Away,
Einstein's Revenge, Yes
No or Maybe?, Betrayal,
London 516433.
Side Two: An Eye For
An Eye, Russian Witch
Doctor, Bomb the
Righteous, White Lies, As
Far as the Mind Can See,
Cosmic Blood Brothers,
I'm Outa Here!

Put Your Glam Rags On
1973 AMT Records AMT
5099LP
Side One: Put Your Glam
Rags On, Don't Leave
– Dance! Shadow Of A
Silver Thought, Death
Vampire.
Side Two: Do the Rocket,
The Happy Medium,
Midnight Walker, My
New Dance, Liza in
Leather, Vertigo City (Get
Back On The Floor)

The Slim Hipped Hipster
and The Juxta-Posers
1974 AMT Records AMT
5111LP
Side One: I'm The
Cubist Funk Master,
Slap Your Mamma, Just
as I thought, Dig Deep,
Marijuana Girl, If You're
Out There You're in Here!
Side Two: San Francisco
Party, Ride to Saturn, The
Best at the Boogie, Who's
Jiving Who?, Black is
Gold, Rapid Fire.

Swimming the River of
the Soul
1975 AMT Records AMT
5199LP
Side One: The Great
Unknown, Here We
Come, Come, Come.,
Time and Tide Parts 1-3.
Side Two: Swimming, The
River, The Soul, Marble
City, The End.

Silver Soul Jet Stream
1977 AMT Records AMT
5226LP
Side One: Moving
Mountains, Was it
Something I Said, Who's
Fooling Who?, Just
Because, Pulse.
Side Two: Silver Soul Jet

Stream, Galaxy Funk-Up,
Get On the Track!, Cheap
Chains

Zac's Back. The Best of
Zac B and The Now
1981 AMT Records AMT
7001LP
Side One: Where are
my Wings, Brave the
Spotlight, High as You
Can Go, An Eye for an
Eye, Sensimilija, Cosmic
Blood Brothers, The
Cloud Walkers, Don't
Leave – Dance!, You Can
Laugh.
Side Two: Put Your Glam
Rags On, Do the Rocket,
Black is Gold, Ride to
Saturn, Here We Come,
Come, Come, Rapid Fire,
Just Because.

PRODUCED BY ZACHARY BEKELE

The Deep End – The Dog
Stars
1975 AMT Records AMT
3442LP
Side One: My Machine*,
Sun & Sex, Freeze!, The
Factory, Gun Culture,
Raging Bull.
Side Two: Justice, Just
Is*, Race Riot, History
Lessons (are Never
Learnt), Homicide City*,
Berwick Street Jam, The
Deep End.

*Songs co-written by
Zachary B

APPENDIX 2

Further Extracts from *The KUU Hypothesis*
Answers are Only Ever Provisional

There are no moral absolutes, only specific solutions to specific dilemmas. Even then, more than one proposed solution could be the 'right' one. The value of an answer is often wholly contingent on the future outcome, therefore how can its rightness be quantified in advance of that outcome? The most truthful response to a friend's moral dilemma is the one least likely to be given: "I don't know what you should do – how could I?"

The Good Book Test

I was having a debate with a Christian friend and so used the KUU method of opening the Bible at random to find something significant. I landed on this passage, which is part of the small print of the Ten Commandments. Exodus 21:35:

"If a man beats his male or female slave with a rod and the slave dies as a result, he must be punished, but he is not to be punished if the slave gets up after a day or two, since the slave is his property."

You may already know that this god has no problem with slavery – it's a way of life in the Bible – but here He's actually advocating the beating of a slave within an inch of their life, as long as they recover after a few days. And don't, whatever you do, dream of exercising your free will by considering any other god for worship – here's another passage landed on at random. Exodus 20:3:

"You shall not bow down to them or worship them; for I, the LORD (His capitals) your God, am a jealous God, punishing the children for the sins of the fathers to the third and fourth generation of those who hated me..."

Like a psychotic terrorist, God holds a gun to your children's heads, and – being omnipresent – also your children's children's heads, forever and ever, Amen – just to secure your adoration.

Faith and Fear

Faith dispenses with the need for reason or argument. Faith is seen (by the faithful) as a virtue, and – by definition – cannot be shaken by contrary evidence, however strong that evidence might be – and usually is. The problem today is that evidence is so abundant and overwhelming, that surely even the most fervent supporter of their deity has to adjust their God-view to take into account such things as a new dinosaur or devastating natural disaster? But no siree! Faith itself just won't shift – it's the nature of the beast. Fear is the foundation stone of faith, and it's a fear that takes several forms: fear of death, fear of eternal punishment, and a more general fear of God Himself.

The Love/Hate or RESPECT Tripod

We can schizophrenically swing between love and hate in our one-to-one relationships until one of us leaves. If we were to swap the word 'respect' for the word 'love' then there's less far to fall if it all goes horribly wrong. If we fall out of respect with someone, rather than out of love with him or her, we're less likely to throw all his or her clothes out of the window. We have been brainwashed since birth by a million pop songs and a thousand films to believe that love is a bed of roses, or a basket of kittens. As for Respect, all we've got is Aretha:

"R – E – S – P – E – C – T, *Find out what it means to me.*"

Respect requires that we acknowledge our fellow human being's right to dignity, space and opinions: taking things any further is optional. There is no dignity for the abused wife, the lovesick teenager or the hopeless romantic. Love – that cruel illusion – has dealt them a terrible blow. If you give another person respect it's no skin off your nose, and you've given them something more valuable than gold. But if you say you love them, their expectations go through the roof. We shouldn't stop loving – that would be counter-productive and impractical – but we need to think it through more often.

In the Beginning was the Tripod

The tripod was probably there at the birth of civilisation. That is, the first time one man was civil to another man. In the depths of a dark forest, or in the hostile chill of a desert night, you'd have seen its three legs astride the glowing embers of a fire, its apex supporting a bubbling pot of meat and vegetables. Our lone Nomad would have built this basic yet stable construction as the obvious solution for slow cooking, so that leftovers of a large kill could be preserved for another day. Then along came Nomad 2, drawn to investigate first by the distant glow, and then by the warmth and delicious smells, put down his weapons in return for food, warmth and – as a by-product of these practicalities – fireside companionship. Also as a by-product of such meetings, language and music may have made their first appearances. Later, when conversation faltered and voices became hoarse from singing, Nomad 3 would show up; two's company, three's a society! The potential confrontation of two suspicious individuals immediately dispelled by the arrival of a third party.

The Political Tripod

Two parties are thought, quite reasonably, to be better than a dictatorship. However, with a left and a right party, each party can still – as history has shown us – end up becoming the most extreme manifestation of its ideals. Although Fascism and Communism were, in theory, diametrically opposed, in practice their fate was identical: brutal totalitarian dictatorships. The tribal-binary opposition of Left and Right in politics is an illusion perpetuated by our cunning rulers who know that we peasants like a good fight. Totalitarianism then sneaks in the backdoor while we are busy on the streets waving our red or blue flags.

The Price of Self-awareness is Knowledge

The difference between us and our fellow creatures on Earth is that we know death is waiting for us. How could our innocent, dumb, scared, mammalian brains adapt to such devastating knowledge? How could the gift of a sense of our past and future come at such a horrible price? So we had to invent the notion of an afterlife to prevent existential meltdown. We know this now, so we need to move on and let go of God's instruction manuals. Think about it: they turned up very late in the day (on average, only two thousand years ago, which – in relation to a human history of some hundred thousand years and a prehistory of millions of years – is only a blink of an eye) and they're filled with enough ambiguities and inconsistencies to keep us fighting and killing each other over their true meaning, until Hell freezes over: How can these books be the work of a caring god who wants His unambiguous truths spread across the globe?

Meaning has to be Worked at...
and Played at

Contrary to what every other religion tells you, things might
not happen for a reason. Even Cosmic Nudges (the one flimsy
thread that connects us to our hypothetical deity) rarely seem
to have symbolic meaning or lead directly to great changes in
an individual's life. The message seems to be that we are on
our own to create reason for ourselves. From reason stems
meaning, and meaning in turn gives us a sense of purpose.
In other words, we each need to be our own God, or play at
being our own God.

The KUUist's History of
Western Civilisation

Although we have a biologist's/anthropologist's history of
the evolution of mankind, we don't have a parallel history of
mankind's emotional and intellectual development.

So here's a version of that:

PD: (Pre-Darwin), was mankind's childhood when almost
everyone believed in some kind of supernatural, overseeing
being.

Then, **AD** (After-Darwin), most of Western civilisation has
been in a kind of stroppy teenager phase – some of us have let
go of our mythical beings, and are struggling with adulthood,
but the majority are still throwing tantrums, slamming doors,
and saying "My God is better than your God".

So now we need to move on to full maturity with AK (after-
KUUism), where the search for meaning can continue
unhampered by the notion that we already have all the answers.

Meaning is not a single arrived-at destination. Meaning can arrive in one life-changing, revelatory moment, but it's more likely to creep up on you incrementally. So be grateful for whatever meaning you can lay your hands on. Etc, etc Amen!

Martians would be KUUists

Martians wouldn't find *The KUU Hypothesis* any more far fetched than any of the established holy texts – it's all just daydreaming. I am merely stating the case for the KUU because no one else is going to do it.

Faith or Belief is Never an Intellectually Arrived at Choice

It is rooted in the individual's genetic predisposition to believe, along with their cultural background. To put it another way, an individual's nature, along with their contingent circumstances, predetermines whether or not their life will have a spiritual dimension. However, being a KUUist only takes an open mind and a sense of humour.

A Four-Four World

Music originated with rhythm; rhythm equals dance. The Western world feared that the primal beat of rock 'n' roll would cause the collapse of civilisation. This superstition didn't dissipate until the arrival of late twentieth century popular music. Previously, the dominant culture of classical music did everything to suppress or belittle music in which rhythm played a dominant role. They probably feared that dancing would liberate our God-enslaved souls. So don't pray, dance!

Acknowledgements

Often the first piece of advice given to new writers is to join a writers group, but I'm not a group kind of person, so I had to think of another way of getting constructive feedback during the five years it took me to knock this novel into shape.

The first draft was dismissed by the late Charlie Gillett (1942-2010) with the words, "I couldn't get passed page 20" – which was exactly what I needed to hear from someone whose judgement and good taste I respected so much. It spurred me on to eventually produce something Charlie thoroughly enjoyed.

But there were many other guinea pigs whose comments led me to tighten up the plot, improve the definition of a character or two, or cut back on the adjectives. Even those guinea pigs that fell off the wheel before reaching the end (I'm talking about you, Andy, June and Peter) were helpful because my failure to sufficiently convince them to keep turning the pages, let me know that there was still a lot of work to be done on the manuscript.

But whatever your input was, I'd like to thank Justin Adams, Jim Bob, Mick Brown, John Butterworth, John Caldwell, Russ Coffey, Nick Coleman, Graham Crowley, David Cummins, Joe and Michelle Cushley, Emma David, WPietro DiMascio, Maxine Doray, Norman Druker, Justin Earl, Will Firth, Tim Footman, Salena Godden, Johnny Green, Simon Holland, Chetna Kapacee, Lopa Kathari, Ian Macpherson, Jonathan Main, Joe Muggs, Patrick Neate, Gordon Neil, Linda and Stephen Oliver, Nigel Osborne, Chris Potts, Rich Rainlore, Jamie Renton, Chris Roberts, David Severn, Jenny Shephard, Graeme Thomson, Mic White, and Nigel Williamson. I'd also like to say a special thank you to my wife, Marcia, for putting up with me talking about little else but this book for so long, and my editor Leila Dewji for (hopefully) spotting all the typos and offering indispensable advice on ways to clarify certain aspects of the novel's plot that I had simply overlooked. This novel writing business isn't easy, you know.

Howard Male, May 2012.

For more information on this novel, an interview with the author, and much else besides visit
http://etcetcamen. com/